LUCKY TURTLE

LUCKY TURTLE

∼∼∼

a novel by

Bill Roorbach

ALGONQUIN BOOKS
OF CHAPEL HILL 2022

Published by
Algonquin Books of Chapel Hill
Post Office Box 2225
Chapel Hill, North Carolina 27515-2225

a division of
Workman Publishing
225 Varick Street
New York, New York 10014

This is a work of fiction. While, as in all fiction, the literary perceptions and insights are based on experience, all names, characters, places, and incidents either are products of the author's imagination or are used fictitiously.

LIBRARY OF CONGRESS CATALOGING-IN-PUBLICATION DATA

Names: Roorbach, Bill, author.
Title: Lucky turtle : a novel / by Bill Roorbach.
Description: First Edition. | Chapel Hill, North Carolina : Algonquin Books of Chapel Hill, 2022. | Summary: "When privileged white sixteen-year-old Cindra is sent to a reform camp in Montana, she becomes transfixed by Lucky, a mysterious camp employee. As the connection between them grows, Lucky and Cindra become lovers and escape into the Rocky Mountains to create an idyllic life, living off Lucky's vast knowledge of the wilderness."— Provided by publisher.
Identifiers: LCCN 2021057135 | ISBN 9781643750972 (hardcover) | ISBN 9781643752983 (ebook)
Subjects: GSAFD: Love stories.
Classification: LCC PS3568.O6345 L83 2022 | DDC 813/.54—dc23
LC record available at https://lccn.loc.gov/2021057135

10 9 8 7 6 5 4 3 2 1
First Edition

For Uncle Bill

LUCKY TURTLE

PART ONE

Chapter One

I am Cindra Zoeller. I was born in 1980, in Watertown, Massachusetts, outside Boston. I wrote a report in fifth grade so I know Massachusetts is an Algonquian name meaning big little hills. I grew up there sledding the biggest of the little hills and skating on millponds and swimming in the lakes and rivers and the ocean with the other kids, though rarely with my sister, who was much older and mocked my love of the great outdoors, sat home reading, and I will never mention her again. I adored my father, who was a cabinetmaker or, when business was bad, a roofer. He hated roofing. My mother and I did not get along. She broke my ankle once by accident (but in a rage) and did not take me to the doctor. And then, when I was sixteen, I got in trouble.

There, that was fast.

My actual life begins with meeting Lucky, is why I'm hurrying.

Chapter Two

I guess let's start with the hearing. April Fool's Day 1997. Old Watertown Congregational Church, yours truly seated at the head of the immense table in the sacristy, view of God's Acre patched with snow and daffodils, all around me concerned adults: Reverend Turtman (pale, scrawny little twerp with glasses—we kids called him Turdman and took advantage of his good nature), and Mother and dear Pops, and Mr. Hightower, the principal of Watertown High, also Mrs. Small, the vice principal and chief disciplinarian (we called her Mister Large). And the lawyer, our lawyer, our *criminal* lawyer, a distinguished Black man named Mr. Burnett, from a big firm in Boston proper. And Judge Pernal, luckily Pop's golfing pal, Caucasian person tanned to a crisp from his annual Florida trip, several shades darker than Mr. Burnett, whom he clearly looked down upon. Finally Miss Elegant (her actual name, and actually an elegant, if ineffectual, soul), my only institutional ally, my guidance counselor.

It was she who started the proceedings: "Let's all think how we can be of service to Cindy."

"Cindra," my mother said.

"Be of service?" said Mrs. Small. She fairly trembled with indignation.

"You're clear on what you've done?" Judge Pernal said.

"Yes," I said meekly. "And I'm very sorry for it."

"Your friend Dagoberto Murua will get twenty years," he said.

"I'm aware," I said. Lawyer Burnett had coached me: "And I agree that he deserves it."

"Not Cindra's friend," Mr. Burnett said sternly. "Her abuser."

"You were taken advantage of," Pops said sweetly.

"Very much so," said Miss Elegant.

"No, I take responsibility," I said.

Both Mr. Burnett and Judge Pernal nodded at that. Clearly, unlike my Puerto Rican codefendants, I was on the right track, headed for rehabilitation and an eventual return to society. Also, as no one was saying, I was white.

"Armed robbery," my mother said. "Assault with a deadly weapon!" She had been repeating this phrase for weeks.

My father said, "Mother."

Judge Pernal cleared his throat, a man of little drama, chilly gaze. "And Mr. Murua's brother, Guillermo," *Giller-mo*, he pronounced it. "You're aware that for his role he's going to Cutler until he's eighteen, then to State, likely ten years total."

"Aware," I said. Cutler School for Boys, that hellhole, famous for cruelty.

"And that something similar could very easily be your fate."

"I'm aware. Very much so."

Judge Pernal gave me a long look, the very look of justice. "But we do agree that your role in the incident was less than intentional. You held no weapon. You called for an ambulance."

"Hours later," said Vice Principal Small.

"Saving two lives," Pops said.

"Having jeopardized those lives," said Vice Principal Small.

"A fine girl," said Miss Elegant. "All that sunny blond hair."

"Let us stay on track," said Mr. Burnett.

The judge said what everyone already knew he was going to say. That he was saying it in church rather than in his courtroom meant I would avoid having the felony on my record. He read from a handwritten document, tapped the table to accent each item: "We remand you to Camp Challenge in the town of Elk Creek, Montana, voluntary enrollment, two years. No parental contact for the first six months, monthly after that, weekly in your second year. A full courtroom trial if the camp administration is not happy with your progress or you leave those premises for any reason. At Camp Challenge you will pursue and complete your high school certificate. You've missed nearly a year of school—I disagreed with the expulsion, for the record. You will also accelerate your religious studies, investigate college options, and begin to make financial amends to the victims of your associates. Release on your nineteenth birthday, probation thereafter until you reach the age of twenty-one, probation waived if you are enrolled at a four-year college. All Camp Challenge fees and tuition to be paid by your parents, repaid by you at a later date, as per agreement."

Pops wept, the only one.

"Armed robbery," my mother repeated.

"Criminal mischief," said Mr. Burnett to correct the record: a deal was a deal.

"A very adventurous young lady," said Miss Elegant elegantly.

"Remand Thursday," said the judge.

Reverend Turtman cleared his throat, said, "In Jesus's name, let us pray." The mercifully assembled bowed their heads. My father and I hesitated, slight grins as our eyes met and Reverend Turtman began. Finally Pops sighed, bowed his head, first I'd ever seen. Not me. I got an image of vast plains in my head, of snowcapped peaks, of dauntless Blackfeet and Crow and Oglala and Miniconjou warriors on horseback, coup sticks held high. Delusions, in other words. I'd read up extensively on Camp Challenge and on Montana history in the months since the deal had been struck, my only schooling since the crime, and I was ready to put trouble and all these dour adults behind me and start in on what seemed an adventure, nothing a prayer would change.

Chapter Three

A Montana marshal with an actual badge had to fly with me, a very kind and quiet gentleman, from Helena, where the main street was Last Chance Gulch, he said, the only conversation we really had, that and the fact that as a history buff he'd really enjoyed seeing Boston. My parents had paid for that, too. The marshal had a subliminal interest in my chest, his eyes darting furtively. He was a real cowboy, hat and all, very thin and tall, easily forty years old, a weathered artifact. We changed planes at Chicago, changed again at Denver, snowy mountain ranges to the west, bare dry plains to the east, just as on the library maps I'd been examining. A big blue jail bus with a sheriff-badge logo and actual steel bars in the windows met us at the quaint Billings airport, no snow to be seen, almost hot in the sun. The marshal shook my hand in farewell, handcuffed me, draped my coat over my shoulders, and walked me thirty feet to the bus, where the mangy-looking guard unlocked one hand as my coat slid to the dusty ground.

"I'll get it," the guard said, helping me up to the front passenger's seat, where I guessed girls got to sit. He locked the loose end of the handcuffs on the grating behind me such that I couldn't quite rest my hand in my lap. "You gonna be the only female today," he said, and tucked my coat between my legs a little forcefully.

In back, eight or nine prisoners sat with bowed heads, all handcuffed to their seats, about half of them looking to be Blackfeet or Crow or maybe Miniconjou, but what did I know: nothing. The rest were scuffed whites, ancestors from every corner of Europe, one might reasonably guess. There was no talk, none. The guard threw the bus in gear, drove us from jailhouse to prison to courthouse to bus station, dropping men off, picking men up. Everyone was on mumbly good behavior, not a word of defiance. The guard patted my leg at each stop, incrementally higher on my thigh, tugged at my coat so it fell on the floor, patted a little higher, finally eking out a phrase: "Don't get many like you."

"Stop it," I said.

He acted like he hadn't heard but stopped, and that was the end of that. I understood without understanding that as a fresh delinquent I might seem a certain way. But it's not like I didn't know what he was thinking: I'd been secretly dating Dagoberto DeLeon Murua for six months at the time of our crime. Dag was the big brother of Billy Murua, who was a sweet, smart boy I knew from school. I'd call them Afro-Caribbean now, very charming young men, both of them. Billy and Dag were the sons of Jack-Boy, as he was called, the one mechanic in town, a former major-league baseball player out of Puerto Rico who'd been hurt in his second season, specialty in luxury cars, a high-end business, nothing to sniff at income-wise, beloved so long as nothing went wrong. I met Dag at a quarry party, one of the older guys swimming in the hot moonlight. After I'd sidled near, and after some smoldering looks back and forth—Billy's big brother!—he asked me very formally to walk with him under the moon, and there in the field behind the abandoned quarry steam shovel, he took me in his arms and said I was his. Fine with me! I hadn't been soul-kissed as yet, but I was soul-kissed then. He was so bold in everything, once he got going, and yet such a gentleman, none of the rushing hands I'd encountered before, just the very nice, very long kiss and a promise we'd go out.

"My parents will never," I said.

"We'll meet up secret places," he said. "Billy says you are one for adventure."

"He says you are the smartest man he knows."

"He told me you were funny."

"Am I?"

He laughed heartily at that, so I guessed I was.

Yes, and we met. I lied and told him I was seventeen. Even that age gave him pause. But we'd already fallen in love. My great brainstorm was to join the swim team as the coach's assistant (with my bent foot I was no longer competitive). Five a.m. practice, but Coach didn't mind if I turned up late, or even at all, since I had few actual duties. And parents, my parents anyway, didn't think of early morning as a time to get in any trouble. I'd get up to my alarm, dress quick, meet Dag in his muscle car at the corner and straight to his room over Foreign Classics Auto, their garage, his bachelor pad—guy with a plan. He was gentle but insistent, and almost twenty years old, and very experienced, liquid tongue, diagnostic fingers. To be desired like that, to have a secret like him! My body was his, and his appreciation was boundless. He had condoms, which I'd never till then successfully negotiated. He gave me suggestions to please him, and I took pleasure in them all. He pleased me, too, almost embarrassing.

In languid interstices, we looked through his auto magazines and picked out dream cars, not that I knew a thing. Eloquently, he explained fuel injection to me, and cylinder diameters, his expertise and passion like love poems. I brought him a cutting from one of my mother's jade plants, some life for his empty enormous commercial windowsills, and he quizzed me after that, optimum care and maintenance strategies, like a houseplant was a car. I brought him more, all sorts, nearly a plant a visit, and he loved them tenderly, treated me like a master gardener and not only a lover. Till then, I'd been master of nothing and a lover not at all, not like that.

The only commandment was to get to school on time, and occasionally to swim-team practice and the stacking of kickboards, nice ache down low.

A dispute arose with the Mercedes dealership over in Belmont, that's all. Mr. Murua had worked for days hand-milling parts for an antique Bentley, obsolete transmission, got stiffed for the bill, which the skinflint dealer decided was too high. The ol' man was stoic, not one to rock the boat, but Dag believed in family honor. I was the driver, having dropped my mom at the T, the Boston commuter train, five a.m. Dag and his little brother carried baseball bats and used them to smash windows in the big garage doors at the swank dealership—it looked more like a hotel—reached in, unlocked everything, expertly disarmed the alarm system before it could make a peep.

We loaded precision tools into the back of my family car, whole work-boxes filled with metric wrenches, an air compressor worth plenty, boxes of Mercedes parts: payment plus interest. But the owner of the business was there. The one thing you don't plan. Upstairs in his office with his bookkeeper (which of course didn't even make the papers he advertised in so heavily, her baby-doll lingerie never mentioned at the grand jury proceedings—officially they were on the up-and-up, just there extra early doing the books). They hadn't heard a thing but came down half-naked to get more champagne from the waiting-room fridge. Dag, he flipped. At the infidelity as much as anything. He was like that, sternly moral even though he was sleeping with a sixteen-year-old. Bapped the guy in the shoulder with his baseball bat, fended off the girl and her manicured nails. And that would have been it, but the dealer couldn't just be quiet, n-word this and n-word that, thick German accent, fueled by what? Cocaine? Molly? And racism, of course, worse than all other possible poisons combined. So Dag hit him again, this time in the face. Billy grabbed the bat, and believe me, there would have been more damage than the broken jaw if he hadn't, though that's not what the woman testified. She said that Billy kicked her in the neck, not true, that he made sexual slurs. Absolutely not. But there were those hickeys she had to account for. The brothers herded her into the mechanics' bathroom, broke the lockset off with hammers so she couldn't get out. She screamed in there like an old-school movie star. The dealer was unconscious but breathing, his heart pounding away—Billy checked.

I was excited by the violence at first. Burning rubber out of there, I laughed like a gun moll. But then at school, waiting for the doors to open, boys and Mercedes-shop booty safely dropped at the garage, I was hit with what we'd done. Also overcome with anger at Dag, and with remorse. I mean, there was a basically old man maybe dying on an oil-soaked cement floor in a business that wouldn't open for an hour.

As the sun pinkened the sky, Mr. Rolly the custodian unlocked the school doors. I pushed past the other early birds and at the pay phones by the cafeteria called the fire department, asked for an ambulance. I knew it wouldn't be smart to call the police. I gave my name because they asked. I gave my name! Some criminal.

Next thing you know that big blue jail bus was dropping me in handcuffs at a gas station in Billings, Montana (large, long-weathered sign retained as a sick joke: NO INDIANS OR HIPPIES—I guessed there'd never been enough Black people around there to rate a mention), and a van was picking me up, red, white, and blue:

CAMP CHALLENGE

A BRAND-NEW START FOR GIRLS

The driver was my age, maybe a little older, slender, huge cowboy hat and cowboy boots and cowboy buckle. He wore a long black braid tied with rawhide and thicker rawhide bands around his wiry biceps. I supposed he was Crow. Having been grounded for months and my only refuge the Watertown Library, I'd read up on the reservation, which was big as at least half of Massachusetts. I knew Wrangler jeans when I saw them, library or no: big *W* stitched on each back pocket, narrow legs stretching all the way down to cowboy boots, perfectly worn leather. He unlocked my handcuffs, tossed them to the jail-bus guard, closed me in the back of the van. He smelled like some distant burning, I can hardly explain it, studied my eyes whenever I was required to cooperate, didn't put his hands on me, didn't ask any questions, didn't offer any greetings, not a word from his mouth.

And off we went.

The reality hit me hard. No contact with my parents for six months. No contact with Dag ever again, though I'd begun in the months since our crime to despise and not love him, stupid, hotheaded man, and to love his brother, Billy, very sorry for him, the boy I should have been dating.

But Elk Creek was something beautiful to see, a river, really, crashing down the mountain as we ascended, sunshine and plains and vast valleys and mountain ridges, peaks more distant, the air like snapping flags, gusts buffeting the van, not a structure in sight until we came to a fence, a wide steel gate. The driver climbed out and opened it, climbed back in and drove through, climbed out again on the other side, closed the gate again with a clang. I thought it was camp security, and not very effective looking, saw myself tramping down that long road by moonlight—escape. But where would I go?

We turned onto a smaller road to follow a smaller river. The air was dry and very clear and even a little cold. Bright lichens hung from the trees. We rumbled over cattle grates embedded in the road. I asked the driver how far we had to go, shouting through the steel mesh as the van banged over gravel—but he gave me no notice. We climbed up out of the barren plain and into the trees, lots of trees, mostly evergreen—trees I didn't yet know the names of. And wildflowers, some coming up through patches of snow: Indian paintbrush and columbine and that other one, the purple-and-yellow one, very tall. And the constant wind, the van windows cracked open, out of my control, the air chilly, then chillier. The driver braked suddenly, oblivious as I half slid off the big bench seat.

Twelve or more animals like giant deer placidly crossed the road in front of us. The last in line was a big bull with antlers. It stopped and examined the van a long while, finally moved along.

"Elk!" I cried. I'd read of them in one of my library books.

Nothing from the driver. He just continued on. At the top of a long hill, the view opened up to at least eternity, distant mountain ranges, high glaciers, and clouds, and sky. Then a sharp curve and after that a real gate in a real fence, eight feet high, chain link topped with taut strands of barbed wire. The gate was just a steel grid, two sheet-metal turtles riveted onto the face of it, giant turtles communing. We stopped and a guard emerged from the entry booth, an elderly woman who opened the gate dispassionately and waved us through. We pulled up in front of a long log building and stopped again. The driver made no move to get out, to let me out.

A crisp woman in tweeds and sensible shoes, coiffed hair almost black, opened my door. This was Dora Dryden Conover. I recognized her from my obsessive study of the Camp Challenge brochure: founder and director, still a beauty, and let that stand in for warmth. I slid out of the back of the van, stiff legged.

Dora Dryden Conover offered her hand and we shook, firm and dry, just as Daddy had taught me. She said, "Welcome to your new life, Cindra Zoeller." She knew my name, she'd read my file—but she knew nothing about me, her eyes hard as blue ice. I felt my heart sink, looked away.

The driver collected my duffel bag from the van, laid it on the ground beside me. He stood tall and very still, didn't look away but kept my eye, and I felt he saw the person I really was. He had no interest in the story I'd arrived with, only in the story that was to come. I saw that he himself had been buried somewhere deep by some disaster. I vowed right there that I would ferret him out, because deep is where the diamonds are made, and I would need something hard as that if I was going to survive.

Chapter Four

Dora Dryden Conover led me inside the long building, knotty-pine everything. Shortly, a knotty-pine door opened and a tall, pallid white man in a rumpled suit appeared. "Well," he said, "here's a beauty."

"Dr. *Gilbert*," Dora clucked. "This is Cindra."

"Cindra," the doctor said, unchastened.

"We'd better keep this item safe," said Dora, reaching to unclasp my necklace, the only piece of jewelry I'd ever owned, a pearl from my father. I didn't protest—how could I? She gave me an appraising look, said, "Well. I'll leave you to it, Doctor." And pearl already in her pocket, she picked up my duffel bag, opened a different knotty-pine door, marched up a flight of stairs, further doors shutting behind her, footsteps receding.

Dr. Gilbert was another chest looker and more than that. Leave him to what? I fixed my collar, smoothed my pleated church skirt, safely midcalf.

I was to precede him through yet another knotty-pine door and down a long knotty-pine hallway. He aimed me into an airy, capacious dining room, beams and knots and benches and milk machines and raw tables, pine fragrant, reassuring. At the far end under a Red Cross flag, he gripped my arm and guided me through a dutch door, left the top half open, pushed me back into a warren of hallways and little offices, all of it empty, abandoned. It was late in the day, one of the new long days of spring. He indicated an exam room, steered me in there. No windows, fluorescent lights, knotty-pine walls and floor.

"You'll undress," he said. And handed me a cloth hospital gown.

I'd been to a doctor before, complied as modestly as I could. But didn't they usually step out? He sat me down on the table, looked in my throat, ahh, looked in my ears, hmm, put his stethoscope on my chest, moved it all around. Honestly, in the moment it was only mortifying, but thinking about it now I'm filled with rage, this prodding of my nipples one at a time, these sharp pinches. "Sensitive?" he asked.

"No," I lied.

He muttered medical words, took notes. "I'll just palpate," he said, and basically felt me up, very interested in my belly for some reason, higher and lower, and lower yet, pushing hard above my pubic bone, uncomfortable. "Virgin?" he said.

"Yes," I said, though of course that wasn't true by quite a few rugged miles.

He laid me back and put my feet in his stirrups—I mean picked my feet up and put them in—I'd never encountered stirrups. And again, what did I know? He wasn't brief about whatever exam he was committing, and in fact it seemed truly clinical, terrible pressure, a lot of cold lube and prodding. "Nice and pink," he said at last. And gave my pubis a pat. "And a real blondie, to boot."

A double embarrassment in that I knew his words were inappropriate but also, and maybe worse, in that they pleased me, compliments being compliments. I have never told this to anyone. The doctor left, taking the clothes I'd been wearing with him: nice pink skirt, nice pink underpants from Sears, nice pink Keds, all the pink an effort not to seem too criminal. I hadn't taken my socks off, so at least there was that, nice and pink, too. He locked the door behind him. The doors locked from the outside! I waited, looking for something to wipe with—nothing but a corner of their stupid gown—that steady, discomfiting wind in the trees outside.

Chapter Five

Everything took so long. That was one way that camp was going to be different from life. But after a while the lock clattered and the door opened and a nurse stepped in, crisp uniform, pile of clothes and towels and bedding in her arms, smell of fresh laundry.

"Cindy Zoeller?" she said.

"Cindra," I said.

"Let's get dressed," she said.

The nurse wasn't going to go away but handed me clothing one item at a time. I dressed in front of her, working around the gown as modestly as I could, plain gray gigantic underpants, loose gray trousers in cotton with sewn-in elastic waist, gray undershirt, gray button-up shirt with a big CC on the back, smaller CC on the breast pocket, gray baseball cap, CC again, gray socks, which I put on over my own. She didn't notice, thankfully, just handed me a pair of felt clogs, also gray, all while reading the doctor's notes. "You'll need regular gynecological exams," she said. "'Monthly at ovulation,' he says here. You've got a tipped uterus. The doctor is here Wednesdays and Thursdays."

"What is a tipped uterus?"

"Nothing. A lot of the girls have it. He can fix it, though. He generally always puts it right."

Well, it sounded like good news, no idea what she was talking about.

"You look nice in gray," she said, a welcome joke, delivered deadpan.

"Lucky me," I said.

"Do you need a bra?"

"No, not really."

She looked me over, seemed to agree. "Mostly for the flat girls we go with the T-shirt," she said. "You're kind of in between. Bras, you have to sign out."

"I'm fine," I said.

"Because what with the straps they're dangerous."

"T-shirt."

"What size for your sneakers, sweetie?"

Sweetie. I relaxed, said, "Eight?"

"Eight, that's easy. If you're good, you'll get boots, too."

"Great. I'll be good. Do we get our own stuff back? My clothes? My duffel bag? And I left my parka in the first bus, the blue bus." The necklace seemed too precious to even mention.

She went all official. "You get your things back when you're released. You'll get a sweatshirt when they come in—we're out right now. Wrap up in your blanket if we get a cold spell."

"I think it's cold now."

She let herself smile. "It's not cold. Coats we give out in September. Here's your toilet kit." She opened it so I could have a look: paper bag with a short toothbrush, tiny tube of Crest, tiny bar of Ivory soap (known to wreck my skin), a hairbrush with no handle, five enormous sanitary napkins with no brand name. "Not exactly a spa," she said. "When you need more, just ask."

Just ask: Pops crying in the car, Montana marshal beside me, four airports, one blue prison bus, one Camp Challenge van, fourteen hours, belly rumbling.

Evening was upon us, the daylight stretching as never in New England. I said, "Is there anything to eat?"

"There's breakfast in the morning."

"Nothing till then?"

"Like I said, this isn't a hotel."

I remembered what Mr. Burnett had told me, how to get along. I said, "I know. You're absolutely right. I can wait."

"Terrible about the tornadoes," the lady said, offhand.

"Tornadoes?"

"Down south—tore up whole cities. Dozens dead."

Unaccountably, tears started to my eyes: all disasters were my own.

And again, I was locked in the room. The nurse had left her sewing tape and I played with it, rolling it up tight, unspooling it, rolling it up tight, unspooling it, measuring my fingers, the girth of my biceps, the length of my feet, rolling it up tight, unspooling it, what seemed like hours, nodded off.

Suddenly a beautiful young Black woman stood over me, hair tightly braided.

"It'll get better," she said, first thing.

"I was asleep," I said.

"I'm Lioness," she said.

"Linus?"

She had holes in her earlobes where her earrings should have been. She said, "Lioness. Like the cat. Let's get you a bite. Poor thing, you missed dinner."

"I love your braids," I said.

"You wouldn't if you knew how they hurt," she said.

It was like she'd turned off the heat. I'd gotten her name wrong, I'd offered an intimacy I hadn't earned. My heart sank further, right into my gut, and I was crying again.

"Quiet now," she said.

She led me down knotty-pine hallways through several doorways to a vast kitchen attached to the grand mess hall, refrigerators like storage rooms. She dug out an enormous can of peanut butter, a loaf of bread, made me a quick sandwich, poured me a scratched glass of milk from a stainless-steel machine. That was going to be it. We sat at the end of a long table. I ate despite tears.

"You're from back east?" she said, not softening. "What kind of name is Cindra?"

But I couldn't get the answers out, so hungry, so sad. I ate.

At length, Lioness said, "I'm from Texas. Big farm. My boyfriend and I got busted with a bottle of wine and a bag of weed in his pickup, and naked. He got nothing, not even arrested. I got sentenced. Guess who was white."

"You?" I said.

She laughed. That was nice. My tears fled. I wanted to say everything about Dag and Billy and me and all that had gone wrong, but I couldn't get out the first word.

Lioness picked up my plate.

She said, "I'm your cabin sentinel. Which means just a senior inmate. You'll be a sentinel, too, if you stay. We have a nice group. Pride, we're supposed to call it, our pride. We'll meet them later. Are you ready? Let's get your bedding. We got to hurry. It's already last bell. Vespers on the mountain tonight."

I carried my blanket and sheets and my towels, crisply folded, paper bag of toiletries on top. Vespers sounded nice. Lioness walked me under the setting sun through big Ponderosa pines, she called them, orange showing through the bark, sweeping branches that guarded patches of snow. Then almost to the creek and to a well-made cabin in a line of three. "This is Cats," she said.

Inside, there was a tiny woodstove, cold. I counted nine bunks in all, two left to pick from, one a bottom bunk, the other the top bunk of the only triple-decker. Which reached up into the eaves, a high ladder along the bed frame, perfect. "That one," I said.

"You sure, hon? The tree fort? It can be hot up there when they let us have a fire. And it's hot in summer, too."

I climbed up and tried the mattress, crunch of old-school stuffing. It was warm, all right, but very dry, and private, no other girl at your level. Also, there was a small square window, a screened hatch maybe a hand's length on a side, trees out there to drift away in. The little crank was hard to budge, but I worked it, the pane like a wing, the citrus-smelling ponderosa pine like forever.

Chapter Six

Camp Challenge was built on Turtle Butte, a massive mountain sawed off at the top and tilted such that if you climbed (and climbed, snow patches deeper and more plentiful) to the end of the property, you came to a cliff, four- or five-hundred-foot sheer drop, whole mountain ranges marching off into the eastern distance, the Great Plains undulating between and beyond, and darkness at that hour, though the sky was still bright. Lioness had me look over the edge in case I wondered why there was no fence. Bras were dangerous but not cliffs?

"Fuck," I said.

"That's a demerit," she said. "Foul language."

"But."

"That's two. Talking back."

My heart pounded. The trees far below us looked almost soft in the dusk, a warm blanket. "I'm just," I said.

But Lioness smiled, the slowest, most beautiful moment: no such thing as demerits.

So what else had been a joke?

Vespers took place on a bare plateau as resounding stars emerged, the darkness rising in the east as surely as dawn. The chapel consisted of concentric semicircles of benches around a giant firepit, amphitheater seats aimed out at the view. That first night, they had an immodest fire going, and it lit the beaming face of Dora Dryden Conover. She was older than my parents, that dark and glossy hair, Black Irish, my mother would have announced. Everyone turned to watch as Lioness led me shuffling up the slope, all of them in identical gray sweatshirts, right to Dora Dryden Conover's side, she in flowing white.

Dora Dryden Conover bowed slightly, took my hand emphatically, announced, "We have a new arrival!"

"Hey," I said to everyone, and nodded my way around the ring. One hundred twenty girls, I'd read. Sixty on "scholarship," meaning they were wards of the state, the rest of us paying for the privilege of incarceration.

"This is Cindra," Ms. Conover said.

Lioness slipped away, found a seat among the benches.

"We were talking about kindness," Ms. Conover said. Her gaze was compelling. I felt I was falling toward her. She said, "If you'd like to stand, Cindra, that's fine, but there are plenty of places to sit. Franciella, make some room back there, what do you say?"

There was no need for Franciella to make room. I spotted her immediately, an imposing sourpuss with flattened afro, utterly alone, more alone than I. She patted the bench beside her, not friendly, and I took the long walk of shame, sat beside her.

"No whites," she whispered.

But I wasn't taking any more shit, slid a little closer.

Franciella did the same, and suddenly we were touching, knee to knee, hip to hip.

"Kindness," Ms. Conover resumed. "It's part of the human contract, one of the ways we can be more like the Lord, who giveth and giveth again and again, who hath given us all this and who, as we know, can taketh again away."

"Amen," a couple of girls said, one of them passionately.

Someone scoffed.

No reaction from Ms. Conover, who only said, "As Paul said in his letter to the Ephesians, 'Be kind to one another, tenderhearted, forgiving one another, as God in Christ forgave you.'"

It was night, it was dark, the incessant wind had stopped, the sky was vivid. I didn't feel I had been forgiven. I noticed that one of the far benches was entirely occupied by pregnant girls, some of them very far along. Well, that wasn't me.

The passionate girl said, "She opens her mouth with wisdom, and the teaching of kindness is on her tongue."

"Proverbs thirty-one, verse twenty-six," Dora Dryden Conover said.

I was impressed with their knowledge, scoffed anyway.

Franciella whispered, hymn-like, "Please, Cindra, throweth me off the cliffside and into boiling fish oil."

I gave her a quick smile—terrified of getting in trouble, terrified I'd offend her. Her skin was brown and smooth and freckled, shone in the fire-light, her soft arms straining against the sleeves of her T-shirt, maybe no sizes big enough in the camp's careless supply closet. And then I laughed: the image of my throwing this tremendous girl.

And so she laughed.

Ms. Conover fixed us in her gaze. She said, "Can anyone tell a story of a kindness shown them? Either here or back home? Or anywhere?"

"My boyfriend fuck me in the ass," someone shouted.

I tensed up, but everyone laughed, not even cautiously, rambunctiously in fact, even Dora Dryden Conover, who said, "Yes, love is almost always a kindness." Dramatic pause. "Though certain men will want to take kindness to extremes, and it is our job to discourage them. And Cheryl, my dear Cheryl, you get double kitchen tomorrow for reminding us!"

"I'm not sorry, Miss Dora."

"Apology accepted."

General laughter.

The passionate Proverbs person piped up again, a mere silhouette, explosively permed pink hair still holding its own: "My foster parents? They wanted to take us to the graveyard? Where my mother is buried? After my father and everything? And the kindness was that the graveyard man first said it was closed but then let us in."

"Beautiful man!" Ms. Conover exclaimed.

Another girl, younger, white as paper, her skin glowing in starlight, speaking from the pregnant bench: "We found a bunny once and brought it home and nursed it with a bottle of milk."

"Wonderful, wonderful," Dora Dryden Conover said.

"I helped bring the camp horses in that one time, the time they got out," someone behind me said.

Derisive sniggers, whispered conversation.

"Ladies," said Dora Dryden Conover. "That is a kindness that Mr. Marvelette let you help him when you know so little."

Wait. Wasn't that mean in itself, what Dora Dryden Conover had said? Maybe we all thought so. Anyway, there was silence. I couldn't quite listen for wondering about the first example we'd been offered, Cheryl's.

Someone hidden behind taller girls said, "We had a neighbor. He, like, fell or something. And I drove him to the hospital in his car. I was like twelve."

"You were heroic," said Dora Dryden Conover. "But that doesn't explain how you knew how to drive!"

Laughter.

Lioness said, "My principal in junior high didn't tell my parents about this thing that happened."

"What thing?" someone asked kindly.

"I broke something. One of those overhead projectors? I knocked it off the table in anger."

Incredulous, someone said, "And you didn't get suspent?"

"He said he understood."

"He fuck me sooooo gooooood," Cheryl said to laughter, riding her own train of thought.

"Well, Leslie, authority is always in a position to be kind," Ms. Conover said, ignoring Cheryl. "And maybe there was some corner of kindness in your action? A point to be made that could be made only with the help of an overhead projector?"

Lioness was Leslie. She thought about the director's words, said, "No, I was just mean and ornery. And the teacher was so boring. 'We're just going to inspect these transparencies and look for press anomalies."" It was a great imitation of a white, boring teacher.

"In your own way, you were looking out for the others in the class," Ms. Conover said kindly.

"Class in the ass," Cheryl said.

When the laughter died down, Ms. Conover said, "Cheryl Milton. Why do you bring up your boyfriend again? Or I should say former boyfriend, as you won't be seeing him ever again, never."

Silence.

"Everyone, why do you think Cheryl brings up her former boyfriend twice? And inappropriately?"

A voice piped up in the night: "She wants attention?"

"Probably true," Dora Dryden Conover said, total authority. "But often there are many causes for inappropriate behavior, layers of causes and not only one. It's best to know ourselves, to strip pages away, to read down into ourselves, find out what moves us to misbehave."

"Fuck-bitch," Cheryl said sharply.

People gasped: she'd gone too far. All the girls turned subtly—they knew what was coming. I turned, too. Back behind the last benches a couple of big men in light blue uniforms emerged. They'd been back there in the trees. They eased up to Cheryl, no hurry.

"Mother*fucker*," Cheryl shouted, and then kept shouting it as the men picked her up and carried her away. You could tell it happened all the time—no one but Cheryl was overly excited.

"She'll get Vault," Franciella whispered, shuddering.

"May I get a couple of girls for her committee?" Dora Dryden Conover said.

Several raised their hands.

She picked two, said the meeting would be at ten the next morning, all very calm, then back to the evening's program: "Any more stories? Stories of kindness?"

After a prolonged (and to me very pleasant) silence, a pale, frail, big-nosed redhead got to her feet in the firelight. While she gathered her words, the sky darkened perceptibly.

"Kindness," she said finally. And then one phrase at a time, gulps between, something broken in there: "Well, the policeman. That found me after the thing. He was so gentle and kind. The others were rough. And handcuffed me. And said insulting words. But that first policeman. Pulls me out from under the porch. After I been two days down there. And says, 'We're going to find you. The help you need.'"

"You've told us about that man before," Dora Dryden Conover said. "He sounds very professional. Very kind."

"He goes, 'We're going to find you. The help.' And then he picks me up. And carries me all the way. To the police cars. On the other side of the woods. And the whole way just. Just saying very kind things. Like to relax. Not to be too negative to myself. I had an illness. That was what he said. And that we'd get the help I needed. But then he was gone."

"And here you are," said Dora Dryden Conover.

"With two broken arms," said the redhead, holding up a pair of thick plaster casts. "That was the other police."

"Praise the Lord," Franciella whispered extravagantly.

"The other officers weren't so kind," said Dora Dryden Conover.

"What do you mean, Vault?" I whispered to Franciella in the ensuing murmur of affirmation.

She shuddered again: Vault was bad.

I looked to the sky, found a couple of homemade constellations, the one I called Horse and the one I called Volkswagen, both sharing stars with more familiar constellations. Perfect horse, perfect VW bug, perfect night to look—that glorious Montana sky, stars the same as home.

"Cindra," Dora Dryden Conover said. "Let us hear from you. Any stories of kindnesses?"

I started, sat up hard at the sound of my name.

"Any stories of kindness?"

Everyone watched me as I thought. But it wasn't a hard pick: "My father," I said. "He bought me a necklace after I got in trouble. After so much trouble, he bought me a necklace, just a chain with a real pearl."

"A token of forgiveness," someone said.

My face burned hot, but around the chapel and in the light of the fire, 120 miscreant girls held a silence, and this was moving in itself. I wanted Dora to know what that necklace she'd confiscated meant, and this fraught silence was my ally. I cried. I finally cried. And it was plain I wasn't the only one. I heard sobs and several girls blowing their noses.

"Kindness to others is a reflection of our self-love," Dora Dryden Conover said after a long time. "Yes, our self-love. When we can accept ourselves, really look deep down inside and look all around, at the good, at the bad, at the beautiful, at the ugly, at the unspeakable, even, we can see it all for what it is and think, I love this person, I love all that I am, all that God has made me. That's when we can be most kind."

I sobbed, couldn't help it.

"Great performance," my bench-mate whispered. "Dora surely loves you now."

"Shh," I said sharply. I hadn't been acting. I decided to hate Franciella.

"Let us silently pray," Dora Dryden Conover said, and all the girls ducked their heads. My father not only refused to pray but (except for that one time) disdained the display, and like him, I kept my head high during any prayer I happened upon. The silence went on, very long, a real owl hooting in the near distance, a breeze picking up.

Far across the bowed heads, back beyond the last rows of benches, something moved, a kind of burgeoning, and then a presence, the sudden sweeping movement of a big cowboy hat coming off, being laid over a heart. The driver. He stood very still, the only other head unbowed. In the light his face looked complicated, more shy than taciturn. And I saw that as much as I wanted to make him into a romantic Crow brave, he was just another guy with a shitty job.

After the prayer, a real minister came out. Reverend Bridgewater, he said. He was tall and thin, started out with a warm look around, let himself smile like he was seeing old friends. "To love ourselves," he said, "is to love God. And to love God? That is to love the planet. And to love the planet? That is to love ourselves. Which, perforce, my friends, is to love God." And that was it. More than a full circle. He let us think about that, an astonishing long silence under the stars, then he bid us stand and sing "For the Beauty of the Earth." But it was a different melody from the one I knew. Then "Michael Row the Boat Ashore." And finally a hymn few but the reverend and Dora seemed to know. Franciella pretended to sing along but made up her own words, Jesus roasting on a spit, pole up his ass, naked priests hungry for him with forks ready, and fighting over the holy dick, and all in rhyme and fit perfectly to the music, so I decided to like her again. When we sat finally for the benediction, the driver and his giant hat were gone, simply disappeared.

Dora took over: "Lord, let us love ourselves more fully so that we may love You more fully. Let us love the Earth, certainly, but You above all, and let us not let earthly concerns confuse us."

Amen, amen, all around the circle.

After, we broke into groups, Lioness coming straight to me, claiming me, collecting me, the girls in my pack gathering around and closing Franciella out.

And without her, we marched.

In Cats, we quieter girls undressed quickly and I realized what the second T-shirt I'd been issued was for—pajamas. We all wore the same giant underpants. Lioness saw my pink socks. "Uh-oh," she said. Then, "Quick."

I stripped off the socks.

Kitten, a little redheaded girl, took them from me, stuffed them into a hole in her mattress. Seconds later a whistle blew and two stern white women were at the door. Everyone rushed to stand at attention in the limited floor space. "Cats accounted for?" one of them said.

"Cats accounted for," Lioness said.

"Count off!"

And we counted, one through nine.

"New member," the other guard said.

The girl next to me pushed me forward.

"Your name?"

"Cindra," I said.

The guards looked at each other ominously. "Not Cindy?" the freckly one said.

The other one advanced, tall as Franciella, lifted my chin in a roughened hand till I was looking her in the eye.

"Your name," she said.

"Hairball," someone offered.

"Puss 'n' Boots," someone else.

"Tiger *Woodn'ts*," said one of the older girls, and finally everyone cracked up.

But not the guards. They hit the doorframe with their sticks till the girls quieted down.

"You're Sylvester," one of them said. And then they left.

The girls fell or climbed into their bunks. I clambered all the way up and into mine, aware of all the eyes upon me, giggles. The heat at that private altitude felt fine. I was Sylvester the Cat, why not? The little vent window was still cranked open. I could hear some early insect buzzing out in the trees, the wind returning. There was that Montana smell of sage, of dryness, of pine boards, all of it balm. Lioness turned off the light and fell into her bottom bunk, a lot of creaking. I got an image of my father, just how he was, a little stooped, a little distracted, living only for me, he'd have you believe, my daddy out in the yard, thinking hard about something, always thinking hard. That Montana wind was lonely. I thought I'd be the only one crying that night in all of camp, all of Montana, all of the Great Plains, all of the west, but I was not: small sobs came from somewhere below me.

"Chocolate bunnies," Lioness said gently in the dark.

"Chocolate bunnies," repeated a soft, soft voice.

"Ham and beans," someone else said.

"Ham and beans," a couple of voices repeated.

"Cindra, how about you?" Lioness said.

"Fish sticks?"

The cabin erupted in laughter.

"Ah, girl," Lioness said still gently. "You're gonna take some busting."

"Fesh stecks," someone else said to more laughter.

Did I have an accent?

And every time it got quiet someone said it again, more and more exaggerated, gales of fresh laughter.

"Chocolate bunnies," Lioness said at last.

"Chocolate bunnies," the tiny voice said, last word.

Slowly my chest unclenched, my fists. Slowly my thoughts grew abstract, preternatural. And then someone farted, a furious he-man blast, general giggling, disgusted groaning, another fart in competition, tears and bunnies superseded, fesh stecks, too. My little window was square and the stars were out there and I rose to be among them, rose up and rose higher and finally slept, slept at last.

Chapter Seven

Much later I had a therapist who said I liked the boundaries Camp Challenge provided. All I'd said was that I'd liked wearing all gray. And the little window in my bunk. And the regular hours, that kind of thing. I didn't like the boundaries. I didn't argue with the therapist, though. I never argued with him, not till later.

Dora Dryden Conover wasn't bound to her office, she said, so that next morning after breakfast in the mess hall, she took me for what she called a ramble, up the hill to the chapel. She was warm and present but said nothing after shaking my hand and proposing the walk. We sat on the first bench or pew and looked out over the world. At length, tired of waiting for me to say something, she started: "Tell me what you hope from your time here at Challenge."

"Well," I said, searching for what she wanted to hear. "To make myself a better person."

"But you seem like a very fine person. What could happen here to make you better?"

"I'm not much of a team player," I said. Teamwork was in their brochure.

"Oh, well, we do have help for that. What else?"

"Probably I'm not used to living, interacting, and negotiating with others." Also in the brochure.

"Never been to summer camp?"

"Never been."

"Well, this isn't summer camp, is it. But you will live and interact with others. Cats is a nice bunch. Low risk, which I'm assured is your profile.

And among them some of our youngest campers, whom I hope you'll help nurture. That's often the path to betterment—helping others." The sky was an ocean, a blue immensity darker above than at the edges, jagged with mountain ranges north and south, perfectly flat east, curve of the earth.

"Let us pray on your improvement," Ms. Conover said, bowing her head with easy grace.

The wind never stopped, just a steady presence, something you really could mistake for divine, almost maddening, my hair blowing behind me. I bowed my head some but didn't close my eyes, purposely thought of my dad, the necklace he'd given me—wherever Ms. Conover had stored it in the HQ—also his tears as I left. The three years ahead seemed like something more than eternity, and there was that feeling of divinity again, that time itself was so long, and that we were so brief, visions unbidden of the Mercedes dealer lying on cement, Dag naked upon me, his broad chest with its manly mat of tight curls. Suddenly someone plopped down beside me, placed a cool hand on my back, that gap where it was bare between T-shirt and pants.

It was Lioness. She bowed extravagantly to let me know she prayed as I did: theatrical simulation.

Dora Dryden Conover took her time, another eternity, but then she was done, muttered a private amen. "Ah, Ms. Hilton," she said, noticing Lioness. "Have we consulted the roster?"

"There's an opening on laundry duty," Lioness said. She was Leslie Hilton, and her real name seemed a treasure, a secret all my own. "I mean since Cheryl . . ."

"Ah yes," said the boss.

"I'm good with laundry," I said.

"A team player," Ms. Conover said, amused.

Later, after a perfect lunch of bologna sandwiches, we Cats returned to the bunk for siesta. No one napped. The rule was just that we be quiet in our bunks. Some of the girls played cards, some braided a neighbor's hair. And everyone whispered:

"Laundry, bummer." That was Puma, knocking the casts on her arms together. "Glad I was exempt. It's disgusting."

Another white girl, Virginia, said, "You have to ride all the way into Billings every week with the Chief."

"But that's the best part," Ocelot said, the youngest of us, Chicana, eerie green eyes, her head buzzed but super cute, almost a boy herself. "I loved that ride."

Puma said: "Chief Deaf Man."

I said, "He's deaf?"

"Deaf and dumb and also plain dumb."

"His name is Lucky," the girl with the broken arms said. "Have some respect."

"Ha-ha," someone else. "Lucky no one kilt him."

Leslie Hilton said, "He's not deaf, you silly kitties, and he's not stupid. He's only *reticent*. I talk to him often, because he helps coordinate tasks. Lucky is the kindest person you will ever know, and he's good at what he does. Ms. Conover says he's not an Indian or anyway not a full Indian but mixed."

"Dora full of shit," someone said.

"Like, *right*, he's not an Indian," someone else.

"Mixed *up*," Ocelot lisped, missing tooth.

Silence, wind in the high trees, all the girls chastened despite the protests.

After a long time, Puma said, "Hey, Sylvester. Did you meet the doctor?"

"Oh my god," several girls said.

And someone said, "You have a tipped uterus, no doubt!" Everyone tittered, groaned.

I said, "He said so! How did you know?"

Leslie said, "All the pretty white girls have tipped uteruses. We have made a survey."

Ocelot with her lisp said, "He's a perf, that's all."

I said, "What's a perf?" But everyone laughed so hard I let it go, let them think I was being funny.

Chapter Eight

I just tried to do my best at laundry. The sheets weren't bad, but the towels were damp and some of them very smelly, some of them used for cleaning up stuff I didn't even want to know about. I loaded the van, the in-my-estimation definitely Indian driver occasionally gesturing. Crow, someone had said. Lucky, the girls had called him. Evidently, I was to keep the piles discrete. Big towels. Smaller towels. Washcloths. Bottom sheets, top sheets, pillowcases. The sun beat down. The pavilion was so cool, the van was so hot. I ducked back and forth, a good worker. A busty camp guard—just some older white lady you might see at church—stood in the shade, not going to lift a finger. Lucky, too, though you got the idea there was some rule, that he'd have helped if no one were watching. Was he my age? Maybe not. Maybe older, but not by much. Puma had said he was deaf, but Lioness was right—he turned his head at the call of a crow or a camper laughing somewhere distant, also when I clicked my tongue to test him.

When the laundry was loaded, I loped to the washroom, my ankle sore, as it tended to be when my mother came to mind, soaped my hands four times, dried them on my own shirt, raced to the mess hall, everyone already eating. I sat at the only available place, beside sullen Franciella.

She started right in. "You got laundry? Worst job in the neighborhood. Except cesspool. That be worse. But they only make the really *dark* Black girls do that."

"Franciella!"

"The truth be true."

I said, "Why are you talking like that?"

A fresh accent, comically white American: "Citizens of African origin represent point-oh-six percent of the Montana populace. Isn't that how citizens of African origin talk?"

"Oh, shut up," I said. "You are you."

"If you say so," she said, suddenly gentle.

To change the subject I said, "What's your job?"

And another accent, an eerily accurate Dora Dryden Conover: "Oh, me? Dahling, I'm excused from physical labor. I type letters for the director of this rarefied institution. Extravagantly boring letters." And another, a kind of commentator voice: "That lady writes letters at the drop of a hat. She's always trying to win some court case. She owns this place, did you know? Did you know it's tens of thousands of acres? Did you know our own diva Dora played the friend in *The Karter Kids*? Like six years' worth."

"No!"

"Yes indeedy!"

"Wait. You mean she's Donut Dora? No way!"

Finally a normal voice: "And she was lovers with the producer, from age like twelve to like fifteen!"

"The Donut Dora thing?" Couldn't be true, not our Dora Dryden Conover! My mother's favorite television scandal, so *instructive*. "Oh my god!"

Franciella nodded sagely, switched voices again, some kind of secretarial ingenue: "I type ninety words a minute and learn strange things."

After lunch, the busty guard walked me back to the Camp Challenge van, where my wrangler was waiting, eyes averted, impassive under his uncreased, comically tall cowboy hat. The camp guard locked me in back, and Lucky got in, not a word, started up the engine. Behind him but in front of the piles of laundry, I rode to town. Same van all right, pleasantly warm from sitting in the sun all morning, unpleasantly smelly, banging and shuddering on the rough road, little sideways lurches. Lucky rolled his window down, and I breathed in the sagebrush and dust and plain oxygen. The mountains far away moved most slowly, the mountains halfway moved faster, the ridge closest sped in a blur, the roadside weeds invisible, whispering, all of it more wonderful than I remembered from my arrival, quite a lot more wonderful, actually inspiring, like a great drama. In town, Lucky tilted stiffly at the wheel, this way and that as he made a dozen turns through a maze of industrial buildings till finally we stopped at a gate, low cement building with an actual guard, portly white dude who very slowly rose and very slowly unlocked the gate and very slowly waved us in, then very slowly closed the gate behind us.

Lucky let me out of the van via the back doors, stood away. The day was at least ten degrees warmer down here in the valley. The gatekeeper went back to his folding chair in the dust. No one was going to help me at that end either. I'd have thought they'd count the different kinds of pieces—towels, sheets, napkins—but all they did was weigh the piles as I brought them in one load at a time, each pile into the right bin, mindless work, past enormous bales of military uniforms all pressed and ready to go.

When I was done, Lucky hosed the back of the van out. And then at his signal I dried it with two of our own Challenge-soiled towels, tossed them back into the proper bin. An officious small white man arrived. He took my arm brusquely, pulled me into the dispatch room, he called it. He filled the standing order with bundles of gray—towels, sheets, pillowcases—and I carried them to the van, one dense bale at a time. When I was done, the little man beckoned me behind the little counter, pointed to the floor. He'd spread out a blanket and a clean sheet, four or five one-dollar bills arrayed.

He said, "Hey blondie, you like to party?"

I thought it was some kind of punch line, a punch line missing a joke, and I laughed.

"Think it's funny," he said.

"No," I said. He just wasn't scary, like maybe Colonel Sanders on a bad day. I felt sorry for him, couldn't even take it as a compliment, as my mother always instructed.

Back at the van, Lucky helped me in, the first he'd touched me, just a hand under my elbow, strong, unexpectedly soft. The laundry-plant guard very slowly opened the gate. We drove out, taking a different route through the industrial maze.

I felt there'd been an opening. I tried for conversation, said, "Is your name really Lucky?"

No answer. He drove on a disused road along a real river, the Yellowstone, I hoped, opposite direction from camp, pulled off onto a dusty spur that opened into a bottom, sandy tracks, scant undergrowth, big trees, surprising cactuses, the river itself—a slow, deep coursing.

He stopped, and as the dust cloud settled, he climbed out, patting the van like you'd pat a horse, opened my door, breeze a little chilly, handed me my parka—he'd retrieved it somehow, saved it from confiscation. I put it on, my sweet old puffy orange parka, like wrapping up in home.

He sat on the riverbank, flat rock like a bench just big enough for two of us. And so I sat, too, close at his side in the welcome sun, a stiff silence between us, the sound of the insistent wind around us, birds twittering, a crow somewhere.

Lucky—that was his name, all right, unlucky creature—sat up straight, gave a little cough, like preparing to make a speech.

"Yes?" I said.

He coughed again. Then surprised me: "My aunt Maria said you will be my wife."

I wanted to laugh, but then in his gray eyes under the great brim of his ten-gallon hat, I saw he meant it.

"Your wife," I said.

"She said it, yes."

"And how does she know?"

"She knows most things."

Something about the gift of my own parka made me see him softly. We sat a long while, very nice in the sun. Still, when it seemed he was about to say something more, I got up quickly, hurried to the van, climbed in. It wasn't that I didn't trust him. It was that . . . I don't know. Just that he had a heart, and it pounded on his sleeve.

He didn't join me, not right away, but simply kept staring across the river and into the distance another long time, or anyway it seemed long, the van heating in the sun. Finally this Lucky rose in all his angles and cowboy boots and that very tall hat and strode over, no shred of embarrassment at his confession, none of self-consciousness, and climbed into the driver's seat.

"Hoppo!" he said.

Meaning only that it was time to go.

Chapter Nine

I looked for Lucky at vespers each night, no sign. He was narrow hipped and broad shouldered, and he was a guy more or less my age, the only one at camp. I'd have to be careful, I told myself. I'd have to treat him kindly. I might go ahead and be his wife, whatever he meant by that, but I'd have to let him down easy when the time came. Because time was the thing: time was already moving very slowly, and a boyfriend would speed it up. And not just a boyfriend but a Crow boyfriend who some thought holy and most thought laughable and I found sexy, what can I say, a box of broken crayons to draw a new life with, his quietude a thick pad of good paper stolen from the art room, blank and promising. But in my bunk at night, looking out at moonlight through my tiny window, I realized I didn't know Lucky at all, that he was no blank slate but complete in himself, that every thought I'd had about him was nonsense, false superiority, and that made me think of my mother's attitude about nearly everyone, especially those who were kind and gentle and wise and better than she'd ever be, like Miss Elegant. I had a strong hunch I wasn't worthy of the likes of Lucky, so much work to do on my soul. But maybe camp was the place to do it. I remembered all I'd seen in Lucky from the first day, that diamond toughness. I hoped he'd forgive me the broken heart when it came, realized I should probably not allow him closer at all. Look what I'd done to Dag! I skated around on my cheap advantage where better people than I fell through the ice. I resolved to leave Lucky alone, to leave all men alone. To be the person I was here to become.

Come day, though, I sought out the van, contrived to cross its path, but it was the nurse driving the once, Dora the next. Donut Dora, who'd famously lived with a famous TV producer from age twelve to fifteen! This made me like her. I asked everyone what they knew about Lucky, trying to make it seem mere curiosity about his heritage. There were rumors about him, of course. That he was deaf was persistent, also that he'd been found as a baby in the gully by the gate. Some claimed to have heard him speak. But not in English, in tongues. Like that, all rubbish. Every girl had a story, just never her own story. I learned he was forty years old. I learned he was fourteen. I learned he was a banished Crow and heard ten reasons why he'd been banished (killed a man, wasn't really Crow, desecrated their gods, broke himself on drugs and alcohol, etc.). I learned he was a Mexican runaway that Dora had picked up hitchhiking. I learned he was an Italian high-wire kid escaped from the circus. I listened and learned so much contradictory everything about him that he started to be like white noise or white light—he seemed a little bit of everything, a kind of walking purity. Two girls who'd been on laundry, one of them quite beautiful, said he'd never said a single word, never held their eye. And then Ocelot, who said he scared her bad, who said she couldn't get that rigid way he sat out of her head, always his back to her, never a word, whether kind or sharp, just did his job like she was nothing. Every last one of us had thought about Lucky, and who he really was. I, of course, the one with the best story of all, held my tongue.

Chapter Ten

Tuesdays and Thursdays were the guards' days off, alternating basis, and so on those nights there was only one bunk check or, if one of the guards was out sick, none at all. The bunk checks were officially unannounced, but they came at very regular times, two and five in the morning, at a guess—there were no clocks anywhere. And everyone cataloged the comings and goings of the guards, noted their illnesses, their bad moods, their vacations, noted them closely.

"Tonight's kind of a funny night," Leslie Hilton said one chilly Tuesday. All the girls huddled in around me, great smiles. "Belinda's off. No bunk check till dawn. So it's Buddy Night."

"Buddy Night?"

"Buddy Night. You'll see. After lights out."

Just one guard for lights out, and after that I felt I couldn't sleep, but must've, because I woke to the two a.m. guard's pleasant counting, like a story in the night, and then her very gentle, "Cats all in and accounted for."

Soon there was a creaking and a giggling and general hubbub, and someone—Ocelot—was climbing into my bunk. "Buddy," she said, claiming me.

She snuggled up face-to-face, and it was awfully warm and nice, her breath on my throat. "Sly, you have a boyfriend?" she whispered finally.

"I *had* a boyfriend," I murmured.

I liked her green eyes in the faint light. She said, "You in here for him?"

"More like he's in for me. Like, doing hard time. How about you?"

That lisp, so appealing: "I've liked a few boys. But I'm in for my own self. Not like some of you whores. I'm only twelve."

We laughed into one another's warm breaths, super quiet. Twelve!

"Do you want to know my real name?" she whispered. "I know yours, it's Cinderella."

"No, weirdo, it's Cindra!"

"I am Azalia, you weirdo yourself."

"So pretty," I said. "My favorite flower."

I turned over, let her spoon my back, nice enough. There was more creaking, and someone whispering, someone else sighing, then another, different sound, rhythmic. We listened.

"Some of the girls are better buddies than others," Ocelot.

I suddenly knew what she meant. That's how long it took for me to catch on, how worldly I was: not so much as I'd thought. My partner wriggled an arm under me and held my breast quite gently, and I felt her nose on my neck, companionable. It was the nicest thing, just to be warm together. Artless Azalia warmed my back, soon steady breaths, steady rise and fall of her ribs tight behind me.

It was 1997. I was only almost seventeen. That is, I was sixteen, regardless of what I might have told Dag. And just then, in that sweet lisping moment, I felt myself move on, leave the past behind, all that the past had meant. There was nothing so terrible about me. Maybe that had all come from outside.

Chapter Eleven

We Cats woke to an insistent bell every morning. It must have been awfully early, the sky faint pink. You had from first bell to second—maybe a half hour—to dress and wash and get to the mess, where inmates on KP had set the tables. We called ourselves inmates. Dora Dryden Conover called us campers, sometimes guests. She insisted on real tablecloths, even for breakfast, blue things from the linen supply, and cloth napkins, and table settings correct, plus Emily Post manners, including posture. Once we were all in our seats, we said a prayer, Dora going on about the gifts of the day to come. And then silent time, which I used for thoughts of Lucky. His upright bearing. His insular shyness. The directness of his speech when he got to it. That he had zero experience of women, and no ass to speak of. And wanted to marry me. I thought for sure we'd speak of great things. I thought we'd take long walks. I thought he'd teach me kindness. And I in turn could teach him to dance, not that I was so great. We'd sit back-to-back on hidden stone walls in the New England forest and read books, write poems. His energy was nothing like Dag's. I couldn't picture us kissing like Dag and I had done, hours on end, let alone the rest. I pictured Lucky and me talking. I pictured us walking. We'd find apples and pick them off the forest floor. I pictured the various moments a first kiss might happen. You'd pick up your apples and find yourselves face-to-face, like that. But that was as far as I got. Those eyes of his—they stopped me.

The food at camp was surprisingly good. Beef arrived every day from the old Johman Ranch down the mountain, and lots of it. And Idaho potatoes, which is what everyone but everyone called them, including me after a while. The camp gardens and cold frames, kept by the cooks, had radishes and greens already, even as the snowpack lingered in the tree line. The bread was baked on the premises from wheat ground right there between old stone wheels powered by trudging campers. The cooks were three ladies of indeterminate age, two of them sisters, all of them widows, the hubbub had it, yoked shirts and Wrangler jeans, barrel racers long ago, town beauties long ago, dreamers still, with good jobs for that time, that place. They'd say small nice things about the weather or the way you'd done your hair as you collected your food in the cafeteria line, and over many meals you felt you got to know them and started to pretend you'd done something to your hair besides run wet hands through it. The campers would applaud after particularly good meals (we all loved french fries, made with Idaho potatoes), and the cooks would come out of the kitchen and into the dining room, take a bow.

After breakfast each day were chores and, after chores, activities. There was no traditional school, but the Camp Challenge activities still felt like school to me, or maybe church: Reading Club, Math Club, Science, Bible. My favorite was Rim Hike (I'll let you imagine the jokes), out along the very edge of Turtle Butte, which was with Nature Group, a subset of Science, and happened twice a week. Another good one was Cookies and Cakes, a baking class with the kitchen ladies on Wednesdays, when a crowd of us helped make a whole week's desserts. A lot of the girls went for Prayer Group, because you could bow your head and sleep extra. But not even a nap was worth any further brush with religion, not for me. I settled into the routine, with designs on Lucky to sustain me.

Finally it was Tuesday again, my second laundry day. A heat wave had overtaken us. Not unusual in that perch over the sun-rich plains, everyone said. Three days in the high seventies and now high eighties at breakfast and climbing, the last lingering snow drifts fading to nothing. I collected the laundry, filled the cart over and over, cheerfully wheeled it down to the carport, sweating, heart pounding, slightly sick with the heat. Linens collected, I waited for the van, no one watching over me. Shortly, here it came, banging and clattering and throwing up a great cloud of dust, Mr. Lucky at the wheel. My plan sort of died with the reality of him, this stiff wrangler of inmates. Hadn't I learned my lesson? We did everything the same as ever, he watching over me as I loaded the van, then locking me in back alone.

After he'd closed the second gate and driven down the road a mile, he stopped and got out, all business, but let me out the back and opened the front passenger's door, quick nod of the head, just as solemn and proper as ever. He wasn't shy, he wasn't flirtatious, he wasn't anything. Well, very beautiful—something about him, the way his hair was tied, so much care, his tender mouth. My plan fell back into place. I climbed up front, and now we were side by side as on a date, forget about Buddy Night.

"Just say you were carsick," he said after a mile. "If anyone."

"I might actually be carsick," I said. You couldn't make him smile. "Luckily lots of towels." Nothing. Not so much as a glance. I put on a face as serious as his and then silently we went through the long process at the laundry plant. The little functionary barely acknowledged me this time, just did his job. And finally I was done and Lucky was driving again, straight to the river. We found the exact spot where we'd been a week before. He kicked off his cowboy boots, no socks. I slipped off my camp clogs, camp socks, gray upon gray. The sand felt hot and fine between my toes. Sweat rolled down my sides. Sweat beaded on my lip.

Not Lucky's. "Vurry hot," he said.

"Vurry," I said.

He knew he was being teased. He said, "*Vurry* hot for May."

"It's April," I said.

"Even hotter for April." His cheeks rose into his eyes, warm amusement: Was he teasing me back? He'd parted his hair with more care than you'd think. Had he done that for me?

Now I was the awkward one. I said, "It's been hot all week. In Massachusetts, it's still winter, really."

"I thought I might dunk in the river here."

I said, "Now we're talking."

And he said, "Yes." But he meant that we were talking, only that.

"I mean, good idea," I said.

A glance. His eyes were full of sky. I don't know how to say it. He unsnapped his shirt, took it off carefully, folded it, and laid it on his shoes. I left mine on, then realized I couldn't go back to camp with my shirt soaked so pulled it off, held it to my chest in a bunch. But Lucky took no notice. I was the one taking notice: he was thin as a rock star, straight in every line. He hopped a little and got his pants off and he was naked, all muscles and cords, like someone had drawn the lines of him with a sharp marker—or no, painted him with sun and shade in some way. He was just as polite as ever, no eyes for me. The air was hot, vurry hot. I pulled off my pants, too, sat in my big gray official panties, let my shirt drop as he folded his trousers. And found I wasn't embarrassed—most guys would ogle, not Lucky. We were just people with bodies. And so I peeled off my knickers, my mom would have called them, hurried to wade into the current, dove fast where it got deep. And it was so fine, so icy cold, so bracing, more clarity descending. Lucky waded in with his hat on. Just below his nipple he had a scar the size of a nickel, as perfectly round. He was a dunker, not a swimmer, kind of flailed as the water got deep, and so I made some nice crawl strokes past him, showing off. He watched me. Finally he took off his hat, let it float on its brim. He had a bigger scar on his back, skin raised pale in the shape of a state or a country on a map, maybe Missouri or France.

"You were looking very closely," a certain therapist would say, years to come. And I would say, "Vurry," not the right answer judging by the spate of pencil notes those two syllables required. He hated how I pronounced that simple word and how I never stopped saying it like that, *vurry*, like kissing Lucky, your mouth just so. Lucky tried swimming as I did, flung an arm above his head, dropped into the water like a tree falling over, a lot of fancy splashing and kicking, all while he sank. Was he being funny? He finished and wiped his eyes dramatically, found his hat floating a couple of yards downstream, plunked it back on his head, everything dripping. Then, nothing for it, we simply sat in freezing water up to our necks, not too close together, not too far apart, he in his tall hat. My skin clutched my muscles with the cold, my muscles clutched my bones, all the organs inside drew up tight.

That future therapist wanted to linger over the story, juvenile ward naked and shivering with her older guard. But it wasn't like that—guards are prisoners, too. And it wasn't the same category as the camp doctor and his awful ministrations, despite my therapist's professionally rephrased questions, all the note-taking, all the clearings of the throat. I hadn't felt Dag's touch in six months, and I missed all that. What went through my head came through my body first. I felt simply that Lucky might make life at Challenge bearable.

In the Yellowstone River up to my neck, I scooted toward him, scooted a little closer, a little closer yet, and then we were touching. I ducked under the shadowy brim of that tall cowboy hat, gave him a kiss on the lips. And then I kissed him again. Staring off, clearly impressed, he seemed to consider what he might add. Finally he kissed me back, a tiny peck on my lips.

I liked being in charge. And I really was, despite the theories of future therapists. On the hot sand Lucky and I kissed naked and our goosebumps receded, and what was plain was that he'd never been touched at all before. I took his hat off for him, placed it on the sand. And though he kept checking on it, eventually his kisses opened up, and you could number them, the first thirty kisses of his life, then forty, fifty, so on, individual experiences each one, all to be savored later, and for years. I surprised him with my touch. He jumped at each advance. I lay back in the hot, hot sand, and I pulled him onto me and helped him inside, and he was quiet as ever, immediately convulsing so hard that I thought something was wrong, great splash of heat.

He tried to roll off, but I held on to him, one arm across his shoulders, a hand on that rectangular wrangler butt, just the feeling of him on top of me and the hot sand under. Still, I must have conveyed some shred of disappointment.

Because he said, "I don't know how."

"You know something," I said.

He broke out of my embrace and all but catapulted to his feet, stepped and dove back into the river. I followed him into the crystal water and washed myself subtly, and it all just felt so good that I didn't particularly think forward or backward, just as far as the wonderment of his scars: he'd been through things I didn't know. When we were tolerably dry, no further words, he put his hat on, then dressed. I dressed more slowly, followed him to the van. He held my door, no stolen kisses, locked me in, and soon we were back at the gates of Camp Challenge, and then I was unloading the bundles of clean linens as he watched over.

"My old auntie told me," he said.

"Tell your auntie I like her."

"She told me you would come from the sky," he said.

"Tell her she was right. I came from the sky."

"She said I would know you by water."

"Know, as in the Bible, yes?"

A flicker of irritation crossed his face—the Bible, useless. He said, "She said I would see you by fire."

"That's how I first saw you truly. Up there at vespers."

Visibly he liked that—him, too, he'd first seen me truly at vespers. He said, "She said we would be of the earth."

"Your auntie is vurry wise."

He stared off. He didn't like even the hint of a whiff of a shade of joking, not about his auntie, whoever she was. He'd be a great diversion, I'd told myself, and I should keep perspective. But some part of me continued to ring, like a brass bell you could hear just till you couldn't, and then nothing else.

Chapter Twelve

After breakfast every day, we campers divided into three groups, three streams heading to various places. One fine morning, I picked Trail Repair over Poetry, twenty girls or so trudging companionably, Franciella at the rear, where I joined her. She was tallest by far, easily taller than Lucky, who I'd have bet was six-two, though his tall cowboy hat made it hard to tell. Anyway, my eye was at her shoulder. The weather had continued unseasonably hot, and the girl sweated like me, our t-shirts soaked after the first hundred yards. She smelled beautiful, like a garden of deep-belled flowers. Lucky had smelled like Montana itself: that omnipresent sagebrush carried in the constant wind. All I could think about was him, about getting back to him.

Franciella said, "These miscreants refuse to accommodate our lumbering," mocking Ms. Conover's patrician accent so perfectly that I laughed.

Trail Repair was captained by Clay Marvelette, the white-guy stableman, ancient from our perspective, likely in his seventies, well known to have no camper awareness, Dora called it. He led a big, adorable old trail horse named View, who didn't seem to be bothered by the saddle loaded with shovels and pickaxes and full canteens: they moved so fast. Franciella and I fell even farther back. As the rest of the group disappeared over the crest of a ridge, she suddenly pulled my arm and hustled me off the trail, a mighty trundle up the hill on a faint game path, several hundred yards through the last patches of snow to a flat, bare rock in the sun, where she sat, puffing hard, pink in the cheeks, the wind trapped forever in her nimbus of hair.

"I've been doing this," she said.

"You just abandon the group?"

"They never missed me once."

She lay back, and I sat beside her, gradually lay back myself on the moss, wriggling to find my place amid the roots and rocks. There were no clouds in the sky overhead, nothing but blue, that hot, steady wind, scent of dust, a kind of whistling through the long pine needles above.

"Montana," I said.

Franciella groaned extravagantly. "I need more people all around me. And less walking, always walking. And just you wait till real winter. I barely lived through it, honestly. They have dances!"

I was not against dances. I hadn't been to one for ages, not since before Dag, who could hardly take me out in public.

Franciella struggled off the rock, pulled my hand to sit me up, popped me to my feet with a tug. She thought a moment, visibly made a decision. She said, "I want to show you something." She led me another few rocks higher, surprisingly agile, a lot of puffing, yet almost dainty progress. And then, among a group of enormous boulders that offered shelter, a vast metropolis came into view, a city of sticks and rocks and seedpods and flower stems, the petals of pine cones plucked and arranged as roof tiles on a hundred tiny buildings. She'd built fences, smoothed roadways and playing fields, erected clock towers over schools. There was a large number of citizens, she explained, people represented by pebbles, a particular type of red stone for one family, granite pebbles for another, striped stones for a third, and on and on, all with names and histories. They'd spent the winter under family shelters made of flat rocks, like Flintstones houses.

The town was called La Vil.

"Three summers I've been at this," she said, pulling families from storage, uncovering houses, repairing roofs and gardens, tracing roadways clean with her long fingers. "When I can. It's only just come out from under the snow."

She assigned me the Robertsons, who were the striped stones, not too smart but community minded, and soon I was seeing what she was seeing—the sad Robertson daughter, Lulu, the tough Robertson son, Lemuel, the bossy mother Robertson, the saintly father. The game was complex, my Robertson daughter, Lulu, for example, secretly dating an ambitionless granite boy, Ed. Much of the game was finding ways for Lulu and Ed to be together, as his parents, really hard people, didn't approve of his dating stripes. Franciella's people, the Arnays, were the red stones, primarily, and ran the town, spoke quick French, it sounded like. As we repaired the ravages of winter, my new friend filled me in: one young red son was in love with Lulu, and it was thought around town that this might wake up Ed.

Franciella could feel the real minutes going by where I could not. After what seemed like no time at all, she said our visit was done. We found a stopping place in our story and slipped down her path in a hurry, hid behind the root plate of a fallen ponderosa as the group went by, shovels on their shoulders like soldiers, led by an oblivious Mr. Marvelette, all tired and riding now, squeezed in among the empty canteens on his big horse. We took up the rear after they'd passed and simply followed behind them to the dining hall, mixing with the other groups before we got there, dissipating like mismatched molecules in some biology-class broth.

"Where are you from?" I finally blurted, personal inquiry being rude where I came from, the blood rushing to my face.

"New Jersey," Franciella said, hated question.

"But before that?"

"Why do you think there's a before?"

"I don't know. You were speaking French."

She made a fart noise in dismissal, said, "*Your* accent is super funny. What is it?"

"Boston, I guess."

She liked that, all right, said, "Have you ever had a best friend?"

"Just a boyfriend," I said.

She grinned, vulnerable. "So not really."

"Yeah, so not really."

And we entered the mess in the bright afternoon sun. We lined up with the rest of the campers, filled our trays with the rest of them, then sat alone, Francie's table far at the back, no longer forlorn, the Queen of La Vil and me, her acolyte, suddenly best friends, no one the wiser, hot dogs and Idaho fries, not bad. We campers applauded the kitchen ladies, who came out and curtsied hilariously, one, two, three.

Chapter Thirteen

Tuesday couldn't come fast enough, and when it did, it came hot, a stiff and unrelenting wind blowing up from the plains. Sweating, I loaded the laundry in great undifferentiated heaps, Lucky watching by the van as usual, no offer of help, laundry not being his job but driving, any variation sure to raise suspicion.

"I'll separate while you drive," I said, climbing in. "And if we drop it fast and collect the new stuff fast, we might get a whole extra hour at the river."

"It's vurry hot," he said. "Sometimes, see, the van overheats and we find ourselves late back to camp. You just never know. Just takes a time to cool down. Ms. Conover doesn't much mind."

I let myself be flirty with the little plant manager, and he let me drop the rough piles I'd made right into the bins, none of the usual sorting and tallying, gave me our full count of fresh, even helped me carry it all: apparently I'd conquered him.

At the river, well more than an hour early, Lucky and I sat but didn't strip right away, even as hot as it was, as I was. The guy wanted to sit, almost formal.

"I saw my auntie," he said. "It was a long way to go, but I had to ask about you. She says our practice the other day means we're married."

Seriously as he, I said, "No, it doesn't. It just means I like you."

He took that in, brows knitted hard.

I said, "But you have to be more careful, okay?"

"Careful?"

"No shooting off inside."

"I understand," he said.

"Don't be so solemn," I said. "You know, it's supposed to be fun."

"I had some fun, all right." He almost smiled, no he didn't, stood and stripped and swam with his frank boner, neither big nor small. It was really hot down there in the river bottom, so I did the same, swam with his frank boner. On my mind. The water didn't seem to have warmed at all, seemed like the tears of the glaciers high in the distant mountains. On the sand we kissed a long time. I put a finger to the raised scar below his heart.

"I was shot," he said.

That was shocking. I kissed the old scar and then kissed my way up to his neck and then kissed his face. He was all but quivering, entirely under my spell, nothing like Dag had ever been.

He said, "You follow the woman," quoting his revered aunt.

I'd have to get him out from under her spell. "I'll let you know when I'm ready," I said. And then immediately, "I'm ready."

He didn't get the joke.

But we shifted about on the warm sand, kissing, and he climbed atop me, vurry delicate, putting no weight on me, my hands positioning his hips, as he didn't seem to get that either. But then he got it. And splurted before he even got inside me, a generous offering on my thighs.

"Oh dear," he said.

"No, that's okay," I said. I didn't want to laugh. "Just as we were saying."

"Saying what?"

"That you shouldn't do that inside anyway."

"You are in estrus?"

"I'm not a horse, Lucky. Most of the time, like most girls, I can make a baby. And you have to be the one to watch out."

"Okay."

You could see he thought I was wrong about the estrus business. He was so downcast that I kissed him, traced the scar on his back with a finger. I was a little worked up in any case, and as he kissed me (a great, natural kisser, now that he'd had some practice, really tidy and aware of me), I got more so, pulled his leg up between mine and rocked on it.

"You like this," he said, maybe a little incredulous, and still working with the intelligence from his aunt.

"Vurry much," I said. I held his hand on me and showed him as best I could, demonstrated how good it felt, far quicker than usual and quiet as I could manage so as not to frighten him.

"Hoppo!" he said as I crushed harder on his leg. He was in the midst of a revelation, is what that meant, a whole new vocabulary in one ancient word.

My moment had brought him back to attention. Soon we were honestly making love, super slow and super aligned, soul kissing the while, and he was staying with it, staying with me, like it was all a kiss, and really about souls, not forever, not anything like that, but long enough to bring me to a rippler, I still call it, like I'd been a calm pond after the first explosion died down, flat as a mirror, and he'd thrown a stone into me. And that was enough for him—another splash straight up inside me, a thousand degrees.

"Didn't I tell you not to do that!" I cried.

"You don't like to be married?" he said.

"That's something different!" I said.

In the river I washed and washed and he felt free to help some and seemed properly remorseful, also full of respect: I'd taught him a thing or two his aunt didn't even know about. I pushed him in and dove over him, this flailing narrow wrangler, came up behind him and helped him back to shallow water, and there we kissed the longest kiss in the history of kisses, a whole language, taste of the old river, which is mineral and honeysuckle and glacier melt, the taste of winter and rock, and me rippling again, rippling hard.

At about the peak of which we heard a car, the crunching of tires on sand as they left the road, squeak of tired springs.

I got into my T-shirt and loose camp pants all but instantly. Lucky got into the water stark naked, began his splashing imitation of swimming.

I saw my gray panties down on a flat rock, but too late, just sat there like I was watching the show as the car came in view, and it was the police, old gumball-machine light on top, this huge black car with white doors, the whole rocking like an elephant waddling into the center ring at a circus. I waved—nothing wrong here, Officer. But of course there was the camp van, all its doors wide open.

"Cry, don't wave," Lucky said from the water.

And so I cried, no problem, leaned into my knees.

The officer got out of his car, young guy, cop sturdy, outdoorsman, or anyway quite dark from the sun, no urgency, assessing the situation, Lucky wading up out of the river like he'd been swimming all day, naked as a baby mole.

"Jesus, Lucky."

"Officer Boardman, howdy."

"What have we got here?"

"She doesn't want to go back," Lucky said, extra laconic.

"Laundry day," said the cop. And then to me: "I know the feeling, miss. I know it well. I never did want to go to work up there, and I was only a guard, and not for long."

"I thought a swim," Lucky said.

"That's what I was thinking, too," the cop said. And he stripped down just as Lucky had, down to his khaki boxers and his suntan—another ex-Marine become a cop—and dove in, a terrific swimmer with a build like a Jeep.

Chapter Fourteen

Leslie Hilton handed me a letter, the first I'd gotten at daily mail call. My heart jumped to think it might be from my dad, but of course Camp Challenge wouldn't pass such a thing along even if Daddy had had a mind to break the no-contact provision, never. No, it was in a Camp Challenge envelope, just a handwritten note, elegant old-school script, fountain pen. I was to go see Donut Dora before dinner.

Her office was the nicest indoor space in Camp Challenge, occupying the second floor of HQ, several fragrant rooms of log walls and stuffed bookshelves, huge desk made from a slab of pine with the bark still on underneath, view through large windows down the valley and across the whole wide world. This was behind her as she sat at her desk, and she did share its grandeur, her hair carefully French braided away from that famous face, its stony kindness.

"Depression," she said without preamble, "is the common enemy of the girls here, all of you. But when you're new, it's dangerous, insidious, even if routine. Abruptly you're in a bunk with eight other girls and your world is upside down. You miss family and friends. You feel estranged from even the Lord. You are full of remorse. Your heart breaks. Dear girl, we understand."

"I'm feeling okay," I said.

"Tribal Officer Boardman told me otherwise. He said he chanced upon you down at the river? Our employee has been reprimanded for that offense, letting you out of the van, swimming naked in front of you, my goodness. Not you, who could hardly be blamed, you weren't swimming, which I do find exculpatory. Lucky is very simple. If it's hot, one swims."

I flushed. "I'm sorry."

"Officer Boardman said you were crying copious tears."

"I guess I was sad."

"He said you were fully dressed?"

"Oh, Miss Dora. Of course I was!"

"Lucky hasn't the best social skills. He hasn't any social skills. Did he scare you?"

"The driver? He never said a single word, Ms. Conover. Just suddenly there we were on the river, and it was so beautiful."

"You didn't want to come back."

"I didn't mind coming back."

"And don't worry about it happening again. You are relieved of laundry duty."

"Thank you, Ms. Conover," I said. But tears sprang to my eyes, real tears this time, at the thought of the loss of Lucky.

Dora gazed upon me benignly. Finally she said, "Have you prayed on your sadness?"

I sniffled, not a tissue in sight. I tried honesty: "I don't pray, actually."

Dora pounced, a sharp streak plummeting from above, falcon's claws: "You cry instead?"

Crying all the harder, I said, "I don't cry often."

And then there was the soft Dora, face of an angel: "'Is anyone among you suffering? Let him pray.' Did you hear that, Cindra? 'Let him pray.' That's from the book of James, chapter five, verse thirteen. Let. Him. Pray."

I clasped my hands and bowed my head, no way around it, and no way to point out that I wasn't a him. When I peeked, I saw that Dora had bowed her head as well, a gentle muttering, nothing showy. No reason I couldn't bow my head. You could bow your head and not pray. You could bow your head and think of Lucky naked and lying upon you, hot ripples.

"Amen," Dora said at length.

"Amen," I said, straightening, bereft: How would I ever see Lucky again?

"You feel better."

"Blessedly, yes." But then I was crying again.

Dora let me drip and sniffle a while before she said, "Let us try this: I can get you out of the bunk for a night or two a week. Psychological confinement, we call it officially. But truly, it's just a break. Your meals are brought in, your time is your own, there's even a shelf of good books. Also, a private restroom, and a tub, salutary. It's called Solitude, but it's not solitary. I will visit, as will your group leader. We all feel sad at times, but those that go amid the Lord get His blessings. Best if you don't spread the news around, however!"

I was speechless, afraid, didn't want to leave Cats, though a bath sounded nice.

"Salutary?" I managed at length.

"It means healthful."

"Healthful's good."

"Praise Him!"

"Praise him!" I repeated, meaning Lucky.

And Dora took my hand, walked me out of her office and down a knotty-pine hallway, past several closed doors and to the far other end of the building where she opened a knotty-pine door to reveal Solitude, simply an apartment over the infirmary, knotty-pine walls, knotty-pine furniture, woolen blankets, rag-wool carpet, knotty-pine lamp on a knotty-pine table beside the full-size knotty-pine bed, real sheets, two pillows, small knotty-pine desk, knotty-pine bookshelf full of church titles, knotty-pine bathroom. Dora pointed out towel and washcloth, fresh camp garments, and toiletries, including a fresh toothbrush, then bowed her head in prayer, backed out the door, shut it behind her.

I didn't recall taking a vow of silence! I tried the door and realized I was locked in. Well, no matter. After a look around (not much to see— extra blankets in a closet, no hangers, lots of medical pads in great variety, also a pregnancy manual, it looked like, and mothballs in an otherwise empty chest of drawers, a little balcony looking out high over the back ravine, sound of the river), I picked through the bookshelves, pulled out something at random, and then something else, dense philosophy, it looked like, Martin Buber, Miguel de Unamuno, Paul Tillich, philosophers whose names I've never forgotten, read sentences slowly. Later, I pulled down a book of poems by someone called Pablo Neruda, poems in Spanish. Dora's name was in the flyleaf, and a date, December 9, 1969. I had taken Spanish class and knew enough to translate the title, which was *Twenty Love Poems and a Song of . . .* something. That word I didn't know. But I thumbed through and lingered over several poems and did find the word for love a great deal, also a pencil translation in the same hand as on the flyleaf:

I desire your mouth, your voice, your hair.

So Donut Dora was human. There were penciled question marks over some of the words. I read the poem in Spanish then, picking out the odd word, and read Dora's English, checking back and forth. I desire your mouth! *Boca.* I found that word several times in other poems, worked on the sentences that contained it, didn't get far, but far enough. I filled the old claw-foot tub with the hottest hot water, and soon my soiled camp garments lay on the floor beside it. I adored my body back then, but there were no mirrors. I liked to twist a private curl around a finger and tug ever so slightly. I must have been in there two hours, refreshing the hot water intermittently, tugging that curl, various scenarios in which I got to kiss Lucky, squeezing my knees together, making a cow, as we used to call it, I don't know why. Moo. A small red pebble tossed into my still pond, none of the huge stones and boulders Lucky had thrown in.

Dora returned well after dinnertime with a plate of meat loaf and overly much salad. She prayed a little, said, "And how are we feeling?"

"Much better."

I'd put the Neruda away and had laid one of the twelve or so Bibles open on the bed. At least there were good stories in there. Dora bowed her head slightly at the sight of it, still not a word. But now I knew she had once wanted a mouth like I did now. As soon as she left, I pulled the Neruda down, translated painfully, found more kissing, a whole line I could translate from a poem whose title I couldn't make sense of, unending kisses.

Unending! I loved that.

Chapter Fifteen

The next morning Dora slipped into Solitude and woke me with a hand to my forehead. "You're more peaceful," she said. It was true.

"Do you want another night?"

"I think that was just enough," I said.

"All right. Let's give you Friday, too. Two days a week, perhaps, just for a while, as you adjust. Tuesday and Friday for a while?"

"Okay," I said. I never understood language like that: adjusting. I wasn't going to adjust anything, not like you adjust the volume on a TV set. I wasn't going to change at all. I was only going to learn a new world, and then live in it, the same me as ever. "I'd like that."

Dora cast a benevolent eye upon me: God's work practically made her glow.

I was being cossetted, my mom would say, but she'd been raised by Lutherans. It seemed natural enough to me at the time that a blond girl some people thought so pretty would get better treatment than the rest. Some voice in me wants to say, But that didn't make me a bad person, did it? Yes, I was a bad person, ignorance no defense.

Out among the less blessed and less benighted girls, after breakfast I kept an eye peeled for the van, knew where to wait. Soon here it came. Lucky paid me no attention, but then, he couldn't, not if he was in trouble for our swim day. I tried to imagine what discipline they'd given him. Docked his pay? Threatened to fire him? Whatever it was, it was enough to make him disappear into himself. Not that he would have known I was there: he didn't look around at all, didn't even get out of the van. Probably he'd been prohibited from any more contact with the campers, and certainly with me.

I contented myself with staring, no one having prohibited me from anything (the usual double standard—the ethnic kid pays, the white kid skates—but this time enforced by my crying game, and suddenly my complicity stung). I watched the girl on grocery duty loading the empty banana boxes, the meat coolers, the potato sacks neatly folded. She was awkward, clumsy, and slow moving. Her face was puffed from a fistfight before breakfast, but oh, she'd won in the end, given that loudmouth girl a drubbing behind the upper bathhouse—I'd seen it all from a distance, a mean girl from Yonkers who knew how to punch. Lucky wouldn't take a thug like her to the beach, that's all I cared about.

My fellow Cats welcomed me back to the cabin at siesta. "Solitary," I said. They were all sympathetic, plain they'd never been. "There's a bathtub," I said. "There's a clock."

Everyone laughed, hard.

"Nah," Puma said. "Can't fool me. I been. There's only a hole in the floor. There's not even a bed!"

"Solitude," I said. "I meant Solitude."

But that didn't help. More laughter.

The next day I joined the stream of campers heading to soccer league, a huge crowd led by four of the oldest girls who acted as coaches, plus a male guard, a grizzled old gent who acted as referee. Evidently the games were pretty well organized, three standing teams and a perpetual round robin.

I fell behind, fell behind some more, ducked into the forest, my heart pounding. The sports field wasn't far enough away. I crawled farther into the woods, then up the mountain for twenty minutes, then a long way on an elk track, then down the hill again, trying to come out below HQ. There was a garage there, and that, I hoped, was where Lucky would park the van as he came back in from his rounds. I waited in thick underbrush behind a ponderosa pine, held the tree, pressed my cheek on the rough bark, fragrant sap in my hair, sap on my hands, my face, waited more, no idea how much time had elapsed (time not my gift), and just as I was about to give in and flee back up the hill to where I could intercept the soccer crowd Franciella-style, I heard the Camp Challenge van rattling. It parked neatly on the gravel near the garage, and then (thump-thump in my chest) Lucky climbed out.

I burst from hiding to meet him.

"Okay," he said, barely startled. And then, not kidding: "You are off limits."

"I had to see you," I said.

"Oh, I knew we would see each other," he said. "But just maybe not right like this, here in the garage lot."

I said, "You got in trouble?"

"Oh, I'll say. Ms. Conover prayed over me."

"She prayed over me, too."

"She prayed I would learn the difference between a man and a woman."

"She thinks of you a certain way," I said.

"What way?"

"Just, innocent."

He looked puzzled. "No, I was plain guilty," he said.

"I mean, um, simple."

He seemed to take no offense but only laughed and said, "Simple." I hadn't seen him laugh before. "She did not use that word."

"'Very simple,' is what she said."

"Like a trout," Lucky said.

Why was that so funny? We laughed a lot, then stood there a long time. Silence was good with him. Finally, silence not so good with me, I said, "Dora put me in solitary."

Lucky gasped.

Quickly I said, "The one with the bathtub."

"Ah," he said, and dug in his deep overalls pocket, pulled out a large ring of keys, slid them one by one deliberately till he found the one he wanted, held it up for me to see. "You mean Solitude," he said. "The visitor's room. That was where they birthed the babies before the clinic came to Elk River. Sometimes still."

"Friday," I said. I did not want to hear about babies.

Lucky simply walked away.

"You come back here," I said.

He did, part of the way. Then a step more. "Wife," he said.

"Trout," I said. But then despite myself quoted my poet, saying, "'I desire your mouth, your voice, your hair.' Also your unending kisses."

He seemed to keep listening after I was done. Finally he said, "Unending kisses." I like that. Unending. My old auntie said there are two trails ahead of you and me, and we must take care."

"And Dora told me I must pray."

"She mumbles and calls it prayer."

"Better if we two just kiss."

"My aunt says we are married if we want."

"You are plain weird, my not-husband."

The sun was in his eyes. He let the slightest smile come, said, "Plain and weird together. If you like. And simple, too."

I stood up on my toes and kissed his mouth, unending. "Lucky," I said.

"That's my name," he said. "I have a few."

"It's on my mouth," I said. "I'll save the rest for later."

We were this far apart, less than a breath. Aspen leaves shivered in the slight breeze. A squirrel chittered. We only stood there, then only reluctantly parted: the other camp van was coming—with those rough roads, you heard every arrival from far away. Lucky pushed me away with a kind of brusque humor. And so I scrambled back up the steep slope to the elk run, ducked among boulders out of all possible sight. From way up there, I saw the second van pull up. And Dora Dryden Conover herself climbed out, as put together as always, flowing white skirts, a kind of unfolding from the graceless van. She approached Lucky, fierce step.

But it wasn't trouble, or not much. She only gave him a quick hug. And then what seemed a lecture, one long finger aimed at his impassive chest, more like what you'd expect. But then a longer hug, arms around his neck, surprising affection from the boss, shocking, really. I felt ruffled.

But Lucky's name was on my lips, and I directed every thought his way.

Chapter Sixteen

At breakfast, the nurse pulled me aside. "You have your appointment with Dr. Gilbert today," she said. "You'll come with me."

I was already more than a little flummoxed and overheated from Lucky and his kisses, Lucky and his aunt, his embrace with Dora. And on edge, too, a little nauseated as always from breakfast. I followed Nurse through the knotty-pine corridors. Dora was in her office, didn't look up. I realized she would be near, and so I relaxed: she might be chilly, but she was a woman to be trusted. A number of doors down, the nurse showed me into the same small examination room I'd seen before.

"Undress," she said. And handed me a worn hospital gown missing its ties.

It took Dr. Gilbert forever to arrive. He came in dour but looking me up and down grew almost cheerful. He pulled my gown off my shoulders, his breath shifting perceptibly. I tried to notice everything, so if I had to lie later my story would still be true. His hair was quite thick and combed back. He wasn't half bad looking, but his eyes were so unkind, and—something I would learn later—beauty must live in kindness. I felt myself drifting out of the room, and it was like I watched from above, or not even watched but averted my eyes. I remembered all that the girls had said about him.

"Sit up here," he said. And that person down there complied, and he put her feet in the stirrups, leaned in too close between her legs. "Nice and pink," he said. "Let's get a look at that cervix of yours." And he began his prodding. "Relax," he said, and then, incredibly, "It's easier if you like it." And then started petting me.

"You see," he murmured. "You like it quite well."

I felt my power to destroy him, to rescue myself, the other girls, all of us, and it was a sexual power, something I hadn't felt before so explicitly. The courage was not sexual, however, and wavered briefly, was not nice and pink. "Quite well," I lied.

"We'd have to be quiet," he said. "The lock's on the outside, this damn place."

"Like church mice," I said, an expression of my grandmother's. And I whispered: "Like church mice."

He stammered and said, "All right, then," and backed away some. He thought to put a chair in front of the door, pretty ineffectual, good. I tugged my slight robe around me, slid off the table and to my feet. He unzipped, pulled his pants down and over his shoes, hopped about trying to get the legs untangled.

"Shoes, too," I said.

His breath was coming so heavily, I thought he'd die right there, maybe save me some trouble.

His dick was short and purple and rampant. I wish I never saw it, because I can see it now. He struggled with his shirt, so keen to attack me that his basic motor functions weren't working. I dodged, patted the exam table, feigned willingness. Nearly choking, amazed at his luck, he climbed up, lay back at my direction, his skin all mottled and strange with spots and freckles and misplaced hairs. "Come on, pretty," he said.

I kicked his shirt to the corner of the room, stood on his pants, shuffled them backward, away from him. And then I started to scream, just, "Help! Help! Help!" My voice was loud and super strong. I had returned to my body, gulped an enormous breath, willed tears, screamed again.

The doctor sat up with some difficulty. "Stop, stop," he said. He put his fingers to his thin lips.

"Nice and pink," I hissed, and then shouted more: "Help, help!"

Hurried footfalls in the hallway as he lunged for his pants—but I was still standing on them. He pushed me, only wanted those pants. As the door sprang into the chair, I fell, and he fell atop me, and I screamed more.

"Shut up, shut up," he hissed, laying a hand over my mouth.

But Dora was there, banging the chair out of the way with the door, and then the nurse was there, too, and then the secretary, and then the stableman, Clay Marvelette, who must've heard me all the way from outdoors.

"Uterus," the doctor said, trying to rise, his hands on my belly in his desperation to stand, then a grip on my arm.

Spry Mr. Marvelette leapt in, pulled the doctor away from me, and punched him in the nose, all in a flash, great fountains of blood suddenly coursing from the doctor's nostrils. I felt so sad for the little shit, his life rushing past his eyes, his blood down his chin. The secretary inserted herself bravely between him and the stableman, who was ready to give him a good pummeling. Dora pulled me out in the hallway, almost roughly, patted my face, tugged my robe closed brusquely.

"My God," she said, half a prayer.

Tears sprang unbidden to my eyes. "I'm so sorry," I said.

"Oh, child, no. This is not your sin. This is the sin of man. Did he spoil you?"

"She tricked me," the doctor shouted, his voice garbled by fear. And then he said more, total Rumpelstiltskin about a tipped uterus and common examination practices, as if he weren't naked. Thud and crack of knuckles on cheek and a cry as Mr. Marvelette gave him another shot over the secretary's head.

Chapter Seventeen

That certain therapist lingered over the doctor story, whole sessions, always coming back to it. If men were bad, so be it, but if I drew it out of them—well, let's examine that. And he spoke of my beauty, which I was inclined to deny, though I'd traded in it, still was. He was prebuilding his own excuses, arguing in his own defense. I mean, as it turned out.

In Solitude later, where Dora had wordlessly led me, I took another bath. I felt dirty, responsible, felt I couldn't get clean. And yet proud of myself. And queasy over my trickery. Or not so much my trickery, but the thing about me that had drawn that doctor out, you see. And then proud again: after all, I'd done a turn for all the girls, not just myself. That future therapist would have a bullshit name for that, as he did for all his bullshit, a something-something delusion. I had a something-something delusion that I was helping others when in fact all I was doing was feeding my own sick need. First Dag, then the doctor, finally Lucky, no doubt, situations far from parallel, a condition I wouldn't have thought to name but perhaps suspected in some secret, self-abnegating way as I lay there in the cooling bath, distraught, then in the comfortable bed, my gray clothes in a corner.

The first cook brought a lemon tart, the second brought tea, the third a bowl of ice cream. "Always hated that man," the first said. "Good riddance," said the second. And then the third: "Don't know why Ms. Conover ever put up with him." "Brave girl," they all repeated. My allies. I felt I was at a kind of hotel for heroines, sat in the late sun out on the little knotty-pine balcony, breathed the fragrant wind, got a smooth and creamy feeling in my belly: all was well. Then a rumble and a cramp: trouble ahead. And then a sort of percolating triumph: I'd prevailed.

As the sun fell into the trees, Donut Dora knocked, let herself in. "Are you injured?" she asked again.

And again I said no. I said, "You came before he could hurt me. Thank you, thank you."

"Sometimes we find injury in an aftermath," she said, fishing.

"No, fine. I took a bath."

"A bath is balm."

"It was warm, anyway."

She drew herself up, said, "'But every man is tempted, when he is drawn away of his own lust and enticed.' That's James, chapter one, verse fourteen."

"But I didn't entice anyone."

At length, Dora fixed me in those deep, dark eyes. "Dr. Gilbert tells me you invited him to undress."

"Him? Invited him? That old frog?"

"Then how did it happen? Dear girl. Tell me exactly."

"I—I can't!"

"You must, please. It's important."

"Well. He was doing his, his exam, and telling me how pink I was. I mean down there. My eyes were pinched shut. He examined me overly long and told me I liked it, but I did not. And then he told me to wait a minute. And then I don't know what happened."

"He says you tricked him."

"I tricked him? I tricked him? How could I trick him into, into *that*?"

"Exactly my question to him. He did explain."

"Well, explain to me."

"Oh, Cindra. Our job is to keep you safe in the Lord and we have failed. He will be dealt with directly."

"In the Lord," I said, awkward attempt to speak her language.

She took my hands. "Let us pray," she said.

"Lettuce spray," I said soberly, my father's joke.

And I sprayed, my thoughts going everywhere while she prayed, whatever that meant.

Then silently she left.

I bathed again. A knock on the door. The first of the cooks. Then the second, the third, one at a time. A beautiful steak, perfect fries, a salad from their beloved kitchen garden, so early, each saying something in confidence about the doctor, no doubt what they'd been saying to one another: "Now maybe we'll be shut of him," and "He's had quite a number of complaints!" and, too simply, "Men."

At bed check Dora came back, but I was under the covers and feigning sleep. She prayed probably half an hour over me, muttering Bible verses and other inanity, until finally she was gone. The wind outdoors blew all the harder, all the drier. That was my life force. The old clock on the bedside table ticked, tocked. That was my heart. At two in the morning I heard a key in the lock, pinched my eyes ready for more praying, heard the door open, heard faintest footsteps.

Then Lucky's dulcet voice: "They said you were here."

I pulled him down to me, held on tight.

"I will kill him," he said.

"No need," I said. "I've killed him enough." And finally my tears arrived.

"He's an Irish," Lucky told me. He thought that meant more than I thought it did.

Lucky drank maybe a quart of water to wake himself early, undressed and climbed into bed beside me. That night he smelled like pine smoke, must have been tending a fire. I was the water. He didn't touch my body except for a warm, long hand on my back, words in my ear: he was there.

And we did sleep.

Before morning, he woke and pissed a long time in the toilet, a manly sound, and I asked him to hold me, and he did, lying behind me, that hand on my tummy now, not the slightest sexual demand or intimation, just as I would tell my future therapist in rebuttal to his theories—but that future, self-serving therapist would take Lucky's side, a long speech about how some feminine danger to Lucky was implied by what (supposedly) I'd done to Dag, (and definitely) to the doctor. That I drew forbidden men into forbidden situations, something like that, repeated and restated and reframed, and I would strongly and unfortunately believe that future therapist, in fact already believed him before I ever met him, some kind of way of being a woman that had a name, a diagnosis, he called it, and set out to heal me.

Lucky stayed protectively there in my bed in Solitude till the last possible safe second, then rose and dressed and slipped out the door, swept away down the hall and the stairs and into the dawn.

Chapter Eighteen

Dora arrived at first bell, held my hands and prayed over me. "I hardly slept," she said.

"I slept at first," I said, practicing honesty.

"Oh, child."

"Oh, Ms. Conover. Thank you for your prayers."

And she prayed some more, suddenly looking up, revelation: "Your days should be as normal as possible."

And so to breakfast, and then to activities. I picked Prayer Group to please her and because no one would be able to grill me on those pine pews up at the edge of the bluff.

At siesta, finally back in Cats, the girls all gathered around.

"We heard all about it," Leslie said.

"I will kill him," Ocelot said.

"He's already killed," I said. And I told them the story, never an audience more rapt for anything, Leslie pushing for details, Ocelot braiding my hair, stroking it. I described the doctor's short, purple prick to gales of laughter. I told them how I got him to undress, how the door flew open, how Dora tugged my robe closed. They wanted to hear about Clay Marvelette over and over again, how he pulled the doctor off me, how the old man punched the younger in the nose, kapow!

And that was our entire siesta. Before afternoon activity, I found Franciella, and we fell back behind the Trail Repair Group, trotted up her secret path. And she was the perfect companion, as I'd begun to feel filthy again and had no more to say. Silently we worked on a stadium in La Vil, as several of our pebble families had athletic children and a track meet was coming up, almost the Olympics. Francie narrated: "In grade school I was the soccer girl. I won all the races, too. But by junior high I couldn't pass gym. You had to run a mile under eight minutes, and I couldn't run it in twenty. I couldn't walk it!"

"I wasn't the fast one," I said.

"Fuck no, not the way you limp," she said.

"My mother did it. I'll tell you sometime."

We mounted the Games of La Vil, track and field, a lot of it in Franciella's private language, which I felt I had begun to understand, pebble athletes talking to one another behind the other pebbles' backs.

My new friend sensed the time perfectly, and we fell in behind our group as they came back down the slope. And Franciella and I mixed with the crowd milling around HQ, no one the wiser. Before dinner, Dora found me in line, pulled me by the arm, led me to her office. Inside, the big guard stood, Andy, a frosty enormous white guy I knew by sight only and hadn't so much as spoken to.

"Sit," said Dora.

I sat opposite her at her desk, the view behind her. She studied me, whatever shred of kindliness gone from those eyes.

"Tell me the story again," she said.

And I told it again, exactly as I'd told her before, this time with tears.

"Now tell me again," she said. "But this time, the truth. The story you told the Cats today. Which, as you well know, is exactly the story the doctor told."

Betrayed.

She didn't actually want to hear any story, but prayed, enticement the main theme, that I had enticed an innocent soul: "For the lips of an immoral woman drip honey, and her mouth is smoother than oil; but in the end she is bitter as wormwood, sharp as a two-edged sword. Her feet go down to death; her steps lay hold of *hell*."

"Proverbs, chapter five, verses three through five," the big guard informed me.

Dora said, "Very good, Andrew. And do you know Psalm one forty-five, verse twenty?"

He did not.

But Dora did: "The Lord preserves all who love Him; but all the wicked He shall destroy."

And shortly Andy all but pushed me out of her office, led me outdoors, tugged me down the hill in the wind, frog-marched me hundreds of yards to a large storage facility near where I'd found Lucky and the van, an anomalous metal building. Andy was rough but oddly kindly, forceful and determined in the presence of Satan, I began to understand, gave no answer to my protests, pulled me inside the building through a steel door. Just the smell in there—diesel and mice. A second steel door opened on stairs that descended into darkness. Andy flipped a switch, and tube lights blinked on. He urged me down into a dry, clean cement cellar, absolutely empty, then opened the next steel door, pushed me into the small room behind it, the kind of place you'd put a furnace, concrete pad with a hole in the center, a wooden pail of water sitting beside it, square floor, square ceiling, square walls, a perfect, empty cube.

"I haven't had dinner," I said.

Andy fished in his jacket pocket, found half a Snickers bar.

I took it gratefully.

Chapter Nineteen

I slept, but couldn't say how long, only my clothes between me and the concrete. I did jumping jacks to warm myself, counted them to one hundred in a loud voice against the darkness. Time had disappeared in the abyss. I had one of Franciella's pebble people in my pocket, one of the athletes, and played with her. I tossed her, listened to the welcome skittering sound, then searched for her till I found her, feeling all over the cement floor. I drank a little water in the blackness, welcome sounds again. There was nothing for my eyes to get used to, no light at all. I put the bucket in a corner, felt my way to the opposite corner, tossed my pebble. The game was to find the pebble after I missed, over and over again. Out of one hundred throws I hit the water twice. Such a lovely sound, that splash. I drank more, just to hear it gurgle down inside me. I felt with my clog for the hole in the floor when I needed to, peed in there. I lay down on the concrete and kind of slept. Had a day passed? An hour? A week? I ate the Snickers bar in nibbles, finally gobbled the last chunk. Blessed is Andy, for Andy feeds the lowly. I slept, I woke, I did jumping jacks, I tossed the pebble, I sang. Then I heard something that wasn't me. Blinding light under the crack in the door.

Which opened like God parting the clouds, one of those Roman church ceilings: Andy. He had an apple for me, a hunk of bread. Fresh water, new bucket.

"Leave the old one," I begged, a fresh game in mind. But no. He didn't say a single word, didn't answer my questions, which concerned time. How long had I been in, how long did I have to stay here? Silence. "Oh, Andy, Andrew, please talk to me."

Silence, sorrow in his face.

He closed the door, the band of light beneath seeming super faint now, then gone.

I woke without knowing I'd slept, fiercely hungry, tried to gauge the time by that. Was it a dinner kind of hungry? A sound again, and it was Andy at the door. "At least pray over me," I said.

He was wary, I saw, and I realized he'd been warned: I'd try to seduce him. "The Lord bless you and keep you," he said.

"I need a blanket," I said.

He had another apple for me, and two old hamburger buns, fresh water again. And a washcloth. When he was gone I ate the apple and one hamburger bun. I didn't wet the washcloth, but put it over my face in what I hoped was night to keep warm with my breath, my knees doubled up, just enough warmth to sleep, the only source of heat being myself. I slept and woke. I played with my pebble. I drank water. I ate the second bun in tiniest bites, made a game of how long I could wait for the next. I changed the furniture around: ninety shifts of the bucket corner to corner to corner to corner and throw the pebble with only three splashes, three scores, the whole time. The pebble was my girl, won ribbons. I splashed in the bucket with my hands just to hear the sound, to feel something. I found the apple core, ate it: bitter seeds, tough little stem. I counted how many Beatles songs I knew, and could hear them almost as if a record were playing, all the songs in order, every note, like they were playing in my ears.

I slept.

The door opened and in the light, I saw Lucky. Of course I knew it wasn't true, but he held me. It was Lucky, it was really him.

"Hurry," he said.

He emptied the water bucket and took it along. He stuffed the washcloth in his pocket. These were my belongings.

"What day is it?" I said.

"It's night," he said. "You've been down here three. I'm sorry, the key was hard to get."

Lucky locked the door to Vault behind us. That would make a mystery for Andy and his Bible to solve. And we slipped out of there and into the blessed night and hurried in moonlight down through the woods to the road and across it. He knew a place we could cross the creek, and we did, way down the property near the gate, no one in the guardhouse. I dropped into the water, washed the dust off my clothes, out of my hair, took everything off, washed myself clean of all the preceding days as Lucky wrung my camp pants for me, my camp shirt. On the bank, shivering, I damply dressed, a new person, free.

We walked in the woods, then, that soft pine duff—so good on my cramped legs—my body warm again in Lucky's jacket, his arm around me, his hand on my elbow. We clambered over a huge cracked rock, edge of the cliff. Lucky beneath me, a hand on my butt, we inched down a story or more, only the crack to wedge our feet and hands in, then crawl through where it widened, and into a hidden cavern. He had a candle in there and lit it to reveal piles of blankets and multitudes of Camp Challenge sleeping bags all arranged on a great, flat rock like a bed. We fell into them and he wrapped me warmly, nice old blankets and sleeping bags with hunting scenes, fed me bread and American cheese he'd lifted at lunch from the mess.

"Our nest," he said. He was tender and sat close, sweet, warm hand on my back.

We slept.

Chapter Twenty

Morning, and Lucky didn't care about the likely manhunt going on above us. He didn't have a thought about food or of time. He seemed to think we were on our honeymoon. I kept saying, "I have to get out of here." And he didn't say much in reply, except that if we emerged we'd be caught, that we had to wait. He was right, of course, but going from solitary to his cave started to feel freaky, like he was part of the whole monstrous thing, had known every minute for three days exactly where I was and done nothing, nothing, made an excuse out of the key, that it had been hard to find. In the night while he slept (he was as quiet in sleep as in waking), I edged off the mountain of blankets and sleeping bags and old pillows and crept to the queer crevice that was the only exit and saw the fat, waxing moon high in the sky, a million acres lit silver, a million acres you could walk across to the single visible light far across the valley, fifty miles, likely, and my escape.

I climbed out the way we'd climbed in, balanced with a foot on a knob of rock, that steady Montana wind in my face, fingers jammed in a crack in the cliff. No way: Camp Challenge above, pile of rocks far below. And so I watched the valley out there, watched the vastness, let the wind breathe me, that one light winking out like a signal, felt the vastness of the plains open inside me, decided in a rush of feeling that Lucky was vast, too, his heart opening inside mine. I started to slip, but he was there and caught me by the arm and drew me inside our lodge so quietly, let me guide him by the hand back to our bed, and then, despite what future therapists might have to say, we made love, barely awkward at all—we'd missed each other, what syndrome explained that?

"Wife," Lucky said, deep in the night.

And for the first time I said it: "Husband."

And we woke hours later, safe in our nuptial apartment, which was a room in a castle of feeling, the two of us buried in old blankets on that perfectly flat rock, the only level place, safe above the deeply slanting floor, which fell back to a trickle of purest water, plenty of water to keep us alive. Lucky had more camp bread and American cheese, a stack of slices. Standing at our diagonal threshold, almost a sill to lean on, we looked out over our world and fed each other, a sacrament.

But I was starving. "More," I said.

And he gave me more.

"More," I said again.

"My aunt Maria said you'd come to her under a full moon."

"I won't be going to anybody if I starve."

"Food is easy," Lucky said. He seemed to think that was funny. He was naked. I'd never seen anything like him. So narrow, one width from ankles to hips to shoulders. There was more to me than that, though I'd lost some weight. I made a robe of an old sleeping bag, ducks and hunters. I left him there, padded back to the water and drank, moved down to the corner and washed, moved back to the farthest reach and peed. There was a place even farther back for the rest of it, a squat in the dark over the noisy exit of the water. I took my time.

Lucky still stood at our window, so much out there to see.

"Wife," he said.

"Prove it," I said.

And so he did, most carefully.

Chapter Twenty-One

Through our fragment of eastward window, we saw moonlight on the distant snow peaks that evening, then the moon itself, bigger than the night before. Second night, the fears of Vault—the girls had spoken of being put in Vault, and now I knew I'd experienced it—returned like a shadow, my father lost to me, poor Franciella, too. And my belly empty, really hungry. My confidence in Lucky's plan, whatever it might be, was fading.

I said, "Did your aunt forget to tell you to bring enough food with you for more than a day?"

No particular reaction. The moonlight on the plain out there absorbed him fully. And then late that night, an hour of terror when I woke to find him gone, then an hour of remorse: Why was I so mean? An hour of recrimination when he got back, an hour of forgiveness: he'd brought loaves of bread he'd liberated from the camp kitchen, another stack of American cheese, also a slightly limp cabbage and a huge bar of baking chocolate, all he'd been able to get his hands on with the one larder key he had. We started right in, cheese and bread, the chocolate after, so bitter it made us wince but tolerable on the bread, exquisite on Lucky's lips, where I did find his name.

Come dawn, we heard a search party shouting, maybe back up on the road, no danger, but then really close, directly over us, an unknown male's voice calling orders.

"Montana State Highway Patrol," Lucky said, just an observation, no fear, no judgment, his ethereal calm: "No trackers them."

Later, we felt the rumble of large vehicles passing on the camp road, not good, as they brought in more searchers. And then the baying of hounds.

"That's why we walked down the road so far," Lucky said.

"And walked back in the river."

"In the river," he said, "yes."

We hadn't discussed it. But I saw his deep planning suddenly. "And why we leapt from rock to rock," I said.

"Yes, and why we leapt from rock to rock. The high points. Dogs search low."

I had started to like how he repeated me, offered variations on my themes, his quiet way to say he heard you and understood you.

The hounds got louder, then much louder, then quieter, sniffing the ground between the boulders up there, then nothing but the violent pounding of my heart: as a runaway from camp, having violated the terms of my agreement, I faced prison, real prison, real time, like Dag, like his brother, Billy.

Lucky said, "The rock face up there fools the men, but it doesn't fool the dogs. The men call the dogs off, see. And so the dogs learn we are not the quarry."

His small grin calmed me.

We ate a little more chocolate and bread and kissed unending, no sense of time passing, but night came again, and the moon, so close to full. I told Lucky stories of my family, and finally of Dag and all that had led me to Camp Challenge. He listened carefully, his expression unchanging, occasional observations about the conduct of others in his quiet, gravelly voice: "Unfair." "That wasn't right." "Cruel." I told him what had happened with Dr. Gilbert. He'd heard some small piece of it from Dora, he said, that the doctor had tried to kiss me, that's all, and that I'd falsely accused him of worse, which Lucky knew not to believe, and so he'd come to me in the night.

So I told him the whole thing start to finish, from my perfidy right through to my betrayal by Leslie.

He waited a long while, gathering his thoughts, said, "He had it coming."

Late, we started in eating the cabbage, which we both had claimed to hate—but it surprised us with its layers, not many before you came to crisp spiciness, best thing we'd ever eaten, and soon it, too, had to be rationed. We slept almost accidentally, woke in the night, lay like indolent gods, asked each other probing questions, lost in time. Sex was good exercise for the cave bound, good exercise at the vurry least.

The fourth day was surreal conversation and long kisses, half hallucinating. The fourth night was the full moon, and hearing no dogs, we emerged from the nest. The planet beyond the cliff seemed to roll away from us in liquid moonlight. We made two light bedrolls from our favorites of Lucky's blankets, tied them with rope, and dropped them down the cliff along with a Camp Challenge towel Lucky had soaked in the pure water of the cave and tucked into a canvas stuff-sack to make a kind of canteen.

Climbing down was easy enough for Lucky, a terror for me, over a hundred feet, but good footholds and handholds all the way in dry rock, a route Lucky knew well and that no one else had ever known, careful instruction and an occasional strong hand to help me from below. At the bottom we slipped our arms under the ropes on the bedrolls to make knapsacks. Lucky had made the climb in his cowboy boots but took them off now. I tied my Camp Challenge clogs into my bedroll. Neither of us had socks. He carried his boots. The moon was fat and full and climbed the sky.

Lucky said, "We will hurry real slow."

I knew what he meant.

The prairie floor, lightly furred with sweetgrass, was a loose matrix of sand and cinders and coarse gravel, tough on the feet, here and there a pile of antelope pellets or a lone cow pie in moonlight, and if we ambled across it all like wild things, he said, our tracks would soften in the constant wind and be no different from a cow's or a coyote's. We put our shoes on after a few hundred yards, and I walked in his footsteps as best I could. We made large, purposeful ellipticals, always tending east and north, guided by a certain distant peak limned by a million-million stars, no path but Lucky's knowledge, and through the night.

He knew a place he called Halfway Spring, and we slept there an hour or two at dawn among stunted trees in strong wind. Turtle Butte was a night's walk behind us but still seemed close, looked just like its namesake, a friendly looming. I guessed we'd walked ten crooked miles to go forward six. Lucky shrugged at that: those kind of numbers weren't real; we'd walked what we'd walked. And now the challenge was different. Ahead was nothing but bare chaparral whereon we might be easily seen in daylight.

So we stayed put. Sat in the spring pool naked, freezing water, hot sun.

"Wife," he said.

"Husband," I said.

He climbed out of the water, found a stick, scratched a circle around the whole spring pool, and we sat and lay together within its safety.

"Our wedding lodge," Lucky said.

Our wedding lodge. I was not even seventeen, and drunk with our marriage. Even in the moment I knew it, too drunk to worry about sunburn, too drunk to be afraid.

At noon Lucky heard an airplane, five minutes before I heard it. But that gave us time to erase our circle. We dressed and rolled our bedrolls and stuffed them under a creosote bush. I lay down and covered my face while he kicked dust on me for camouflage, and then I climbed under a bush, curled up tight, became a stone among the millions. Of course they'd take a close look at the one spring for miles.

Lucky crouched inside a stunted and cow-coppiced cottonwood tree, made himself one of the twelve trunks of the thing. I could barely see him from ten feet away.

The plane, a blue Cessna, passed over twice, then passed over again a half hour later super low, then, satisfied (even I could read that plane's attitude), flew back to Turtle Butte, flew around it a dozen times at least, distant growl and whine of its engine.

"It's Dick Darnell flying," Lucky said. "He's making a grid. He's vurry smart."

"But you are smarter."

"No, he's a tracker, too. We have to surprise even ourselves with our route."

We ventured out of hiding and ate cabbage and the last piece of bread and kept chipping at the bitter, bitter chocolate, which had become delicious beyond reason, a kind of solidified elixir, sat in the spring pool under a blazing sun, kissing chocolate off each other and sucking prickly pear cactus to sweeten it.

Come night, we waited on the moon, and it looked nearly as full as it had the night before, tiniest decline, clearest sky.

"How much farther," I said.

"About as far as we have to go," he said. "We'll walk most all of the night the way the wind comes, and no resting."

My feet were sore to go with everything else. Lucky chewed a leaf he knew and made a poultice, heavenly, cool and smooth inside my camp clogs, which left about nothing for footprints, but not to Lucky's liking: "You'll have to walk on the heels some." He soaked our canteen towel at the last second before we left. And we walked, me on my heels, a relief to my toes.

After an hour we came to a rough road, crossed it, came up against a formidable wire fence. "Offset," Lucky said.

He'd brought us blind exactly to a wildlife passage, an opening coyote and jackrabbit alike could pass through—just not cattle. We fit fine, crossed onto the next vast ranch. Of course, nothing about the landscape looked different. Lucky picked up the pace. The sky pinkened. I suckled at the towel, which had stayed remarkably damp. Lucky barely touched it.

I thought of my father, couldn't help it. "I'm scared," I said.

"Scared of what?" Lucky said. He scanned the horizon, thinking he'd missed something, not one for abstractions.

Abstractions were my job: "I'm walking away from my family."

He thought about that, said, "Nup. You are walking toward. Count your steps, that will help."

I did, I counted my steps. And counting was calming, he was right, a hundred steps, a thousand. I counted until I didn't, then fresh worries roamed my head: What if Francie's city was found? What would happen to her because they were looking for me?

Shortly there was a glint, dawn sun shining off a car mirror—just an old hulk of a car rotting into the earth, nothing to fear. And then an old washing machine complete with wringer standing forlorn beside a midden of applesauce bottles, all the same brand, thousands of them, it seemed, faded labels, a shock when I finally looked up and saw the vertical planes of a mobile home where for a day and two nights there'd been only distance ahead. The trailer was ancient, curved lines sagging, likely one of the first ever sold, dragged out here at the end of its usefulness, twisted oddly on its axis by a life of accidents, set up high on an outcropping of rock, tall stairway descending from a dented door, seemingly abandoned, and in the midst of what looked to be a junkyard.

We'd come in from the backside, made our way through sere sagebrush and serviceberry around to the front, where everything was suddenly green, a fenced garden, a venerable stand of cottonwood trees, shrubs twisting this way and that: this was another oasis, a hidden spring. The dooryard was cluttered with artistic precision, derelict cars and pickup trucks, an old electric stove, cable spools, a large trampoline frame on its side, about a million shot-up cans. A dusty two-track road snaked out past stacks of old metal roofing and twisted piles of discarded steel gutter. The cottonwood trees abated the constant wind, and trees meant water. A dappled horse was loosely tethered to a post like the one good idea in a faulty argument. At sight of Lucky, it nickered, danced.

"That's Chickadee," he said. The horse, he meant. A tall derrick wind-mill creaked as it rotated, livestock trough beneath receiving a bare trickle of water from the effort, but somehow full. A series of automotive tubes and hoses carried the overflow to a vegetable garden beautifully maintained.

I hurried to the trough, plunged my hands in, nice and cold, washed my face, cupped my hands to drink.

"Nup," Lucky said, surprised I didn't know better. "The animals have been in that water."

But in among the legs of the windmill there was a tap over an old porcelain tub, and that's where we could drink. I thought I'd never stop. I felt myself bloom like the random daffodils I suddenly noticed, licks of bright yellow in the dust. Lucky went to the horse, communed with it face-to-face as I splashed. He seemed to notice nothing else, neither clutter nor beauty, only the horse, left me waiting just the exact few minutes I could handle being apart.

"You'll get to know Chickadee," he said, returning.

The horse didn't like being left behind any more than I had, snorted and stamped.

But Lucky took my hand and led me to the trailer looming on its outcropping, helped me up the tall homemade steps. Inside, it was homey, the floors tilted from whatever misfortune had torqued the trailer but carpeted with stacks of bright weavings and furnished with chairs and an expensive-looking couch and matching coffee table, paintings on the walls, a real living room, redolent of high plains dust and sage smoke, recent cooking. On a shelf squared to reality rather than the ceiling line were a dozen bowling trophies, a bowling bag on the floor below, newest thing in the room.

"She'll be sleeping," Lucky said, not a home you whispered in.

"Your mother?" I said, apprehensive. I wasn't good with older women, and that was a fact.

No answer.

"Lucky, talk to me. Are we on the Reservation?"

"What? The Res? No. This is the Junk Ranch, people call it."

"So it's not, like, your house?"

He clammed up.

There were no clocks in the place, I noticed sharply. I was as hungry for time as for food. Lucky and I perched on the broken couch to await milady's waking, I guessed. We drooped gradually till we were lying down.

"Husband," I said.

"Wife," Lucky said.

"You know you weren't actually married, of course," a certain therapist would later say, perhaps in response to my dreamy tone.

"Wife and husband," I would repeat.

"Our personal mythologies are very rich," that theorist would say after a long silence, then offer me his box of pink Kleenex.

Chapter Twenty-Two

When my husband and I woke, it was late afternoon and there was the smell of baking bread and something that wasn't bacon, but close, some sort of smoky game. An older woman in a flannel shirt and stiff Wrangler jeans was cooking, singing to herself, a braid long as Lucky's down her back. She turned because my eyes were on her and gave me the most direct look I'd ever encountered, a long and lively communication that seemed to open a window into the back yard of the universe.

"Hello there," she said, clearly pleased with what she'd found in me, or among us.

Lucky stirred at that, protective arm around me, recalled where he was. His childhood home, I assumed.

"Hello right back," he said.

"Lucky Turtle," said the woman, immensely fond.

Was he a trout or a turtle? No one was going to say anymore.

"I'm Cindra," I said.

"I'm Cindra," she repeated, extending it like Lucky did, *Cindrawww*.

"We came off the mountain," I said.

"We came off the mountain."

"She'll just echo," Lucky said.

"Thank you for having us," I said.

"You're welcome," she said.

"Ha-ha," I said to Lucky.

"Ha-ha," she said to me.

Lucky and I got untangled, sat up at length.

She shook her head in amusement, older than I thought, quietly examining me. She leaned to me, touched my hair, put a hand to my cheek. "You like to bowl?" she said.

"I'm not so good at it," I said.

"Not so good at it," she said. She wasn't trying for it at all, but there was something so attractive about her, a kind of floating concentration. She patted my shoulders, she checked my ears. "Nearest lanes are in Billings. Thursday leagues, gosh we get home late."

I wasn't going to get anywhere talking about bowling. I said, "You're Lucky's mother?"

She laughed, delighted, took my hands, pulled me to my feet, wrapped me in a delicate hug.

Lucky laughed, but I could see he found me embarrassing or improper, something wrong anyway, a mood crossing his face. "She's Maria," he said. "My auntie."

"Might as well be your mother," she said, imitating his tone, correcting him as he'd corrected me, and I saw it was meant as a lesson or a bit of wisdom for him. She was lanky like him, made me feel short and plump, not true. She pulled Lucky to his feet, pulled him into our embrace. I felt strong currents—truly—colorful and joyous trout children leaping bosom to bosom among us. We held on tight, held on a long while.

So this was Lucky's aunt, nothing daunting, beautiful despite old pox scars, not the great and powerful sage I'd built in my head, who'd been some kind of Earth Mama, languidly Rubenesque. The real woman was burned dark, her flannel shirt faded to faint pink, jeans falling to blue Keds, built narrow as Lucky, her black hair shot with gray. But more importantly her presence: she was fully right there with us, beaming with intelligence and kindness, nothing I'd ever known in an older woman, not like my mother's spare and occasional warmth and hair-trigger wrath, not like Dora Dryden Conover's make-believe kindness, those knives of insight. To meet Aunt Maria, was to long to be her niece, her daughter, her sister, her friend, even her bowling partner.

I could learn to bowl.

Something burning. Her food! She attended to the little gas stove so calmly, turned the burners down, everything apparently in good order. Soon we ate, and I'd never had food that perfect, simple greens from her garden, handfuls of early peas, flavored with I didn't know what magical things.

"Various herbs," she said when I asked. "They have a good selection at the grocery in Billings, big store, cold as a skating rink! Maybe mostly thyme, which my husband likes to grow in the garden here."

She'd made bread, too, and offered honey in rough combs, and some kind of dried and salted meat, fried—that was the bacon-like smell, but it certainly was not bacon. Same answer: her husband. "It's some kind of cowboy meat he makes from game and Jewish salt. I call it poor jerky."

I laughed, but eating that meal opened me to sadness, and I stepped outside to hide my emotion, to absorb it alone under the big sky, hurried down the steps and away from the trailer, fat tears warming my cheeks as I made my way round the junked cars and weed lots, the wild things all foreign to me, the wind in my face now, sagebrush underfoot, the vast flat of the dry and golden reservation ahead of me, the sun grown hot and hard above. I'd find a way to write Uncle Jeff, who never judged me. And he could call Pops, his brother, or pass along a letter. Then Pops would know I loved him, and know where I was, and know that wherever it was it was better than Camp Challenge, and Pops would be glad, and it wouldn't be forever, just as long as necessary, and sweet to be with Lucky. Suddenly, and not so far away, right there out on the plains exactly where I'd been look-ing, an antelope leapt, then another, three and then four and then a wave of them drawing arcs through the sky together, white patterns on buffy flanks, dozens.

Lucky had saved me, Lucky Turtle, okay.

I liked how he hadn't come following me out of the trailer. And I'd have taken that space, too, but there was the grind of an engine and the clattering of bad springs coming our way, plume of dust. I turned and trotted back to Maria's trailer, arrived just as she and Lucky emerged, hands shielding their eyes. On the makeshift stoop Lucky put his hand in my back pocket, gave a squeeze the way he liked to do, his auntie's arm sneaking around him, her long hand finding my shoulder, a squeeze there, too.

I guess I expected the police. But it was just an old pickup with one yellow door, horse trailer banging behind, the whole arrangement creaking to a halt and going silent as the dust carried on in a cloud westward. Chickadee stamped and snorted, sensing company. The horse in the trailer—there was a horse in the trailer!—whinnied as the air cleared and then the whinnying went back and forth between the trailer and Chickadee. The driver swung his door open and climbed down, big man, dusty as his truck, super lean, craggy handsome. And one more wicked jolt: it was Clay Marvelette, the old stableman from Camp Challenge.

My heart pounded—we were caught.

"Lunch is over," Lucky called, sounding for all the world as if he were making a joke.

"Oh, I got food," Clay said. He trundled around to the passenger's door of his impressively battered truck, collected four grocery bags, an awkward embrace, celery sticking up in his face, trundled around the truck, settled the groceries under a thick canvas tarp in the bed, turned to face me.

"I'm not going back," I cried.

He looked surprised, made himself mild, posture and expression both, said, "That's not what I'm here for, miss."

Of course it wasn't. "You punched the doctor," I said.

"I'll punch him again, too," Clay said. "I'll punch him every time I see him, but you can bet I won't see him much. He's gonna be long gone after what I told him yesterday down at the bus station. I told him I'd nail his rooster to a tree and run him round the maypole, that's what I told him."

Maria nodded at that. "So you and Cindra here met at Challenge," she said.

"It's a long story," Clay said.

"Well, very happy," Maria said. "According to Lucky, I been telling him for years this woman was coming."

The groundskeeper laughed heartily. He said, "You been telling everybody all kinds of things, Maria. Something's gotta come true!"

"Something has."

Clay shrugged, hard. He said, "And now they got a second girl missing up there."

I was thought of as missing. I said, "Another girl? Who?"

Clay wished he hadn't mentioned it, I could see. And transparently he tried to keep it light, said, "Yup, another one, already a couple days. Rumor is the two girls run off together, but I don't think so, what with you being one of them. And no one's seen Lucky for days. So the rumor is that Lucky kidnapped 'em."

Lucky was impassive, drew his hand out of my pocket.

I said, "Do you know which girl?"

"Ah, you know, that large-format gal, can't recall her name. New Jersey. Mean as the first serpent, that one."

"Not Franciella!" I said.

Lucky said, "Probably dead in Vault."

Clay thought about that a minute—not impossible, that's what his hesitation said. "Franciella, yup. I believe that's her name."

I said, "Well, I'll bet I know where to find her. I mean if it's Franciella Goldfarb? And if she's not in Vault? Which she's not. She built a town, this miniature town. It's really well hidden. Up in the rocks on the way up to whatever that trail was. Clay? You were doing trail repair farther along. We left your group."

"I got no camper sense," Clay said ruefully.

"Those big rocks up high on the right."

"Oh, yes, back up in there. The Sentinels," he said.

"Wouldn't get in the airport van," Lucky said. He acted different around

Clay, sounded different: "That's what I recall. The marshal had to man-handle her. She bit him. She has a mouth on her. Teeth and words I never heard."

"Words for every hole in man and woman alike," Clay said.

Lucky didn't care for that. "They'll find her," he said.

"And they'll treat her fair," Clay said.

"If she isn't dead," Lucky said.

"She is not," said Maria.

"She is not," I said.

"I trust your instinct," Clay said. "And now, you best trust mine."

Clay was Maria's husband, I suddenly realized. He clapped his knobby hands. He said, "Cuz, pardners, we got to go. Pretty much right now. They've swarmed the camp. Another girl gone missing? And you know they're going to want to parlay with me. So I gotta be able to say I was delivering horses, hear me? And you best believe none of us three Camp Challenge alumnids can be here."

Maria gripped Lucky's shoulder, spoke so tenderly: "No, you can't be here with your little wife."

"We best do some sweeping," Lucky said, not tender, just business. He meant our footprints from the yard, every sign of our presence.

"Now I call that an expedience," said Clay Marvelette.

They were all so laconic that I didn't get it was an emergency. But suddenly we were loading blankets and provisions and whatever clothes Maria could spare for me (two shirts, a pair of ancient jeans, a heavy sweater, two pair socks, hallelujah, then finally, and best of all, an old pair of sneakers), loading it all into Clay's truck, while meanwhile Clay collected tools, scratching his head, wandering off, returning with an axe or a length of rope or a pair of rusty buckets, Lucky sweeping the yard, sweeping out every step we'd stepped, including my foray into the junk. The wind picked up the dust he raised and obscured the marks of sweeping, just as planned. Maria handed me garden seeds in used envelopes, each tagged in her florid handwriting with dates not too old. They sounded like baby-rattles, filled my pockets.

"Stuff that'll grow quick," she said. "Get it in the ground soon. Next to your brook up there so it's simple to water." She filled the two buckets with composted horse manure. "Just to get you two started."

"What brook? Up where? Started what?"

No answer, just the tender, prolonged regard.

Well, I'd done plenty of gardening—my dad was the neighborhood pro.

Lucky opened the trailer doors, and I was surprised to see that the horse in the trailer was View, my favorite from camp. Old View! Lucky and Maria loaded Chickadee in while Clay retrieved a saddle so worn it had holes in it where your saddle sores would be. But the leather shone with care, and the traces looked new.

Clay gave me a long inspection. I must have looked new, too, bewildered, even terrified. He said, "You'll be safe down wilderness way, more than a million acres." And he said the dead-white-guy name of the wilderness, which I won't, wanting no one to go looking, not even now.

I wanted to pretend my confusion was amusement, something about the horse: "It's View," I said.

"Yes," he said. "You have the horse eye."

I said, "How did you get him away from there?"

"Oh, it's not what you think," he said. "The horses are mine. Leased to the camp, and cheap, too. That Dora's a skinflint. But they come and go on my plan. This one here is my beauty. And due for what they call a saddle-batical."

"My beauty," Maria said.

The horses stamped and nickered, seemed pleased to be together.

"Onward," Clay said again. He leaned just so and kissed Maria's mouth. By the kiss you could see everything about them: the camp stableman and Lucky's aunt were a way-long-term couple and thoroughly in love even so.

"Well, then," Lucky said.

Lucky's aunt kissed both of his cheeks, then held his face in her hands. "I told you," she said.

Then she kissed both of mine, held my face a long time, started nodding, kissed me again, this time square on the mouth. "This one," she said, "has a baby inside."

"This one does not," I said.

"So much for premlanition," Clay said.

"This is no premonition," his wife said, "this is right now."

"This is not," I said.

"And the baby will be a man one day and come back here to see me."

"Full of visions," Clay said with a chuckle. Amused, not dismissive.

A great pause as the universe settled back in around us.

Clay killed his grin. He said, "We gotta go. We gotta go right now."

Maria put her hand on my belly. "Yes, the boy will be back. A lot of trouble in between. But this one inside here, he is coming back to this ranch a man."

We regarded one another for the longest moment, and then I reached to hug her, kissed her cheeks as she had kissed mine, as I had never done anyone. I said, "One thing at a time, dear Maria."

Everyone laughed at that. Well, not Lucky Turtle. As if I were some delicate lady with child, he helped me up into the cab of the huge pickup, climbed in himself. Clay and Maria shared another long kiss, and then he joined Lucky and me in the cab, started the engine, jammed in the clutch.

"And baby makes three," Clay said as he pulled out, hearty laugh.

"And baby makes three," I said, to complete the ridiculous joke.

Chapter Twenty-Three

Horseman and helper Clay Marvelette drove intently, bouncing that old truck out on a long, rutted trail, miles, finally reached a gravel road, then after another five or so miles west, actual pavement, finally a sad-looking casino. And then we were off the ranch and onto the Federal highway, Clay called it, the sun suddenly falling enough toward the horizon that it lit all the world below the clouds golden and unreal, long shadows ahead.

Clay said, "I'll wager Maria is talking to the sheriff right now, that's how close we cut it."

And Lucky said, "She'll have him in her front pocket."

Clay liked that. "They both got bowling league tomorrow," he said. "He'll never catch up to her."

I kept feeling my perfectly planar tummy, ridiculous idea, no room for any babies in there. Many miles and the highway curved and curved again, following the course of a river. Clay steered off a lonely exit, crossed a bridge south, cut onto a dirt road by a tumbling brook, then higher into the mountains, three more turns on obscure roads, shot-up little government signs pointing the way to the Far Turtle Wilderness, as Lucky declared we'd call it—the government signs were just wrong—higher and higher and eventually over a bald pass through snow fields, then down again, my sadness all gone, the mountains like a painting I'd once seen, two more roads, not a house, not a barn, not a human thing, then up a sharply articulated valley, another painting, vast meadows strewn in wildflowers, snowfields high above, not a word among us, just the most agreeable companionship, these men who would hide in caves for me, punch a doctor for me, rescue me from Vault, risk their jobs for me.

"Can you feel it?" Lucky said suddenly.

"Feel what?" I said.

"The baby," Lucky said.

"Will you stop!" But we were laughing.

Clay dismissed Lucky, too, said, "It ain't like Maria's never been wrong about nothing."

"Oh, it isn't?" Lucky said.

"She's wrong about this," I said.

"And you'd be the one to know," Clay said.

I didn't know anything.

We fell back into our silence. Lucky put his hand on my leg, slowly worked it up till it settled right exactly there, just a comfortable pressure, nothing more, Maria's old jeans. I felt us merge again, Lucky and me, whatever disjunction between us having bounced right out of the truck somewhere along the way.

Clay drove, oblivious, a man in his midseventies, it's hard to remember, a man who'd been working all day, but even as the sun fell and evening grew he was so resolute, so untiring in that heaving, rattling truck, all projects and stamina, the horse trailer pulling us right and pulling us left, constant corrections of the wheel. The moon rose ahead of us big as a barn, and in moonlight we came to a ranch gate. Lucky got out and opened it. Clay drove across the cattle guard, collected Lucky once he'd closed the gate again, drove higher among towers of moonlit rock, then suddenly sharply higher, snow in the crevices, bright glaciers on high. At length we arrived at a modest clearing settled in a bowl among knobs and knolls rising and rising higher to jagged peaks in one direction, a drop-off back the way we'd come, moonlighty view out across the world. You could see a single set of headlights probably dozens of miles away, someone driving somewhere that had nothing to do with us.

"Home sweet home," Clay said.

"Just as Maria said," Lucky told him. "All those years ago."

Clay sighed—my kind of skeptic. He said, "Maria? She's never even been here, bub. She never been anywhere to describe anything, a hut being a hut."

Suddenly I noticed the cabin, a low dark shape across the way, no more than that.

Lucky said, "She told me I would come to this vurry home. With a wife and fine horses and a baby and enough food to last."

Clay was amused by that. We had enough food for a week at best. We did not have a baby.

He said, "How'd she say it all come out?"

PART TWO

Chapter Twenty-Four

My son, Rick, who's now in his early twenties, began having these weird dreams about age twelve, more than a decade ago—cityscapes and maps, and things happening within the maps and cityscapes, not the usual people things, but his kind of drama: cities growing, new buildings, new forms of transportation, whole neighborhoods rising and falling and being replaced. And to capture the dreams he started drawing and mapping, annotating and labeling, studying isometric and axonometric drawing technique from dense books (always in the library, that one), something more than a hobby, maybe a compulsion, not yet a profession—he could hardly explain it. He'd wake in the middle of the night and draw these *places*: seaports, back alleys, the interiors of warehouses, the holds of ships, fantastical trade routes, topographical prospects, fanciful factories making products he named but couldn't explain—never just the one elevation, but each new structure turned this way and that (including inside out, which has a name I forget), Rapidographed skylines, penciled blueprints, vivid Sharpie-colored waterfronts, towering cardboard models of great bridges. And Conté crayon renderings of abstract spaces, mind as matter, all brick red. And vehicles, too, crazy-looking things, also the highways and tracks and air cushions they traveled on. He developed a blocky, perfect handwriting to emulate the lettering he found on blueprints.

He was on the way to a doctorate in engineering and a power career in planning, but I didn't know that then and saw him more as a budding artist. He didn't care much for that idea, nor for art class—instead, he excelled at math, excelled at physics, surpassed not only his teachers' expectations but their abilities, took classes at the local branch of the state college, wrecked the grading curve, internships and summer programs at the likes of MIT and UCLA. Girls meant nothing to him unless they could factor fractals; on his walls were no bikinis but posters of infrastructure, infrastructure only, and that eighties boy band, now that I think about it, New Kids on the Block, obscenely cute young men looking over their shoulders and past the lens and into my son's heart, unbeknownst to me.

Even that poster was buried under the large sheets of art paper I'd get him, later whole rolls of paper, more and more expensive: Canson, Strathmore, Fabriano. Weekends I'd venture into his stinking room with snacks (I allowed apples, peanut butter, celery sticks, never a bit of sugar— he could fly off the handle on the basis of a single jelly bean), and if I'd knocked on his door at the proper juncture he'd give me a tour of his world in progress, a world without people, only spaces, all of them carefully measured, every sheet of paper related to the next, washes of watercolor to provide atmosphere, his notations in a mysterious hand, little English, languages he'd dreamed, copious paragraphs, my magical boy, his hair black as the sky between stars on a clear winter's night, his eyes blue as my father's, honestly more beautiful than handsome, and tall, his hair in a braid down his long back, pudgy for years, till through this or that boyfriend he discovered the gym and got plain big.

Proud parent, I let it all just burgeon, bemused on the one hand, concerned on the other. I mean, you picture your kid playing soccer or at least excelling at chess. Then one hot August evening, the latest roll of expensive paper having reached into our hallway and unrolled out the sliding doors to our deck, I was stopped by a mountain-scape, beautifully if a little schematically rendered (but shaded with gouache watercolors, subtlest hues), marching lines of mountains, something familiar in those peaks and valleys.

"Now where is this?" I said.

"Here," he said, pointing to the next blank place on the paper. And right in front of me he started drawing close up, scratching with his pencils, erasing to make highlights, a few strokes of color, wetting his thumb to shade it all in: a kind of bluff coming into focus, endless mountains behind, and then a new angle and the bluff again and all the mountains around it, then a new angle, then another, dazzling speed and confidence, till the bluff took center stage, a landform like no other, a turtle's shell and straining neck, legs made of cliffs. I gave a shriek, scared the poor kid, cried out again, covered my mouth, and couldn't help it, burst into tears, didn't mean to be dramatic, fell to my knees, put my cheek on the ground, longform tears, the boy hugging my shoulders.

Turtle Butte.

Chapter Twenty-Five

As Clay Marvelette drove away a wave of remorse broke over me, nearly knocked me down: I was going to be alone with my new husband in that all but wilderness. And though he was truly my husband, I didn't really know him. Lucky had climbed an enormous boulder, stood up there surveying the vast bowl of stars above us. I'd gotten used to the oceanic sky, but at that elevation there was something more to see.

You could hear Clay's truck and the horse trailer a long time, banging and rattling back down the mountain. He'd left View and Chickadee in an old hand-fenced corral, just a big circle of tall, straight poles, all grown up inside with tall mountain grasses that delighted the beasts, who set immediately to tearing it up, crunching and grinding with their teeth in the otherwise silence. In the wind, maybe because of the wind, and in the darkness, foreboding washed back over me, made my stomach heave.

Touch the horses, caress their velvet nostrils, gulping breaths, all of us uneasy. Until the edge of the earth out there lightened, lightened more, and quickly the moon rose over the Great Plains, past full, a bath of soothing light. Lucky slipped up behind. He knew not to hold me or say any words. After a while instead he took my hand in his and led me to the herder's hut, this barely visible hovel, nothing but a pair of moonlit rectangles, the only straight lines around, heavy logs chinked with mud, rudimentary porch, the door an elk hide hung with nails, heavy and hairy, still animal smelling, thumping in the wind. Lucky pulled it aside to darkness, but also a bit of the heat of the day in a wave of rustic scents: mouse pee and plain dirt, fresh fir tips laid like a carpet.

Someone, I slowly saw, had gotten us set up—the bed a wooden pallet with old sleeping bags and good blankets in a pile on top, always the good blankets, Maria's loom. And as my eyes adjusted further, two rectangles of faint light emerged, moonlit portals, glass bubbly as a brook, one looking out front to where Clay had unloaded everything, the other to the back, slender pines dancing in the wind. Someone had kindly left a box of matches, and Lucky tried ten on his zipper, heartening stench of spent sulfur, just patiently striking them, sprays of failed sparks in green before one finally exploded.

He lit a candle and that single flame reflected in his eyes. He was so patient, lifting the mashed wick of another candle with the tip of his big knife. Sudden details: mismatched cabinets clinging haphazardly to the old log walls, woodbox full of pale splits, tiny homemade-looking sheet-metal woodstove, not likely big enough even for that small room in winter, meant to get hunters through hunting season at best. Kerosene lamp on a high shelf, reservoir half-full, glass sooted but elegant in shape, the only elegance in the place. One chair, a dinette piece from some distant era. Matching dinette table, chromed legs blooming with rust.

"Married people," said my husband, taking it all in.

Outside again we lifted the last bales of Clay's Junk Ranch hay into the makeshift rick, sorted halters from the hasty unloading, laid them over the fence beside the worn saddle Clay had donated. He'd been transparently in a hurry, caring but distracted, a law-abiding man who knew he was aiding and abetting. "Okay then," he kept repeating. And at last: "I'll stop back over in one week. Don't forget to count your days. Days is the first thing you'll lose."

Lucky wanted to carry me inside the hut, new bride. And so I let him, that easy strength, held the wild-smelling elk hide for him as we passed through, let him put me down on my feet on the wobbly dinette table, which put my hips in his face. He worked my jeans off half an inch at a time.

Later, we were extravagantly hungry. For our first meal in the wilderness, my husband said, he wanted to honor the old-timers. He found a can of baked beans and a can of brown bread, old hunting-camp provisions, quick and easy, opened them with his heavy homemade knife, expert. Clay trusted in Lucky's skills, just dropping us off like that. This hut, Clay had said, was owned by the grandson of the settlers who'd built it, a rare camp easement within the million-acre wilderness. The grandson was a kindred spirit, a great friend to Clay when they were young, the father, now deceased, like a father to Clay, and so Clay looked after the place, didn't require thanks. The grandson lived in New Orleans, owned famous restaurants, hadn't come around for years. And Clay had dug out a business card, the landowner's name emblazoned, handed it to Lucky. Lucky handed it straight to me, who could read.

"Don't lose it," Clay said. "That there is your proof you ain't squatting."

Lucky assembled a fire, tried to light it with our candle, which took a drip to the wick and sputtered out. He checked the matchbox, but he'd emptied it lighting the stupid candle. He felt his way around the few cabinets, checked the windowsills, nothing. He was unconcerned: "No matches."

"No shit, Sherlock."

He'd no clue what that meant, just the tone, which he countered with quietude.

We ate the beans cold, pretty good. The canned bread was like cake, packed in a kind of syrup, cheered me. But the hovel was still dark.

"What's your next trick," I said, unkind as my mom.

That stopped my husband banging around. Businesslike, he pulled me out of the one chair, slung me kicking over his shoulder, carried me out onto the cockeyed porch where, without setting me down, he gathered the pile of canteens Clay had left. And then he bounced me across the yard to the corral, dropped me like a sack of grain, canteens arrayed on top. The horses came to the fence, peered over at me, seemingly amused. Well, it was comical. And the night was so alive with wind that I forgot whatever complaint I'd had and fell into giggles. The moon, for one thing. Just past full and already half-high, the surrounding world cast from pewter, distant peaks bright as day, firs and pines and aspens all swaying and whistling and defining a large, scruffy clearing—ours!—boulders and stumps and sticks and fragrant sage, the sudden hoot of an owl, stars muted by the bright, bright moon and as familiar, exhilarating.

Lucky Turtle helped me to my feet, poked a finger in the fob pocket of his jeans, dramatically drew out a delicate, long gold chain, and finally a single fat pearl: my necklace! I gasped. "My dad gave that to me!"

"Ms. Conover's desk," Lucky said. He'd kept it lovingly, not a knot, not a tangle, opened the little ingenious clasp in a practiced way, put the chain around my neck, fastened it easily. He said, "A marriage gift, then. From your pops."

I plucked the pearl off my chest, put it to my lips, put it to his. "Pops and you," I said.

"Let's water these horses," my husband said.

Chickadee and View seemed to know Lucky and to adore him, stepped out of the corral when he lifted the boards that made the gate, took their halters willingly, walked with us out of the clearing and down a path into the moonlit course of a strong brook, and down to where it pooled in a tight clearing. The horses drank. We drank, too, and filled the canteens. Lucky rustled his way into the dense branches of some droopy, dark trees, emerged with strips of bark.

"Smell," he said. "White cedar. The underneath bark makes good tinder when it's a long time dead."

"Not without a match," I said.

Wordlessly, suddenly, he leapt onto View's bare back, reached for my hand, and despite my awkward jump pulled me up behind him, the horse beneath me all rolling muscle, that mat of horsehair both prickly and soft, hot with life. And neither slowly nor quickly we rode back to the clearing, pretty romantic, Chickadee bringing up the rear.

Back in the hut, Lucky unloaded his pockets, arranged a small puff of the cedar shreds atop the woodstove, pulled out his knife, used the back of that thick blade to strike bright sparks off a quartz chunk embedded in the cement of the chimney for the purpose. Simple as that—knife, quartz, sparks, tinder. He blew the sparks into flames, placed the flames inside the stove under the fire he'd already built, fed the flames carefully, and soon there was light, and soon again the warmth that went with it. He relit the fated candle. My pearl caught the candlelight, opalescent.

Later, capable Lucky wanted to sleep out under the stars, and so we did, pile of blankets and old sleeping bags in the dusty yard, the horses nickering in the corral, that encompassing hum you hear late at night—the world turning, Lucky called it—and we listened. Oh, and of course we made love, vurry slow, vurry quiet, not to miss a thing.

"I hope we see the bear," Lucky said.

"There's a bear?"

"There's generally a bear," he said.

Chapter Twenty-Six

I woke in a tangle of blankets and bright sunshine, barely sure where I was, this new good dream or that old bad one, Lucky already up and out. I checked for my necklace, brought the familiar pearl to my lips, thrust myself free of the bedding, hopped naked and barefoot on cold rock to a spot the horses couldn't see, peed heedlessly among boulders so big they were like parked planets, wafted back to the hut, a couple of clunky pirouettes, song in my heart. The elk-hide door hung like a curtain, the fur soft one way, stiff the other. I couldn't get enough of petting it, called Lucky's name into the gloomy interior. Of course he didn't answer. Why would he be inside when there was this outer world, this private sky, these scents of heaven (Ponderosa pine and sagebrush and ageless dust)—those mountains distant, these mountains close, our view all new, as if last night's moon had taken parts of the landscape away with it and the morning sun had brought along its own new features. Also its own steady wind, this daytime tremble of aspens, the seed heads of the thin grasses outside the corral clittering.

The horses—our horses!—stamped and snorted to call me over. But something clanged and we all turned: Lucky down in the brook trail, swinging his knife like a machete, working our direction, cleanly cutting whip-like sticks from tall shrubs, his dark belly taut and flexing, Wranglers low on his hips, a hot day coming. I ran to him, startled him grabbing hold, this naked, barefoot girl grabbing hold and hanging on, knife and sticks still in his hands—didn't matter, he held me, too, squeezed me between his elbows, fresh smell of the whips he'd been cutting.

"Nannyberry," he said breaking our embrace. He showed me his sticks.

Like the horses, I adored him. "How can you tell? No flowers? Barely any leaves. Just basically sticks? And you can tell."

He shrugged. Nannyberry was nannyberry.

Don't ask me what was so erotic about that.

We hadn't even known each other six weeks.

We tottered as a unit back to our mound of blankets and made love in a way I still remember, something new: forwardly, Lucky called it when later it came to words.

After, he dressed while I washed as best I could, found his shirt at the foot of our makeshift outdoor bed, his Wranglers underneath. My clothes were in the hut—my new clothes, I mean, not the Camp Challenge grays, which just became part of the bedding. Maria's castoffs seemed like raiment, one piece at a time out of their grocery bag, flannel shirt and jeans too long, thick socks, sneakers worn in. Lucky searched the cabinets, found an old woven dish towel. I sat beside him out on the bit of porch, rolling my cuffs just so, tying the sneakers again more neatly, as he went about unraveling the towel, making a gradual ball of string. Next he quick-whittled one of his nannyberry sticks smooth, trimmed the tip to make what looked to be a fat toothpick, super sharp at both ends, and carved a groove around the fat middle of it. He tied the end of his dish towel string in the toothpick's groove, tied the other end to his nannyberry stick, then, still barefoot, still shirtless, marched off the way we'd gone with the horses in the night, not a word, no sense in his mind that there might have been anything to discuss, off down the brook trail.

I ignored the horses who stamped again to call me over—no fair that Lucky had left us—pinned the elk-hide door aside with a stick to let in some light, inspected our new home, just a room and another room, one like a kitchen, one with that sort-of bed, that little window, square of blue sky. The lower cabinets were newly stocked with staples, canvas sacks and cans, cardboard boxes: flour, salt, sugar, rice, two cases condensed milk, dry beans in several varieties, shortening, a paper bag of what I thought were white carrots. Parsnips, as Lucky would soon explain, and a bundle of green onions, the only things available so early in the Montana spring from Maria's garden. Two pounds home-cured bacon, wrapped in plain paper, wow. Lucky laughed when I worried about refrigeration—the stuff was indestructible, he said, a staple of stagecoach days: salt and smoke. I realized there'd been a plan in place from before my rescue. I thought suddenly of a banana, just the flavor and texture of a banana, wanted it so badly! I thought of orange juice. I thought of coffee. No such luck, just the ghosts of flavors. I thought to make pancakes, but I was dependent on a recipe or Bisquick. I opened a can of condensed milk. Not what I expected. Kind of a sweet pudding, which I ate with a spoon, la-la-la! Then opened and ate another.

On the little porch I felt my freedom again and began to laugh. The sun rose higher, its voyage west, rode the ridge to the south into the sky—suddenly the day was hot. I wanted Lucky back for kisses. I wanted to cook for him, surprise him, play house, forwardly screw all day, why not? And pancakes I could fake.

Back in the small kitchen feeling really good, I built up our fire and put the huge iron pan on to heat, then mixed flour with water in an old coffee can till it seemed about right. I put shortening in the pan and it sputtered and spread, next poured a neat blob of my batter into the heat. After a few minutes there were still no bubbles, but I flipped the pancake anyway, using the side of a strop-worn knife, cooked the other side, took it off the heat. It was wafer thin, turned crisp as a cracker as it cooled. Never mind—as my dad always said, the first pancake you throw away. I cooked all the batter like that and the pancakes only seemed to get crisper, something missing.

Lucky returned just as worry at his absence had crossed into my brain, returned with his nannyberry pole and three small rainbow trout, beautiful creatures that had swallowed his toothpick thing and then been unable to disgorge it, he explained, the "gig" turning sidewise in their throats. He was a miracle, and he was back. He'd already cleaned the fishes, leaving the heads on.

I wanted to demonstrate my actual cooking skills, so I put more Crisco in the pan and threw the fish on and salted them heavily and turned them before they burned—super quick. I'd cooked fish more than once with my dad on campfires.

And we sat out in the sun on the porch, I on the one chair, he on the woodbox, and didn't we eat all of his fish upon all of my crackers, which weren't bad at all, snapped in our teeth with sharp reports. The trout was so delectable. I said, "Fish and crackers." And for some reason that was the funniest thing either of us had ever heard. We laughed and laughed and couldn't look at each other in case we'd laugh more and choke. We hadn't yet laughed like that together, I realized, so completely unguarded, no one around.

"For pancakes you need eggs," he said after a long while.

Why was that even funny? "Eggs," I choked out, erupting. "I knew that!" No, I didn't, and that was funny, too.

Lucky knew and kept it up: "And a certain kind of rock, busted to powder! My grandfather showed me." His laugh was so unexpected, a giggle and bray.

That was it for the fun. We had a stare. I had always won these things, famous in high school, but Lucky really was a turtle, never blinked.

Chapter Twenty-Seven

Same day? The next? One of the early ones, anyway—Lucky had already ranged far down-brook to fish, so the two of us hiked up-brook to explore. There wasn't a sign of a human, not in the forest around us, not out across the vast world beyond, no one, and we made our way up the slope alongside the diminishing brook for miles, for hours, drinking from it when we were thirsty, nibbling at my failed pancakes, good crackers.

"Look at Lazy resting on the wind," Lucky said, and pointed to a hawk riding high thermals. He spotted mule-deer sign, and elk, and black bear scat, and then enormous paw prints in the mud where grizzlies had crossed. "Our friends!" he cried.

We came to a rocky meadow that afforded a view both north and east across the plains far below, and it was more spectacular even than the vespers view at camp. I trotted ahead, another high viewpoint, stood among craggy rocks, the sound of water dripping below, a spring. From there Turtle Butte was visible, my last connection to what had seemed reality, its turtle head high, perfect convex shell, legs of rockfall, walking eternally, much farther away than I would have imagined, light-years, and even something so imposing was insignificant compared with the great mountain ranges beyond, black mood descending, sudden as a storm. I was a missing person. Franciella was a missing person. I thought of all the Camp Challenge people over there going about their days without me, without Franciella. And that led me back to Watertown and Massachusetts and my father and his days, Daddy, who'd no doubt heard from Camp Challenge about my disappearance. I cried all the harder, his pearl at my throat. What even day was it? We hadn't counted at all. Could it be May sixteenth? May sixteenth was my birthday.

Lucky caught up. He knew not to paw me. Just waited, watched the world.

Which for me had been constricted to *him*. I said, "I don't even know your last name. Is it Turtle? Don't tell me it's actually Turtle."

"It's Sing," he said.

"Oh, stop," I said.

I must continually remind myself that I was either only just seventeen or soon to be. My period was late. I hadn't even had one since *before*—before Montana, before Lucky, before all of it. We'd been worse than careless from the first. Well, push that away. Lots of reasons a girl might skip a month, even two. I walked off, Lucky following at a distance, respectful.

The hut was the same when we got back down there, nothing but a hovel, logs chinked with mud and grass, a place for castoffs and losers. I said all that, repeated it, pushed my way inside. "*Castoffs*," I said. "*Losers*."

Lucky came in behind me, drew his knife, a stout homemade thing, the blade hooked from sharpening, balanced it on his fingers for me to see how fine, suddenly flipped it hard, spun it into the dirt floor where it stuck, quivering.

"This is our lodge!" he cried.

"Hovel," I said angrily.

Lucky, so patient. I guess I'd expected him to be mad, too. He just waited till I'd settled down. Knew enough not to try to hold me, not to say anything, the knife in the floor between us.

"Do you know the story of Crazy Horse?" he said finally.

I did, from all my reading. He was the magnificent chief of the Oglala band of the Lakota people, a warrior, and not only that but one of the great generals of history, so what?

Lucky said, "Hoppo! That was the battle cry of Crazy Horse. But in the end, he knew his people were done, and he came in to talk peace. The Blue Coats tricked him into a cell at their fort down there in Nebraska, twelve

Indian men it took to pin him, a betrayal. And you know what he did? In front of all those men? In front of all the Blue Coats? In front of all of the future world? Well, he stabbed his coup stick into the dirt floor, and he said, 'This is my lodge.' He was still himself, is what that meant. And so the cell went away, and the bars of the cell, and the fort itself, and Crazy Horse was home. No matter if some strangers had built a fort around him. He was home, always home."

"We should water the horses," I said, no great chief.

Sweet, dappled Chickadee was calm, happy to see me. But View remained wary, made sure Chickadee was between him and me, or that Lucky was. Slowly lightening up, Lucky's story having had its effect, I said, "Do you think View hates camp girls? You'd certainly think so, all those seasons of shit riders taking lessons they don't want."

"Ah, he's just shy," Lucky said.

"Today might be my birthday," I said. I wanted a birthday.

Lucky looked stricken, said, "At Challenge they'd all sing. There'd be cake."

I didn't want to ride, and so we walked the horses down to the brook. Lucky carried a scant couple of buckets of old horse manure from the corral. Of course he hadn't only been fishing that morning but had hacked away brook-side wildflowers and dug a garden plot in the sandy, silty soil above a deep pool. We added in the buckets of manure.

I started to mark rows the way my grandfather had done, but Lucky didn't plant in rows, he just opened his auntie's old junk-mail envelopes and broadcast seeds willy-nilly, lettuces and radishes and beets and kales and chards and various herbs. I recognized a few of the seeds from gardening with Pops, all of the earliest stuff, little spears, discs, fans, tiny pearls of rust, black grains like sand. Maria had said not to eat the baby onions but plant them, and I did, pushing Lucky away, the only straight rows in our garden. We drew buckets of water from the brook and dampened the soil nicely, and somehow the damp earth filled me with the feeling that we were going to be really okay.

Inside, later, it was dark enough that my husband lit a bit of tinder, then a candle, then the kerosene lamp. Its light was even more golden than the late rays of sunset. The floor, I hadn't noticed earlier, was just packed dirt, hard as concrete. The roof and the ceiling, I realized, were one and the same, a single thickness of corrugated metal.

Not a winter abode. But then, it wasn't winter, and my possibly being seventeen wasn't more than a week or two off, a few weeks off at most.

"This is our lodge," I said, trying it out.

"You know how to make rice?" Lucky said.

"I know how to make love," I said.

"Hoppo!" Lucky cried.

Later, a pretty good dinner with pretty good rice, I sat on the hard bed and felt terribly displaced again. I wanted my father, wanted my life from before all these boys had come to explode it, closely pictured my room at home, scraps of my old security blanket hidden from Mom under my mattress, poster of Kurt Cobain in a handsome phase, Foo Fighters, too, my CD rack all women, however: Alanis Morissette, Lauryn Hill, Sarah McLachlan, on and on. All of them gone to me.

Chapter Twenty-Eight

Day by day Lucky and I created our world. The horses quickly trimmed down all the fresh grass in their paddock and surrounds, so to save the hay Clay had left, we brought them higher into the mountains, me on Chickadee with the worn saddle over one of Clay's thick horse blankets. I'd ridden a little as a kid and found that if I pretended as I had back then that I was capable and unafraid, it came true, Chickadee easy in any case, my legs wide in the saddle, that bumpy, rolling gait. Lucky rode View with only a blanket, the two of them thoroughly aligned.

We happened on a tilted mountain meadow with its own brooklet, and while the horses ate, Lucky and I drank the freezing water. We hadn't eaten a thing since morning crackers. But my husband plucked greens out of the water, really delicious, almost spicy. Cress, I'd learn later. He'd collected new young puffballs, too, mushrooms like softballs, dense and spongy, sliced them into discs with his knife, fried them up, made sandwiches with bitter dandelion greens, weird at first, then to crave—he'd brought extra along.

We climbed back on the horses and rode down into a fresh valley. "Yes, well, it's hard to get lost here," Lucky said as if we'd already been speaking of it. He knew I was worried. He pointed out landmarks even I had noticed. A stone spire down the way we'd come, a tree with a broken top ahead.

"What if later on you can't see them?"

"Well, then there's the sun, pay attention. And the wind. Straight from there."

"What if the wind dies?"

"You track yourself back."

"What if it's night?"

"If it's night, the same."

There was a purple kind of shoot growing in a bog. Not delicious. And on a slope over the brook a patch of wild onion. I closed my eyes and bit into one of the bulbs, super strong, a kind of fiery grass. Lucky dug enough for dinner and no more.

"Tomorrow I'll hunt," he said.

"You don't have a gun," I said.

"Too much noise if I did."

"So how do you propose to hunt? We don't have *anything.*"

"We have me." His immodesty was disarming. Because it was the simple truth. On a dry rock face, he found some of the powdery mineral he wanted, let me taste. Vurry sour. "I don't know the name," he said, filling a pocket. "But it makes a biscuit rise tall."

"This is the stuff you were talking about."

"My grandpa's rock."

Suddenly I was annoyed. I didn't want to seem impressed. Something in me was telling me I'd given him too much. I hadn't been a moody person back home, not really, and my irritation took me by surprise. I clamped my mouth shut upon it.

And Lucky was quiet, too, quiet the whole ride home, like a mist had come between us. We stopped wordlessly over a pool in the brook where he pulled out his gig and string and fished, three little brook trout, one after the next. He spoke privately to each fish before dispatching it, a sharp whack of its head on a rock. I remained unimpressed, unaccountably irritated.

In silence we rode. Soon he spotted nettles, pulled his jacket sleeves over his hands to avoid the stings, gathered a thick bundle. And that was dinner, once we were back and had a campfire built up against a boulder, a couple of flat rocks to sit on, nettles boiled in a steel bucket, trout fried on a stray piece of iron with one piece of our bacon for grease and the wild onions for flavor, real food, powerfully tasty after the long day and all the work that had brought it to us. My mood lifted some. Lucky's, too.

"I'll make biscuits in the morning," I said. "Tell me about your grandfather."

"What do you want to know?"

I said, "I don't know, Lucky. Whatever you want to tell. What's he like? Where does he live? Do you see him? These are not hard questions."

"He doesn't live, Cindra. He's been dead a while. I see him most days, though. Today I saw him in his rock, and you were there, too."

"I'm sorry. It must be hard."

"No, it's easy enough."

We watched the fire. We watched it a long time. Lucky added sticks. Embers fell, sparks took to the sky.

I said, "Oh, Lucky. You have to talk."

"Talk what?"

"Talk your grandfather. Was he tall like you? Was he quiet like you? What was his name?"

"Ah. He was not tall. He was not quiet. He told good stories that I haven't forgotten. He was called Robert. But his true name was Far Turtle." And then the silence settled back in. My husband watched the fire as if he were reading it.

"Oh," I said. "Far Turtle. Like our wilderness!"

"Exact," Lucky said, and put a finger to his chest, the scar I was always touching. "My grandfather. He died on the same day this happened to me, and the same way, same men, too. They shot him in the back."

"Who? Who shot him?"

Clouds crossed my husband's face. He pressed on that scar, said, "Some pretty bad people. White people. They wanted what he had. The land and all that was under it. The Free Men, they called themselves, militia types. But really they were just poachers and speculators and marched around with a flag and old guns." And then nothing, our talk being over.

I wasn't used to silences. Dag had been an explainer, my father con-
fessional. After a long time, my husband remembered to eat, finished his
nettles, sucked at what I'd left of the delicate trout till there was nothing but
fin and skeleton.

He saw I needed words, generously said, "Far Turtle worked on the
railroad, fixing the tracks and passes. He came from far away. He met my
auntie's sister, who was called Walks Far and was much older. That's all I
know."

"Your aunt Maria."

He clammed up, rose to bank the fire.

A little miffed, I arranged our blankets on the pine duff, a softer spot
than the night before, flatter. Separately, we climbed in under and among
the neat pile of Maria's coarse blankets and old sleeping bags. He'd already
said that we'd sleep beneath the stars till some reason came not to do so,
like rain, or cold, a bear. We lay on our backs a little apart. But wasn't the
night spectacular! Heat radiated from the earth beneath us, all that stone.
The stars wheeled above. I could see them in Lucky's eyes. A breeze rattled
the leaves of the aspens overhead. I bit Lucky's shoulder. Nothing. I bit him
more.

"Tell me about your own grandfather," he said.

I played it like Lucky, pushed away from him. At last I said, "My grand-
fathers are both dead. My father is super fine and most alive. He's far away,
in Massachusetts."

"But what is his name?"

"His name is Hates Roofing."

"I know Massachusetts," Lucky said, missing my joke. He said, "A lot of
campers have come from there. And history, Paul Revere and the lanterns
and such. The ocean is there."

I didn't want to talk about Massachusetts. I didn't want to talk about
my father. My father made me sad. And so finally I understood Lucky's
reticence. Still, I shook him a little, like words were acorns and he a strong
tree: "Now you."

The coals he'd banked under the ashes sighed, the heat emanated, the blankets were warm. He said, "Maria told me this bedtime story many times. After my father was gone, and my mother drifted from us: Once there was no world, and no America, and no Montana. Only the sun and the stars. And then later there was land. And later after that the water and the animals and the birds and the people. One day Raven got an itch to build a nest. She collected sticks and grass and feathers and moss. And then she laid five eggs in her nest. Oh, and she sat there day after day. But she got bored waiting and flew off. Hawk saw the empty nest and truly hated that the eggs were left behind. And though she was vurry busy with all the things that hawks must do, she sat on those eggs till they were hatched. And then she stayed with the chicks until they were big and ready to fly. Raven returned and she croaked and cawed: Those are my children! But Hawk said, Oh, they're yours, are they? Go ahead then, ask them who is their mother. And Raven asked the babies. And the babies said, Hawk is our mother."

The stars turned above us. Somewhere far away packs of coyotes or maybe wolves took turns across the miles, howling and waiting till somewhere closer a pack howled back. Lucky's breath shifted. And that quickly, he was out. I was far from sleep, terrible thoughts of my Raven mother. My emotions bubbled up, boiled over, my loneliness become complete. What terrible mistake had I made? And suddenly I decided I was *bloated*, my mother's code word, that I must be about to get my period, and realized I had nothing for it, nothing, not a napkin, not a tampon, not so much as a towel.

And I ruminated on that, and ruminated in widening spirals, but at some point must have slept. In the earliest morning, just the pink of dawn, and contrite, I woke my husband. We'd worn our clothes to bed, but they loosened as we snuggled, and loosened more, that big buckle of his like a door latch.

"You have secrets," I said.

"You have fury," he said.

But soon we were meadows of welcome skin, and the camp jays began to call and Lucky peeled me out of my Wranglers, which were Maria's, and a little angrily and a little secretly we began to make love. I wanted to boss him and so I climbed on top of him and pinned his arms and pushed myself on him a little roughly. I expected a bloody mess after and then I would explain my predicament, but there was no mess beyond the usual. I must have sighed at the delay, my tummy round with it.

"What is it," Lucky said.

"You wouldn't understand," I told him.

"Likely true," he said.

I stood shedding coarse blankets, and naked but for socks I staggered away, suddenly dizzy, unaccountably frightened, a thorough, terrible confusion in my head as if I were caught in a dream, a dream of vast, shattered spaces, took two steps fleeing it, then vomited, dropped to my knees and vomited again, right on the plain dirt.

So much for bossing Lucky.

Chapter Twenty-Nine

Ricky loved Legos well past the Legos-loving age. He was online way before the rest of us. When I was still printing out emails on our dot-matrix printer so they'd seem more like good old-fashioned letters, he was writing code, communicating with the world via his own inventions. Anyway, he signed himself up online for local Lego competitions somehow, won prizes, worked himself up the Northeastern Region leader board, all unbeknownst to me, and one fine Saturday morning—he was already thirteen—looked up from pancakes and announced he needed a ride to New York City.

"As in New York City?" I said.

His sort-of stepfather, Walter, peered around his newspaper—an actual paper one delivered to our suburban sidewalk—said, "No."

"It's Legos," Ricky said. "It's at the Hyatt, right next to Grand Central Station, so that's easy. The grand prize is a full scholarship."

"To Lego U? I don't think so," Walter said. "Absolutely not."

Ricky was never an emotional arguer. Patiently, he said, "No, it's a scholarship to a summer engineering program at UCLA. Also a crate of Legos, plus all expenses paid to the World Series of Legos. I mean if you win first prize."

"Legos don't come in crates," Walter said.

Ricky said, "It's a city competition. You get two days, you create a city. It must have infrastructure, services, and a history. You get to name it, too. There's like a pile of every imaginable Lego piece in the middle of the room. One kid from every state. I'll be representing Massachusetts. And you're right, Legos don't come in a crate, but all the pieces used in the competition are going into actual wooden crates after and the top finishers get crates. It's a *scholarship*, you guys."

I said, "Of course you can go. And of course I'll drive you. Or better yet, we'll take the train. Right to Grand Central. We'll make an adventure of it. We'll book a room at the Hyatt. Walter, come with us, we'll make it an adventure."

Walter receded his chin a notch farther, said, "Amtrak goes to Penn Station."

"Momma, please," Rick said. "There won't be any adventure. I have to build a city. That's the whole adventure. We already have a room. At the Hyatt. I won it in the last competition so I could be part of this one. I'm a *Legos Star*. Trademark."

Walter snapped his paper, disappeared behind it. His way when defeated was silence, and he didn't say a single further word. Our house was nice, smelled nice with breakfast—cinnamon, coffee—big eastern trees outside untroubled by loggers. Our town was hardly real anymore, just a few T stops from where I'd grown up, the main street practically a mall now, only high-end clothing for sale. The stuff of life—food, hardware, regular jeans, regular socks, books, movies—all that had been pushed to the outskirts, to one-story buildings surrounded by parking lots. Even a home wasn't a home anymore but a storehouse for excess commodities and soaring disaffection. In case I sound bitter, I was not, because there was my son, who'd explained all this philosophy to me, my love and my light:

"Ricky, sweetie," I said, "you should tell us these things. Like that you won. How wonderful! When is this?"

"It's tomorrow," he said. "But registration is tonight. We have to leave *right now*."

And so I flung things we might need in Walter's big plaid suitcase, twenty minutes tops, planning our escape: taxi to the T, T to South Station, Amtrak to Penn Station, Times Square shuttle to Grand Central, walkway to the Hyatt.

"You should warn us in advance," I said once we were safely on the train. "Your father doesn't like surprises."

"He's not my father," Ricky said, a new refrain since he'd skipped eighth grade and gotten placed among the geeks at the O'Bryant High School of Math and Science.

I ignored the truth: Walter, in fact, was not Ricky's father. Instead, I said, "And what if I'd had plans?"

"I'm your plan," Ricky said.

Also the truth.

Chapter Thirty

Clay had been right. We lost track of time. Lucky was unconcerned, but I came up with a game to help mark it, a kind of history of our exile, every night after dinner numbering our days in faulty fashion (we seldom could agree) and saying what happened on each. Day Five, for example, was Hot Tub, though he said Ten. In any case, this day or that, we smelled sulfur on a walk down below our swimming hole in the brook and then kept smelling it.

"Brimstone," Lucky said happily. He pulled off his cowboy boots so he could feel the water temperature, took my arm and walked me back up-brook till we found a hot current. From there we followed a mossy, steaming rivulet high into the hillside a quarter mile, steep going, but after a struggle, rocks falling behind us, we found the source, a font of clear water too hot to touch.

We set to work building a dam, making a hot tub. Soon it had filled and cleared and soon we were naked and steaming. I'd stopped worrying about when my period might come—in the summer sometimes it just didn't, that's all. I tried not to think much about the vomiting each morning, always following a disruption in mood. There was nothing to be done in any case. Purposeful denial, I chalked my symptoms up to anxiety—my parents, for one example, didn't even know where I was. Lucky thought I needed meat. And so Day Seven (by my contested reckoning) was Tracking, Lucky showing me how Clay had taught him to follow a deer, a bear, an elk, a horse, a man, then challenging me to find him, a game of hide-and-seek over miles of unmarked terrain, me stopping before a transcendent view under high sun to puke in my apparently great need for protein, then carrying on.

Nights had no numbers. I put on Daddy's necklace and rolled the pearl between thumb and finger, sometimes hours before it went back in its hiding place, a large knothole by the bed. Lucky liked to touch it, too, liked when it was all I had on, my hip bones lately disappearing like rocks in the tide. At night you could look out across the plains in all directions in the dark and not find a human light under all the light of the heavens, crashingly brilliant stars almost always, though often enough you might spot a pair of headlights way down there on the highway proceeding one direction for half an hour, then receding in red for another, never closer or farther.

Day Perhaps Eight was Clay Didn't Come—he'd said a week—and more tracking, more puking. Day Nine-ish, let's see, that was actual Hunting for Meat. And for me, Worrying Intensely about Clay. Which went away after I ralphed. And more tracking, the lessons taking hold.

"You're getting so good you could follow a mouse to town," Lucky said, rare compliment.

I glowed, said, "If there were a town."

He didn't like leaving our lodge unattended when we went on excursions, so I wrote a note on an old envelope we found amid the paper scrap in the kindling box. I tried for tough-guy talk and tough-guy spelling, too, clipped it to the elk-hide door with a clothespin whenever we left:

WELCOM BRONCO: MAKE YOURSELF AT HOME,

IF YOU FIT IN THE DOOR.

BACK IN 5 MINITS!

Day Nine was also Sleep Inside, or maybe that was Ten. Lucky wanted to call it Seventy-Seven, finding that number auspicious. Whatever the accounting, Lucky hung all the blankets and sleeping bags on tree limbs for the afternoon and in our bedroom built a kind of box of spruce boughs filled with fragrant pine needles to replace the old pallet, wood we could use to build other things. I liked it outside, but the thought of bears had grown each night. Lucky didn't care about bears but certainly about inter-lopers. There was no Bronco to protect us, and our own note had pointed that out to him. There were good reasons a person might turn up, and bad reasons, too, so Lucky expounded. "Rather greet 'em in a doorway," he said. And it was sweet inside that night and a little warmer, and the mattress of pine needles squeaked just a certain way and made music and fragrance when we gave it a whirl.

Day Twelve. Yes, Day Twelve was Exploring, a morning ride over the ridge we hadn't seen past—more of the same out there, peaks and long val-leys, the foot of a glacier, snow to bring home in Lucky's hat, which he wore on his head to keep cool, the drips running down his forehead comically.

"Good meat," Lucky said, surveying the valley below, meaning future hunting. That made me feel sick, and after a while I vomited voluptuously, Lucky holding my hair for me. And then of course I craved meat, all the long ride home. We foraged dandelion and sorrel and unnamed greens (clubs, we called one of them), collected a few mushrooms he seemed to know weren't poison, cooked them on our fire with a parsimonious half strip of bacon, which was getting used up—a half pound left, now packed in the remainder of Lucky's snow.

Day Fourteen was a big one: Viking Spear, Lucky stripping and sharpen-ing one of the dozens of saplings he'd cut on Day One, which we'd named Adjusting, hardwood grown up where beavers had cleaned out the woods around their abandoned bog. He practiced all afternoon, chucking that wobbling javelin at various targets, and after a few days he was able to kill a certain rotted stump pretty effectively from twenty paces, then thirty. He changed his grip, he whittled away the wobble left-handedly, he changed his stance, he developed a three-step windup, he developed a quieter sta-tionary throw, he hit that stump from forty paces, then fifty, sixty the limit.

I just wanted to lie down, and that's what I did, a warm spot in the sun where I studied my husband minutely: maybe we were spending too much time together? I vowed walks on my own but found I couldn't be without him.

And about there I began to falter in the marking of days. I seem to have several Days Fourteen in memory. One of the later ones was Trap Day, I having gotten more than a little obsessed with the idea of fresh meat, and still no sign of Clay. And trout had grown less plentiful, what with fishing day after day in the same brook. But then Lucky made a cunning box with sticks he'd whittled and tied with strips of inner cedar bark and weighted with rocks from the creek, triggered by a simple lever he'd invented wakeful the next night, then carved in the morning, fifteen minutes of focused work. The bait I invented: doughy pellets of the biscuits I'd perfected with the help of Grandpa Turtle. I dreamed of vinegar, kept searching the cabinets for a forgotten bottle, none.

On a different Day Fourteen, Lucky packed the traps on Chickadee and climbed on View. I didn't want to be alone, so climbed up behind him, my arms tight around his chest, cheek on his back, heels gripping the big horse, no path but our own, till we happened across an active beaver bog, dam at the far end. And there he set the traps.

Day Twelve or Twenty or whatever it was was First Morning Apart but could have been called Cindra Accepts that She's Pregnant. Anyway, Lucky went on foot to look for meat. He carried his spear lightly. You couldn't want the food too much: intent tipped off the animals as surely as scent. I wandered a mile downhill to a place we hadn't yet seen, found berries, just a handful ripe, but a trove imminent. And despite my sense of isolation, I liked being alone. I wished I knew mushrooms, found a patch of thick brown things growing in a fairy circle, but Lucky had already said no to that sort. Still I sat in the circle and felt something powerful coalescing under my breastbone, a fierce joy that produced tears, and then the weight both metaphorical and real in my belly, the sense of a *we*, and more tears, and laughter: this *we* would be fine. And then I puked and kept puking, worse than previous days. Standing, I was disoriented but started walking anyway, warm sun in my face, maybe a mile—not more than that—before I realized I was lost, no familiar landmark, all the terrain the same, the spruce trees knotted the same, the sagebrush standing the same, this pile of rocks and odd boulder just like the next pile of rocks and odd boulder, no familiar peaks in sight, nothing. But I was a tracker, I told myself: I could track myself home. I put the sun behind me and followed my own clumsy tracks straight back to the fairy circle and thence to the trail, which was our road, two rutted lanes. I spun in joyous circles till I was dizzy, sat down right in the dirt, lay there and looked up into the sky. Curiously, it was pure blue at the top, lighter at the horizon. I thought of the bowl the ancient Greeks saw up there, a kind of dome between the earth and heaven's light.

And then I heard a shot. An unmistakable gunshot. Just one, with impressive echoes. My gut clenched. I stood. Should I make myself visible or invisible? I listened, listened the longest time, nothing more. The shot had been from way over there—to the east, and down the mountain, maybe far down the mountain. It had been neither loud nor quiet, yet in my heart I could still hear it. Visible, I thought, and walked up the mountain square in the trail, hurrying only a little, working to remember the name on the business card Clay had entrusted to me, couldn't call it to mind.

I reached the clearing before Lucky was home, stood with the horses ten minutes, letting my fear abate. And it abated. I built a fire outdoors—visible, yes, that was my decision—and boiled the beans we'd soaked that morning. They'd been dried fresh just the previous summer, and Clay had said they'd cook faster than we knew, whatever that meant. I felt myself a rice expert by then and started some rice, too.

The rice was ready but the beans weren't, and I had barfed some time before and was starved and now remembered the shot again. A bad half hour, then suddenly Lucky materialized—silent approach, that pro (I jumped nearly into the fire, I was so startled). He shook his Viking spear over his head, he danced a little, he held a rabbit aloft, already cleaned and gutted, the fur peeled down like a sock to reveal meat and sinew, shook that spear outrageously, comically. The words poured out of him in a rare, excited tumble: "From fifty paces away! Straight through, and running, too. Gave himself to us." Then more solemnly: "Now this spear has killed, we name it . . ."

And then he thought and thought, couldn't think of the right thing, left the rabbit on a big rock in front of me, nothing I'd ever eaten—it didn't even look like food. I was sad for the bunny, and sadness for me was never far from anger.

"I heard a gunshot," I said.

Lucky paced, oblivious. "Name it, name it," he called.

"Bunny Slayer," I shot back, witheringly I thought, maybe wanting a fight, but Lucky's humor didn't extend toward sarcasm, and he missed my meanness.

"Bunny Slayer!" he repeated.

"But wasn't it called Viking?"

He missed my tone again. "Oh, that's what we played as boys. We'd use cow horns and make hats and chase each other around."

"You and your grandfather?"

"Me and my friend."

"You had a friend?"

But that's all he'd say, danced off shaking his spear and leaping up on rocks and shouting its new name to all the Norse gods, I supposed. By the time he was done, homemade ritual, there was no joke, only a spear with a spirit alive inside, a sharpened, wind-worthy stick all but howling with blood lust, also protection. "Bunny Slayer!" he shouted.

And that sent my bad mood flying out across the meadow to clatter harmless on the rocks. "Bunny Slayer!" I shouted back less meanly.

Lucky liked that. He said, "You heard a gunshot?" He stood close, put his hands delicately to my ears.

"I did, I heard a gunshot."

"I suppose we might sometimes," he said. And wryly, "Perhaps it was Bronco."

I'd thought he'd be freaked out. I thought he'd want full information. But that was the extent of his interest, much less fear: sometimes in the wilderness, you might hear a shot. My own worry fled.

He built the fire up over my coals—the rice was done, the beans were far from—then let it burn down, speaking of the trees that had lived and died to bring us that heat, which was of course a Lucky thought, always thinking of every cycle, never the straight lines.

He said, "I remember my grandfather roasting rabbits, quite a few. He called the recipe French rabbit after some trapper he knew when he was young." And then he demonstrated the old man's way, how he arranged the coals, how he added fresh wood at the end for smokiness, how he banked the whole thing down.

I said, "Far Turtle."

And Lucky smiled at that. "I'm glad you know him," he said.

"Robert Sing. And he knew Walks Far. And Walks Far was Maria's much older sister, and Maria is your great-aunt?"

"I call Maria my aunt, yes, and she is great."

"So she's not your aunt?"

"She's my Hawk mother, how's that?"

"That's really interesting and a little annoying. That you won't tell me anything. What about your Raven mother, Lucky? Is your Raven mother around?"

He didn't like the pressure. But liking me, he said, "Yes, in a way. Grandfather called her Hard Turtle, but that was a joke only for me. Sometimes I still say it in my heart. She drifted from me after he died."

"She was traumatized."

"I don't know that one."

"Her heart was hurt."

"No, her heart was hard."

I pulled up my shirt. I put Lucky's cool hand under my navel. He held it there, warming.

I said, "Sweetie, Lucky, your auntie was right."

"Yes, she was," he said. "There's a boy in here, and we will name him Mountain Turtle."

"Mountain Turtle. Fine with me."

Lucky was pleased: "And just like Maria said, he will return as a man and meet her."

"Return from where?"

"From where he will be."

"And we are happy?"

"We are vurry happy."

"I'm sorry your mother was so hard."

He thought a long time, at last said, "Still is."

The smoke was sweet. The beans might not get done, but little matter.

My husband wrapped the poor rabbit extravagantly in our remaining bacon and wound it all in place with onion grass and whole branches of Montana sage à la French trapper, then rolled the entire package thickly in large dandelion leaves we'd collected, tied it into a bundle with cedar bark, soaked the bundle in water he'd carried up from the brook, dug a hole in the banked coals, dropped the rabbit in, covered it, built up the fire, which soon put the beans to a hard boil.

I put the rice on. Rice was my job.

And in no more than twenty minutes we feasted. The beans were perfect, somehow perfect. The rabbit was delectable. Every bite for my baby, I told myself. I gorged on rice and beans, wished for more meat: a bunny ain't much.

"Many a man with a rifle," Lucky said, musing.

Yes, many a man with a rifle.

Does everyone keep a list in her head of the best sex of her life? I only bring it up because that unnumbered night remains the very pinnacle, with quite a few dozen close runners-up, all Lucky.

Chapter Thirty-One

Lucky and I missed the afternoon of Day Probably Not Seventeen to his moodiness over Clay, the way I kept talking about Clay, how we needed Clay, how I wished he'd turn up already. Likely something to do with the gunshot I'd heard, that I wasn't over the gunshot, that in my mind I kept relating the gunshot (it was really loud, it echoed) to Lucky's scar and the fate of his grandfather, which annoyed him: there was then, and there was now. I didn't know the word *anxiety*, gave great credence to fear. Maybe my talk got spiky. Anyway, I kept yammering about Clay, the safety of Clay, and when was he going to come?

Lucky couldn't quite find the words, or hardly any, but he didn't want Clay.

And that was the numberless day you don't have sex for the first time since you could, monumental crossroads. But next morning, first waking, we climbed on one another, almost wrestled, me pinning him at last.

After, I felt better about absolutely everything, and then more than that, perfectly perfect, and then more than perfectly perfect, something like beatific, harps playing, celestial voices in chorus. Yes, pregnancy hormones. No, I did not know about such things, gave Lucky all the credit. Inside at the tin stove, he'd started breakfast and laughed when I grabbed holt of him (he said "holt"), embraced him, held on tight. And he was all sweetness and light again, and we were all laughter again, and soon again it was just we two again, and soon again I understood Lucky's horror of dependence on anything or anyone but the two of us and our otherworldly love, our splendid isolation inside each other's hearts.

I kept thinking of vinegar, just the way it curled your tongue. I kept thinking of my parents, whom I'd be turning into grandparents, a forceful realization. As the sun came up over the ridge, I said, "I need to write my dad. And I have had this idea: I could mail it to my uncle. Clay could post it. And you know, let Clay address the envelope."

"Let Clay or beg Clay?"

"Beg him, I guess. If he ever even shows up again. Don't make it a case, would you not?"

He would not. He collected some poison berries he knew would make good, lasting purple ink and found a wide strip of birch bark to write on and an owl feather for a quill, super soft, a guy who could find owl feathers.

I tried to strike a jocular tone, but it all seemed so serious, words that in a week or two my father might touch with a finger one by one and read, words that would make him cry, words that he would no doubt withhold from my mother, good: she was hateful. And if I tried, maybe Daddy would laugh as well, a laugh I could hear. As I wrote I felt the directness of our connection, words on birchbark bridging time and space:

Our Father Who Aren't in Heaven: By now you know I left Camp Challenge. But this was only because of severe mistreatment. Now I'm far from there and you shouldn't look for me or worry. I'm safe and sound with a friend I love and plenty of good food. Okay, a husband. And I've a baby in my belly. This is a lot of news, I know. I'll get to see you again before too long. I hope Uncle Jeff gives you this note. It's peaceful here and I feel the best in my life except for when I was with you, of course, and I sorely miss you. Tell Mom I'm fine.

I knew my uncle's address by heart, wrote it at the top of the letter. I thought Clay could copy it onto an envelope, find a stamp and hand it off to a third person that might mail it under their own return address, confuse whoever might be watching. And Uncle Jeff, well, he'd give it to Dad with utmost secrecy, one of their frequent fishing trips, say, deep in some north woods.

And now that I was writing again, reading rushed to mind. How I missed reading! Our lodge needed books. When I said it aloud, Lucky said, "How 'bout you write them."

"How about you?"

"You know I can't."

"So I'll take dictation. You talk, I write it down."

"And what should I say?"

"The story of you."

"Nup."

"The story of you and me, then."

"Once upon a time," Lucky said, not the slightest hesitation, "two vurry fine people rode two vurry fine horses for most of a day. They put down gravity traps and didn't get home till supper."

"And that's the end?"

"That's the end for now."

"Then what is the beginning?"

"We haven't gotten to the beginning. Not yet."

Well, that was the name of Day Quite Possibly Eighteen, I decided: Letter to Daddy.

Chapter Thirty-Two

The middle of some subsequent night—okay, morning, the sky lightening in the east—Lucky and I heard a vehicle bouncing up the road far below, and exactly as we'd planned in the event of an intruder, and relieved at the early warning, and of course thinking of that gunshot I'd heard, we pegged our note for the imaginary Bronco to the doorframe and slipped out of our lodge and up the mountain several hundred yards to an overlook Lucky had picked, a high bluff well off our normal routes and near a complex rock formation to retreat to just in case and, from there (if needed), an illogical route eastward, illogical so that a logical man wouldn't follow, Lucky the tracker thinking backward.

"It's Clay," he said, listening. From up on the bluff I knew immediately as the old truck came heaving into view that Lucky was right: it was Clay Marvelette, great gusting sighs from yours truly at the sight of those dented fenders and the mismatched driver's door, we imagining what we'd have done if he'd been some stranger or the police. We gave it a minute, but there were no tricks, no one from camp pulling up behind, no cops. We watched the dusty vehicle approach the horse pen, watched it rock to a stop, watched Clay climb out all weary and crooked, watched his quick powwow there with View and Chickadee, then that stiff-legged stride to our lodge, posture suddenly wary.

"See, he's vexed," Lucky said.

Clay didn't like the looks of our note, true, or anyway he studied it a long moment, crumpled it.

And just then Lucky whooped, a feral cry, and poor Clay jumped, backed under the cover of our tiny porch, scanned the landscape. Lucky and I whooped more, hurtled down the slope, rocks and loose till rolling down ahead of us.

"You just leave the horses?" Clay said when we got there.

"We didn't get much warning," Lucky told him.

"Next time let 'em out of the corral so they can't just be commandeered, boy."

"Next time let 'em out of the corral, boy," Lucky repeated, both of them edgy like I'd never seen or imagined possible from either of them.

We met in a knot. I hugged the handsome old man, like hugging the corner of a barn. He smelled of horses and gunpowder. And then we just stood there, no one with anything to say.

But after a while Clay started: "I really done it this time."

And just then the passenger's door of Clay's truck squealed open. A grand pause, like nature herself had stopped. Not a birdcall, not a whisper of wind.

And then—and then Franciella got herself turned correctly and slid out of that cab. She slammed the truck door dramatically. "*Bonjour, mes amis!*" she called. And marched up the hill to join us. Steep grade at high altitude, and yet she barely puffed, nearly ran at the end, pulled me away from Clay and into a massive embrace. She smelled like sage, she smelled like bear oil. The bear oil was the clue: she'd been staying at Maria's.

"Franciella," I said, incredulous.

"You're from New Jersey," Lucky said, always with the pertinent observation.

Franciella looked him up and down. Something different about her—had she lost weight? She said, "He speaks! The kidnapper!"

"Oh, he speaks, all right," Clay said.

Franciella had clearly been outdoors, and a lot—her skin was burned mahogany, freckles arisen, sun-bleached springs of hair flying every which way. Her thighs were massive as ever, but muscles stood out. Her face was almost disturbingly narrow, like she was someone else, her own sister, perhaps. Also, something psychical, but that you could see and feel and hear:

she'd thrown off captivity, abundant life and light in her eyes, unveiled brilliance, what I'd only barely seen emerge in La Vil.

Clay cleared his throat, steered a course through his thoughts: "I found her in her little conurbation there, the one you told me about, her little impressive metropolis." Sweet man, digging for complimentary phrases. "Just like you said. Right amazing."

Her own words tumbled: "I made a kind of shelter. Biggest structure in La Vil. Like an arena. My idea was lie in there and to starve and freeze and die. Because you were gone, Cindra. People said you expired in Vault!" She burst into tears.

I started to tears, too: evidently we'd been closer than I'd let myself believe.

Clay said, "She was passed clean out."

"I ran out of water. I had only one Dixie cup of bug juice from mess, less than half, because I spilled it all out walking up there in the dark."

Clay said, "I often park up that way. Got her loaded in the truck under a blanket, sleeping beauty. Then, see, I just drove out per usual, quitting time. And we absquatulated. Straight to Maria's. And didn't Maria fix this young lady right up. Pulse of forty-two. A good many nights, couple hundred gallons of water. Couple bites of food."

I said, "You met Lucky's aunt!"

"She more than met her," Clay said. "The two of them nearly used up all the words. Secrets were imparted."

Franciella, animated like I'd never seen her, clearly as fond of Clay as I was, fell into patter: "Yes, yes. Maria is beautiful to talk with. She kept saying there'd be a wedding one day and that you and I'd have sons who'd build a kinder world and love their moms. And that my own mom watched over me, and for the first time, you guys, I truly knew it. And Maria nursed me right back, didn't she, Clay. All those perfect greens and funny teas."

"She did."

Then some new voice she'd come up with in imitation of Clay: "And then I was sitting up again and this cowboy here promenaded all through his world of junk, a little longer each day till I'd been certified Okay to Travel, and so we packed up his buggy and now he's brought me here."

Lucky took her in—the girl was utterly changed since whatever long ago day he'd taken her off the marshal's hands. He turned visibly to his own thoughts, a leap of light-years.

Clay grew grave. To me, he said, "I'm going to have to leave this loquacious Lilliputian here. She's not well yet, but she's on her way. She's got to drink water. That's the main thing. And not get too cold. And gradually start to eat normal. All right? You hear me? I'm going to have to get going pretty quick here. Before anyone back camp-wise knows I'm gone. What I'm saying is, Francie here is staying with you." He'd been sidling down the hill toward his truck so subtly I was surprised we'd arrived there, all of us following his increments, so many Scottie-dog magnets following a block of steel. At the truck Clay lifted out two boxes of food—milk and bacon and yeast and oats, big block of cheese, boxes of pasta, treasure. Last was a glass jug of homemade vinegar.

"Oh, Clay," I said, thrilled with it all, but especially the vinegar. I hugged him hard, corner of a barn. "We'll take good care of Francie."

"She's talkative," he said.

Lucky tossed the brown-paper packet of bacon unhappily hand to hand: I was making us beholden, that's what he thought.

But Clay was used to Lucky. He moved his tarp back farther and dug out a hundred-pound bag of white flour, SURPLUS stenciled on it in huge letters, hefted it out of the bed easily, dropped it on Lucky's shoulder. Sullen Lucky, not a flinch, not a word, carried the huge bag and the packet of bacon up the long hill to the lodge and inside.

Last there were two fine bales of hay, and Clay hefted them, too, tossed them out onto the trail.

"We've barely used even one yet," I said.

"Well, good," Clay said. "You can't have too much hay." And then, with Lucky out of sight, he gave me a paper package, which I understood from his delicacy I was not to open in front of him.

"Okay then," he said.

"You're itching to go," Franciella said.

"Yes, mademoiselle," he said.

He gave me short hug, more of a shoulder squeeze. Last gesture, like I'd been waiting forever, I tucked my letter in his shirt pocket, whispered in his ear.

"Yes, I will," he said, simple as that, securing the letter with a pat. "I'll mail it from down in Wyoming next week. But you'll owe me two bits." And he dug under the tarp once more, came up with a large and lumpen burlap sack emitting a subtle mutter. "Almost forgot," he said. "Laying hens. Maria had quite a few extra. Miss Francie here confabulated a flock for you. It's her gift, too."

"Oh, Clay. Oh, Francie. I've been dreaming of eggs."

Franciella shrugged, proud of herself, proudly took charge of the birds, hurried with them in their sack up the hill to the little broken woodshed, a perfect henhouse—Clay must have told her all about it—trotted up that hill to put the chickens to home. A different shape altogether, that woman, something athletic emerging. I saw her then as a grown-up, old and wise, but I look back now and see a child, the two overlaid in memory like colors.

Clay had me alone, said, "I'm working on what we'll do."

"What we'll do what?"

"What we'll do come winter." He broke eye contact, looked to our lodge, where Lucky had disappeared, my husband likely unpacking all the gifts, which seemed bounty. Franciella stood in the dooryard up there examin-ing the woodshed, sack of chickens now jumping in her hands, a lot of squawking.

Clay found my eye again, said, "You won't understand it, but Lucky don't want my help. He don't want anybody's help. And what I know he thinks you're going to do is the two of you are going to spend the winter here. But that's just not going to work, and don't you let him convince you neither. He'll be huffy. Like right now. You see he's not coming out to say goodbye. You see he's not said thanks for anything. And now look what I've done."

"What have you done?"

He pointed up the hill to Franciella, who was expertly pulling chickens out of the bag by the feet and sticking them in the shed one by one.

"Clay, don't worry," I said. "We'll see to Franciella."

"I'm afraid Franciella's gonna see to you!"

We laughed: true enough.

I said, "I'm glad to have her."

"She's surely fond of you."

"And Lucky will be okay, don't worry."

"I'm worried plenty. But I will have a plan. Next time." He plucked a downy feather off his shoulder. He examined the trunk of a nearby tree. He had a look at the sky, a look at the ground, finally landed on me. Enough with the parlay: it really was time to go.

He edged toward his truck, said, "Oh—almost forgot. Something you'll maybe recognize. Box musta fell off the laundry van." And retrieved a carton holding twenty gray T-shirts, all size medium, then a paper package with two dozen pair gray panties, size extra small, useless, except perhaps as washrags—okay then! There were Camp Challenge sheets, too, and blankets for Francie, a growing stack in my arms.

"Thank you, thank you," I said. "And thank you from Lucky, too, even if he can't say it."

Wry as always: "I'll accept that and say you're welcome." He climbed in the truck, shut the door. I stood there by his open window. I wanted to say a list—rope, and string, and a jackknife of some kind for me, a packet of fishhooks, a book to read. But was that asking too much? The words caught in my throat: yes, it was asking too much. Lucky really did want to be self-sufficient. Just a funny wedge I didn't expect, coming in between these two, and maybe now if I weren't careful, between Lucky and me. And Franciella—of all people—Francie, come to share our little paradise. How would Lucky take that?

Clay coughed and said, "Oh, and Maria said to tell you: we're not made of cash, but maybe the rope. Fishhooks I got. Surely a jackknife."

I had not said any of that about what we needed out loud. None of it. I had not. Shocked, I tried to find the right reply, but Clay just started the truck and turned the heavy steering wheel, backed up, suddenly stopped again with a jolt, the old truck rocking on its springs: "Oh, and shoot. One more thing. Maria said you'd like this here." And he handed me a fat, foxed paperback book.

Some mysteries you just had to accept. He balanced the pawed old volume on the stack of goodies already in my arms. I laughed out loud: *Hawaii*, by James Michener. "My god, it's huge," I said.

He grinned. "I'll tell Maria you said so. She been reading that one thirty years."

He clacked his workaday truck back into gear, spun the tires in the dust, hurtled off in his own cloud and back down the mountain, the suspension clattering and banging, its own personal song, as Lucky had pointed out.

I shuffled up the hill, suddenly exhausted. A chicken had escaped, Franciella chasing it comically, shouting at it, words I'd never heard: where had she gotten so familiar with chickens? And Lucky burst out of our lodge, all cheerful energy again, now that Clay was gone, helped the new woman catch that bird. I dropped the other stuff on the porch, clutched the book to my chest.

Winter. I hadn't really thought about that.

Worse, I'd forgotten to ask what day it was, and Francie didn't know.

Chapter Thirty-Three

After another ecstatic sip of vinegar, I hid my treasure—*Hawaii*—under the corner of our bed, Lucky and Franciella distracted in the construction of hers, right there in the kitchen, fir boughs and cedar bark on the packed dirt, all filled in with pine needles and covered with Camp Challenge sheets and the fresh blankets from Maria.

In the morning, I insisted Francie go with Lucky on his fishing rounds. I just wanted some time alone. She was reluctant, but he pulled her along, and soon they were laughing, crossing out of the meadow and down along the brook.

Blessed solitude, a silence of sounds: View whinnying, Chickadee kicking at the corral, a gray jay piping, actual chickadees, males, reclaiming territory with their two strongest notes. I heard the wind. Always the wind. I heard a commotion among the hens, remembered we now had hens, just as we now had Franciella. I sipped vinegar like a guilty wino, built up the fire, heated some water, washed up, all the while entertaining specific moments from the deep night. Lucky was willing to kiss me everywhere, to kiss me with his whole person. I was a wife now, grown past all fumbling, awakening at all hours from the wildest pregnant sex dreams, and Lucky mostly ready.

Using his powdered white rock—his grandfather's rock—and fresh, fresh milk, I invented a new batter for biscuits, got them in the little woodstove. Then a quick visit with the horses, Chickadee's sweet soft nose. View stood as always where I couldn't reach him, just off the smaller horse's flank. I imagined he was jealous of me, she my cheering section, and we whispered back and forth.

"Oh, Chickadee, what is wrong with me?"

I'd never had a horse stand so still for me, not ever, not that I'd had many chances, but I held sweet Chickadee in the wind, super comforting that she loved me, too, and found me blameless, even after all that had happened.

"We'll go to the hot springs later," I told her.

Then crack, and crack again, two unmistakable gunshots, much closer than the single blast I'd heard the week before. I jumped and Chickadee flinched and we both listened, the whole forest gone silent. We listened forever, then a little more.

The biscuits! I raced to the lodge, but they'd already started to burn. I wrapped my hands in our one towel and yanked the car-part pan out, ran them outside, dumped them on the little porch. They rolled this way and that, puffily misshapen, only slightly burned, now that I looked, my first baking success ever. The towel was hot. I threw it off. Bolt of fear—what if you burned your hands out here? And the shots! Who was shooting? But the biscuits, fragrant, steaming. The towel smoked. I stomped it. Down by the corral Chickadee stamped, View snorted. So much for peace.

Soon Lucky and Francie were back, Lucky with the usual string of fish flashing in the sun as he held them up, Franciella jogging ahead of him at the sight of me, real locomotion—that new physique came with capabilities.

"Lucky caught fish!" she cried like a little kid. "And I found these . . . um, *fraises*!" She showed me her T-shirt, rolled up and full of tiny strawberries. Lucky sidled up behind her, handed me his string of five little trout. He didn't have manners, shoved past Francie to kiss me. Well, yes, to that.

"I heard a gunshot," I said in his mouth, intimate tones, purposely excluding Francie, I'm afraid. "Two gunshots, I mean."

He'd heard it too, of course. Without alarm, and without saying a thing, he strode to the corral, shoved open the gate, threw the blanket on View. He kicked the gate bars closed and then horse and rider were away, Chickadee nickering at the fence, left behind. She'd heard the shots, too, knew exactly what Lucky and View were up to.

Francie said, "Where's Long Braid gone?"

"He thinks he knows where there are more berries," I said, instantly guilty at dissembling. "And don't call him Long Braid."

"He called me Brown Bear, what's the difference?"

"And when did he call you that?"

She didn't answer but lifted a tiny delicate strawberry, put it on my tongue, ambrosial. I remembered why I liked her, embarrassed to recall my initial sense of superiority back at Camp Challenge. She leaned into me, enveloped me, held on tight. That berry—it was as if she'd kissed me. She smelled like the brook. Twinge of jealousy in my throat—she'd been down there with my husband.

Not long and he was back. He was such a beautiful rider, so relaxed as he came into sight, rolling with the horse up the trail past the new barrier— three enormous boulders he'd levered into place using a pole and fulcrum somehow—straight to the corral, sliding off View at the gate and pulling his riding blanket with him, no showing off for the women on the porch, biscuits lined up now on the railing. Lucky closed the corral gate after View with a few words and then a pat on the nose for Chickadee, who'd charged up to them in protest—left behind! He put his finger on his own nose the way he did when it was time for him to talk more than the usual: "Yup, a poacher. I found the pile of innards, mule deer is all. Foot sign everywhere, boot about so big, the ones you get at Big Western cheap. Pointy toe. Heavy man, not too tall, so. He parked his truck at the second bend after the brook down there. He just loaded his deer and left. That's how poachers do it, mostly, load the meat and go. Bleed it at home. But it won't taste good, I'll tell you that. Didn't even try to hide his tracks. That kind of man."

"So you're saying there was a man?" Francie said.

"A poacher," I said.

"Are those biscuits?" Lucky said, delight growing on his face.

"With your grandfather's rock."

He beamed. "Now see?"

After breakfast, a feast of fish and bread, I remembered the kraft-paper package from Clay, retrieved it from the shelf over our bed, brought it out to the porch, out to my family, untied the string. Inside, a note in Clay's square hand, back of an envelope: "For you and baby." And more wrapped items. A three-pack of big white panties. A chunk of black glass, super smooth, which Lucky said was arrowhead obsidian from the Yellowstone. And then, even more beautiful, a sky-blue, vastly oversize T-shirt: maternity clothes. And finally, wrapped in used Christmas paper, a pair of pink socks, my own from home. Impossible, since I'd abandoned them at camp, but there they were, dear emblems of the previous life. I wouldn't wear them. I'd make a purse of them for my necklace. I put them on my hands for the moment, like elegant little mittens.

Chapter Thirty-Four

Despite all her excitement at joining us, Franciella's freedom had come at a cost—she wasn't a cowgirl, not a country girl, and that life wasn't for her: too much work.

She couldn't ride a horse and wouldn't try; she wouldn't cook or forage without a lot of pressure. She groaned at every effort, complained about having to use the outhouse (as if the bathhouse at Challenge were any better), complained about the cold at night and complained about the heat of the day, complained about having to search for food. She missed the kitchen ladies, missed La Vil, missed the bustle of all those girls she loved to hate, seemed to transfer all that emotion to everything about our existence. And she knew her only other choice was prison. She'd been busted originally, as far as I could make out, for armed robbery or possibly manslaughter in an odd case involving her grandfather as both complainant and accomplice. So she was stuck. As were we. With her. Thanks to Clay. Or thanks to me, who'd told Clay where to find her.

She wore a pair of XS gray Camp Challenge panties on her head, cuter than it sounds, all those curls, wore my new T-shirt, which fit her like a short dress, and showed off fulsome boobs. She and Lucky were stiff with each other still, but he always had a parting eye for her as she strutted past, that constant pacing. She slept thickly at night and well into morning, snoring under a beautifully woven but unraveling blanket Maria had donated, a big deal, that blanket, deeply generous, but Franciella complained of the wool smell and itching. Lucky was never irritable about her, though, not even a frown. And, the more she was around, the more he couldn't keep his eyes off her. And worst of all, her face, more radiant by the day, her health returning, her eyes grown incandescent.

I sought out time alone, made blessed excursions for solitude (*Hawaii* in the hot springs, *Hawaii* in the high meadow, pages flying past, a solid thousand of them, and Michener's brand of history, too, the most vivid pictures in my head, beautiful Polynesian people naked among the abundance, vile missionaries bent on reforming them while fucking them and fucking them over, heroes and villains and too many men, really—I wanted to read about women, women in charge as among the Hawaiians—and just the ocean, the beauty of the encompassing ocean. But Franciella started following me, watched as I read, watched as I worked the garden down by the brook.

"Water!" I commanded, trying to make it fun.

"Water!" she commanded right back, and headed for the brook, waded into the deepest pool, stood there dreaming, then singing, then sitting, then slipping underwater.

But at length she filled the large bark vessel Lucky had made, took her time pouring where I pointed, a satisfying puddle that I directed to the radishes with the point of a stick. Which caught her interest—what if you dug a little trench here, and made a little holding pond there? And miracle, she went for more water, and then more again, the whole time singing: something about Mama Wata, whoever that was, a repetitious drone, which I took up as well: Mama, Mama Wata!

We had tiny lettuce almost ready to trim and eat, Mama Wata, we had onion shoots, Mama Wata, we had radishes almost ready to pull, and beet greens fully ready to go. I weeded and banked and babied every radish, explaining as she returned, bucket more-and-more carefully full: the girl understood irrigation. I sent her after the next thing, fertilizer, long explanation, Mama Wata, and still singing, she ventured out in wider and wider and less and less reluctant circles, collecting old elk and mule deer and moose droppings, plentiful, the more to work into Papa Té. And that was the job that won her over—she was a collector, loved the chance to seek.

"Food is shit," she said, dropping off the fourth bucketful, actually amazed, and charging out for more.

That got me past my nauseated irritation and back to liking her. Also back to work, digging, chopping, crumbling old, dry moose balls into the moist earth, the most loving details adding up to a kind of fury: Mama Wata, Papa Dirt.

"My mother would sing it," she said, though I hadn't asked.

What secrets had she imparted to Maria?

Later, back in our clearing, we found that Lucky had built us a picnic table, rough proportions, the four mighty legs simply lodgepole logs buried in the rocky ground, the top and benches ingeniously axe-split and axe-joined lodgepole pine. He called it Family Table. And then so did we. And that's where we ate every single subsequent night and every single noon, most mornings. I don't remember a drop of rain that summer, but there must have been some. The firepit was just the one the settlers had used, the hunters after, a ring of stones around a natural scoop in the bedrock and up against a huge boulder that threw heat back in your face.

And good, because some of the nights were chilly, even cold. Lucky barely seemed to notice, wore the same tough old shirt, the same old Wranglers, this beanpole philosopher, director of our evening talks, with questions like "Is a person above a deer?" He thought we humans were a particular kind of angel, fallen back to earth from a greater state. I had learned a small amount in Mr. Orr's English class about the Massachusetts hero Thoreau (no idea he was wider known), announced that I was no angel but Emerson's ruined god, by which I meant goddess, as Emerson had forgotten some of us, the ones who could make new beings. Francie, wrapped up in Maria's blanket, said she'd started to believe in a kind of purgatory, and that's where we were, enjoying our year and a day before heaven or hell, having dearly departed the land of mortals.

I make us sound unserious, but we were not, big questions among all the stars up there like city windows I'd seen once from a skyscraper: whole lives lived in there, whole hidden yearnings, nothing but what was known, sudden blinkings out.

The poison berries to make ink grew in thickets in the shade under a cliff above a bog, and I collected them and collected long strips of birchbark, determined to keep some kind of record of our days. I'd sharpened my owl feather all the way up to the first downy barbs, so Lucky found me a tougher hawk feather, keener point that lasted longer, but I could think of nothing interesting to write sitting there at Family Table, quill poised, purple-bright ink dripping. I'd been taxing my memory, writing down the numbered days and the things we'd done on each, all of it hopelessly tangled. Lucky was against all the recording—the days should be burned as they came.

DAY MAYBE THIRTY-FOUR: HAWK FEATHER SILENT

And that bit of birch bark started the night's fire, Lucky blowing it up into flames from banked coals. And on that Day Maybe Thirty-Four, after dinner in firelight, I got my materials out, asked Francie to tell me something so I could write it down, something not to be burned. "Something you've thought or done, for example."

"Tell your first day in Montana," Lucky said.

We all liked that story, had heard it more than once.

Francie didn't hesitate: "Well, a marshal put me on a bus and brought me to a place and we met an Indian dude there in his Indian van and he was very scary and didn't say one word."

"That was me," Lucky said happily.

"Lucky is not scary," I said.

"And not an Indian," he said, adopting my tone.

Francie and I laughed at that and then laughed more: Lucky's serious demeanor, like he hadn't made a joke.

Dutifully I wrote down Francie's words, each phrase requiring a dip of the thin berry ink, a slow process. Skritching, Lucky called it, after the sound. I changed some things, like making Francie's *very* into *vurry*, all deviations causing a riot of argument and laughter that lasted into the evening, with Lucky insisting the ink couldn't hold him and insisting even so that I read the whole thing over and over again, amazed I'd captured something of Francie with such blunt instruments, ink and hawk feather, that she'd become mine in some way.

Late, Lucky pulled out his knife, sharpened my quill for me.

"Now it's my turn," he said. He seemed about to speak, about to speak for fifteen minutes, half an hour, firelight dying in his face, his whole entire life on his face.

"When you were a boy," Francie prompted at long last.

"When I was a boy," Lucky said, and waited patiently as I wrote it. "When I was a boy, I had a friend named Aarto."

I wrote that much, but then, a miracle, my husband kept going, talking faster and faster. And with Francie's help I got it written down. We took turns, read it aloud over and over, and Lucky was amazed. Francie or me, it was his voice in those ink marks:

Aarto's last name was Johman and he was least of three brothers and had a vurry nice mother. His grandfather was my grandfather's friend, and his father, too. We would roam everywhere before he had to go to school. I wasn't allowed there because of some kind of test, and I wasn't allowed in the Indian school either. We made ships out of tin cans and built dams and played San Francisco, where my father lived and met my mother, and built fancy trains, one boxcar at a time out of old shingles and spools and things, and Grandfather helped and told us stories: he worked on the railroad and that's how he came to Montana and met Walks Far, who'd got sick and died with a lot of her people, who were Crow. He was blamed for the sickness and had to leave. Maria was just a girl and mourned them both.

There'd been an owl, we heard it in the night down below us some-where, an insistent hooting.

"Came to Montana from where?" Francie said.

"We will skritch more later," Lucky said, clamming up, tending the fire, walking off.

I remember that night as a scent, smoke first, then Montana sagebrush, that distant but forever threat of autumn in the air, and a passion caught in that scent, just a feeling that still wells up in me when I smell anything remotely like it, all of us purely alive and lit up by the fire like fresh devils in the dark.

Chapter Thirty-Five

The Lego competition was well run, vurry colorful, big work-tables set up in the hotel ballroom, enormous bins of every conceivable Lego shape in the middle of the room, *twenty-two builders twelve to eighteen years old from eleven northeastern states and the District of Columbia* racing back and forth from their four-by-eight plywood tables to refill the little official totes they'd been given, part of the fun and what passed for exercise in this world of brains.

Ricky went instantly to work and over the two days (minus required but terrifyingly brief sleep and food breaks) built a cityscape complete with sculpture garden and public transportation, also schools and museums, banks and government. Banks? Government? Surely that wasn't what they were looking for. But I wasn't allowed to counsel him or get closer than the rope line placed at fifteen feet, not that he'd have allowed me closer in any case.

So I watched other kids at work, a special interest in the girls, only three. I didn't notice a particular difference among the creations of male and female—Legos are mostly right angles, after all, and enforce a certain rigidity. Walter, a rigid person, had started out liking them, little blocks of character, to his thinking. But as Ricky had grown more and more epicene (Walter's way to say *queer*), all toys were to blame. At the rope barrier in front of a particular table, I watched a busy young woman—the only Black competitor—use all green pieces, absolutely nothing but green, a curious illusion of curved lines where there were none, nice.

Sunday afternoon the judges began to make the rounds, taking notes on clipboards, asking terse questions. That night over pizza at the so-called completion party, the participants sat in a semicircle for the prize announcements, friendly but separate, not a giggle or shout among them, serious Lego talk, phrases among the parents like "Which is yours?" and "Where is New Canaan?" and "Gifted-and-talented program," a blur of conversation I stayed out of.

The young woman with the all-green city won the Concept Award. She was a senior at a DC city school. A large Asian-American kid, sixteen, won the Practical Engineering Award—his city floated a yard off his table on Lego pylons. A slight white girl won the Aesthetics Award, a contiguous rainbow running through every structure. They did win crates of Legos, *Walter*, along with the scholarships, maybe smaller scholarships than Ricky had hoped, but. He won Grand Overall Champion. So along with the crate of Legos and the UCLA summer-program scholarship, he won a solar motor scooter, a gorgeously awkward blue thing I'd noticed parked in the lobby with other engineering miracles. A solar motor scooter! The judges' statement commended him for including banking, medical, and financial, on having a traffic circulation plan. Good I hadn't been able to advise him.

Polite applause. Sudden loud rock music, the kids and large numbers of siblings leaping to their feet only to stand awkwardly as three of them energetically danced, a lot of tension to dispel or perhaps hold on to.

On the train home, back yards and back alleys and warehouse districts speeding by in a blur, I tried to explain that the scooter would be delivered safely. After an anxious half hour of back-and-forth, alternately bumping and speeding on the sad Amtrak rails, I tried a new tack, said, "Your dad would be so proud of you."

And it worked—the motor scooter was forgotten. And then the most companionable ride, lots to see through New Haven, lights and clever drawbridges and a barge out on the bay. When the night was dark again, the train tracks carrying us through dense forest, Ricky said, "My dad is Lucky Turtle."

And I said, "Yes, that's right."

"And I am Mountain Turtle."

"Yes, honey, yes you are."

"And he's my father, but he died."

"Yes, sweetie, it's vurry sad."

"Call me Mountain Turtle."

"Mountain Turtle, yes. I love you, Mountain Turtle."

"And then you met Walter?"

"I knew Walter before your father was dead."

"And Walter was helpful, and so when Lucky Turtle died you went with him?"

"Yes, like that. You weren't even two when we moved in with him."

"From that school. I remember just a few things. There was a gate with a buzzer and we lived right in the school buildings."

"You remember that?"

"And that really nice lady with the cookies."

"Oh, gosh. Junie the Moonie. She was awful, always giving you treats!"

"And I remember getting my own bed—a big-boy bed—in Walter's house."

"Those were all big events, Mountain Turtle. And super-early memories! My own earliest is maybe the front seat of an old car my parents had."

"But I don't remember a wedding. You and Walter. Wouldn't I remember your wedding? If I remember big events?"

"We didn't have one, sweetie. We're not married and never will be."

"But why not, if we're a family? He always says we're a family. I mean, we are a family, right?"

"We are."

"So why not a wedding?"

"Because."

"Because you don't believe my father is dead."

"No, honey. Yes. No."

"No, you think he's alive. And I do, too. I feel that he is, and vurry strongly."

"You say that word like him, *vurry*."

"I say it like you, Mommy."

"Yes, you do. He's gone, Ricky. Mountain Turtle, I mean. Lucky is gone. It's sad. But for us he's alive always, okay?"

"Okay."

Walter had shown me the death certificate, signed by a prison warden out there in old Montana. Walter had gone to great lengths. Why? He thought if Lucky were dead, I might marry Himself. And Lucky was dead—Walter proved it to me—but I did not marry Walter because I didn't believe it, not in my heart. Smart Mountain Turtle.

Also, I didn't love Walter. I just needed him.

What to say to Ricky? He'd reached the age of truth. "Your father was a beautiful man," I said.

The train swayed and clacked, moving quickly through dark realms, Connecticut, Rhode Island.

"What does beautiful even mean," Ricky said.

"Well, fair to look at, but that becomes a metaphor to mean he was fair in all things."

"Fair just means beautiful, when it doesn't mean just."

"That is almost a poem," I said. "And you say you're an engineer."

"I just wish I could see him," Ricky said. "In the Legos today? As I was finishing? I thought he was there. He was there in my city, if only I could build the spot where he needed to stand."

"Yes, of course he was there."

"But the time limit came and I couldn't build the spot."

"You built a beautiful thing. And your father was there. And he was vurry proud of you."

"It was fair to look at."

"That's a line from your poem."

"Yes it is." Silence, the train tracks clacking. "A kid called me a bad name, Mom. At the thing."

"Oh, little creeps and cruds. And their parents, too. Which kid?"

"Oh, I don't know. It was no big deal."

I said, "It's a big deal in the scheme of things but doesn't have to be a big deal in your heart. I'll lodge a complaint. You remember that boy at that camp?"

"Biomechanics Camp? Yes, I remember him, he called me the n-word."

"And Walter said something."

"Yes, I know, and then I felt bad because the next day that kid was gone. He didn't come back. And Mom, the thing is, I liked him. I didn't want him in trouble."

I boiled a little, then boiled a lot, those parents, train in the dark, tried to think which kid, which entitled, overpraised, fear-fucking kid in that crowd? A face came to mind. But what if I was wrong?

I said, "Does your city have a name?"

"It does, but I can't say it."

"Oh, honey. I know just what you mean."

"It was fag. He called me a fag. I ignored him. Like Walter always tells me. And anyway, I'm not even sure what that word means. I mean, I know what it means. But I'm not sure what it means for me. Or I mean the nicer word."

"Well, you don't need to know. Not yet. If you're gay or not. You'll know when you know."

"I guess I know. I guess it's all right, though. I just want to know why he would say that, and like being gay is something bad. So just never mind."

"That's the point, though. He's the bad guy, not you. You, you're something really wonderful and maybe one pinch different, and that boy was afraid. I think I do mind. I think I do mind vurry much. I think his parents need to know."

"It's called Turtle City. That's the secret name."

I thought about that a few miles. The relative light of the Boston suburbs grew. The tracks were smooth, then rough, the train quiet, then rattling. "That's a great name for your city. It doesn't have to be a secret," I said.

"Well, not from you. Mom, I'm glad you're not mad."

"Of course I'm not mad. I'm glad you told me, honey. And I'm glad you know the right word is gay, a happy word for a super-nice thing. And you don't have to know or not know, that's not the point."

"Well, I know. And I'm glad you know. But let's not get him in trouble."

"Okay, if that's your wish. If you change your mind, just tell me. And you can tell me or ask me anything, anything at all. And if anyone else says any mean thing, you tell me that, too."

He said, "There are many things you haven't told me."

"That is true. Yes. And I'm going to. But let me tell you slowly."

"Like for instance. Where was my father from? You always said Montana."

"Well, that's true."

"That he was Crow."

"His heart was, yes. His aunt Maria was Crow. Really she was his adoptive mom."

"And his father was unknown."

"Not unknown, exactly. Just died quite young. It's not clear about him. He was called Thomas Sing. I don't know his turtle name. His father, Lucky's beloved Grandpa, had a girlfriend in San Francisco, and she might have been Thomas's mother."

"But Walter said Thomas Sing was Chinese, that Lucky's."

"Well, yes, that might be true. Taishanese, the part that was Robert's blood, Far Turtle's. That's one of the old Chinese tribes, you could say. Lucky Turtle's grandfather immigrated to the US nearly a century ago. He took the name Robert Sing, but back home in China he had been called Far Turtle. In Chinese, of course. Thomas Sing was his son, and not impossible that Thomas was the son of Walks Far. But much more likely a girlfriend in San Francisco who also died or just went missing. Many people died at that time, all sorts of diseases. Many went missing, too. That's the part we don't know."

"And so, Far Turtle raised Thomas Sing mostly in San Francisco, and when Thomas was just a teenager he met my grandmother, whoever she was, but her parents didn't like he was Chinese and split them up. And so Thomas went to war."

"You're forgetting about his cameras."

"Right—he took pictures in the war. And then he died."

"Yes, he died in Vietnam."

"And he died never knowing she was pregnant! So Lucky's mom, my grandmother, ran away and came back to Montana with Far Turtle? To Maria's place?"

"To Turtle Butte Ranch, quite close, which wise Far Turtle had purchased during the Depression with railroad and gambling savings. They made a home there. Your grandmother gave birth to your father there. But then Lucky got very close to Maria growing up. She raised him in many ways after Far Turtle died. In many ways he was abandoned by his birth mom after Far Turtle was gone. He called Maria his aunt and his Hawk mother."

"Hawk mother."

"Like, his soul mother."

"Walter said this was all a fantasy of yours. You want Lucky to be exotic, but he's really just a kind of bum. He said not to bring it up with you."

"Walter is full of it. I will have a word with Walter. And we won't let him triangulate." *Triangulate*—that was another of Walter's words.

"Are you going to clam up?"

Yes, I was going to clam up. I said, "Who you are is my son. And Lucky's. And you want to know what you are? What you are is beautiful. A little of this, and a little of that, and a *lot* of me."

"I'm Mountain Turtle."

"Yes, that's you."

"And guess what?"

"What?"

"I'm the Northeastern Region Legos Grand Champ."

"Ha-ha, you certainly are."

"And my father would be vurry proud."

We laughed as the train pitched, yawed, the lights of our car blinking off, blinking back on, the squealing of brakes and whistle of the train, then everything smooth again, like we'd crossed from that century into this.

"The scooter will come all right, though," Ricky said after a while.

"Yes, the scooter will come in two weeks, just like they said."

"I'm going to tell Lucky Turtle about it in my dreams tonight."

"I think Lucky Turtle will hear you."

"And the scooter will come?"

I tugged him in close. The train rumbled and coursed through the businesslike, world-beaten stretch through Providence. We had forty-five minutes, no more. Walter would be waiting at the gate. He would be proud. He would be curious about our days, about the competition, he would promise to help assemble the scooter and to help Ricky learn to ride it. He was a pretty good dad, even though he wasn't a dad at all, not in his own mind, not in Ricky's.

The scooter never came.

Walter denied canceling it, but.

Chapter Thirty-Six

I tried to interest Lucky in another story-making night, but he wouldn't tell us any more—nothing to write down, anyway. And Francie didn't see the point of writing down her story, a long discussion. She won by asking me to tell my story and she'd skritch it on birchbark, but all I could get myself to say was stuff they already knew: my time since I'd arrived at camp. And then she wouldn't write it but tried to draw it, and soon we were trying to make black ink from charcoal and canned lard and tea, hopeless—funny cartoons, though, that disappeared within hours but came back if you burned the bark.

"Things don't want to last," Lucky said.

"And yet," Francie said.

And we sang, taking turns as the jukebox. Lucky knew few songs, mostly hymns, and took to making up more. We'd catch some corner of his tuneless tunes and repetitious lyrics ("Three people in the mountain / Three people in the wood / Three people in the mountain / Three people and two hor-ses"), sing them for what seemed hours, alternately hilarious and serious, droning at times, trying for grand harmony at others, faces close, or shouting them out, running to far corners of the meadow, making it a dance, "Three people in the mountain / Three people in the wood / Three people and two hor-ses." The horses, now that we mentioned them, seemed annoyed to be kept awake.

Around then, the weather changed for a dog days week or two, the far mountains growing hazy with rare humidity. Lightning flashed at the lost edges of the universe, an indistinct and continuous rumble of distant thunder, the wind shifting up from the south and growing lazy, and hot, hot. We swam in a tarn Lucky had found, ice floe still floating—you could stand together on one end and sink it like a raft, or jump at opposite ends, get it moving, one edge of the pond to the other till your feet were frozen, lips blue, then hurry to the hot springs, overheat, hurry down to the brook, cool off, back up to the tarn and play iceberg, high summer.

One of those hot nights after we'd eaten (Francie's rice and peas, which meant rice and beans, variations of which were our fad for weeks, flavored with things Lucky found per his grandfather's lessons—mushrooms, stiff leaves, roots, flowers, bits of a certain stone, charred wood), I reached under Family Table, found the tattered tome I'd stashed, drew it out into the firelight dramatically. "*Hawaii,*" I announced: my big surprise. Not that they hadn't seen it, just that I'd held it so close.

"Oh, Maman," Franciella said, excited.

Lucky wanted to touch the book. It had come from Maria. He paced with it, traced the map-like image on the cover with his finger, riffled the pages, sniffed them skeptically, said, "A lot of words and bear grease, also flowers, all those petals she kept."

"Are you being funny?" Francie said.

"I'm going to read to you," I said.

"No, instead let's sing," Lucky said.

Before he could think of a song, though, or suffer further disastrous associations with Maria's attempts at schooling after his multiple expulsions or Camp Challenge church lessons, I started in, reading out loud, dramatic voice, deep as I could make it:

Millions upon millions of years ago, when the continents were already formed and the principle features of the earth had been decided, there existed, then as now, one aspect of the world that dwarfed all others.

"The oceans!" Lucky cried.

Exactly right, Grasshopper. The vurry next line, in fact. I was past being surprised by my husband. He finally sat, listened closely, settled down, head on his fists on the table across from me, Francie at my side, snuggling close. I read to them an hour, so it felt, thirty introductory pages, some of them pretty dense, not much story as yet. But my audience was rapt and immediately hooked.

And so *Hawaii* became our nightly habit, a long half hour or so of reading under the stars and in firelight, another half hour of reliving, rereading, discussing, pulling apart. I did not think the book was perfect, and so repaired certain sentences as I read, skipped long asides. Lucky shouted out comically during fights to the death, cheered on escapes, returned all insults, grew excited by nearly every development, sometimes stood and howled, furious. He could not separate himself from the story. He became extremely stressed by action scenes, inconsolably depressed by all the cultural conflict, righteous over the imposition of authority, tearful at unfairness, silly with love scenes.

Michener was strong medicine. We'd get in bed and wait for Francie to snore, and then I'd put my necklace on my naked neck, my pink socks on my naked feet and we'd make love long and vurry slowly, Lucky forward. I worried Francie would hear us in the night, that it would make her lonely, or that she'd mock us, I don't know, but the snoring never abated, fireworks, dams breaking, herds stampeding, and all that.

It was hard to remember silence.

Chapter Thirty-Seven

Franciella grew stronger yet, walked taller, started to glow from the vurry soul and outward, those eyes of hers flashing less anger and more kindness, her skin growing dark from sunshine, especially dark when laid by mine, which was perpetually burned bright pink, the million freckles running together. She whistled, she waved from across the yard, she laughed with herself. She had ideas, crackled with ambition. And she began for the first time to look her age, which was young, seventeen like me. She could roll a log and dig a pit and move a rock, all right.

Not half kidding, I accused Lucky of ogling her.

"You look at her, too," he said.

"Okay, I mean gawk," I said.

"I don't know that one."

I demonstrated, looked him up and down, lingering on his zipper.

"She is interesting to see," he said.

Beauty unleashed, I thought, and in that she was much like Lucky—my husband!—who also stood taller, gazed more directly, held forth more eloquently than he had at Camp Challenge, his skin the same as always, the outdoor man, brown as bark. I found him almost painfully beautiful. But Franciella barely tolerated him, made fun of his oddball pronouncements, bent locutions.

She was, however, fascinated by his animal traps, set to work improving them, set to work whenever he was gone, chopping and carving and fitting, and within a couple of weeks at most had built four traps in ascending sizes, beautiful pine things like furniture, using nothing but various branches she'd found on the ground, also Lucky's big knife, an ancient screwdriver for a chisel, a little iron skillet as a hammer, a couple dozen sixpenny nails from a can in the larder. She showed Lucky her improvements. He simply nodded in admiration, offered improvements of his own, showed her where the real hammer was. She was defensive, even pissed at the advice, but Lucky didn't understand that either and persisted, which eventually made her laugh, and together they got the job done, went off in the forest to set traps, a chore she'd avoided till then.

I'd a baby in my belly, and—having not puked in a week—this was pure joy. I sat at the table and read *Hawaii*, staying ahead of my audience. When I finished the book, great sigh of satisfaction, I started right in again. I liked the feeling of being alone around the lodge, made food that was only for me, drowned it in vinegar, sang songs from *Kiss of the Spider Woman*, a wildly inappropriate musical my dad had taken me to for my thirteenth birthday, thinking it was like *Beauty and the Beast*, hot tickets from a cabinetry client, memorable trip to New York.

The traps worked. Soon, we had more regular small meat, as Lucky called it—a lot of marmots, which were a kind of ground squirrel, good to eat if Lucky was the chef rather than I, and certainly not Francie. And then, in higher country, spruce grouse, which Lucky cooked, too, fat birds that tasted like Jesus ascending, as Franciella put it, first in Creole, then French, then to our laughter in English. That was Day Fifty-Five or Sixty or maybe Sixty-Five (who could count so high): Spruce Grouse. And Lucky showed Franciella how to track, a little more each day, making me jealous. I loved his stories of her incompetence, forgive me, but I did. I made ink and collected birchbark. I made lists. Things Lucky said. French words from Francie. Birds that visited. Foods I would love to have. Like that, our disappearing ink.

The wapiti weren't home, as Lucky put it, the elk, but there was deer sign everywhere, and so deer were what he most wanted to kill, the most nutrition for the work, not that he put it that way. I didn't think I'd ever had more pure fun than tracking, better even than sports in high school.

I'd played field hockey before my ankle injury, and wasn't too bad at it, and a good game gave you a rush. Tracking was like that, when you followed a coyote, say, and the sign kept getting fresher, and then there she was, scrawny thing staring back at you across a brook.

"Hey, Coyote," Lucky would say, not so much as twitching his spear in the animal's direction. So I got to look a long time, these staring creatures still trying to fatten back up after the long winter, each animal part of a system, integral, neither good nor evil. I, of course, spouted on in that vein over a dinner that included a real salad of garden greens, our own eggs, and a fatly dripping grouse caught in the gravity traps, till Lucky got to what I was trying to say: "Just is."

Which was his motto, when you thought about it: Just is.

And Francie went about building herself a room in the lodge, at first full of the old complaints, then excited, then obsessed. Lucky helped her cut some of the thinner lodgepole pines to be found down in the valley just off our road, whacking with the bowie knife Clay had brought, truly gifted with that thing, the wood soft enough that he could bring a tree down in three strokes, whack it into a pole in three more. They dragged the poles up nine or eleven at a time behind View, who seemed truly to enjoy the work.

One afternoon they were taking a long time, and I started to picture terrible injuries, or maybe that poacher and his gun. I climbed on Chickadee, using the corral fence for a boost, my first mount ever on my own, my first ride ever solo, and she was vurry sweet, only hurried as we got close, a canter that scared me and that I couldn't talk her out of, even when she ducked off the road and into the forest. Shortly we came to the lodgepole pinewoods, all those perfectly straight and tall and narrow trees. And there was View, standing stolid, already tied into a fresh travois. I climbed off Chickadee and untied View, wanted the horses along, just in case of something bad. I walked them into the wood past fresh stumps following sign, finally over a rise and mound of great rocks. And there were Lucky and Franciella, out of the range of their log stand, face-to-face on their feet and super close, holding each other by the elbows.

My heart pounded.

"What are you doing?" I cried.

"Kissing," Lucky said, the big dope: he'd fallen from grace and didn't even know.

Francie shoved him away, stood away, nowhere to hide.

"I've never," she cried, deep flush. And burst into tears.

The nervous horses watched. They knew so much about emotion, felt it cross the understory—it reached me, it reached them, we patted the dirt with our hooves.

Lucky merely crossed his arms, guiltier than he let on—you did what you did, but he well knew that there were things you didn't. And there we were: two horses, three people, wind in the treetops, felled lodgepoles behind us.

"You *idiots*," I shouted, and stormed away past the animals. View gave me the widest of his wide-eyed looks.

I marched into the woods, no clue where I was, rushed back, tried to mount Chickadee, who did have a clue, but I could not mount—no fence rail to help, one try, two, my kick simply too slight. I tried again, but weakly, slithered to the ground, crying in a heap, felt Lucky's hand upon my back, didn't throw it off.

That night instead of *Hawaii*, we had a long talk. Francie had been curious, that's all, and Lucky didn't see the problem.

"My grandfather," Francie started, but couldn't finish: just that a kiss had even been possible after that monster, that suddenly it was possible again, and she'd wanted her first, whom else to ask in a world with one man? My anger fled, this new woman in our midst, this world like a galloping horse I didn't know how to stop. In the end we agreed that nothing so terrible had happened, agreed that Lucky and I needed to take Francie's loneliness into account, agreed Francie wasn't to blame. All that because Francie was distraught, far more upset than I.

Lucky, later, I took by the throat, surprising him. "If you ever," I said.

"I understand," he said.

"I don't think you do."

"She has a nice mouth."

The truth, at least, was the truth.

I tightened my grip, tightened some more, tightened till his eyes bugged out, then let go.

Chapter Thirty-Eight

Morning at last and Lucky and I mounted the horses and left Francie to her project, which was coming along rapidly, expertly, a door already cut into the back wall of our lodge, a platform of poles in place. She was our sister and not just some roommate. At last Lucky was contrite. It had never occurred to him that what we had wasn't only given to us but *entrusted*, as I kept saying, something to *maintain* like the vurry coals of our life-giving fire, *precious*: he'd thrown a bucket of water on them, that's what I told him, *pissed* on them, I'd said into his tears. And with that, my rage had abated, sleep overcome me.

I felt suddenly queasy, nothing worse—progress in my increasingly acknowledged pregnancy—then just as suddenly fine again, jazzed, in fact, and felt good on Chickadee, the little horse who loved me, and then exhausted again. I all but slept a mile or so, woke to worry: How did women give birth to baby after baby, and how would I get this baby from the inside to the outside through that tiny gate? Lucky let Chickadee take the lead and so I found myself in the beauty of the earth and we rocked up the ridge into a sharp, dry wind like a hot river flowing up over the mountain.

"You'll never do that again?" I said.

"No, never," Lucky said.

Only the second girl he'd ever kissed, give him credit.

No sign of humans, but Lucky pointed out a single sharp and distinctive deer print in dust. And then a series of depressions in a carpet of moss, then bitten twigs and blades of grass, then another print, a hank of tail hair on a prickly pear thorn, finally droppings, a neat pile of oval balls. We rode slowly, Lucky keeping View in check with clacks of his tongue,

I imitating Lucky, the deer sign growing fresher—an hour, then two and three. I'd become a good rider, vurry relaxed, no sores. We emerged into a bigger valley, several brooks coalescing, beauty almost shocking. Lucky stayed focused on the ground.

We climbed an escarpment and up into a wood.

"Here," he said gently.

He slid off View, lifted me down from Chickadee. We long-tied the horses to separate trees in good forage, then walked, following extremely subtle deer sign. He pointed, tsked: our animal had taken a plunge just there into a bramble of berries. We plunged, too, battled through the prickers, then into the shade of aspens that did truly quake, the bright vertical light of their trunks like beacons. And step-by-step in silence to a small clearing.

"Doe," Lucky breathed.

We'd been so quiet and stayed so calm and unhurried that the pretty thing didn't bolt but only turned her ears back. She sniffed the breeze audibly. We breathed with the animal, took short steps in no particular direction, put our heads down, pretending to graze, I realized, watchful but engrossed in our forage. She put her ears down gradually, then her head, grazed with us, Lucky and I moving separately and a bare few steps at a time, crabwise, backward, diagonally, step, graze, wait, step, ever closer to the food (the food, Lucky called her!), just gentle creatures taking sustenance, nothing this wilderness deer had ever seen before, no perceivable threat.

Lucky flexed from his toes to his arm, then suddenly unspooled, flung Bunny Slayer, all one left-handed motion, a good shot, too, or at any rate super close to the deer, mere microns over the top of her back, even ruffling her hollow body hairs. She bolted, of course, complete silence and complete motion all at once, as the sharpened stick clattered harmlessly on the rocks.

Lucky was unperturbed: "Most you miss," he said. And, "She only thinks a branch fell. She thinks we're running away, too. She won't go far."

And here came the irritation: "Oh, Lucky. Do deer think their way through every incident with man and stick?"

"They see is how they think," said Lucky.

They see is how they think. Just is. She has a beautiful mouth.

You get my drift: maddening.

Lucky retrieved Bunny Slayer, quickly resharpened the point with his trusty knife, chipped at the shaft to correct the flight. We retrieved the horses and followed that generous deer for another hour, never in the slightest hurry, merely a day's work in progress, my irritation giving way to the job at hand, mountain and forest all around us in wind, sudden distant views, exaltation.

My stupid husband was forgiven. I leaned hard across the horses to give him a kiss. A long kiss, to go with the day. He approached kissing the way he approached other projects, something you finished. So after a while, the horses still ambling, he pulled me easily out of my saddle and onto View in front of him, reached around to put his hand in my pants a while, sweet ripples even as the horses climbed airy talus slopes. I reached back, his kisses at my neck. All the while we traced the edges of a bog, moving slowly as the high clouds drifting above, Lucky keeping track of deer sign, keeping track of Chickadee, who kept trying to pass, I panting.

"It's all one thing," Lucky said.

Another mile or two and I was ready to head back to our clearing, the lodge. But I didn't say it, instead grew irritable once again. We don't always give thanks for the gifts we're given, and probably all but never in the moment. I'll say it now, to all the powers and the six directions: Thank you. Various troubles notwithstanding.

"Here," Lucky said, that voice like a breath. "Smell."

Sure enough, there was something, a scent maybe, not us, something a little like that of the elk-hide door, a little like pee, so faint I didn't believe in it.

"They smell is how they think," I said.

Lucky squeezed me happily, abruptly lifted me off View and put me on my feet on the ground in Chickadee's face, climbed down beside me, all in a motion. I fastened my Wranglers as he tied the horses, he fastened his, and we crept forward along a ledge and into a tiny, sunny meadow. And there, once again, was the food. Lucky signaled and so I grazed my way into the sun. The little deer was alert, eyed me as I moved away from her, stepped incrementally herself—away from me, downwind and toward Lucky just as he'd planned—her ears twitching and turning, tuning in far stations.

I sidled and grazed and saw that in effect I was cutting off her escape. And now pity took over, and horror. Tears came that suddenly, and if I hadn't been hungry, hadn't needed what she so freely offered, well—in the face of my hunger, all precepts fled.

The little doe made another couple of steps away from me, twitched to discourage an insect, then simply accepted me and grazed, more and more intent on the pretty grasses. And then I myself was simply grazing, preoccupied with my grazing, examining individual blades of grass, a mood like daydreaming, a good, long, unmarked time.

Because of his skill, I didn't notice Lucky's appearance over the ridge. But I felt the little deer tense, tensed myself, some feral corner in me, and then, with no further warning, the thud of impact. The animal collapsed to her front knees, then to one side, the spear holding her half upright as—beautiful creature built from mountains and valleys and brooks and wildflower meadows and sky—she became wind.

Chapter Thirty-Nine

Late in the afternoon, the deer bled and dressed and the meat Lucky wanted cleverly packed up in her hide, we rode home—the first I'd called it home—first to our hot spring, where we didn't make love, worth mentioning since it was out of the ordinary. When we climbed back down, we found the horses excited, halters twisted. Lucky dropped to his knees as if shot, crawled up into the grasses.

"Here," he said.

And in the mud of the brook at the far reach of hoofprints there was something even I could read, a print from the heel of a boot, then another, plus pointed toe.

"That poacher," Lucky said. He traced the tracks, clues I couldn't see at all. "Afraid of us," he said. "See how he hurried through."

Chickadee had blood dripping down both flanks from the meat package and did look fearsome.

Lucky tracked the interloper down the trail, then back up. The man had skirted the horses, leaving our path and taking to the woods, still headed toward our clearing.

"Oh, Lucky," I said.

"He would have stayed to visit, if he wasn't such a man." Such a man—that meant a poacher. "Yes, and with a child."

"A child?"

"Yes, see here—this small foot. His son, who he's pulling along."

"His son," I said, a little doubtful.

"Who he's pulling along—see how he's tripping here."

The child had peed, is how he knew it was a boy.

We remounted, the two of us on View, Chickadee carrying the meat, rode at the same pace as ever, straight up along the brook, man sign all the way, and little-boy sign, too, so obvious now: having encountered our horses, the poacher had been alarmed, more so with his child along, had hurried, the kid small enough to carry at times, half running, that's what the sign said, jogging straight to our clearing, where he'd seen the lodge or heard Francie at work, put the boy down, watched and listened a while, then gathered the boy and scrambled up the slope to hide among the boulders that watched over us, over Francie all alone there.

At the clearing, we saw Francie's pile of poles much diminished, saw that her new room had grown some, an oddly elegant appendage on the back of the lodge. She didn't answer our shouts.

Lucky was calm as always, put me on the ground beside him, that smooth strength. He said, "Walk Chickadee down and go after Francie. She won't be far. See? Her big feet go that way." I hadn't seen—but down the old jeep trail there was in fact the faintest kickings of gravel. Lucky didn't waste a second but urged View up to the rocks and out of sight. Heart pounding, I led Chickadee down the road, seeking sign: here a stone turned, the ground slightly darker beneath; there a wand of timothy grass Francie had chewed; further along disturbed moss on a rock where she must have rested; finally the woman herself among large ponderosa pines, low branches, pulling down Day-Glo staghorn lichens to chink between the logs of her addition, the T-shirt in her arms already stuffed like the body of a scarecrow.

"Francie!" I called.

She startled to see me, but mildly—it wasn't like she was kissing Lucky.

"Did you see anyone?"

"What? No, no one," she called.

Chickadee snorted to see her approach, happy horse.

Francie showed me the lichens. She said, "Lucky says these will swell with rain."

I said, "We tracked the poacher!"

She said, "Looks to me as if you killed the poacher."

That bundle, leaking blood on Chickadee's back.

We laughed pretty hard and embraced in sudden affection, the pillow of lichen coming between us, more laughter, or relief, same.

Home, we led Chickadee to the Family Fire, untied the heavy meat bundle, pushed it off onto the table. Francie went to work with her load of lichen, stuffing the cracks between the newest poles of her bedroom. I put Chickadee in the corral.

Just as the renewed thought of bears arose, a little mind-mixed with the poacher's presence, I heard Lucky charging up the road on View. You have to be a hell of a rider to gallop like that in loose gravel—hell of a horse, too. Lucky was one, View was the other. They pulled up hard in dust at the corral gate.

"Saw him drive off," Lucky called, more excited than he wanted to let on. "That selfsame blue truck. Just a man finding animals like us. Showing his son the way to do it, so."

"So why are you so excited?"

He didn't answer, took some thoughtful breaths, dismounted, put View in the corral. "Chickadee needs scrubbing," he said.

He was excited because life was exciting, that's why he was excited. He didn't ask about Francie. He knew Francie was fine. He just shouted to her to watch the meat. She waved, a handful of bright lichen for emphasis. Without a further word, Lucky and I put View in the corral and together we led Chickadee down to the brook, stripped to our skin, that cold water, that hot day, exciting in its own way, washed the beautiful horse at length, Lucky having persuaded her in some expert way to lie down in the pool. She'd be dry in the sun and wind by dark, Lucky explained, and wouldn't catch a chill in the night. We dressed without drying, which was the Lucky way. I led Chickadee back up while my husband, barefoot, bare-chested, pulled out that busy knife of his and cut whip sticks, as he called them, straight switches of some streamside viburnum.

Shortly we were back in our clearing. At Family Table, Lucky dumped his bundle of sticks, pulled out that knife, sparked tinder into flames, no more trouble than striking a match and, though the day was still warm, built up a conflagration (as Clay might have called it). He didn't explain things, just gave me chores: "Collect some sagebrush wands."

"Wands," I said.

"Like so," he said, vague demonstration of the proper length.

I knew their use would soon be revealed. "How many?"

"Let the plant say."

Let the plant say. "And what about that man?"

"Nothing about him."

"And on to the next thing? Just like that?"

"Just like this." And he continued his work.

I felt my irritation bubble. But the poacher had a little son, how scary could he be, guy with a kid? Scary enough! Add bears. And my rumbling stomach. Were we going to eat our venison or not? Well, sagebrush was everywhere—just a matter of attending to the fragrant edges of our clearing, and once again in the doing my moodiness fled.

Lucky, meanwhile, sliced and carved and barked his sticks, no tool but his knife, razor and axe and hammer all in one. I cycled back to drop off sage in piles, inspected his work, still a mystery, slits and slots and notches, sharpened ends, long strips of bark to make twine, total focus as he fitted and lashed the sticks into a tall, rectangular grid. When he was done, he lifted it whole, that's how light. He leaned it against the sunny side of the boulder close behind the fire ring, safely away from the flames but in their smoke and heat and in the sun. He opened the meat pack, spread the venison strips he'd cut in the field onto the stones of the firepit, rinsed them in brook water, salted them heavily, flipped them like pages of a long book, salted them front and back, one by one married them to my sage wands by pressing the dry leaves and stems against the sticky meat—the exact number, as it happened, the plant having told me (ha-ha), and one by one hung them on his rack till it was full, size perfect.

Any trace of blood from the meat was consumed in the fire—that's why he'd salted it on the stones of the fire ring. Meanwhile, the meat on the rack no longer glistened, drying quickly in the near-desert wind. The deer's hide had gone stiff and gross, was to be washed in the brook and tanned in some way he knew and useful for vurry soft gloves he said he knew how to make—that was our conversation: a day's living in the wild, pretty absorbing.

Lucky carved another spit and speared the roasts he'd cut, suspended them over hottest coals to sear them, then lowered the meat, threw soaked sage leaves and cedar bark and salt over it, then hot ash, and more hot ash, then live coals, built the fire up a little around it all, left the meat to cook, the original slow roaster.

Our kettle was the bottom of an old boiler, like a witch's cauldron, too heavy to lift. It lived next to the fire. To use it you built the fire out around it. And Lucky did that. He poured the blood-pinkened brook water in and added the bones and a mound of fat and meat scraps and fistfuls of onion grass and sage.

"Clay's Stew," he said.

Gradually we added two huge cans of surplus beans from the larder, two huge cans of tomatoes, several handfuls of rice from the hundred-pound surplus sack, a handful of salt, all kinds of ground pepper, plus the wilder things Lucky knew, forays long and short, roots and buds and fungi and the usual burnt stick—I never learned what kind. Later, like sooner, was an abstraction. Poacher and bears were abstractions. The child in my belly and the day of its birth, abstractions.

Lucky, however, was quite real.

He leaned back, elbows behind him on the table, scar prominent on his chest, a human like none I'd ever known, not in body, not in spirit, not in mind.

Francie had finished her chinking, moseyed over.

"Better wash that deerskin," she said.

And so the two of us went down to the brook, washed the hide together in our exhaustion, washed it and scraped it and rubbed it and rinsed it, not much talk, washed that pretty hide till it was ready to be hung high over the fire late that night—that's how Lucky said it was done: smoke it hard so the bear wouldn't know, the bear and the vulture, too.

We rinsed the hide and rinsed it again, heaved it up on the rocks.

"To live is a lot of work," Francie said.

"There's your bumper sticker."

We washed ourselves in the next pool up. Naked didn't mean much anymore. Bears, the poacher, the idea of winter, none of it meant much. We dressed, and clothes didn't mean much either. Francie and I carried that damp, clean hide back up to Lucky, found him seated at Family Table, calmly at work on another drying rack. I sat close beside him. Francie sat across. He just kept working. Our happiness was complete. The sun would soon set and we'd have a feast of roast venison in sage and cedar, kettle of venison stew to eat for a week. We'd hang the deer hide high above the fire in a makeshift ceremony, and later we'd have our time with *Hawaii*, finally to bed in the lodge, Francie among the bones of her new room.

Francie leaned and touched my nose with a finger. She touched Lucky's nose, too. And oddly, in that moment, I felt the first movement in my womb, just a flutter, just a mouse running in the rafters.

Chapter Forty

At Family Table the next day (a day unnumbered and unnamed), Lucky peeled long strips of bark from sticks he'd soaked, the sun strong, too, the wind stronger, object clear: show ourselves and Clay that we could survive winter right here at home. The venison dried behind us—couldn't be left in case of bears, coyotes, ravens, and gray jays, especially gray jays—and for the next several days Lucky would be bringing the whole rack into the lodge for sleepovers till the jerky was ready to wrap in cedar bark and pack away in the rafters. I'd been on guard duty but, tired of being alone, had complained, and so Lucky had upon the instant come up with another project: cordage, he called it. Francie mocked the simple braiding he'd shown us and demonstrated her method, an ingenious eight-strand weave she'd learned from a craft book alone in her room as a young teen. My job was only to hold the loose end tight against her pulling—languorous duty, all of us silent for so long.

"Franciella, tell us the story of you," Lucky said suddenly, second day of our employment.

"She's not a radio," I said.

Lucky liked that. He said, "It's all a radio if you just tune in."

Francie braided as if she hadn't heard. She was keen on the rope, which was over twenty feet long by then, three Francie wingspans. Her fingers were long, her nails carefully filed on a stone, her cloud of hair carefully split by a straight part and pulled to one side. Back at Camp Challenge, they wouldn't recognize her.

And it was fifteen minutes, a foot of rope, before she said: "I started out in Haiti. But when I was five or maybe six my *maman* died, my mommy. With the hundreds. There was a hurricane, not so bad, but then the rain came, days of it, and everything flooded. I was so little. She was trying to come home, but the brook had become a river. My grandmother and I found her washed up against the stones at the bottom of the hill, all broken. And so I came to live with my father, that's all. I hadn't ever met him. A nice Jewish man from Short Hills. He'd been to Haiti as a relief worker. One of the many, many Anse-à-Veau earthquakes. I am the result of an aftershock. So said my *maman*."

Francie thought quite a while, another few inches of rope, another few sticks on the fire. Then, slowly, no detriment to her task, long pauses as new strips of bark were worked into the weave, no lumps: "There's an earthquake and a hurricane and terrible floods in the same week. Your mother goes missing, turns up dead, and you're an orphan of the village. Not much changes, in some ways. Everyone still knows you. No one feels very sorry for you. But I had a father in the US. And the sweet neighbor lady wrote a letter in English and soon a letter came back, and my father came to take me home. Well, to his home, New Jersey. It was paradise at first. So busy and orderly with beautiful gardens and huge houses and one town richer than the next. Also places to eat. McDonald's, wow! And American school, no uniforms, no order, no nuns. I missed everything, though. I missed my *maman*. I didn't thrive, really. Suddenly I was not just a girl but a Black girl, and people let me know. I'd never heard some of those names they called me. My father worked constantly. My Jewish grandfather was a terrible babysitter. I was alone so much. I didn't fit in. My teachers were nice, though. I was always closest to the teachers. Then junior high, I just kind of fell apart. My grandfather convinced my father I needed, like, a warm vacation. I was such a sad girl. My father was clueless, too, or supposedly clueless. He thought a trip to California would straighten me out. So I flew with this grandfather I barely knew. I'm thirteen. And we stayed with his friend, a foreign kind of guy with sharp eyebrows. But first night, the friend was demanding high payment for something. Like, a lot of money, I forget how much. And shouting and threatening. And I was in this little room all frightened. And my American grandfather—this man I barely knew—he told me it was something about rent, but there was something *dyabolik* going on, you know. A kind of exchange going on. But just a day later—we didn't even get to Disneyland, which I'd been promised—this man took me driving to see the Pacific Ocean. My grandfather had to go somewhere. I was real scared. But the man was very nice to me. Nicer than my grandfather. Really nice. We got ice cream. We ate more McDonald's, which is all I wanted. I was okay, I was even thrilled. I'd never seen anyone surfing, or anyone lying about on any beaches, or any beaches at all, really—I was an inland girl back home, a country girl, the beach for tourists and princesses. In California we swam. We watched the surfers. From a kind of bluff over the ocean at a kind of place a normal American family might go camping. There were palm trees down on the beach and a giant kind of pine trees on the bluff. And maybe a picnic table. And I don't remember the rest. Only the sky, because I disappeared up into the pine trees when this man started doing what he was going to do. The man was old like my grandfather. And here's the big problem—maybe it *was* my grandfather? That's what all these men said in court, that the friend with the sharp eyebrows was murdered in some way. And that things had gone on with my grandfather—were they saying he did the killing? They made me try to remember in court, but I could not. Anyway, my grandfather was the one in trouble. But somehow he figured out how to blame me. And even in family matters Black people never win, in case you didn't know. He got time served. I got Camp Challenge and ten years correctional after I turn eighteen, would have left for that pretty soon. Correctional, as in prison."

She'd talked for near eighteen inches, the cording supple and wet on the ground at my feet. "And that's why I'm here," Franciella said.

"That's one rough story of you," Lucky said.

"I wish I remembered Haiti better," Francie said. "My *maman* was really gentle. I still know some of her songs."

She kept braiding, then tried to sing, but her tears began to fall, and they got worked into the cordage along with mine, along with Lucky's, who cried if we did. Francie made a rueful joke about it, about wetting the cordage, but Lucky said tears made it stronger.

Only slowly, three feet of new cordage or more, did the swaying aspens and the perfect rack of jerky and the sage on the wind and the distant calling of ravens and the gray jays hopping expectantly come back into my heart, and this shred and that strand of happiness, each of us adding a little without words till that was a braid strong as any: we were alive, and things that had happened long before were not.

"Your turn," Francie said to Lucky after a long time. "Story of you."

"Nup," Lucky said.

Chapter Forty-One

Ricky's interest in his father's story continued. I wished I had those birchbark broadsheets, our later writings, too, because the details escaped me. Was my answer to all of Mountain Turtle's questions, which came in waves as his curiosity grew. When my dad passed away, Ricky's grandpa, the boy's questions shifted to that generation. My dad had loved him a lot, I assured him. My mother remarried, moved far away. She had loved Ricky only reluctantly, I didn't tell him: illegitimate. We talked a lot about where my parents were from, about how they'd met. Cabinetmaker, bookkeeper at the Watertown lumberyard, their parents all of them solid German stock who'd perhaps expected more success—anyway, my parents weren't much of *my* life either.

As for Lucky's heritage, which is to say Ricky's, I want to say I didn't lie to the boy, that in my trauma I simply reverted to the story I'd told myself at the outset, a good story, and maybe truest in the end, that Lucky didn't know his folks but only his grandfather, Far Turtle, and his aunt Maria, that Lucky had worked at a correctional camp, that I had attended that camp. So Ricky got to know the whole truth as I had: gradually.

He was still asking questions in high school, but rarely, almost formally, more interested in mechanical systems than his heritage, at least for the time being.

Based on an MIT summer course and a paper he'd written subsequently, Ricky was invited to apply and then accepted to MIT Engineering, an accelerated bachelor of science program that let him take courses there during his junior year in high school, not too difficult to do from Watertown, take early graduation from his proud public school, then move on. Wonderful, but it meant all our talk of college visits, the fun of all that travel, was moot.

"So instead," Ricky said one day, not even seventeen, "I want to see Montana. I want to see Turtle Butte. Camp Challenge."

Heat pounded in my neck, and it wasn't just the coffee. I said, "You'll have to do something wrong for that, I'm afraid."

"No, I've looked it up. It closed in 2009. There was a land dispute and a law case and it's still under review."

I tried to counter his growing intensity. "Oh, sweetie. You've seen it. You've been drawing it for years. It's in your heart already."

"I want to see the Yellowstone River, where you and my father sat."

"I have told you too much."

"Please, let's go. For my birthday."

"That's a big present."

"For your birthday, too, then."

"Walter won't allow it."

"Walter will," he said.

"Maybe if we don't say Montana."

"What, is he jealous?"

"It's complicated," I said.

"But we can go?"

"Let me think about it."

"That means yes."

He wasn't wrong. That meant yes. But with no car and only Walter's credit cards, closely monitored, I didn't see a path west.

In the days after, and the weeks, Ricky began to braid his growing hair: he wanted to look more like Lucky as I'd described him. He ate less, he exercised, he wore leather thongs around his biceps, Lucky's affectation. I attributed this in part to a boy he'd met at MIT—he'd begun to have sex, a mother could tell. At first fantastically, then more and more seriously, we planned a trip. My rule was we couldn't lie to Walter. But then Walter announced his attendance at a conference in Geneva, mid-August. I caught him in the driveway when he was late for work, blurted that Ricky and I wanted a trip, too.

"Where on earth would you go?" he said, that certain needling manner, and his constant theme: I was incapable.

"Montana."

"Montana."

"Ricky wants to get a sense of his heritage, is all."

"Richard's heritage is here, Cindy. All the heritage he needs is here." Big sweeping gesture around the suburban yard where we were standing.

"If we drive, it will be fairly inexpensive," I said.

"If you had a car." Said with his hand on the door of his new Prius.

"We'll work everything out," I said.

"The answer is no," he said. And climbed in the Prius and whispered out of there angrily.

But Ricky planned away, route, meals, stops, cheap stays, the works. I got excited despite myself, his adolescent energy. I wished we could call Maria, plan a visit, but Maria was off the grid, way off. If she was even alive. Ninety years old at least. Clay had had a business, but I wasn't even sure what it was, beyond horses. Anyway, searching the internet yielded nothing. And nothing about Camp Challenge, just a survivors' group, tantalizing but defunct. I put away grocery money. I bought camping equipment. I packed closely. I didn't lie.

At last the day came. Ricky and I drove Walter to Logan Airport in his Prius, dawn flight, then rushed home, loaded up quickly, and off we drove, as many miles as possible day one, Ricky using his lettering skills to alter Walter's mileage notebook despite his mother's not-at-*all* theatrical disapproval, midnight nap in a Walmart lot somewhere east of Chicago, predawn start and onward, increasing excitement, aching bones, great efficiency, windblown night and hot shower at the Peeling Paint Motel somewhere in South Dakota, tumbleweeds knocking at the door.

In the morning, Mountain Turtle dressed carefully in Wranglers and pocket T-shirt, braided his hair, fastened leather bands around his biceps. He did not look much like Lucky, nor much like anyone else, a big person, solemn in his devotion. I dressed, too, as if for a reunion, Mystique blouse half-open, my old Wranglers tight to my hips, the vurry Wranglers, cuffs frayed, only a little too tight, zipper stuck half-mast, pockets worn soft, corrective hiking boots pink as peonies.

Not even noon and there it was, rising unchanged from the greater shapes around it: Turtle Butte, center of our vision for a hundred miles, perceptibly growing. Ricky, driving, clicked the music off, took my hand, squeezed hard, drove.

Camp Challenge was abandoned, the structures vandalized, picked over, building materials scavenged, windows smashed, satanic symbols, firepits and condom wrappers. We parked at the Admin building and walked uphill. The Cats cabin had been wrecked, door swung open, the bunks atumble, mouse-eaten mattresses strewn, only my triple bunk still standing, bolted to the wall for safety. I climbed the plain ladder and fell onto that familiar mattress, lay on my back. My tiny window was still there, maybe the only glass left in the place. I cranked it open, waft of sage.

"Mom, I'm sad," Ricky said.

"It's okay to be sad," I said. "I'm sad, too."

We hiked up to chapel, which he'd drawn, too, so much I'd told him, so much I'd not, nothing changed there, the hopeful amphitheater of pine benches, the tall pine cross, the forever view back across the plains we'd only just traversed. We took out our lunch, sat on the exact pew where Francie and I had met. I told him more about her, that I'd loved her.

"Let's find her," he said.

"Honey."

"I mean, why not?"

"I don't know where to look."

"It's weird," he said. "I sort of thought we'd find all of them here."

"We sort of did."

"It's beautiful, though. Mom, this chapel, so high up."

"It was important to the Crow, too," I said. "A holy place."

"Still and always," Ricky said.

We walked back down to the car, took our time. Each building had a little funny story. I didn't tell him about Doctor Nice and Pink. But I told him about laundry. I told him about Vault. We got in the car at Admin and drove down to see it, Ricky fascinated. The steel building was still there, locked up tight, maybe the only intact building in the whole place. Despite some years of graffiti, it had that inviolable look.

"Mom, what did you do wrong? Solitary confinement!"

"Hey. Your mom did nothing. They were just bad people."

"Don't be cross."

"Let's go find Maria," I said. "I mean if we can. I'm getting the creeps here."

"You miss Lucky Turtle."

"Sweetie, yes. I miss Lucky. And you know. I need coffee."

"Coffee makes you anxious."

That building, Vault. It had been a crossroads, the bridge between this life and that. The long hell of solitary, then paradise so brief. All that incomprehensible graffiti, symbols and tags and just plain splashes, bullet holes, too, once you looked. Someone had written a name in pink paint: BECKY. Someone else had written a slogan in black: I DIED HERE.

Chapter Forty-Two

I started a stick calendar on the thick duff under the lodgepole pines, my private place within sight of the lodge. I thought of it as a kind of attic I could slip away to among all the old things, the duff a soft, old carpet on which to work the 1000-piece puzzle of my life, and I visited near every day. With a butter knife Lucky had sharpened for me, I cut sticks a foot long and whittled the bark off, made neat groups of seven to represent weeks, remembering our days as best I could, special rocks and pretty pebbles to mark highlights—like Hot Springs Discovery or First Venison or Francie's Arrival.

My best guess was that we'd made it almost to August. Neither Lucky nor Francie took the slightest interest. But I couldn't take their way—*just is*—because the current moment progressed, the past receded, things were coming at us from the future, clearer and larger as they came closer, like asteroids that would most likely miss us but might also blow us up. Still, my belly was rounder, my heart more content, a feeling of permanence settling in, that this was my place in the world, my calendar growing like a patchwork quilt, our beautiful days.

So, call it the Bad Morning, a rare windless morning, hot, peaceful, chores to attend to. Lucky was off hunting, wapiti his obsession. Full of confidence, he'd taken both horses, one to ride, one to carry the meat he was so sure he'd get.

I visited the calendar, placed a stick for yesterday, a piece of antler to represent whatever it was that had happened the day before, the happening now forgotten but the antler clear as the moon on a cold night.

After Calendar I spent a pleasant hour picking berries, tart things Lucky called redbugs, hard not to eat them all. At Family Table I worked a while stripping a big bundle of unusual pine cones Lucky had collected, special whitebark pines he'd spotted somewhere and climbed. Under the inter-leaved scales were fat pine nuts, hard again not to eat every last one—first I'd ever heard of them. When the sun finally rose over the ridge, I built up the fire, dragged the drying rack out of the lodge, delicious, peppery jerky I wasn't to eat if we were going to have food for winter. But just a little shred. And just a few berries. And just a spoonful of pine nuts. I boiled water in our one pot and made tea from raspberry leaves—Pregnant Tea, Lucky called it, magic from Maria. And I sat at the table, then climbed up and lay on it with *Hawaii*, third time through, all indolence: someone had to guard the jerky against bears and jays and not only my appetite, which was prodigious.

I chewed, I read.

Francie returned from the garden under high sun with a nice pile of greens, then went to work on La Gran Vil, as she had started calling our place, singing happily, happily finishing her chinking, happily layering long swaths of cedar bark like palm fronds over her poles, at least something like her earliest memories, her mother's village in Haiti, the homes of elderly people she'd visited with her sainted mother. Francie had her period, I remember that, likely so long delayed because of her exposure and severe dehydration during her last days at Challenge—we'd discussed what to do.

A fetus was inside me, and growing every day, and though my puk-ing was done, it was replaced by strange pains and sleeplessness, anxious midnight maundering, kicks and punches. The only thing I knew about pregnancy was what had already happened. About childbirth I knew noth-ing, except that in old novels mothers died, of course they did. The baby was in me and would have to come out. By day I was more sanguine, and more in love than I'd ever thought possible. With Lucky, of course, but also with our world. Our world, including Francie. And with the concept inside me as well: a boy, just as Maria had said, half me and half Lucky.

We'd eaten lunch and were cleaning up when I heard it—something different from the wind, just faintly at first. Then louder. A vehicle. Miles of warning.

"It's Clay," Francie said, delighted. We'd begged him for chocolate, for candles, for baseball caps, the sun forever in our eyes, and maybe Maria would have thought of some of the woman things we lacked.

Just listen, that's what Lucky always said. So I just did, shushing Francie. And okay, this vehicle sounded clunky, whereas Clay's sounded brighter on its springs, a twittering above all the squeaks, this one making lower tones, a kind of booming on the bumps, someone making slow progress, more careful of the roots and rocks and ruts than Clay had ever been. The wind had picked up, the heat rising up through the afternoon, seemed to carry the unwelcome sounds.

An interloper. We'd gone over it a million times. I banked the fire quickly as I could, covered the soup pot, put our message up on the elk-hide door: Bronco would be back soon. I kept Francie's hand so she wouldn't get distracted. She insisted on retrieving the old pickle jar we used for water, filled it from the heavy bark vessel Lucky had made.

We clambered up the ridge, I more sluggish than a mere moon cycle before, short of breath, slipping and sweating. Just as we got to our overlook a pickup pulled right up to Lucky's boulders, parked in plain sight, just where Lucky had said a bad person would not: good.

A man climbed out, stocky, large, open stance, the friendly vibration outdoor people often emanate, cowboy hat cocked back so you could see his face. Lucky and I had talked about this at length, especially long for Lucky: a bad person would hesitate, look all around, hide under the brim of his hat. And Lucky had said wait—wait to see if the caller stepped away from his vehicle and made himself visible, vulnerable, and if so, then carefully observe the way he walked: his intentions would be in his walk. This man proceeded slowly, not strutting or shouting out, stopping well before the dooryard, respectful, not furtive, not official either, something open and friendly about him.

Francie was at my shoulder, put her broad hands on me. "He can help us," she said.

"Quiet," I said.

"We need things," she said.

The interloper lingered some, then seemed to notice the corral, sidled over there, kicked at the fresh hay bales, then seemed suddenly to notice the lodge—it wasn't easy to spot—walked on up there, stood just off the little porch, hands in pockets, inspecting our note, nodding his head as if Bronco were a friend of his, too.

And that's when he would have turned around and shambled back down the hill and gotten in his truck and driven off, but Franciella shouted, "Halloo!"

The interloper shielded his eyes, looked the wrong direction, stiffened in his boots.

And Francie took off running down the steep hill, likely feeling the same warm vibe as me but also eager to meet whoever might be met, her usual restraint forgotten.

"Francie!" I shouted, starting after her. But she was already on the brook path, this thundering woman, carrying long strips of new cedar bark for her bedroom project, the long ends trailing behind her—always with the focus.

"Halloo!" she shouted again.

The interloper flinched hard, spun the right direction, spotted her coming, crouched small, put a hand at his belt in back—in case you'd wondered where his gun was hidden. You saw his beat of surprise: She was tall. She was brown. A lot of woman.

"Howdy-ho," the man called, trying not to sound scared.

She raced right to him as I picked my way more carefully through the rocks. I couldn't hear, of course, but saw that words were passing between them, friendly enough words, it appeared, their heads nodding. Francie pointed downward, she pointed upward. She walked with the man to our lodge—he a match for her in physique—opened the elk-hide door for him, goddamn her: too friendly, and she shouldn't forget how exotic she might seem and that a person just like her was missing.

A minute, that's all, half a minute, and they were back outside where she showed him the outdoor portion of her new room. Well, so that's what they'd been talking about. He pointed at bindings and measured invisible things with his hands—building advice, okay. And you saw Franciella take exception to something he'd said—that defensive pose, hands up between them. But then they were laughing. I hadn't often heard Franciella laugh, I realized, not like that, a bark and a chortle and a bubbling cascade, carried like a falcon soaring on a breeze and, to my ears, surprisingly happy, and I knew why: a sudden man in a world with but one.

I made my way down from my aerie and into the yard, greeted them both.

"Well-well," the interloper said, eyeballing me bodily.

He was the poacher: following his every step in the dust were the exact boot prints Lucky had pointed out.

"Don't look now, but she's having a baby," Franciella said.

"Goes without saying," the man said, certain chastening tone, patronizing air that he wanted to draw me into, create a team. We were one thing, Francie another. He extended his hand, the gentlest gesture, kept his eyes on mine. But when that attempt failed, so transparent, his brand of seduction, he again took in my belly, my chest.

I stood up straight, titties first for the gold (as my gym coach had liked to say), posture as challenge.

He grew careful, said, "Just come up ta fish. That's my church, the brook."

"How do you do," I said.

"I do just fine," he said. "I am Mr. Drinkins. Dale Drinkins."

"This is Mrs. Franciella," I said.

"How do you do," Franciella said, mocking me.

"I do just fine," Mr. Drinkins said again. "Just fine indeed.

"Is it Sunday?" Franciella said.

"It's Sunday," said Mr. Drinkins.

"What's the date?" Franciella said.

"It's August seventeenth."

August seventeenth. I'd been off by several weeks, still had us back in July, had just lost time. My heart sank. We all stood an awkward minute.

But then politely our visitor said, "Now, what religion is that there?" And he indicated our bonnets, pairs of XS gray panties we'd taken to wearing on our heads, low-rent wimples, the leg holes like crests—two makes a cult.

Franciella studied the man, clearly liked what she saw, why? He was middle aged, paunchy, unshaven, smelled like deer lure and aftershave, seemed nice for all that. She said, "Where did you come from?"

And the man said, "If I may, I was talking to your missus."

Francie stood up tall, taller than him. "My missus?" she said. "My *missus*? So we have your answer: you came from the, like, nineteenth century."

His faced flushed perceptibly, not embarrassment, exactly, but what?

"You talk to us both," I said.

He tried to regain ground: "About the headgear," he said. "What religion?"

"Testamentals," Francie said, so quick.

He thought a moment, said, "So you ladies homestead up here."

"It's the old family place," I said. "We are here just through summer, as we go back to the . . . the mission . . . in fall."

Francie had already forgiven him, or pretended: she was crafty, I knew. "Down in Haiti," she said brightly. "You know our country?"

Lights went on in his eyes, our presence making some kind of sense to him suddenly. He said, "I hear it's dangerous down there South America way," he said.

"Not with Bronco along," I said. "No worse than here."

Mr. Dale Drinkins said, "I didn't notice any wedding rings." He turned his own, a thin band of gold.

"Don't be coarse," I said. "We don't believe in jewelry of any kind."

"I stand corrected." He gave Franciella yet another long look up and down, all shrewd. I'd read him wrong—there was nothing nice about him.

"Bronco can be a tad jealous," I said.

Francie took my cue, bless her: "Yes, he threw someone in the ocean once."

He thought about that, clearly wasn't buying it, small smile—an operator, my father would have called him. He said, "I noticed they were off with the horses."

I said, "Off with the horses, yes." Good, he thought there were two men. I remembered he'd skirted the horses when Lucky and I were at the hot spring. He had a young son. I breathed a little easier, just remembering that. A man with a kid. A man with a name.

Mr. Drinkins said, "Off poaching, I suppose."

I said, "Takes one to know one."

He said, "Man's got to eat." He'd walked right by our garden, I realized.

"Well," I said, brainstorm. "It's about time for morning devotions. One hour. If you'll join us."

One of the hens began squawking in the makeshift coop.

"Someone laid an egg," Mr. Drinkins said.

Francie grinned at that.

Mr. Drinkins grinned back, said, "No, no devotions for me."

We all just stood in silence. The wind blew. Our visitor studied Franciella, studied her up and down. Finally he said, "Well, if ya need me, I'm around. This has been my stomping grounds these many years. Did I say my name? Dale. Dale Drinkins."

I said, "Yes, you said your name."

"So I did. Did I get your'n?"

"Mrs. Bronco," I said.

Mr. Drinkins offered his hand, but I didn't take it, something sour filling the air between us. The hand hovered. Francie turned away, bless her.

I said, "Do you have a child with you?"

"Neither with me nor without," he said surprised, or acting so.

"You had a child with you the other day. When you were spying."

He flinched. He flushed once again. And after a long standoff, he turned, sudden emotion—the observer observed—and marched himself down the hill. No look back, he climbed in his truck, started it up with a roar, and drove back down the trail and out of sight, cloud of dust lingering.

"Testamentals," Francie said.

We fell into giggles, uncontrollable glee: the plan had worked. Somehow the plan had worked. And here came that full laugh again, a waterfall hitting rocks, great splashes and booms, the joke still growing, and growing some more: there was a man, and he wasn't Lucky.

Lucky for his part was gruff, hearing about our visitor. He didn't rest, didn't eat, but rode right back out on View to track him. Not long and he was back: "He drove down to the creek there and got out and stood a long time, then he drove off. He's the poacher, all right. He is dreaming about us now, and they're not good dreams: snakes and wolves."

Francie said, "If we fight him, he'll fight back. If we act like friends, he'll help us. And, honestly, family, we could use a few things."

"That poacher will tell people," Lucky said. "And people will know who we are. And who we are is you two in trouble and the whole world looking for you."

"That's what I'm saying," Francie said. "We can't afford enemies—and you only need one. He won't tell people if we're friends. If he sees us as his friends, he might even help us. He seemed inclined to help us. We need to have friends. And who else have we got?"

Lucky and Francie stared one another down. But in the end Lucky let her win, a whole plan unfolding without a word: if it came to it, Francie would befriend Mr. Drinkins. That is, if he wasn't already in town reporting us, asking after rewards.

My husband was dour through the evening like I'd never seen him, dour even after a long chapter of *Hawaii*.

"Not a good day to count time by," Lucky said late, and to sleep without lovemaking.

The next couple of days Lucky and Franciella built simple machines, levers and fulcrums, ramps and pulleys, clever work harnesses for the horses, who were willing, used them all in various combinations to nudge boulders down the hill and back into the road below our curve such that anyone arriving would have to leave any vehicle and appear first on foot.

Chapter Forty-Three

We Testamentals lost track of the days again, and lived by the moon, but I guessed if that reach of time needed a name, I would call it Gold. Lucky lay with his ear on my belly, heard a heartbeat beneath mine. And, oh, the kicking in there when Lucky spoke, or even more so, chanted. Because I wouldn't call it singing. Two-note ditties about what baby would see when he opened his eyes to the world for the first time: blue sky, for one thing, and the dark of night pricked by stars. Baby was a he, we knew: Maria had told us so.

In her new room, Franciella slept contentedly on a mat of pine boughs and soft mosses too small for her, Challenge sheets, an Aunt Maria blanket pulled to her chin, freckles blooming on her cheeks. I liked to peek in and see her, so far from who I thought she was that first day at the Camp Challenge chapel. She'd developed a Cindra persona to use when teasing me that made Lucky laugh and laugh. Did I really emit such superior airs? It was as if she'd channeled my mother somehow, these imitations of me were so far off the mark! And though Francie could still be aloof, she was also more vulnerable than I'd realized, occasionally sulky, more often mewling like a kitten for attention. And at times, she was a warm listener, listened at length to whatever I had to say, never an opinion if I didn't ask for one. In that, I guess, she was not a man. And not as tough as she let on. Nor as experienced as I'd assumed, my unconscious racism gradually revealed to me, so gradually that really only now do I grasp how I'd bought into the mythology of Black women's sexual prowess. Where had I even learned that? Everywhere and nowhere, I guess, from the halls of my high school to our tattered history books, and definitely from pop culture. Francie, in fact, was far less experienced than I, far more innocent than I'd been for years, despite my pretending even to myself. Right there in the wilderness my mythologies broke, fell in shards at my feet only to be reassembled over the coming decades as wisdom but in that moment left me struggling to catch up to myself as I grew. Francie had never had a lover, I had to keep reminding myself, only abuse, which as an even younger girl she may or may not have unconsciously mistaken for love, and which maybe, just perhaps, made a man like Drinkins seem possible to her. But this, too, did not come to me in the moment like some explosive revelation. Just this: that kiss with Lucky had been her first. And as revelation enough, had made me more tender toward her, which in turn brought us closer, and brought her into focus: she was who she was. All the other, previous words came from a different world.

"I thought white people weren't capable of love," she said on one of our walks, way over behind the tall ridges, a couple of miles from the lodge, searching for mushrooms, ambling, holding hands. I'd been talking about my dad, missing him. "Or really any feeling at all. Until I met you, I mean."

"That's so. So sad," I said.

"But true," she said. "I wanted to tell you one true thing. To make you understand."

"I think I do understand. I really think I do. And I do love you."

At the intensity of that we separated for a moment, she this way up the path, I that way into an aspen copse, arriving simultaneously upon opposite ends of a fallen oyster log—hundreds of the beautiful mushrooms growing in shelves upon each other. Lucky would be delighted: he wanted to dry huge amounts of fungus ahead of winter the way Clay had taught him. Wordlessly, delighted at the bounty, Francie and I filled our Camp Challenge pillowcases, met in the middle.

"Tell me something true," Francie said, still annoyed with me. "I mean true like that, that I made you understand."

"Well." I thought a long time, the fresh smell of the oysters, anise-like, slightly fishy. "I didn't think I'd like you."

"Not until you saw La Vil."

"Yes, La Vil was a miracle. But I liked you before that."

"And now you love me."

"Yes. I do. And you love me. But, one more true thing, I'm worried about you. Because of that man."

"Dale Drinkins," Francie said, so dreamily, but just to twit me.

At dinner that night she brought up the poacher again, just out of the blue, lull in our talk of food, food, food, Lucky already racking mushrooms to dry in the sun next day, brought him up as if the discussion had never been tabled.

"I say we keep Dale Drinkins close," she said.

"What does that even mean?" I said.

"He said he'd bring us apples," Francie said. "He said he'd bring me nails."

"And when did he say all that?"

"In my room. When I showed him my room. How I'm building my room. See, we might not like him, and he might not like you, but he likes me, some version of me that he's inventing, and as shitty as that is, it means I can control him, and we could use some help."

"He's not welcome here," Lucky said darkly. "He'll bring trouble."

"Unless he thinks there's something for him here," Francie said. "Otherwise, why would he not just turn us in? Am I repeating myself? I'm repeating myself."

"It's best to say such things twice," Lucky said pondering.

"You've got a plan," I said.

Francie only shrugged.

Lucky had had more to say, but now he nodded. He liked a plan.

That night in *Hawaii* a volcano was erupting. There was sex in a grotto. There were whole sections about food. I read, my family listened, the night grew long, the fire to coals, the poacher out of mind.

This was heaven.

Truly.

I was in a brief but beautiful phase of pregnancy, the world and everything in it glowing with meaning and strange powers, my dreams having burgeoned into cinema, reel after reel in Panavision, new worlds to explore, doors opening in our scruffy lodge to ballrooms, spiral stairs, attics full of toys and peculiar foreign money and gifts in blue wrappings. And often lavish feasts that included mostly high-layered hamburgers in toasted buns and precarious scoops of ice cream, a recurring lobster roll from Benny's Clam Shanty back home, with fries.

In the morning with a scrap of moon low in the sky, Francie got up early to take off on some brilliant mission, Lucky and I back to sleep spooned tight. She was still nowhere to be found when Lucky and I rose, wonderful, just Lucky and me sitting on the rickety porch sipping hot aspen-twig water—we were rationing coffee and tea.

"I dreamed a bird," I said. "I think last night."

"He had something to say."

"No, just a bird in the wind over a field. And speeding clouds."

"Which direction?"

"Oh, Lucky. I don't have a built-in dream compass. I think the bird was you."

"I dreamed bobcats heading south," he said. "Down into the Yellowstone."

"Don't you ever dream of me?"

"I'm dreaming of you right now." That sly smile, rising into his cheeks.

The aspen-twig water tasted vaguely of root beer. Lucky drank out of my cup when his old can was empty, then sauntered to the fire, filled both again, nice and hot. Back, he sat vurry close, pulled my leg over his. I put my arm around his neck—just wanted him closer, as close as we could get, and then even a little closer than that.

He said, "One time after a heavy storm at Maria's, I found two tired hummingbirds on the ground. They must have been blown up and down the plain all night long. I held them in my two hands in front of the morning fire. Like nothing, those two, soft as petals, tiny hearts tick-ticking. Breathing hard, but just lying there. After a long time, one of them got up. Then the other. They gripped onto my fingerprints with those tiny claws.

They tried out their wings some and flicked those long tongues. Then buzz-buzz and they were gone."

"Messengers," I said.

"Just birds," said he, placing kisses upon my throat.

Okay, yes to that, but I sat up quick, a conversation planned: "Lucky, I'm worried about winter."

"It will come."

"I know it will come. I'm just worried about this baby." Pat-pat on my tummy. "Having this baby, I mean. In winter, all alone here."

"Francie will be here. I will be here."

"Oh, Lucky." I pictured Clay in his truck, the bed loaded with bags of chicken feed, a pyramid of hay bales. But Clay hadn't turned up for more than a month, in my estimation, maybe a lot more. And he'd never be able to reach us in winter. Lucky only looked ahead a day, two or three at the most, and the idea of a month was just foolish to him, the moon being new every time, a year even more so.

"I've seen many a birth," he said. "They had their babies in Solitude. Ms. Conover made me help a few times in winter when the staff was low. I'll boil my knife and cut the cord and tie it. There'll be a mess to clean up, but nothing so bad as a horse. And the pain won't linger."

"I can't imagine the pain at all."

"You won't have to imagine."

"Oh, Lucky."

"I try you."

"You do."

"I don't try to try you."

"You compared me to a horse!" I punched his chest, pushed him away from me, untangled my leg from his, but as soon as we were separated, I grabbed hold again and pulled him back violently, comically (or anyway he laughed), suddenly wept, my mouth at his ear. I was in nothing but my maternity T, he just in pants, his chest dark from the sun. He held my arms so I wouldn't pummel him, pulled me in, held me and kissed my throat again a long while. We talked into each other's mouths, he promising it would all come out just fine, sentences chopped off clean, just the two of us side by side on the rustic porch in hot morning sun, shedding what little clothes.

"You'll sound like that," Lucky said.

Chapter Forty-Four

Lucky and I heard no truck, noticed nothing, that was the strange thing. We were people who listened, but even sitting out on the little porch we heard nothing at all until we heard Franciella's shout as she trotted in from the brook path, all out of breath: "Visitor!"

I tugged my shirt on, burst inside through the elk flap, found my pants, my sneakers, pulled my Maria brush through my hormone-luxuriant hair (twigs falling out), pulled on an XS panty bonnet, realized my shirt was filthy, exchanged it for a fresh one, Camp Challenge gray, too tight, my breasts grown enormous, or so it suddenly seemed.

I emerged in a rush to see Lucky meeting Francie out in the yard, urgent tones. But there was no time to enact a plan: up from the brook path, Mr. Drinkins appeared, encumbered by a large backpack. He must have been camping, I thought, camping in the high valley, must have left his truck far below, so startling to see him. But wait—it wasn't like it had just happened that way—we were well beyond coincidence: Dale Drinkins knew where to find us. And Francie: he'd found her first and together they'd walked up along the brook trail before she'd broken away to come warn us, so it seemed.

Lucky had pulled on his one shirt, stood there tall beside her in his Wranglers and cowboy boots, long, long hair in blackest braids tight as rope—my work—braids pulled forward onto his chest for power. I hurried to join them. Clearly in all his spying, Dale Drinkins hadn't yet seen Lucky, approached warily, looked him up and down.

"Well, you're back," I said.

"Howdy," Mr. Drinkins said.

"Well, so," my husband said, a neutral couple of syllables.

"Injun," Mr. Drinkins said.

"His name is Lucky," Franciella said. "Lucky, this is Dale."

Dale? She was using his first name? Oh, no, no. It all came plain as the view out across the Great Plains. She'd been making friends, all right. Sudden vision of the day before, when she'd left before Lucky and I woke, had gotten home much later than usual, not a berry in her basket, and all mysterious, uncharacteristically reserved.

"Where's this Bronco?" our visitor said cagily. "I'm here to meet this Bronco."

"No, no, no, you're not," Franciella said bravely.

He tried to look like a guy joking, tried a joke: "Bronco and not his sidekick here." He pushed past me, got in Lucky's face, all like he was kidding, kept trying, kept digging himself in: "You wouldn't want ol' Bronco thinking you got his girl with child, here, would you?"

Lucky was serene, a little amused maybe, half a head taller than Mr. Drinkins, who was half a body bigger but encumbered by his huge backpack. A push and he'd go down.

Mr. Drinkins's voice rose, comedy having failed him: "Speaky English?"

"Dale," Franciella said firmly. Yes, she'd met up with him, knew him better than we did, had some vague power over him.

"Bronco will be back in half an hour," I said evenly. "But you'd better be gone after the things you've said."

Mr. Drinkins smiled, just teeth: "What'd I say but the truth?"

"Dale," Francie said. "We talked about this."

Oh? They'd talked about this?

"Yep," he said, still in Lucky's face. "Yep, we did. And you said there wasn't no Bronco but just the Injun."

"I told you no such thing," Francie said.

"There's a Bronco," I said evenly.

"But no Injun," Lucky said evenly.

Dale Drinkins rose on his toes, couldn't find words, hands clenching into fists, face hot as a car-part frying pan.

I stepped between them, said, "Time to move on, Dale Drinkins. Time to head on home to your wife and your boy. Bronco's going to be vurry unhappy, you causing trouble like this."

"There's no such man," Mr. Drinkins said.

"Dale Drinkins!" Francie barked.

And it was like he'd been slapped. He stepped backwards, attempted a winning shrug. "I just want to help," he said. "Help you ladies." His face was square and burned and not half handsome, something likable there despite himself. Was he even Francie's height? He had a crush, that's what was going on. "Help you with what-have-you."

"We don't need any sidekick," Lucky said. "We got Bronco and he's all the sidekick we can use."

Dale Drinkins turned slowly. He struggled out of his backpack straps, put it heavy on the ground, let his gaze rise to Lucky's, couldn't keep Lucky's eye, so steady, turned to me instead, tugged his fat wallet from deep in his front pants pocket, extracted a folded bit of newsprint, slowly opened it, a long column neatly cut, held it up to show me, wouldn't let me touch it:

CAMP CHALLENGE RESIDENTS MISSING: SUSPECT AT LARGE

"Done a little research," he said.

He wouldn't hand over the clipping, so I read it aloud as he held it, rock-steady hands to belie his nerves. None of it was accurate. The "suspect" was someone known as "The Turtle," an "indigent youth lately of Crow Nation and a sometime Camp Challenge employee." The crime was kidnapping. Or, if it had been an escape, aiding and abetting.

"All nonsense," I said, pushing the clipping out of my face.

Dale Drinkins read the rest out loud: "Investigators want to know how two incar . . . incarcerated juveniles left Camp Challenge unseen. Sheriff's deputy Gordon Sam would not rule out foul play. Mr. Turtle is considered armed and dangerous." Dale Drinkins repeated that, then softened, stepped close to me, whispered conspiratorially: "Miss, honestly. These Crow, they are animals. They'll cut your throat in the night."

"Enough," I said. "Just stop."

He said, "They'll steal the underpants off your head."

I couldn't help it, laughed. "Bronco will be back," I said. I said it loudly, to counteract the whispering, the wedge he was always wielding: divide and conquer.

"My sidekick," Lucky said.

"So good day to you, Dale," Francie said.

Dale Drinkins reached for her hand. "I'll take care of you," he said hotly.

Francie scoffed, so subtly: he'd have to do better than that. But yes, definitely: they'd been talking. She said, "On your way."

"Done," he said. Deflated, dismissed, he lifted that heavy backpack, slipped his arms in the straps, adjusted his balance, threw out his chest, walked down our road and away.

Lucky couldn't help a slow smile: Francie had cast a spell.

Chapter Forty-Five

Ricky drove so slowly, always cautious, more so behind the wheel. An enormous pickup got on our tail on the Elk Creek Road, passed at last, American flag snapping in its bed. Hypervigilance, I believe it's called, my neck bent to watch that grille in the passenger's side mirror, my fear for my son.

I had a smaller worry, too, which edged forward as my old militia phobia receded: money. We hadn't spent much and yet it was more than I'd planned, mostly food along the way, and gas, and that motel. I kept trying to add up what it might take to get home, couldn't get a number small enough that we wouldn't have to use my credit cards, charges I'd have to explain to Walter. Well, better to ask forgiveness than permission, as my late uncle Jeff so often said. I rehearsed scenes, no fun. Walter had made it impossible for me to work, then lorded money over me. I'd been weak, dependent, credulous: I was not the fragile thing he made me out to be. Montana made me remember.

Back on the highway I realized my sense of where to find Maria's was only approximate. Thirty miles or so back to the west, and the familiar exit toward Turtle Butte was clear enough. But then it was just miles of dust, that thrilling landscape.

Ahead a young man with swimmer's shoulders and a buzz cut came into view, stood by a little car waving emphatically. I thought the little car a good sign. Ricky pulled over neatly right beside him. Nothing for it, nervous suburban lady, I rolled my window down.

"Hi guys," the young man said, handsome. "You headed to Maria's?"

"Marvelette Ranch," I said, because that's what I'd planned.

"She said you'd be coming."

"Wait, what?" Ricky said.

But I wasn't surprised at all.

"I'm Born on Bison," the young man said. "Bob."

"Mountain Turtle," Ricky said. "And this is my mom."

"Cindrawww," the young man said uncannily—but he was only imitating Maria.

I must have looked skeptical.

Or anyway, he explained: "The Crow council's been trying for years to reach out to Maria, more or less bring her home—we've got great assisted living there in Crow Agency—or at least get her some elder services out here at the ranch. Lately she's been more accepting. I'm just trying to help. That's my goal. Our goal. And today my task was to get out here and wave you folks down."

"Thank you," Ricky said to counter my suspicious foot tapping.

Bob got it, though: we were all protective of Maria.

He said, "When I was little my grandparents would take me over here to see her sometimes. She was the lady that lived on the Junk Ranch. My grandpa called her Lives in Box. The schoolkids call her Mrs. Marvelette. She used to do the school bowling trips every spring. She calls me Gutter Ball sometimes to this day. My dad still calls her auntie. She's kind of famous. So was Clay—if you needed to junk your car or wanted a hunk of metal, boy, this was the place."

"Clay Marvelette," my son said—he knew the name, all right.

Bob said, "She shouldn't really be out here alone."

"Alone," I said.

"She'll tell you all about it," Bob said. He climbed in his car and drove as slowly as Ricky, led us to a hidden turn past a NO DUMPING sign and then south, Turtle Butte directly in front of us, the wind behind us hard, dust covering the windshield such that I reached over and turned the wipers on.

Had Clay passed? Tears started to my eyes.

"So cool we were up there," Ricky said.

"See that sort of black streak?" I said. "And then to the right there's a crack?"

"Mom, I'm driving."

"That's where your father and I climbed down."

He liked that.

Naturally my heart was atumble. I wiped my eyes. I would not cry.

Soon enough Ricky spotted the first metallic glimmers of Clay's collection, flashes of sunlight off chrome and old mirrors and windows, then an absurd long line of purple garden spheres on cement pedestals, finally a tall gate made of airplane wings.

From there the driveway skirted the junk mountain, bigger than ever. Maria's dooryard was just as I remembered, right down to the old trampoline frame in the yard, where Ricky chose to stop—there was no defined parking area. Her vintage mobile home had been jacked level up on its outcropping and painted bright yellow, the stairs rebuilt at a gentler incline.

As we climbed out of the car, the high door opened.

Maria was tall as ever, unbowed, her eyes ablaze as always, possibly the same flannel shirt as ever, that skeptical air, hair white as clouds, brushed long and pulled forward over one shoulder. She ignored me, looked Ricky up and down.

"Well, there he is," she said, unamazed, unfazed—she'd been living with the future all her life. "Come on up. The girls bring dinner at four-thirty, and then it's bath and all the stretching we do. I have a thing with my wrist. There's a little time for a visit, though."

We climbed the steps, so much more solid than I recalled. Bob watched, bemused, then started the bath, Clay's ingenious system, absurdly high hand pump top of a ladder, dedicated drum, hot, fast softwood fire, release warmed water strategically into the galvanized farm tub placed just so— once I'd bathed in it, too.

Slowly, Maria put a hand to Ricky's cheek. "I knew you'd be back," she said. "Maybe not even soon as this."

Now that I looked, she was frail—she'd never been frail. And definitely weary. But who wasn't tired, so late in the afternoon?

"You didn't go up on the butte now," she said.

"Yes, we did," Ricky told her. "Turtle Butte."

She took Ricky's arms by the elbows, said, "Look at you, pretty as your father."

"How'd you know to send Born on Bison?" I said.

She tore her eyes from my son. "Oh, Bobby," she said. "He's full of it, he's out here every day. He may be studying history at that Little Big Horn College, but he's like Lucky, wants everything to be a sign. Tell me something, Mountain Turtle."

Ricky tried studiously to remain unamazed, but said, "You know my name."

"Yes, yes, of course I do, nephew, your name was there before you. Tell me one thing."

Not a blink of hesitation: "I'm in an engineering program this summer. I'm interested in materials. I'll be going to MIT. I love your husband's junk collection. You could build a whole town."

"The mysteries of Marvelette," Maria said fondly.

"Tell *us* one thing," Ricky said, quick to the game.

Maria thought a long time, couldn't find the words. Finally she said, "Lucky's not here. I think you thought you'd find him. He lives in that city, what's it called. Where Far Turtle lived some. With the red bridge. Gosh my memory."

"You mean San Francisco?"

"Yes, that's it. San Francisco. Of course. I dreamed it. Many times. And I dreamed this very moment. I remember everything you say while you say it. Dinner is at four-thirty. Bath after. And of course the stretching."

"Seems a little early for dinner," Ricky said. How was he so good at this? My heart pounded. Lucky was not alive. I'd seen his death certificate. I'd seen it many times. I'd seen it recently. I'd seen it just before this trip. I'd been pulling it out of its hiding place to keep myself convinced, keep myself centered, a neatly typed form, turning yellow. Reality, Walter called it. Ricky had never seen that piece of paper. I'd have to show him when we were home. Reality had its place, I was starting to learn. Maybe Maria had dreamed the past, Far Turtle in San Francisco, his son Thomas Sing, too. Had Lucky ever even been there?

Maria had been standing long enough, threw a sigh, backed up cautiously through her door, accepting our hands, backed right through the trailer till she bumped her bed and sat. Her breaths came slowly. I tried to match mine, slow, slower. It worked. At length, she said, "Turtle Butte, Turtle Butte. Been a mess up there since Clay died, that's what I hear."

"Clay passed? I'm so sorry."

"Yes. But I wouldn't say passed. That sounds too peaceful. They killed him."

"What? No." I felt my chest would cave, gasped. "Who killed him? Maria, who killed Clay?" Now the tears did come.

Ricky put his arm around me, his first gesture as a man.

Maria lay back, found her pillow, pulled her legs up, eyes tight shut, crossed her hands over her thin chest said, "Those Free Men, that's who. Brought him home dead in the back of his own truck. Already ruled a suicide by that coroner of theirs. They own all of Elk Creek now, all the county government. They got Clay's horses, too, bought 'em up at auction, I couldn't stop it. Not View, though, View had already died. Buried out there somewhere. And you knew Chickadee, too. She was here the whole time. I kept her a while. Now she's over there safe at Crow Agency with Bob's dad. I guess he still rides her some, tough old girl. So they didn't get her, is the good news."

Ricky put my hand over hers on her chest and then his own long hand on mine. Her heart was under there, still beating.

I said, "Maria, I'm so sorry."

"He'd go see Lucky up in prison there where they put him."

Cindra, breathe slowly. "Oh, good. Oh, I'm so glad of that."

"Then something or other happened. They moved Lucky somewheres."

"He passed, too, Maria."

"No, I've dreamed him. Dreamed him often. You'll find him years to come," she said. "That city with the bridge. Just as I said. Years to come. Not today. Not tomorrow. But you will find him. The seventh day you arrive. That city. The big one. San Francisco."

Ricky put his cheek to hers. He squeezed our hands. He wasn't like me, carried off by my sadness. He was right there in that room. "Yes, Auntie," Ricky said. "We will find him, we'll find him on the seventh day."

"That your mother arrives," Maria repeated. Then, "I'd better get ready. Dinner is four thirty." She threw off our hands, pushed us away, strong as ever, sat up quick. "Look in that drawer there before you go."

The dresser. Three drawers. I opened the top one.

"To the right, there under the scarf," she said.

A paper bag worn leathery. Inside it, a long box as for old-school dress gloves, my name written on top, dark pencil, my father's unmistakable, slightly childish hand. I knew exactly what I would find inside: cash. The next item was a green notebook, Bic pen stuck deep in the spiral. And a kid's pink sock, just one, my pearl inside, my pearl from Daddy.

"That all came back with Chickadee," Maria said.

"Chickadee?" Ricky said.

"I'll explain later," I said, and held the pearl in my hand, bigger than I remembered, clutched it to my breast, wept again. "Maria, my god, my god. You saved it all these years! I don't know how to thank you."

She pried the necklace from my fingers, gave the pearl a polish on the stiff flannel of her shirt, opened the clasp easily, put the chain around my neck, closed the clasp. "Back to rights," she said. "Now. Look in the bottom drawer, deep in there."

I pulled it open, pushed the Wranglers aside, a dozen pairs, all worn the same. Underneath, I found a flat steel lockbox. I drew it out—heavy—put it on her lap. She spun the numbers carelessly, the latch popped open.

"Contraband," she said. Inside was a big old gun.

I recognized it immediately.

She said, "That came back with Chickadee, too. Yours, if you want it."

"I do not."

"We do *not*," Ricky said.

I heard a car coming, coming all the way along, a big old model, it sounded like, lifters clattering. I closed the gun box, spun the numbers, put it back.

Shortly there was laughter outside, Bob greeting three young women who offloaded a cooler and fresh towels and linens, a clean stack of flannel shirts. "Dinnertime," one of them called gaily, pink scrubs and bright running shoes.

"Just hang on," Maria called standing easily, lady in her nineties. "These folks are just about to go!"

The water cauldron was already steaming, olden routine, Clay's genius. One of the young women laid out a queenly bath on the bench Clay had carved from Yellowstone River willow: robe, towels, soap, shampoo. The others spread a tablecloth on Clay's steel worktable, laid out a modest meal.

At the tall bookcase by the door, bowling trophies all polished and put in line, Maria paused. She looked things over—pretty rocks and feathers, her bracelets, her rings, a few dozen romance novels, trashiest sort, then selected one foxed and colorful volume, tugged it out, showed me, the cover familiar as a face: *Hawaii*.

"I was glad to get this one back," she said, putting it in my hands. "But you can borrow it one more time."

Ricky helped her down the stairs. Bob introduced the young Crow women very briefly, two of them at college with him, one working at the nursing home on the Res, each shaking Ricky's hand, each more or less oblivious of me, my red eyes, Maria impatient. A schedule was a schedule, and it was time for dinner.

"Gotta go," Bob said. "I'll be late for class." He took Ricky in a muscular hug, said goodbye, and was off.

Then so were we, not so much as a wave from Maria, who had moved on.

In the car Ricky and I were silent, moved to introspection.

The highway sign in bright sun broke the spell.

"Wow," Ricky said.

I showed him the money, my father's gift, maybe less than it had seemed back in the day, but plenty for a big night in Billings. Later I'd explain it to him: my dad had loved me so. But I didn't want to get into Pops, not on this night, not riding in the Prius of the shithead I'd forced on Ricky. But my son wasn't curious, talked into his phone, asked the lady in there for best Billings hotels, liked the sound of the Big West Resort, rang them up, told them we were coming, just like that, all of it the cash treat of Hates Roofing, my beautiful dad.

"San Francisco," Ricky said. "I sort of believe her."

"She's just an old woman," I said. "Can be a little silly. Your dad is dead." I didn't even believe myself: such was Maria's power.

"My famous sort-of aunt," Ricky said.

"Yes, sweetie, yes. That's the true part. Maria is your aunt. Not sort of. She was your father's Hawk mother. And Maria is alive. And you got to meet her."

"Sister of Walks Far," he intoned, like a special we'd seen on TV.

I don't know what was so funny about that, but we laughed for miles in that long, long afternoon light, late summer, the highway east as straight as a Viking spear, Billings growing on the horizon like five movie sets stuck together, different eras.

"Thank goodness for Born on Bison," Ricky said at last.

"Yes," I said. "Thank goodness."

"Maybe there's more we could do to help."

"Maybe so," I said.

"Like, what about that gun?"

"Maria loves a secret," I said.

"Lots to discuss," Ricky said.

The hotel was nice, really nice. The room was enormous, the shower so hot and hard, the restaurant nearly empty, big western-style steaks, big beautiful old beds, soft sheets, eighty-five bucks inclusive, *Hawaii* all to myself while Ricky bathed forever, giant claw-foot tub, nagging sense that I ought to be digging up roots for breakfast, collecting sagebrush, sleeping on a rock, penance for surviving.

Chapter Forty-Six

In the days after Francie's poacher left, things got back to normal—building, gathering, hunting, gardening, horses, hot spring, *Hawaii*.

Lucky spent a whole morning ceremonially and mysteriously building something. "A pyre," I kept joking to no response, a tipi of sticks to begin, a fortress of pitchy ponderosa logs around that. But instead of lighting the thing, he rode off on View, heading down the mountain on our road. Not a word. If he wandered down to the range land, he might be seen, might be tracked. I thought to jump on Chickadee and chase him down, but I dithered too long to possibly catch up, and that little horse would gallop me right into the treetops trying.

Francie was cutting a window into her addition—apparently Mr. Drinkins had promised panes of glass, not good. But she'd more or less convinced us that it was best to appease him, take his presents, let him have his crush on her. She felt herself in control, and I wanted her to have that. In truth, Dale Drinkins's coming back with glass was less worrisome than all the other possible things he might bring. Even Lucky had endorsed the idea: Francie Power. Still, it's not fair I called him "Francie's poacher" before and here I emphatically take that back. Dale Drinkins was nobody's fault, only his own.

But now the pyre. Lucky saw fire as a way to create space with Maria, as best I understood it. I was realizing that he invented his own rituals, strung from various sources. His grandfather had revered fire for all its usefulness, one of the pillars of truth, whatever that meant (and Lucky couldn't explain). They lit candles for their ancestors, offered gifts of food, those ancestors very real to a boy, populating not only his imagination but his world: there weren't other children around, just the inmates of Camp Challenge.

I pried the rest out of him in small, hot pieces: after Lucky's grandfather was murdered, and after his traumatized mother had grown so hard, Maria and he had developed fresh rituals. Maria was all he had, emotionally speaking, and she knew it. Other abandoned kids might phone a beloved aunt, even write letters back and forth (and today, of course, text and email and all the rest), but those options weren't available. What was available was Maria's hearth. She told Lucky to build a fire whenever they were apart and he needed her, which was often, really most of the time. What he told the fire, she said, the fire would in turn tell her. It wasn't so different from her lighting candles in church. Intention to pray, she called it. And what she told her fire, which in one form or another was always burning, the fire would tell him. You could see how an isolated, traumatized, and badly injured boy would come to believe in it absolutely, how plain comforting it would be to gain Maria's presence that way when he couldn't see her regularly, especially in winter, when he saw her not at all. And as it happened, through all his seasons till he met me, he built a fire most days. Didn't matter where. Strike sparks in tinder, whistle up the flames, speak your heart.

I'd told him about the ancient Greeks, how they'd believed in four elements, something like the four directions he was always talking about (or six, when he counted up and down). There was earth, there was air, there was water, there was fire. And so in the wilderness he began to talk with all of them. It wasn't nutty, it was very sweet, and it soothed us all. His grandpa was earth, he decided, and always there for comfort. He himself was air, blowing in and out of things, picking up the dust in capricious whirlwinds, carrying fire into the sky, driving the rain, carrying water as clouds. That was me, water, and wasn't I sloshing with it.

We discussed all this at Family Table after *Hawaii*, discussed it many nights. "So if you're air and Cindra's water," Francie had said on one of them, "what am I?"

"Whatever you like," Lucky said. He hadn't meant to leave her out, he'd only run out of elements.

"I think wood," Francie said, not at all sardonic. "Soft as it grows, hard when the time comes, portable, super sturdy, good for many things, direction always up, prone to flame."

Lucky thought about that approvingly, said, "Prone to Maria, you mean."

"To Maria," Francie and I repeated.

To Lucky, this was revelation: we really were a family.

The poacher had brought something home to him, it seemed: we were people who needed things, who needed help, better to ask the elements than stand on pride. Lucky had had an idea, something inexpressible that had to do with his aunt, with bringing her powers to all of us, and that for some unstated reason required his riding View hard down our road at first light, that pounding of hooves rising from my worried dreams. Later that morning, awake-worrying about Lucky riding many miles down into the range lands, I couldn't stay at my own task, which was cutting thin strips from our deer hide at Family Table.

Instead, I toddled down to the lodge to stand in Francie's doorway, light already coming in a fresh window hole, which she was endeavoring to square up with nothing but an axe and my sharpened butter knife, tying off loose pole ends with our cordage, making a frame with logs she'd axe-split to make rough boards. She measured from fingertips to shoulder repeatedly, tongue in her teeth as I watched.

"Are you just going to stare," she said.

"I'm worried about Lucky," I said. "He rode off and I just don't know what he thinks he's doing."

She worked, tying off a piece of our cordage, pulling a corner of the window opening into square. At length she said, "Have you worried about him before?"

"Yes, of course I have."

"And then everything was fine?"

The little knife had been sharpened so often by then that the blade had a hook in it. Francie shaped a stick of wood, tried it in the window opening, whittled at it some more, tried again, back and forth from knife to opening several times till the fit was perfect. Soon I was her helper, felt my worry flee ahead of the small tasks she gave me.

Time for a windowsill. I handed my irritable boss the pounded old axe Lucky had sharpened, held the board for her, a board she'd made from a lodgepole log, four short chops to create a join, the little knife to carve it clean, a nice tight fit, kicks and karate chops to knock it into place, and suddenly the floppy window frame snapped to attention, rigid and true, self-portrait.

Lucky returned. Of course he returned. Returned triumphant, he and View thundering up the trail in a cloud of dust and spray of gravel, a regular cigarette commercial. "Hoppo!" he shouted.

"Hoppo!" Francie shouted back.

I just sighed, so angry, as snorting and wild eyed as View. I squared around, hands on hips, belly thrust.

"You will tell me where you are going!"

"I'm not going, I'm here," he said affably.

"Enough of that," Francie said, suddenly taking my side, and hard: "You will tell her from now on!"

Emboldened I cried, "Where on earth have you been!"

And Lucky, not susceptible to tone, never defensive, simply answered: "On earth I have been down to the fence line. It's a long way. All of the morning, and now the afternoon."

"Wait," I said, "You rode to the ranches? Those cowboys, if they caught you, if they even just saw you? We don't need their meat." He was forever talking about hijacking a steer if we got desperate in the winter, making it look like wolf work, meals for months.

"No, Cindra, *chwing*," he said, drawing out that last word, the new one.

"What the hell," Francie said.

Chickadee over in the corral liked the drama, wanted View back, pawed the dirt, threw her head down, threw it back, View the same. Lucky dismounted, threw the traces to the ground, pulled a bark folder from his capacious pocket, opened it to reveal several dozen delicate long-stemmed, atrociously fragrant mushrooms. "Found down on the cow pats," he said.

"Mushrooms?" Francie said. "You rode to the ranches for mushrooms?"

"No, for visions," Lucky told her. "And saw nobody but cattle."

"*Merde alors!*" Francie said, suddenly awed. "Magic mushrooms?"

"The same," Lucky said, plucking one from the folder and swallowing it down whole, not a grimace. "*Chwing*, Maria always called it, don't know why. Clay didn't like us eating them, so mostly we did not."

And standing right there beside the work of our long day, View back at the fence kissing on Chickadee, Francie and Lucky and I choked down mushrooms one by one, Lucky dosing us by bodyweight, not a thought for my pregnancy: four for me, eight for himself, twelve for Franciella, who retched but kept trying.

"Now we just wait," Lucky said.

So meanwhile Francie showed him her work on the windows, all but the glass in place, then we filed up to Family Table, sat atop it back-to-back-to-back in a clover, Lucky called it. In a clover you took turns speaking leaf-to-leaf-to-leaf, the things of the day, as Lucky called them, thought by thought by thought creating a spiral that seemed to rise into the air above our little knot.

"Everything is *so normal*," I said.

Francie said, "You don't say things are normal when they're normal, my friend!"

But they *were*, just normal, maybe funnier, like that clover was lover with a *c* in front, as Francie suddenly said, which I didn't get till she wrote it in the air over our heads. Then there was the pyre Lucky had built, which he wanted to finish, and so in a knot we examined it a long time, beautiful construction on the bald rock above the firepit. Francie was first to begin giggling, then I. Lucky was not a giggler even in those circumstances but pulled his big, bighted knife, banged sparks off the quartz he'd placed just so, sparks like amusing revelations falling into tinder already placed as well, and we blew into the sparks in the tinder, taking turns, and when the tinder burst into flames we died from the beauty of it, no more giggling, Lucky's tough hands babying the flame in its ball of tender tinder and handing it off into the heart of the lodge he'd built, the tender heart, which lit slowly then quickly, and boom, the inner tipi of kindling lit, then the log fortress around it. I've always loved things we build just to destroy. And I said that, and it seemed profound.

And Francie got big eyes and said, "Yes, like meals."

"And sandcastles," I said.

"And friendships," Francie said. Then, "Just kidding sorry."

"Like the world," Lucky said, conversation stopper.

"Something has to be real," I said after a while.

"Something is real," Lucky said, unimaginably comforting.

Silence took over. And heat, the heat of the fire. And it was as if my thought had been transmitted to the others. Anyway, we all backed away from the conflagration and started laughing at once, Lucky, too, and Francie vomited, and so we all laughed more, watching one another through the increasing flames. Lucky vomited, too, but neatly. I escaped that fate, lately an expert at nausea, and there was inside me another giggling presence, the baby who would come back to Aunt Maria a man. After an hour what had been funny and light began to seem something grand and absurd, cells dividing inside me to make another person? Crazy. Then more absurd: Was this person me or not? I could almost feel him growing, formulating his own answer: Nope.

"We listen to the fire," Lucky said.

"We listen to the fire," I repeated.

"We listen to the fire," Franciella said.

So Lucky could proceed: "Hawk Mother," he said, not like praying, but only conversing.

I'm not kidding, the fire leapt at that and the sparks reached so vurry high, some raining back down, and the smile on my face seemed to apply to my whole body, which I felt floating, just ever so slightly floating off the earth. And then it struck me just what a great word *fire* was, a word that reached high all the way up into space and all the way to the sun, a word that dug down into the ground, and a word that was but letters, words being things unto themselves, and not only the things they attempted to say, a bottomless deep thought I couldn't quite follow, just that all the elements were one.

"Oh, Hawk Mother," said Franciella. She'd always made fun, but she had liked Maria during the healing time at the Junk Ranch after her rescue by Clay and did not seem to be making fun now. Because in the climbing light, in the surrounding warmth, in the smoke as well, Maria's presence was full and real. As the fire burned down we edged closer to the warmth, and Franciella closer to me and Lucky till we were in a knot, the flower of the clover, Lucky said, and we spent the night like that, the three of us blooming in awe of the single everything, or anyway, that was how Franciella said it, better than I.

"Send us wisdom," Lucky said.

"Send us Bronco," Francie said. "Send us chocolate in great amounts."

Lucky didn't like her kidding. He didn't like it one bit.

"I miss my dad," I said, to bring it back down.

And then we all sat there, the mood turned glum, my fault, the three of us more separate, holding on to our knees, edging closer to the fire as it died, that modicum of warmth as the sky lightened, lavenders and pinks and finally yellows and then the sun herself (Francie had said the sun was womanly), the fire to ashes, a sense of returning to something, not just Family Table but the mountain, the planet, a place we would never see the same way again.

Out of nowhere, Francie said, "She was small and fit and important in the village. She sat with the priest every morning. She visited the people who were struggling—the priest let her know in quiet ways. My *grandmère* didn't much like the priest, but she liked my mother visiting all the people, and that's how they got along, different centuries. My *grandpè* stayed to himself. My father was just a thought, a thought about New Jersey, and you'd hear that name on the radio sometimes or in a song, what's that guy."

"Bruce Springsteen," I said.

"Yes, and once my father sent a note to us. It made my mother so angry. But I kept it a while till Grandmère found it and buried it in the ground with a word. She didn't think he was so bad. Just American, which meant something like indifferent, not worse than that, but bad enough."

The coals of the spent fire were so layered, so many shades of heat. We stared a long time.

"My mom?" I said. But I couldn't finish and eventually said so.

"The fire heard you," Lucky said.

Francie said, "Yes, the fire, what's left of it."

And bluntly Lucky said, "Ms. Conover is my mother."

"Ha-ha," Francie said.

I took a long time to find words, finally said, "But you're serious."

"My Raven mother," he said.

"Your Raven mother," I repeated.

He said, "My Hawk mother is Maria."

"That's just a parable," I said.

"A parable?" Lucky said.

"A story. Like with a lesson. But still just a story."

Lucky stood and took a few steps away, crossed his arms over his chest, just seemed so calm, so settled in himself, and yet he'd stirred a great storm in me, of which he couldn't be oblivious (that's why he'd gotten up, stepped away), first a puff of wind, then a dark cloud, then chaos.

He was my husband, but I didn't know him. That had been a given till that moment, a kind of gentle given, that there were things about even the people closest to you that you didn't know, maybe couldn't know, but now it was more than a given, it was a kind of shuddering, monstrous truth, swallowing me up.

"View wants to be put in," Francie said, as much as to say that she had no clue what we were going on about.

"But Francie," I said. "Dora?"

"Yes, I know. It's too much to consider. Three years I typed for that lady and never one peep." She rose unsteadily and made an elliptical approach to the corral, seemingly forever.

I said, "Lucky."

And he said, "Wife."

I said, "Dora is your mother."

"Yup," he said quietly.

We watched as View greeted Francie, as Francie opened the bars of the gate to the corral, as View stepped in, as Chickadee greeted View. I said, "Lucky, sweetie, who are you, then?"

"I am Lucky Turtle," he said.

Not everything is what you think, as my dad would often say. It's what he said to my mother when I got in trouble, when all my secrets had come to light, said it in anger when she blew up, her anger uncontainable, said it as if it were she and not I at fault: *Not everything is what you think, Margie.* It hadn't made sense then, but it made sense now. *Not everything is what you think.* I couldn't hold the thought, however. I'd deal with the thought when I could. For now, sun heating the plains, the rising morning wind began and ashes rose from the firepit in small twisters, sparks flying inside them, making coils of light, the elements as one. I was alone, was my thought, I was nothing, like steam.

Francie made her way back, expired with a wooden clunk upon Family Table. I put her between me and Lucky, curled away from both of them. Lucky wafted back and climbed on, too, shipwrecked sailor on a raft, and I the stormy sea.

Chapter Forty-Seven

Early evening we woke famished, the world still a revelation of light and wind, but easier now, clarity almost cheerful. We rolled sheepishly off the table one by one by one, not clear what might be next. Lucky wandered a distance, just stood there, arms folded, searching the sky for birds. After outhouse, Francie toddled the other direction, then hurried—she'd gotten some kind of idea. I'd gotten good at pancakes now that there were eggs, and after thinking about them a long time, I got started, bustling between henhouse and lodge and perfect hot coals, making a triple batch, happy to be alone with the ingredients, the practical science, Robert Sing's magical powder pounded from rocks (later I'd learn it was called baking soda!), powdered milk, handfuls of flour, and water just so, the car-part griddle heated hot, greased with lard. Lucky, whistling his two notes like a nesting chickadee, collected sticks so as not to deplete our growing supply of firewood, tidied the firepit—ashes were everywhere. When my pancakes were done, he stirred the coals, added wood, called up flames. Francie returned with chinking material though she'd declared the chinking done, went out for berries, soon rushed back, only half a bucket, panicked: it was hard to be alone with your mind full of sticks and stars. She ducked into the henhouse, ducked out, T-shirt pouched full of all the eggs I hadn't taken. Lucky scrambled all of them atop our last piece of bacon, threw in a handful of the magic mushrooms, not a word. Pancakes and berries, bacon-y eggs, psilocybin, what was so hilarious about that? My tormentor was his mother: Donut Dora. There's a giggle that's a scream. We ate, every bite a revelation—we were machines

made of molecules that needed more molecules to keep going. The darkness in me receded further, nearly gone.

Shortly we heard an engine down in the valley, a kind of drumming.
Lucky, with his exquisite ears, could hear the skip of the fan belt and the
particular clonk of the bed on a broken bushing, knew what a bushing was,
knew that this was, at long last, Clay.

Clay's door slammed with its particular creak and ring. The man himself
trundled around the corner, a couple of packages in hand, clearly surprised
by my headlong race to greet him.

Clay said, "This is for you," and handed me a small package, just a rect-
angle of kraft paper tied in string, nice heft. I started to say something, but
he interrupted: "Just quick let me tell you. Open it on your own. You can
see the inside piece is addressed to Kristina Johman, is how we done it,
good friend in Sweden, but it's for you. You can see this piece here is post-
marked *from* Sweden. Is how your father done it, too. Your uncle musta
done the sending and sent it along to Kristina—that's who sent this piece
here, see—and number-one Johman son, Aimo, musta gave it to number-
three Johman son, Aarto, who brought it to me, and now here we are,
epistle in hand."

"Oh, Clay," I told him, "I haven't the faintest idea of what you're saying,"
and hugged his neck so hard he had to stretch it out when I let go.

"Okay, hi," Lucky said, three hot syllables, and wary.

"Yeah, boy, hi," Clay told him, his own three syllables, equally serious.

"Aarto?" Lucky said.

Clay nodded, these mysterious men.

Francie just stared.

I put the packet atop my belly under my big T-shirt, let it balance there,
a bit of my father close to his grandson as my thoughts continued to rush:
what a terrific grandpa he was going to be! My dad, my sweet dad.

"I'm sorry once again it's been so long," Clay mumbled, a prepared
speech to cover his discomfiture, as if we'd turned into different people.

And maybe we had, Lucky all erect and straightforward, Francie fit, me a few sizes larger around the middle, all of us glassy eyed. He offered the other package, which turned out to be a huge block of half-sweet chocolate. He must have been surprised again by our squeals of wonder, the way we tore the paper, put hands to the chocolate, felt it as if it were a beloved face and we were blind. His smile, it was like the sun coming out. And in the heat of the day the chocolate melted onto our fingers, smearing our faces thoroughly, a little too much shit looking not to be funny—shit that was some kind of holy, Clay looking on.

"US government surplus," he said to tamp us down a little. He didn't want us to think he'd gone out of his way for us. "Twenty pounds. Maria said get it. Even if it is just kitchen chocolate."

"Cindra asked out loud for chocolate just last night," Francie said.

"That was you!" I said.

Clay shrugged. He knew what Francie was getting at: Maria's powers. But Clay would deny being some kind of spiritual agent and Maria was just Maria and so it just wasn't something anyone was going to wax on about.

I felt my string-tied package, my private wish, balanced on my belly.

Down the hill, another door slammed.

"Something to tell you," Clay said.

Just then a strapping blond man turned the corner below, as startling as if the chocolate had gotten up and waltzed. At the sight of us, the man began to run. Then sprinting faster, a great athlete, he must be, racing that steep grade like that, and at altitude. He didn't stop either, but barreled right into Lucky, grabbed him up, threw him over his shoulder, made a few laps around the rest of us, poor Lucky bouncing like a lanky sack of beans.

"Ya, Aarto," Lucky kept saying, purely laconic.

The blond giant put him back on his feet, and the two of them embraced, Lucky still quiet, the stranger bouncing up and down in excitement, then reaching and grabbing Franciella impulsively—Franciella, who was not impulsive and resisted—then reaching again and catching me into the scrum, lifted us all off our feet, unalloyed enthusiasm, completely oblivious of how any of us might be feeling about things, strong and solid as a steam shovel.

Clay said, "Watch that one, Aarto—she's with child."

But baby was safe—what I'd been protecting was Daddy's gift.

Aarto let me go, trying to sober—we were the high ones!—couldn't do it, grabbed me up again, baby and package and all, fresh laughter, Lucky falling into it, too, face covered in chocolate, and then Franciella, same, laughing hard, all of us squeezed together. Daddy's gift box fell to the ground. I wriggled after it, and Clay helped me escape, grabbed the box, handed it back to me, he laughing now, too, not like him, but entirely like him, too, I guessed, both things at once. Now Aarto got Clay in a bear hug, and the two of them fell to the ground shouting with laughter, or maybe Clay was protesting: Aarto was enormous. Lucky joined the melee, a lot of rolling around, Aarto pinned but briefly, two men not enough. Slowly, slowly, we all subsided. At a safe distance, Franciella sat herself up. Aarto shook off his opponents, rose easily to his feet and went to her, helped her to her feet, a lot of muscular woman, nearly big as he, but seemingly light as air.

Suddenly they all seemed to see one another, and everything went serious.

"You're here," Franciella said. Her face said the rest: wishes didn't come true, not like that, how stupid, and how was she going to wish for something she'd never known and anyway didn't want? But the chocolate.

"I'm Aarto," the enormous man said heartily. Teeth like a beaver's!

Clay felt responsible, that you could just see, and he set himself square on his feet to give a speech to Francie and me.

"Aarto," he said, "is the grandson of old Aapo Johman, a great friend to Lucky's grandfather—who fate chased far—and, later, neighbor and protector to Lucky. Aarto in turn was best friend to Lucky, boyhood pals and partners in mayhem."

"Yes, true," Lucky said happily.

"I seek asylum," Aarto said, all but formally.

Clay liked that. "If you'll have him. Maria thought a week was about plenty at our house."

"If you'll have me," Aarto said truly.

Well, not much question of that: we would have him.

Clay seemed to think he had to sell the idea. He said, "Aarto's got his own tent and a good knife. And he's on the strong side, as you've not failed to witness. Plus he's a bit at loose ends."

We'd all edged down the trail alongside as Clay spoke, following him. Back at his truck he pulled out Aarto's backpack, as big and pregnant as I was. Aarto slipped into the straps easily. He would be ours! I felt the giggles rolling up inside me.

"Welp," Clay said, then remembered something. From under a shiny new grader blade in the bed of his truck, narrating all the way—he and Aarto had gone to an auction in Billings for cover in case they were watched—Clay dug out fresh gifts. First, twelve-packs of cheap T-shirts and panties, rainbow of colors, Billings Five and Dime. Then, a multipack of cheap soap. Next, he produced seven or eight grocery bags stuffed with brightly colored clothing, said, "Maria got these things at the church bazaar. Ten cents a sack. Treasure and Trash, it's called, and I guess she acquired a lot of both. You'll see."

Franciella and I ripped into the bags. Three old flannel shirts, size 3XB, worn soft at the cuffs and collars by some enormous stranger. Next, a pair of pink overalls, which Clay called "overhauls," Maria's try at maternity wear. But I dropped my Challenge pants right there and changed, like heaven, that soft denim, and just the pinkness of the pink. And Francie pulled on an outsize pair of gray college sweatpants, GRIZZLIES emblazoned in huge bloodred letters down one leg.

"How about that," Aarto said.

"Ten cents a sack," Clay repeated. And while Aarto and Lucky dug through the next bag—a towel, a pair of winter-looking boots maybe my size, a pullover sweatshirt, Grizzlies again, Clay poked me with a Bic pen, handed me almost secretively a pale green spiral notebook, then the pen itself, then three pencils with erasers, one at a time.

I hugged Clay's poor neck again, put the package from my father and the glorious notebook and holy pencils in my new and capacious overhaul pockets.

"It were but ten cents a bag," Clay repeated yet again.

Lucky grew serious: "We got a man tracking us," he said.

"Well, not tracking," Francie said. "He *found* us."

"Dale Drinkins," Lucky said. "That's his name."

Clay flinched, and I could practically hear his dear heart shift, saw the blood pulsing in his neck, the hot color coming to his cheeks, emotion like a rifle shot. He gathered his thoughts a moment.

"Okay, now listen," he said. "I don't know the man, but I've heard of him, all right. He's trying to get standing with them militia boys. He's got truck with the Nations. Some think he's one of them killed those women up there at Blackfeet, not that the law is pressing to find out. A bunch of them been harassing Maria and me all these years, running off my horses, and harassing Dora, too, well, harassing everyone who isn't one of them, filing claims against all our deeds, these historic ranches, chasing me up to Challenge, stopping Dora on the road. It came to an end there after what happened to Lucky when he was little, and what happened to Far Turtle, no charges filed, Lucky will remember, but now it's started up again, this questing for natural resources, as they call the rain and the gold, and of course the range wars eternal, and now this natural gas, unnatural as it is, and their belief that it's meant for them as white men predestined, and I believe he's one of them, having moved on from simple mischief to outright fraud and misrepresentation. All innocent at the County Ag meeting with his son, but then I come out and my tires are slashed. Their threats are no match for Maria, of course. She tells me ignore 'em. Works for her! But a bunch of them have started back in harassing Dora, too, up there at Challenge. They're making much of you missing girls. Trying to gin up some kind of forfeiture having to do with negligence, some nonsense like that. One's up for judge, Dean Kellogg. Another has been sheriff a long time now, a Mr. Brown. And the mayor of Elk River, what's his name, little glad-hander. They ganged up and voted him in. Drinkins, he'd like to think he's one of them. And if he's up here finding you it's not coinciden-shal, I can tell you that. A scheme is afoot."

"I can handle Dale Drinkins," Francie said.

"We'll push east," Lucky said. "We'll pack up today and go."

"Mr. Drinkins has got a crush," I said, not wanting to push east, whatever that might mean. "He's got a crush on Francie." That sounded like a song, so I said it again, almost singing: "Mr. Drinkins has got a crush. He's got a crush on Francie!"

Clay stroked his chin, much to consider, this distasteful world. He said, "Well, that I don't doubt. He's a ladies' man, all right, but it never comes out good for the ladies. I mentioned those Blackfeet gals, didn't I?"

Francie appealed to Lucky. "It's best we keep him close, then."

Lucky wouldn't keep her eye. So she appealed to Aarto, stepped up in his face. She said, "It's best we keep him close."

"Dale Drinkins got a crush," I sang. "He's got a crush on Francie."

"Quiet, now," Aarto said.

Clay said, "He's nobody's friend, miss, and for him a crush will just turn cruel. You'd do well to keep him not so much close as at bay."

At bay? Handle him? Push east? More lines for my song. Aarto the size of a Norse god with teeth to match. Nothing made sense. The taste of the mushrooms filled my being, metal at my tongue. Lucky was trying to say something, and I knew what it would be: "We gotta move on."

I gasped, bolt of light, our solution right at hand: Aarto was Bronco!

"Listen," Clay said sharply. "Drinkins is no lark. He made trouble at Crow Agency way back when, he made trouble up there at Blackfeet more recent. What's he doing always there where he's not supposed to be? He's visiting this person and that person unwelcomely and why? The tribal police used to arrest him for lurking and trespassing and harassment of this kind and that, but since he's not Native they have to turn him over to the county, and the sheriff drops charges. He made trouble up in Kalispell, too, truckload of fillies. Who all get arrested, while he heads home. He's lowered his profile but he's upped the ante, is my guess. You listen to me, you kids. He's eyeing that Free Men's Militia. He's trying to get standing and won't stop at nothing. The Free Men are against the very existence of Native anything, even the Reservations, those old accords. But they can only chip at the edges, you know, as Reservation law is strong, and it's Federal, where they can't touch. They think they're living in 1880, trying to undo all that, and maybe they are, maybe they did turn back the clock. It's getting hard for Maria even to bowl without some jackass saying something invidinous. She can shut 'em down with a glance, that one. But try being a young Crow these days, just going about your business."

"Yes, try that," Lucky said.

"Aarto is Bronco!" I nearly shouted. Why didn't Clay get it?

Lucky did. His mouth opened like something had exploded inside it.

Francie, too. She began to bounce.

"Bronco!" they said together, extravagant whispers, repeated it.

Clay lectured on, his perfect control cracking along with his voice. "Dale Drinkins did not just happen upon you folks up here and that's what I have to say."

I said, "Don't you get it? We can stay right here! Bronco has arrived!"

Clay deflated like a knifed tire, studied our faces: we'd gone crazy, that was obvious, cabin fever, mountain madness. He shook his head. He cleared his throat. He scratched under his hat like a boulder about to talk, and that was funny, too. Finally, seeing all was lost, he said, "Okay, I didn't want to scare anyone, but best say it: police have come by the homestead four times looking for Lucky, looking for you."

At that, Francie plucked the big Stetson out of Clay's hands, punched the careful pinch out of its crown, plunked it on Aarto's head. Aarto grinned despite himself, those beaver incisors, took a cowboy stance, hands on hips, head thrown back. He yodeled, enormous teeth like Chiclets. Big, professional fists. He took a clownish bow like he was in on the game.

"Bronco," we cried.

"Aarto, don't encourage 'em," Clay said. "You're supposed to be the sensible addition."

Aarto tried to look serious.

"Gotta go," Clay said. He turned hard away from us, climbed in his truck, started it up and rolled out of there, that broken bushing banging.

The trees above us shook with wind.

Chapter Forty-Eight

The next morning was old by the time Lucky and I rose. We'd pretty well melted into each other in the night after an early bedtime, no supper but the chocolate, discovered new corners of compatibility in misplaced districts of our psyches, our bodies. For a while we'd called back and forth with Franciella in her unfinished room. Francie, who kept excoriating Clay over the issue of Mr. Drinkins. Aarto had refused mushrooms and gone off into the gathering dusk with his bedroll and backpack to make camp up by the spires—he wanted first sun come morning. I felt so good and safe in bed, just that that huge Viking was up there watching over us. I reasoned with Francie—Clay had made good points—all the while pushing the thought of Momma Dora away. Quietly I petted my husband whom I loved so much, however he was made. Francie shut up after a while and shortly snored, then outslept us.

The morning was bright, but I'd had ominous dreams and a formless dread lingered. Shortly, though, there was a whoop and the heightening beat of size 16 huaraches pounding the dry earth. Aarto and Lucky were immediately boys again, a lot of shouting and laughter, the two of them racing up the mountain with hatchet and machete and Lucky's trusty knife to find a certain kind of tree. Francie, foul mood, went back to lichen-chinking her bedroom. I rather frenetically—my brain and bones feeling fried—made yet another batch of biscuits, the two of us calling back and forth.

"Dale brought us apples," she kept saying.

"Apples have a kind of bad history," I said.

She said, "Yes, I guess. And there was that little folded fuck-you clipping."

I said, "Blackmail, basically. Or barter. He's a poacher for real. He's try-ing to poach you, my love. Or trade us for some favor in town."

"But our power is in knowing all that. Knowing all that, we control him. We turn him loyal. He helps us. Doesn't turn us in or whatever it is he has in mind."

"He has Francie in mind."

"And so, you see, we get to stay."

Her argument seemed suddenly compelling. To stay was all I wanted.

We could hear the men up there under the cliff, chopping and slashing and hooting. Soon they were back with long wands of pale wood to set soaking in the brook, Aarto glistening with sweat, his shirt discarded.

"Shouldn't that man be in a museum," Francie said.

I didn't want to like Aarto either, competition for Lucky's affection, but what a specimen! I said, "He's Bronco, no four walls can contain him!"

"He's awful," she said. "Those teeth. He could bite down trees and make a dam."

Lucky had told me the plan. The plan was that we'd make a plan soon, with Aarto, who understood such things, since Clay thought we shouldn't stay. If Drinkins never returned, we could call it a false alarm. Clay had had to make an extreme case so that we'd heed him even a little, was Lucky's theory. But, Lucky said, putting his weight on me forwardly, we lovers were wise, two heads better than one, two hearts. And then in the night he'd whispered in case the snores were a cover: "Francie's but one and thinks for herself, mistakes her powers. Clay is part of Maria and thinks for them, mistrusts the youngers, mistakes their powers."

I whispered, too: "And what about Aarto?"

"Aarto won't mistake his powers but use them for me, his old friend who knew his father, and for you and for us." Meaning the baby.

"So you're saying you don't think Francie can control Mr. Drinkins, but that despite what Clay's saying, you and Aarto can."

"Yes, exact."

Noontime, their switches cut and soaking, whatever project in progress, the boys mounted the horses and galloped like movie stars up into the
mountain. Poor View seemed strained under that giant of a man, but he
knew Aarto and served him gladly—more old friends.

"Ugh, why?" Francie asked as we bent in the garden. "Why do we need
Aarto?"

I'd been arguing that a feast was in order, a feast for our new friend. I
said, "Bronco, you mean."

Later in the afternoon the boys came thundering back, basket of
brightly speckled trout from some far brook, survival baskets they'd
woven themselves that selfsame afternoon from reeds Aarto knew. They'd
cleaned the fish where they'd caught them so bears could feed far from us,
fish guts being fragrant and a lure, bears bringing luck, if not too close.
They'd cut prickly pear, too, found some un-magic mushrooms for eating,
just the sight of which made my brain prick and sparkle.

We built up the fire and made a true feast as night came in, and a chill,
the mountain season changing. Aarto had a magic trick where he'd palm
a biscuit somehow and make it disappear, then find it again on Francie's
shoulder, on top of her head, on the knee of her new sweatpants. She
laughed reluctantly, then less so, and after a while the two of them laughed
so hard they couldn't eat, closer and closer on their side of the table. The
fish was cooked a way Aarto knew and better than how I'd done it in earlier
days, so crisp that you ate the skin, too, the skeletons coming out whole.
The prickly pear was sweet and juicy and the strangest thing I'd ever tasted,
a roasted fruit. And mushrooms in their own broth, hearty as beef stock.
Aarto made a rice pudding, too, full of raisins Clay had delivered. As for
me there was the new jug of vinegar, like ambrosia to sip and with which to
dress my greens and small carrots and the many wild things, and everyone
shouted with indignation when I said it was only mine.

Late, we sat with our backs to each other, four-leaf clover on Family
Table, and talked head-to-head-to-head-to-head, necks all thrown back to
touch temples and crowns and watch for shooting stars, shouted at each

display. Aarto explained meteor showers, said this one was called Perseid. But Lucky had grown moody: it seemed we took turns doing that.

"Who really knows the doings of the stars?" he said.

"Let's tell stories," Francie said, bless her.

"Our stories are all the same," Lucky said. "Rock stays still, river moves."

We thought about that, our backs all stiff against one another suddenly, the flow of time all around us.

"Aarto, okay," Francie said quickly. "Guess my story."

"You're Haitian from New Jersey," Aarto said. "Clay told me."

"Is that my story? Is it really? In Haiti they called me the American. When I was a little girl."

"Well, it's your sort-of story. When I was in Haiti, I was also the American."

"You big Swede. You were in Haiti? Why?"

"The American intervention, do you recall? To put Aristide back in power."

"I don't recall. Not at all. My sort-of story. And 'American intervention'! What an awful phrase! But what were *you* doing there?"

"Well, to understand, you have to know I'm a dual US and Swedish citizen."

Francie squirmed so hard I thought the rest of us would fall off the table: "Part awful, part lawful," she said.

Aarto took a breath that filled his trunk and pushed us apart farther yet.

"He's Special Forces," Lucky said darkly.

"They put me in with the Swedish peacekeepers, but I'm US military. I admit it. Lucky, I admit it. It's a secret, okay, don't tell. But freely I admit it."

Francie pressed back into us by way of a promise: she'd never tell. "But wait just a second. How old were you? How old are you now?"

"Not so old. I was twenty-three."

"So you're what, like middle aged? I'm seventeen. Well, eighteen before long."

"Only eighteen? You wear it strong." Phrases like that in their odd-ness made you hear Aarto's accent. He saw we were amazed at how old he was, at his military exploits, continued on more proudly, clearly annoying Lucky, whose back stiffened once again: "So, my dear Francie, if you and I had been seen together in Haiti, people would have all pointed and said, Look at the Americans!"

"And maybe, Kill the Americans!"

"And we'd shout, Wrong Americans!"

The stars were so particular above. We pressed our backs hard together, spines and muscle, the strangest feeling.

Aarto said, "I am just back from Guatemala, a verification mission, wrong Swedish!"

"Swede!" Francie corrected, so boisterously.

"Yes," Aarto said, "wrong either way. We were peacekeepers in the hot-test spots, and it was rough. I've been a lot of places. Somalia was one, the year before your Haiti. And Bosnia-Herzegovina before that. In Sarajevo I was undercover, you might say, still US Special Forces, but I could go where the Swedish peacekeepers went. Peacekeepers were unarmed. We had white helmets. We had the Swedish flag on our shirts. We took fire. My job was to take the insoorgents out."

"Insurgents," Francie corrected, not so boisterous. "You took them out?"

"When we were fired upon, yes. That was my job. At night to go find them. Not very peacekeeper, more US Special Forces."

I said, "Lucky, what year were you born? You always say you don't know."

Lucky was silent, shoulders gone square.

"Younger than me," Aarto said. "By less than a year. Like Irish twins."

I said, "How old are you, Lucky Turtle?"

"Younger than him," Lucky said, nodding his head back to bump Aarto's, the old friend clearly bugging him.

"I'm twenty-five," Aarto said quite proudly.

"Old man!" Francie said.

"Francie and I are seventeen," I said again.

"So Lucky's like, what, twenty-four?" Francie said. "Lucky? You're like twenty-four?"

"We're who we are, just the same," Lucky said.

Why did my chest roar? My ears pound? He wasn't wrong: he was still just Lucky. And in my heart, of course I'd known he was older.

"You killed people," Franciella said to Aarto.

"As I was trained," Aarto said. "Just those that presented a mortal threat, however." These things he spoke of had just happened, when you thought about it, recent history.

"And now you're back," I said.

"Yes, now I'm back. They fly you where you want to go upon discharge, honorable. I hurried to Maria's. I needed her medicine. That's all I can say. I needed her hand on my shoulder. I've done wrong. I can't even tell you all of it."

"We don't want to know *any* of it," I said.

"Yes, you've said enough for now," Francie said.

Aarto gestured in the air above us. His hands were enormous. I kept noticing them. He had an accent only when passionate, like he was singing the American words, perfect English however, nearly always—he'd grown up with my husband, was taken back to Sweden by his mom, this Kristina, only after Lucky was shot, I remembered that now, Aarto being part of Lucky's story.

"I'm discharged from Swedish service, too," he said. "Gold Medal of Merit with Swords. Highest honor in Sweden. I won't brag, not much. But we Swedish are the peacekeepers. The US won't acknowledge me, of course. That was my work. The peace was my intention."

Francie twisted and craned, examined his face. She said, "How did you kill them? The people who presented mortal danger?"

He raised his hands up high above our four-leaf clover, flexed them open, squeezed them back to fists, flexed them open, touched his fingertips to form a large sphere, which he then collapsed, sudden force.

"I can't say," he said. "I took a vow. Now I'm honorably discharged, and it was all a secret, though here I am telling you too much. I was a peace-keeper. And now the peace is won. That's all you get to know."

A dozen stars fell, marked the passing time.

I said, "Did you know Dora?" My own train of thought.

"Of course," Aarto said. "She was the boss up there on the butte."

Lucky shifted away from us. I put a hand on his leg to keep him beside me, but he rose. "Hoppo!" he said, a call to action aimed at Aarto—they'd talked earlier of night-climbing up in the spires, as if there weren't danger enough.

Our clover leaf broke up.

But Aarto wasn't going along with Lucky, only laughed. The firelight caught something in his face, high cheekbones, strong chin. He was no lug, manikin handsome as he was. His teeth threatened to push open his lips and let his secrets fall out. I can't forget the teeth.

"Did seeing Maria help?" Francie said to him, suddenly soft, soft like I'd never seen. "Maria had the right words?" Her own face was full and bright, her hair just so, and the preternatural eyebrows—had she been primping?

Yes, she'd been primping!

"I am forgiven," Aarto said.

He took Lucky's hand, pulled him forcefully back down to sitting, took my hand, pulled our hands together under his own. Francie added hers, this durable-looking knot, four hands.

"We're the wrong Americans," she said.

"We wear it strong," Aarto said.

"All forgiven," Lucky said grumpily.

But Aarto had won him over.

And under the stars we clasped all our hands together and bowed so our foreheads were touching, closing together like the prickly pear flowers did at night up among the rocks in the meadow tops.

After a while Francie said, "Cindra, get the quill. Get your little knife so we can sharpen it," a comic command.

Even Lucky laughed. Slowly we all got up, bowed to one another, knights of the Family Table, no ladies. The men peed off in the weeds like boys, great splashing disregard. We women were more private. In the lodge I found the package from my father, held it, kissed it—I'd open it sometime when I was alone. The hawk quill had frayed, the berry ink was used up, the night was no longer young. But wait. Oh my gosh, wait. The new notebook, the Bic pen! A little sparkling psilocybin flashback, an extended giggle, nothing funny exactly, then a kind of charged weariness. It was a dress-up night! I found my pearl, strung it about my neck, expert with the clasp, tied a kid-knitted scarf from one of Maria's ten-cent bags around my waist. We hadn't yet used our candles but tonight was all about light, and you couldn't conserve everything forever—in the drawer of the little table by the brave stove I found two stout blue ones, gritty from long storage, stuck them under my arm. Back at Family Table, I set them in knotholes. Aarto pulled his big Zippo out, military emblem memorable, metallic snap of its lid, explosion of flame. I opened the virgin notebook, surprised to see my own handwriting. Apparently I'd done some doodling the night before after Clay had left, crossed out false starts. I turned to a clean page, made a title:

THE STORY OF YOU

The blue Bic ink was so strong and so thick and so blue after the poison-berry ink, the lines it made so true. I held it hovering.

"Your story," Francie said to Lucky.

Stars fell.

Lucky's voice, his particular growl: "I am Lucky Turtle, grandson of Far Turtle, who was called Robert Sing, and who was from Shenzhen, Guangdong, south China, an ocean city."

I said, "So your last name isn't Turtle, but Sing?"

"Yes, Sing," Aarto said. "The rest meant Lucky Turtle, but it's lost."

"It's not lost," Lucky said. "Only forgotten. Grandfather said he'd tell me when I was married. But then he died."

"Wait," I said.

"Let him tell," Francie said.

"Let him tell? I had no idea, Chinese. First Dora? Then you're twenty-four? Now this?"

"What's the difference?" Francie said. "Just write."

Aarto spelled the Chinese city, the province.

Lucky's grandfather, Chinese!

I wrote down the place-names through gathering tears: Chinese was fine, Chinese plus Dora was fine, but misleading everyone was not. I saw again Lucky's embrace with Ms. Conover, as he called her, that hug in the garage lot at Challenge, now explained.

"Carry on," Francie said to Lucky.

And Lucky did, Aarto filling in more and more till it was just Aarto talking, the comforting Bic pen flying. The gist, some I'd heard before, not all, not all at *all*:

Lucky's grandfather, Far Turtle, paid to be stowed away in a barrel and smuggled into the Port of San Francisco, year unknown, but likely mid-1920s. He took the name Robert—he'd always been Sing, the rest now forgotten, though it meant Far Turtle—made his way to Seattle and soon found work on the Great Northern Railroad, became a foreman on the repair crew—the able ones rose fast because workers died daily. Within a few years he was maintenance boss, the highest a nonwhite could rise, and assigned a task no one higher up in the company wanted, to meet the Crow delegation at a government hearing. The new spur to Billings had illegally crossed Crow land, some problem like that. The hearing was a lost cause. Far Turtle took the Crow side, got fired as soon as the executives heard. So in brotherhood the delegation brought him back to the winter village, and the tribe took him in. Soon he met Walks Far. And soon again they became close, shared shelter through the long winter, even took in her youngest sister, Maria, only ten, neglected baby of their enormous extended family, already a talent on horseback, beloved of Walks Far. The idyll was short lived: Far Turtle had brought sickness, or anyway was blamed, and Walks

Far died in the spring along with a dozen other young people. Far Turtle was banished, left the reservation south on foot, and even mourning, wanting to die himself, he found his way around the imposing but auspiciously named Turtle Butte and south again to the Johman Ranch and Aapo Johman, whom he knew as a friend to the Nation, soon to be his own spirit brother. Aapo was Aarto's grandpa, always called the Swede.

In her own mourning, poor Maria, now eleven, dove inward, focused on her love of horses, remained in her sister's dwelling, separated herself from her family and the greater community as best she could—she was a kid, after all, and needed looking after—so furious at Far Turtle's banishment. She rebelled, went Christian, dropped her Crow name never to say it again, took the name Maria, communed with horses, and after a few isolated years rode her favorite several days into Billings, where the Sisters of Christian Charity took her in, still a horse-and-buggy operation, and where the girl (not incidentally) could tend to their teams.

"Wait," Francie said. "She lived alone at eleven?"

"Well," Aarto said, "no one was alone on the Reservation, not really."

"She lived alone," Lucky said. "Because her heart was with Walks Far."

"And she rode her horse for days?"

"Just so," Lucky said.

Lucky's grandfather, feeling himself a burden to Aapo and family in that drought time, ventured back to San Francisco where he rented a stall at one of the precursors to the Alemany Farmer's Market with the last of his railroad cash. He sold oranges from the San Fernando Valley at little profit but also ran a game of pai gow. Trickier than poker, it looked harmless as dominoes to the city inspectors, the occasional cop. He made a small fortune, then over the years a large one, spent almost none of it, lived in a hovel by the tracks, kept American bills in a carefully modified orange crate, visions of Walks Far both day and night.

As the Great Depression wore on, less and less profit to be had, Far Turtle returned to Montana, used his fortune to buy the hopeless and isolated Turtle Butte from the Swede, who in friendship divided it off from his more productive ranchlands to the south. The price was exactly the amount in Far Turtle's money belt, minus enough to build some sheds, bring in livestock, shore up the rude settler's hut, one day perhaps to build a home, raise a family, if home and family would be Far Turtle's fate. The deed went in Joh Johman's name, the Swede's son (Aarto's father!), then a young man, because nonwhite individuals and especially Chinese could not own land, not at that time. The rest was all handshakes. Far Turtle spent the summer and fall up on the Butte, hunting, fishing, nursing his broken heart—Walks Far had been his one true love. Come cold weather he returned to San Francisco, rebuilt his gambling enterprise.

Over time young Maria became the Orphan School's entry in the local rodeo, a champion barrel racer at fifteen or sixteen, also a beauty that the sisters protected with iron determination. On the ever-expanding rodeo circuit she met one Clay Marvelette, already legendary, scion of one of the vast old historic ranches, mistrusted by the Sisters of Christian Charity but known to be a perfect gentleman, moot in any case: whites did not mix romantically with Indians. The Montana anti-miscegenation law of 1909 had seen to that.

But one rodeo season followed another, and when his family's drought-broken old ranch came to Clay upon his father's unexpected death and his mother's abdication, he invited Maria to come share it with him, even brought a tourist's crashed mobile home to the ranch, made repairs, perched it on an outcropping of rock so his beloved could see back to the Nation, where her heart still dwelt with Walks Far. He was sixteen, she perhaps a little older. They raised horses, grew what little food, hunted the rest, traded in scrap metal, scratched out a living, rode as a show pair on the rodeo circuit, their love an open secret—happy people, as Lucky called them.

Though he was some ten years older, Joh Johman was a frequent visitor to the burgeoning Junk Ranch, gift of cattle from his father, gift of horses, gift of companionship. For Clay and Maria's part, they found Joh a rodeo girl from Miles City, Kristina Coolidge, tough and robust, and attended the horseback wedding.

Another wedding guest was Far Turtle, with another open secret: he owned Turtle Butte. Maria rejoiced at their reunion, and the old railroad man spent several weeks with them at Marvelette Ranch, trips up to the butte to plan: he lacked only a helpmate, though no doubt he might find someone in San Francisco, where reluctantly he returned. He'd have been barely forty, Clay not even twenty, Joh not thirty, both of the younger men potential cannon fodder: the talk was of the war in Europe, the Battle of Britain raging. Norway had fallen to the Nazis, and Joh was enraged that Sweden had stayed neutral, though Aapo was sanguine: How bad could it be? Plenty to argue over. Soon there'd be a draft. The boys spoke of enlisting, should it come to that, and surely it would. The couples put off dreams of family: children would have to wait.

After Japan bombed Pearl Harbor, Far Turtle down there in San Francisco felt himself subtly, then fiercely, unwelcome in the city and, despite a patriotic impulse as the US entered the war, unable to enlist—illegal alien—and so in the summer of 1942, among hoboes in a boxcar, he returned to Montana, not too far from the new Japanese internment camp at Heart Mountain in Wyoming, if you want to understand his reception. Clay and Joh had indeed taken up arms by then, already shipped out, the African theater about to explode. Far Turtle didn't dare show himself in town but helped Maria Marvelette and Kristina Johman keep their respective ranches going. He abandoned the settler's hut, built a modest but proper home on Turtle Butte, dreamed of raising a family there: Maria said that would happen, once their ranchers came home, and she was confident they would, that all of them would at last raise families together.

After the war, Joh and Clay indeed returned home, silent about their experiences but not undamaged. Far Turtle continued on, hermit of the butte. The years passed. Far Turtle helped on the ranches, he prepared for his promised family, he grew more and more isolated, though in dreams he saw turtle children. But where could he go to find a wife? In town he was heckled and chased.

On the Johman Ranch a child was born to tragedy, far from any hospital: Kristina hemorrhaged and died, but baby Aimo lived, Aarto's oldest sibling. Joh waited a decent seven years, invited a second cousin from the village of Arild in Sweden to come be his wife. Old Aapo arranged it: that was the way. The new Kristina was less robust than the first, practically a child herself, not so happy on horseback, but cheerful and excitable and dazzled by cowboy Joh and soon another wedding. The baby, when it came, would be called Aapo after its grandpa: the Swede had been matchmaker, the Swede had been midwife, the Swede was entitled.

Maria and Clay never did have a child, weren't able, not something polite people discussed.

One year, finally, there was a thresher to pick up off the docks in San Francisco, freight charges to avoid. Far Turtle and Joh drove down together, apparently a trip of deep philosophy and meaning, these two serious men. And in San Francisco Joh announced he was leaving his old friend there. "Return to us married," he said.

San Francisco was utterly changed, pai gow no longer a safe occupation. The Paulist Brothers of St. Mary's took Far Turtle in, heart of the city. Once again he was Robert Sing. You found your destiny by being of help, and there was no end of refugees, runaways, beatniks, addicts, bums. He translated where he could (he did speak hobo, along with several Chinese dialects, scraps of Crow, also poetry, which bridged every gap), helped the monks build a soup kitchen, became their employee, lived in a tiny flat they provided.

"You guys," I said.

"Just write," Francie said. "Nothing has changed."

"Everything has changed."

"Only perception," Francie said.

I thought about that, said, "What else have we got?"

Again a sparkling resurgence of the psilocybin: we listeners were all feeling it.

"Write," Francie said.

I wrote, the ball of the Bic dreamy-smooth on the precisely lined paper, kept stealing glances at Lucky, who fidgeted, unlike him. He studied Aarto closely: What revelations were next?

Well, there was the question of the boy who would become Lucky's father. Lucky thought Walks Far had had a son and that Maria had cared for that son. Maria had always denied this, Aarto said, and the timing would be impossible, decades off, but Lucky was a person who believed what he believed. Aarto let him say his piece, claim his aunt. Lucky was also a person who didn't argue, just let Aarto have his turn. And Aarto didn't correct Lucky, exactly, instead offered his parallel story, which he told with flair and gravitas, tales handed down: there'd been a woman in San Francisco, a victim of marital abuse who'd come to the church in distress, run away from Florida. Aarto's father had always said the woman was Black.

"He wanted to explain me," Lucky said.

"No one ever could," Aarto said kindly.

"You guys," I said.

"Just write," Francie said.

The woman's name was Martha Jefferson, and she stayed in the woman's shelter a while, became indispensable in the church, was known for her intellect, wrote poetry, wrote song lyrics that Far Turtle sang into old age. No, Aarto didn't know any. She was near forty but soon pregnant, and the unlikely couple took a pretty apartment at the edge of old Chinatown, where no one minded their living together. Well, one person: the remorseful husband she'd left back in Tampa, constant letters, promises. This would have been 1954. They named the baby boy Thomas, after her father. In Far Turtle's heart the child was American Turtle always, but wanting to fit in, Thomas would eventually reject that name. When baby was two, Far Turtle moved his family to Turtle Butte. Martha hated it there from the start. Like Far Turtle, she could not go into town, not even for church: a movement had arisen, soon to be called the Free Men, and it was racist, white supremacist, anti-intellectual, nationalist, misguided. Martha and Far Turtle lasted not more than a year there, lonely and at odds, then, baby Thomas in tow, back to San Francisco. Where something again had changed. The Paulist

Brothers were not so welcoming, a new bishop: there were fears of communism to consider, and not only miscegenation. The letters from Martha's husband came rubber-banded together, dozens at a time, crazy old fool, she called him, but a little too fondly. Then one night, Thomas barely out of diapers, Martha Jefferson was gone, nothing but an apologetic note, never to be heard from again: the bishop had told her to rejoin her husband, rejoin him at all costs.

"Her name was May," Lucky said. "And Jefferson was only that husband's name."

Aarto nodded, and I noticed: Lucky knew the story. He knew the story well.

But it was Aarto who continued: for Robert Sing, Far Turtle, it was back to pai gow. Nothing like the profits of his earlier reign, and beatings now from both police and competition, protection money extracted by the sudden gangs, no more pretty apartment, but back to the shack encampment near the railyard.

Years passed, just father and son, a couple of attempts at living in Montana, the boy in constant trouble wherever they went, unable to stay in school—mixed-race children were not truly welcome either place. When he was twelve, Maria bought Thomas a box camera, nearly a toy. But he found himself in that lens, documented everything around them. And back to San Francisco, another makeshift shack. Robert Sing found ways to run his game, and pai gow paid for film, for cameras, some new piece of equipment every year.

Calling in a debt, sometime in the spring of 1971, Far Turtle got Thomas a job as apprentice to the Chinese gardener of a great mansion where a movie mogul lived. The mogul housed starlets there, far from the safety of their parents, and one of them was Dora Dryden Conover, who'd been in many films and TV shows as the best friend, as the perky deb, as the devoted daughter, soon to become Donut Dora on *The Karter Kids*, oh my god. That's me saying that. Aarto was unimpressed; Lucky claimed never to have seen the show; Francie had seen it all right, found it stupid.

But cut to the chase: Thomas and Dora met on the grounds of that mansion and fell in love. She later often spoke of his beauty. A secret love enacted, as I imagined it, in the cabanas of the swimming pool, in the garden shacks, in the billiards room when the mogul was off on one of his many trips. All of which came to a shocking end when the mogul was busted by his fourth wife for molesting half a dozen child actresses kept in various mansions around the world. Dora was just one of them.

The newspapers portrayed Dora as a temptress, the mogul her victim. Of course, her career was ruined, while his continued on. Her parents made many attempts to collect her after that, but she'd run off with Thomas to the shack by the railyards, tight quarters, so romantic, unfindable. Far Turtle was already past his sixties, when you think about it, their teacher and nurse and cook and cleaner and guardian, kindly, compassionate, permissive by default. How Dora must have stood out in those grimy alleys! She and Thomas spent indolent days in the shack while Robert ran his game, spent their midnights in the Haight, the summer of love having faded to a tawdry scene, certainly drugs. Also, Dora's notoriety: a hundred schemes were hatched, rockers and players and conmen abounded. But Thomas had a head on his shoulders, as Aarto put it, quoting family lore: Dora was going to get back into movies, on her own terms, and under Thomas Sing's camera.

Dora's parents must have hated the photos: *Time* magazine, just for one, and every tabloid, the most lurid stories: the Donut Girl and her exotic-looking lover, rumored variously to be a pimp, an opium addict, a pinko. The Conovers, prairie nobility, hired a detective, who bludgeoned Thomas and stuffed Dora in a car in front of the Filmore West on a show night, spirited her back home to the Midwest, threats of more violence if he tried to find her. Devastated, nothing for it, all of eighteen, still ambitious for his camera, and perhaps wanting to impress Dora's folks, Thomas signed on with the Department of the Army's Special Photographic Office as a photo assistant, a soldier, that is, if somewhat glorified, soon shipped to Vietnam, where within months his unit was wiped out. Suddenly—Imagine this,

Aarto said—he was a combat photographer, the youngest ever to serve, bumped to sergeant, then lieutenant on the basis of his courageous and yet loyal documentation. Meanwhile Dora, newly sixteen, found she was pregnant, and her parents insisted she abort. She feigned obedience, traveled with them to Mexico, left the clinic via a side door, nothing but a hospital gown, thumbed her way back to the States, back to San Francisco, back to Robert Sing, Far Turtle, the only loving care she'd ever known.

To escape her parents, to protect her from all the malign forces, to keep her safe till Thomas's return, Far Turtle took her to Montana, where he and his daughter-in-law made a home up there on the butte. Joh Johman, son of Aapo, started them off with a few head of cattle. Clay, now married to Maria officially (the Montana anti-miscegenation law having been repealed in 1953) gave him horses and a series of rescued farm vehicles. Donut Dora took to ranch life, pregnant on horseback, the apple of Far Turtle's eye, finally a queen. Far Turtle imagined his son's chastened return from Vietnam, imagined that the family would take up ranching, maybe make movies: What place more beautiful for that? Then word came that Thomas had been killed in action, those famous last images of ARVN fighters bursting into his tent.

Not long after that, in October 1972, Dora gave birth to their son.

"And that was me," Lucky said.

"Wrong American," Aarto and Francie sang.

"You guys," I said. "Not funny. I want to talk. I want to talk about *perception*."

But Aarto took up the story again: After Far Turtle's friend (and Aarto's grandpa), Aapo, died, Lucky just a few months old, Far Turtle took over Aapo's sheep operation, a scant living in wool and lambs. Dora found she enjoyed training the horses, riding the horses, working with the cattle. Joh Johman had two grown sons, Aimo with Kristina the first, Aapo II with the second and current Kristina, also a small child, their accident, and that was Aarto, who they felt had the spirit of Aapo I, the Swede. As the years passed, Kristina and Dora became friendly. Aarto and Lucky played all day. Robert Sing and Joh Johman and Joh's older sons and Clay Marvelette worked side by side by side on all three enormous ranches, mutual benefit, a great neighborly enterprise that attracted attention for its success: a Chinese, a Swede, the Injun-loving junkman Clay. The bad wheels, already long in motion, began to turn faster, hastened by the spike in gold and copper prices and the search for rare metals needed in electronics (palladium, molybdenum, lithium, and good old Montana platinum)—trespassing speculators dropped test pits everywhere, but especially where they thought the owners less than human. Corporate purses were unlimited, and greed unlimited, too. Word got out: Turtle Butte was practically made of metal, no one up there but coolies and whores and half-breeds.

High atop that great hidden wealth, and so far oblivious, Dora got an idea. Starting with the few small buildings, Clay's horses and machinery, and all good intentions, she began a camp for girls who found themselves in trouble as she'd been. She used her fame as a redeemed woman to attract donations, and soon Camp Challenge was building its first dormitory, and not much later, the mess hall, the chapel. Dora knew how to approach wealthy people, and success bred success. Soon courts of law and social workers had learned of Camp Challenge—an unbroken stream of deserving young women, many pregnant, all in trouble, commenced. Foundation and government grants followed.

The mixed family and their magnanimous enterprise were tolerated in town, tolerated at best. But those rare metals, especially palladium and lithium! Those trespassing miners dug pits on the butte. Realtors made absurdly low offers, then absurdly high. Robert Sing refused them all. Joh Johman stood tall—his own land was also under assault. Clay Marvelette actually chased men off the butte, disarmed one and beat him with his own rifle stock, got arrested, got let off with a warning, not *Don't assault miners*, but something more refined: *Don't protect Robert Sing.*

Members of the reimagined Free Men's Militia began paying visits. Once a loose political confederation, it was now a cabal that included businessmen and politicians and bankers and sheriffs—thugs who started making threats disguised as offers. Turtle Butte Ranch came under legal attack alongside an orchestrated onslaught of rumors about the girls that Camp Challenge housed and helped: baby killings, sex rings, witches' covens, body parts bought and sold. Given her notoriety, Donut Dora's character wasn't hard to impugn. Dark arts. Black girls pregnant on the butte. Chinese communists loose on the range.

Simple things: an approved loan was withheld. Building supplies already ordered and paid for never materialized. Permits were pulled. Fines levied. Then nastier: threatening broadsides appeared under the wipers of Dora's old car in town. Sheep were shot, their heads stuck on fence posts, outbuildings burned, more and deeper rogue mining pits dug, bedrock blasted with dynamite in search of those rare metals, access roads brazenly cut through the forest, camp employees chased down and beaten in town, employees arrested. And then came the specious lawsuits against their land, dismissed one by one, but at great expense, and corrupt new judges on the horizon.

Courageous Far Turtle went to the county meeting, gave a speech, that they were all visitors here, that there were no aliens, that men should live as friends. One month later he was shot in the back at the door of the original little house, which he shared with Lucky. For appearances having absolutely to do with race, Dora had moved into her own space up at HQ. Two pregnant campers were shot, too, out in the kitchen garden. And Lucky, ten or eleven years old, out on his horse counting stock, was shot through the chest, miraculously survived, trauma that would live on within him.

There was a brief investigation over the two pregnant girls; the white girl proved to be indigent, so no matter, and really no investigation at all over the Black girl. Sheriff Brown himself came to investigate the death of Far Turtle, cursory visit. He suggested Dora had done it, murdered the girls to cover her crime. She was known in town to be a little crazy, he reminded her. She could be charged at any time, he said, a jury seated, the right judge found. The evidence was strong.

Another offer on the ranch came in, lower than ever. Which Dora refused.

All of this done by the Free Men.

"But Aarto," Francie said. "Now let Lucky speak. This is the story of him."

"Nup," Lucky said, just as always. But he thought a long time, a finger on his chest, pressing that scar hard, then harder, like he was trying to hold it all in.

"Please," Francie said.

"It will help me," I said.

And so he spoke, and I wrote:

I was just a kid, rode down to move the sheep up closer to camp as there'd been many shot in those weeks. My horse, Tortoise, big kind roan of Clay's, half-broke, left the road and I just let him. That horse knew where the sheep were every minute. After a while we heard a truck coming, and that was not unusual. But they drove right into the meadow behind us and several men jumped out. I pulled the reins hard and Tortoise reared and leapt. The men scattered and off we ran. A shot and Tortoise dropped from under me. We rolled, I broke my leg. I knew it right then, could barely stand, but I did. And the main guy says, Injun. And another says, he's just a fucking kid. I heard the other one shoot, felt a punch in the chest, not worse than that. Then like a branding iron stuck straight through me. I fell and played dead, but I was not. They hurried out of there, up to camp as it turned out, and shot my grandfather for owning his own land, and shot two pregnant girls for no reason at all.

The stars had stopped falling, just the Milky Way up there so crisp, and turning. The fire had died to coals like always and the wind had picked up some the same, aspens clattering back in the grove. Lucky stood, stretched, closed his eyes, still a finger on his chest. He'd pulled those braids forward for power. His face was made from multitudes.

"Wrong American," Francie said.

"Wrong American," Aarto repeated.

"Just Lucky," my husband said.

Chapter Forty-Nine

Midmorning, energy unflagging, Lucky finished shaping his version of the mysterious objects he and Aarto had been carving from their special wood, soaked a couple of nights now in the brook. He held it up for me to see: nothing but a board with notches. "Come watch," he said, ceremoniously collecting Doe Slayer from the powerful boulder he always leaned her on beyond the corral. View and Chickadee looking on, he weighed the spear in his hands and plugged her butt into a notch at one end of the board he'd carved. He held the other end in a pitcher's grip, one finger keeping that Viking spear steady. Then, suddenly, he took two Asgardian strides and released the spear same as ever, but with the new board flipping forward and providing leverage that increased force in some mathematical way Aarto had been trying to explain, futile. Whatever the physics, Doe Slayer flew several stories in the air above the stump Lucky had been aiming at and deep into the woods.

"Hoppo!" he shouted.

The two of us spent the next half hour searching, found Doe Slayer buried in the duff, unharmed. Next try, Lucky stepped back a hundred paces, clear to the edge of the trail. Magnificent athlete, he made sure I was observing, only then wound up, double stepped, flung again, slipped the throwing board just so, landed Doe Slayer quivering a few yards off target. But only a few. Determined, he flung her again and again from an impossible distance till he was missing the rotten stump by only feet, then inches. The first time he actually hit that stump, the spear went straight through, landed softly in the dirt behind.

Lucky hid his elation, but I was filled with such pride and such love and such proprietary zeal that I rushed him, hugged him, kissed his neck.

"Now enough of that," he said.

"No, Lucky Turtle Sing," I said, then corrected: "Never, Sing Lucky Turtle!"

Suddenly here came Aarto, wearing Clay's ten-gallon hat, formerly a dignified object, now a comical prop. Aarto lumbered straight to me all pretend bowlegged, reached down from the heights to fold me up in his arms. "Franciella and me," he announced, "we climbed the highest rock and watched the sunrise." He pointed to a stone spire high as a church steeple.

That was one hairy climb, if they'd really done it. I said, "Cool. Where is she?"

"Fie faan!" he cried, spinning to see: she wasn't behind him! He spun and ran, fantastical lope toward the head of the brook trail. Where he collided with our Francie, who grabbed him up in a bear hug and wrassled him to the ground, like felling a tree with bent branches, such laughter.

"Sunrise," she called, in case I'd doubted Aarto: "We climbed the highest rock!"

Lovers.

Chapter Fifty

One morning not so many seasons ago, I found Walter lying on his side on the kitchen floor like someone doing physical therapy, top arm stretched high, bottom arm stretched behind, legs as if in stride. I said, "Walter, you're on the floor."

He couldn't reply, though his eyes rather angrily found mine.

I shouted for Ricky, but of course Ricky wasn't home—he was a third-year grad student at Berkeley, having finished early at MIT, a program that migrated top scholars into top graduate schools. Berkeley Engineering, in this case, just coincidence that it was only a bridge away from where we both irrationally believed Lucky lived. Lucky was dead: I had to keep telling this to both of us.

I'd built a fire just the night before in Walter's beloved fireplace and stared into it long, glass of wine, thinking of Lucky, thinking of what Maria had said those few years before, that Lucky lived, my passionate, recurring conviction that Lucky was alive, that I could feel him alive, that at times he thought of me. I had not asked the fire for anything.

I had not.

But Walter had had a stroke. On account of which Ricky came home for a week, and was such a thoroughgoing help, all the back and forth to Mass Medical, coming up with all sorts of solutions I'd never have thought of: Walter couldn't speak, but he could blink expressively and he could wriggle his left hand a little. Ricky used Walter's tormented face to open Walter's phone (face ID seems normal now but was new and thrilling to me then, I'm slow) and showed Walter his list of contacts. And Walter was able to touch certain names and the two of them made a list, not that long, and

FaceTimed people, also new to me. Ricky would explain the stroke, and then these friends and associates could say a few encouraging things. More important, Walter could see their faces, pretty sweet, even I thought so, and with Ricky's help, impart messages. They didn't know they were saying goodbye, but the day after Ricky left, Walter took a turn for the worse.

In the meantime, thank goodness, I'd let go of my resentment, let bygones be bygones, forgiven him. I thanked him each day for all he'd done for us, kissed his cheek each evening as I left the ICU, felt my guilt afresh—I'd used him, used him a long time, had I not? His eyes were lively each morning when I stopped in, seemed filled with gratitude as well, the anger having fled us all. We'd been friends, in the end, and not only room-mates. He'd done so much for me, no matter his motives. Once we'd been lovers. And then he was dead. Mourning even the unbeloved takes all one's heart. Where Walter was once, there was no Walter now. I cried more than I would have dreamed, this man who'd been my savior, then my bane.

I went through all the motions, so many forms, so many questions, so many numbers, insurance issues I'd never considered, so many papers to look through. With the help of Walter's church and his many work col-leagues and not a few of his old patients and even Facebook "friends," Ricky managed from afar to arrange a funeral much bigger than I'd antici-pated, came home again, no mention of the stress it must have caused him. Walter's people were kind enough. I was sad, I was grateful, also amazed how few of them I'd met. It's hard to remember that gratitude: my fury has regrown since then.

Ricky headed back to California: he had students now, a lab to run, papers in the works, projects in the real world. And then it was Cindra alone, like I'd never been. The only job, I began to realize, was to get out of there: close the house, close it fast and sell it fast and go west. Why west? Ricky was out there, and Ricky was all I had, unless I had Lucky, who was out there as well, I truly believed, believed without admitting it, delusion being shameful, ask Walter, the town with the red bridge (offi-cially International Orange, according to Ricky, who was big on facts). My

magical thinking was aimed at Lucky, that old mourning, and not at resur-
recting Walter, the new.

One of the many things to do was to find Walter's will. Since we'd never
married (and as he'd often warned me), I needed a will to prove ownership of the house I'd lived in for some fifteen years. Without that I couldn't
even get the deed from the county registrar. Walter's lawyer was unfriendly,
when I found him. He had a copy of the will, but I'd need my own lawyer
to obtain it. I remembered that Ricky's Legos coach, Carl "Ronnie" Ronson
(his card said, still in the junk drawer), was a lawyer, and sure enough,
he was available, sweet bespectacled bird. Not the right kind of law, but
he agreed to help me pro bono, remembered Walter as a prick. And sure
enough, when the will was unlocked, its provisions presented to me by
email, Walter had left me nothing. Ricky got title to the aging Prius, and
that was absolutely it. Everything else went to Walter's sister, nicknamed
Bossy, of course, who hadn't even attended his funeral, widow of a scion,
rich as Jesus. Her lawyers swooped in, and suddenly I had nine months
and a day to vacate. Well, Bossy, I'll see your nine months and make it two
months, keep your stinking day.

Deep in Walter's desk—nothing else of any interest at all, that's the kind
of man—I found a file folder labeled TURTLE DEATH CERTIFICATE. I drew
it out, needed reminding once more. Lucky was dead. I'd been letting my
shameful fantasies run away with me. Out on Walter's sunporch I held the
folder a long time, finally cracked it open. And there was the familiar form,
several copies, in fact (efficient man), the last with a typed addendum:
"Lucky Turtle dead of blunt force trauma, Montana State Prison, 1/31/2005."
Yes, that's what Walter had told me. Beaten to death in a prison fight. I just
hadn't seen it in type. Once again, I cried. I couldn't help but imagine what
must have happened, that dank old prison, practically a cinema reel after
all that time. I kept looking and looking at the form. That last copy also
bore a pink sticky note, coarse handwriting, distinctly not Walter's.

Done, it said.

Done.

That's all. It stuck with me. Stuck to my sadness. Didn't sit right. What was done? Was something done to Lucky? Was Walter involved in some way? I couldn't let it go: beaten to death in prison, peaceable Lucky. Done by whom? No, no. It was just some clerk. Like, here's the form, stop pestering me, okay?

Done.

Chapter Fifty-One

Time folded in on itself. The days had names as always: Aarto Fell; Cindra Rode View; Francie Found Blue Ice. She really did, she found diamond-clear turquoise-blue ice in a high tarn that didn't get sun, brought us back ten pounds. And Aarto fell from a lightning-blasted ponderosa, trying to locate the wapiti herd—knocked the breath out of himself, nothing worse. And I climbed on View and rode him to the high meadow, just the two of us, always the way to make friends with a divo: quality time. I felt he knew I was pregnant, anyway he was gentle with me, sweet boy.

We Testamentals had cucumbers, first a few, then a million, the garden throwing bounty. Cucumbers were our new fruit, the various wild berries having gone by, and we munched cucumbers all day, beautiful crisp cucumbers cold from the night. I hoarded my vinegar stash: no pickles, no way. We ate together most mornings, biscuits and eggs, sometimes a trout, sometimes a strip of dried venison, nice and chewy. After breakfast, we more or less disbanded, had our separate or paired adventures, came together again for dinner, fire time, stories from *Hawaii*. We'd survived well into September, Aarto let us know, the evenings coming early, the chill getting deeper, my hip bones long gone. I already felt I'd known Aarto years, booming laugh in the yard, a mountain range of a man. I'd stopped noticing those huge teeth in favor of the blue intelligence in his eyes, the kindness unhidden, the damage somewhere deep.

Aarto had been to college and finished. He told us that Michener was a hack, that *Hawaii* was imperialist apologetics. Instead of that dreck, we should stick to our own stories. He pushed Lucky, and Lucky sometimes relented, and so we heard in smallest increments the further life of Lucky, who'd spent whole weeks and sometimes months with Maria and Clay, who'd grown apart from Dora, who had more or less disowned him even as her precepts broke down: Camp Challenge had changed from a charitable enterprise to a hard-core business, and he from beloved son to useful employee, at least officially. Lucky didn't find this remarkable.

What had happened? "I just loved Maria more," he said, characteristically looking inside.

Aarto had a stronger explanation, at least to my ear and heart: Lucky represented all the worst things that had ever happened to Dora Dryden Conover. She'd already distanced herself, seeing herself a lady now, the proper daughter of her proper parents, who were among the camp's benefactors, and who'd never accepted her son, never forgiven those dark days.

Aarto took up residence in Francie's room, and Lucky and I were fascinated, mock scandalized. But there was never a sound of lovemaking from in there, just laughter, the loud thuds of wrassling, a comic charade, punches and standoffs and chases out the door and through the clearing, ticklings and spankings and roughhousing and frequent appeals to the ref, myself. I did chance to witness a kiss one morning, the two of them off in the trees, Aarto ducking at her, quick smack on her lips, she slapping him, the two of them roaring with laughter or love or whatever it was.

Anyway, breakfast—late September, if my calendar was close—skin of ice on the water buckets, fires roaring in both stove and pit, the horses snorting clouds, ten trout Aarto and Lucky had caught that dawn in some new pool they'd found, each of us carefully tending our own couple or three fish, which we skewered through the pucker on willow wands and held high over Lucky's perfect coals, add biscuits, add cukes cut in slices, add the first of my ripe tomatoes, so late, plants protected from frost by the heat-retaining rocks we'd piled around them, add whatever greens: loooocious, as Aarto proclaimed, grand man. Oh, and didn't we voluptuaries eat! That was an Aarto word, the boy with the education: we were sybarites, we were epicureans, we were hedonists, each word a conversation.

Late, Aarto produced the package from my father, the package I had carefully hidden in among the boughs and mosses that made Lucky's and my bed, held it in the air.

"No," I said. "You wretch." My mother's word!

"It's time," he said.

"I'm saving it," I said. "You have no right!" How strong I was at seventeen, how willing to do battle. Another strength (or was it a weakness?) was self-abnegation. I'd held that package back from myself, keeping its promise intact as long as I could, knowing it would most likely disappoint: things did.

Aarto got down on one knee, handed the box back like it was a crown and I the new queen. Maybe he was right: it was time. In the face of his pretend humility, I untied the string, slipped the box from the grocery-bag kraft paper, lifted the clever lid, sudden scent of Daddy at his worktable. The box was familiar, had played a role in childhood games—a pair of Mom's dress gloves had come in it a decade before, the gloves long gone. Inside I found two envelopes, one thick as my thumb, the other thin as a letter. Under those, perfectly fitting the old box, a movie-theater-size double packet of Bit-O-Honey, which Daddy knew was my favorite, always forbidden me by our dentist, more so by Mom. I thought of Doctor Mack and what would happen if any of us Testamentals got a toothache but opened the candy anyway and ripped a piece off its waxed paper and put it on my tongue. My fellow worshippers watched rapt, none having ever seen the stuff. So after a while of keeping them in suspense, I unwrapped three pieces and placed each on proffered tongues.

"You let it melt," I said. "Do not be losing fillings!"

"What do you mean?" Lucky said, he of the perfect teeth, he who then wept at the beautiful sweetness.

Candy on my tongue, I opened the thicker envelope, tearing it slowly, savoring the moment. And inside was money. A lot of money. Five- and ten- and twenty-dollar bills, stacked with the faces up, grimy bills and clean, money my father had likely gathered from all over, careful man.

We didn't count it. It had no value on that high ridge. The tears started to come before I even opened the next envelope, his own sweet handwriting, swift and tilted like running, a lot to say. And I read aloud:

Love Bug: You can scarcely imagine the veritable flood of relief when your uncle Jeffrey dropped your good letter with me. We had only just heard you had gone missing from Camp Challenge, a grave worry, which you in your consideration have relieved. The camp people said not to come, that there was no reason to come to Montana. And so because of that, your mother forbade me the trip. She did prevail. You'll say, "So what else is new, Mr. Milquetoast?" Honey, my heart was broken, thinking you were in danger. And of course, my heart is still broken, knowing you needed my help. I have not shared your fine, fine epistle with Mommy, you'll be glad to know. She'd set the Mounties out looking for you, and probably sic them on your uncle and me, too. I did tell her I had a dream that you were fine, and you know how she feels about dreams. So she does know you are fine.

No news here in particular. Your mother is deep into her garden club activities. I do all the actual gardening. Just as it always was, so shall it always be. The car windshield was cracked but I found one super cheap at the junkyard over in Saugus and the fellow helped me install it, and it hardly leaks at all. That is a joke. It does not leak. New job at the cabinet shop over on Route 1 there is unremarkable, but they pay me each Friday. And that's "All the News That's Fit to Print."

All right, then, one more item: Your friend I won't name with the new shag haircut (at least new when you left) got into a certain college, one you and I talked about, in a place where fall would be beautiful and the Atlantic Ocean not far, a college that a certain friend of mine attended. I thought it was not impossible you could turn up in such a place this fall, and so I approached your friend and her new haircut (she looks like Jane Fonda, only quite a bit smarter) and suggested she look out for you come September. This was just an idea, no pressure of any kind should be inferred.

The moolah behind door number two is not to say I don't think you can take care of yourself, but only to help you avoid desperate measures. From what you said in your letter, "you" is a "we" at this point, so please do share the wealth, and pass on my unquestioning love to any who love you.

For my part, I love you dearly and miss you terribly and can't wait for the day we get this all cleared up and over with. But for now, some Bit-O-Honey, which I hope says the rest. Love, Your ever-loving Daddy-o

Now it was Francie's turn to weep. Lucky only seemed puzzled, my father's fancy prose.

"Who is this mysterious friend he writes about," Aarto said.

"No mystery," I said. "The friend is Missy MacRae. She looks nothing like Jane Fonda. But she mocked her *Klute* haircut in front of my dad one time. Oh, she made him laugh. Now he calls her Hanoi Jane. And she's going to Tulane, in New Orleans. Missy is the best girl ever. Daddy knows that. He's just trying to find a safe way to meet."

"New Orleans," Francie said.

"Just a place. Just in case," Aarto said.

Lucky repeated the rhyme. "When will you go?" he said darkly.

"Oh, Lucky," I said. "If I ever go—a big if—it's because you are coming with. You understand, right? It's you and me together."

He didn't look consoled.

Francie reached across the table and swiped the packet of money, weighed it in her hands like it was gold, counted it out loud. One thousand eighteen, a vast fortune, the seventeen I would have gotten for my birthday, plus one to grow on. Then add a thousand bucks! Enough to begin life in a new place, somewhere like New Orleans, where winter wasn't killing, and no one would think to look for us, and no one would look twice at a mixed couple. A place you might find a doctor who'd deliver your mixed baby without judgment, a doctor who might be mixed herself. A doctor who'd never worked at any camp. I'd have to impart all that to Lucky slowly, as necessary, if necessary.

The moon was half gone and appeared quickly at the far horizon, lit the night. We four Testamentals pressed closer to the fire, squeezed together for the warmth, everyone on the same side of Family Table, the long bench.

"Brothers and sisters," Aarto said, "we need to make a plan. In case these Free Men come for us, or ambitious Dale Drinkins. We all heard what Clay said."

No, we really hadn't, everyone so ripped on mushrooms.

Indefatigable Francie said, "Dale Drinkins will help us."

"He might," Aarto said without emotion. "Or he might use us to gain himself a higher position in the Free Men, as Clay explained."

Francie said, "No. That's wrong. Dale will help us. Not because he's good, but because he wants something, too. He'll be back with glass for my windows."

"Oh, Francie," I said.

"Where is New Orleans?" Lucky said, a little choked.

"Southeast," Aarto told him. "A city of music and balconies, parades and golden necklaces you wear in piles around your neck."

Lucky grew dark. He'd dreamed we'd go west. He didn't care for riches.

Francie said, "This is not necessary, Aarto. Dale Drinkins will do what I say. He thinks he's manipulating me. But he's in my power, you listen."

I said, "Wait, Franciella. Why would that little fireplug do what you say?"

"Ha-ha. Why would he not? You should see how he grovels."

"Now when-all was this?" Aarto said, playing Bronco. He drew himself up like a cowboy about to bust up a saloon.

"When he was here. And I told him, Leave Lucky alone. I told him it was none of his business if Lucky and Cindra were together."

Aarto said, "Panes of glass. And leave Lucky alone."

"Dale Drinkins will be back," Lucky said quietly.

"I can hold him off," Francie said. "That's what I'm trying to tell you. If he comes, I mean. I told him, glass. Bring that glass to show you care about me. That's my plan. Because he does care about me. He has to think he's ours. He is definitely coming back, and in peace. Thanks to me. Give me credit. I'm buying time. And now we've got Bronco, too."

Aarto said, "Francie's right. We must buy time."

"Time for what?" I said.

"Time to leave," Lucky said. "Because they'll come over the mountain. Dale Drinkins, he knows this territory. He'll bring his people, this militia. They will break into two parties, I'm sure of it. One will climb up the brook, here." He pointed darkly. "Another over the mountain there."

"Pincers," Aarto said impressed.

Francie said, "Okay? You guys? He'll come back. He'll bring glass. That buys time. We can do this right. Trust me."

"New Orleans," Lucky said, like you or I would say Jupiter, or Neptune.

Chapter Fifty-Two

Lucky and Aarto weren't finding any meat, but the wapiti herd, they thought, should be moving soon. The fall mating time was near, and they'd heard the bull elk whistling. They began to go out together before light. They were so intimate, talked in their old, secret child language, vurry rapid, Lucky at ease.

Francie had grown proprietary with the garden—down there daily, returning with bounty. She'd built walls all around our beds, improved her ingenious irrigation system, banked in our onions, which had grown fat, bossed me around, mulching everything against frost, and how had she ever learned that except from me?

I was entering a phase of pregnant lassitude, felt mostly like lying down, sipping vinegar—I still had half my bootleg bottle. But one crisp morning, yet another brisk day coming—could it be October?—I thought to take a hot bath, left Francie in the garden, wandered with *Hawaii* (Aarto be damned—I loved that book) up the grade to the hot spring, stripped off my overhauls and heavy thrift-store sweater, sank into the water incrementally, lay there a while trying to read but distracted by a certain fantasy I'd been having—New Orleans, a visit from my father, a baby in arms, an iron balustrade from a photo I'd seen once, a busy street, trombone music background, surely a trombone, my husband out there on the *balcon* in his braids in the sunshine, never a shirt, the world smiling up at him: beautiful Lucky, home at last, home with his wife, his baby, the ripples building, a curl to tug, the hot water suffusing every cell, the crowns of my trees in the wind, Jesus.

I heard Francie too late—she was a delicate walker when she wanted to be, a tracker, a stalker—she'd found me with ease.

"The princess," she said.

"The goddess," I sighed. Our joke, but it was true, her new shape all squeezed into a gray T-shirt and her Grizzlies sweats—masculine, feminine, soft and so hard—I couldn't even picture the person I'd met first day at Camp Challenge.

"Come garden with me," she said. "You looked boiled."

"I'm boiled," I said. "But climb in."

"No, round pumpkin! Let us go! The green things miss you. They ask every day. Where is our sister? Just reading her dirty book and pleasuring herself in her bath when she already got it *twice* last night?" She grinned in the way that closed her eyes tight. She rolled up her pants legs, kicked off her clogs, sat on the wall behind me (she'd made beautiful rock walls here at the spring, too, deepened our tub), combed my hair luxuriously with her fingers, pulled it back into a bulky pony, secured it with one of her deer-hide thongs, which she'd taken to wearing around each biceps like Lucky.

"Are you pregnant on purpose?"

"Weirdo, yes. Or mostly yes. Just that Lucky didn't know anything."

"Aarto knows things."

I had to get out of the heat. I half stood, still embarrassed, flushed from within and without, dressed quickly, rolled my overhaul legs, sat beside my friend, not too close, our feet in hot water.

In a tumble she said, "Aarto had a girl back in Sweden, but she dumped him years ago and he's been a soldier since."

"Smooth talker, those big teeth."

"Do you know they teach sex in school over there in Sweden? A whole month on where to kiss a girl!"

"Well, let him go ahead and practice!"

"I'll punch him in the nose."

"You're allowed to be affectionate."

"He talks to me, and that's a credit. He's very smart. His hands are as big as windmills. I just don't trust someone so nice."

"That says you trust the wrong men. And look where it's got you!"

"It's got me right here in these mountains, *mignonne*. With stupid *you*."

"It was nice till you showed up."

"So *mean*!"

"I'm trying to be so mean that you trust me."

At length she said, "Don't worry. I don't trust Dale. I don't. At first I thought I knew who he was."

"He was spying on us! From the very, the *vurry* first!"

"Let me speak. At first I thought I knew who he was, but that article he brought. You already knew, okay—wise, wise Cindra—but that revealed him to me, okay? He thought he'd treat you and me differently and that would work, like you with all your blond knots and waves would respond to blackmail and me, I'd respond to, you know, seduction. Like we wouldn't be loyal to one another, like we'd steer two courses with him. He said all kinds of things. And I do admit that at first I kind of fell for it. The attention. But not the bullshit, so don't accuse me. Like, I could live in their house? Like, his wife wouldn't know? I'd take care of the boy, take care of the house—they have a whole back room. He thinks I'd like that? He'd sneak back and be my lover? That's when I started to plan. Because I knew we needed help, but I also thought we had to keep that man close. Aarto wasn't here yet, remember. You were not supportive, remember. But Dale Drinkins would have already turned us in if it weren't for me. Apples are not the issue. Glass is not the issue. The issue is we aren't safe."

"Okay. All right. But yes, I wasn't supportive. Because, wait. When was it he said all this, anyway? And why do you call him Dale?"

"He has to be controlled. That is what I realized. And that is my plan. And I deserve your thanks." She kicked the water of the hot spring, waft of sulfur, rainbow drops in the bushes all around. "The lady that lives in the back room now? Blackfeet. Her name is Eleanor. She's going to move. You shouldn't hear the names he calls her. You give me credit, all I've stomached!

He really thinks I'll be the one to take her place. He can't turn you in till he has me in his house. That's his plan. And our plan has to be to take advantage of his plan. I told him I'd move in when the snow came. And so that's when we must plan to leave. Your thanks, I'm waiting."

"Francie, I'm so angry. You don't plan in secret. When did you talk to him? What did he try? When did you punch him in the nose? When did you hear about his poor Blackfeet *servant*? When, when, when? I've asked you before and you don't answer."

"Well, things changed. Didn't you hear me? Now it's *our* plan. I came up here to tell you. And yes I'll answer: he came upon me in the garden."

"You're writing a fairy tale, came upon you."

"The fairy tale is done, believe me."

"He came upon you, then what?"

"Then we talked a long time. That day he visited, that's all. Before he showed himself—that article, okay? I thought, he's a man. He came up to the lodge. He met you and Lucky. After we talked down there. After he tried to kiss me. And after I punched him in the nose."

"And now he's yours to control? A punch in the nose?"

"Perversely, yes."

"And what good is that, controlling some pervert?"

"I have bought time. I keep saying it. And as everyone is telling you, we need to get ready. We need to be ready to go. When snow flies. Or maybe before. Because Dale Drinkins is going to get more than a bloody nose if Aarto has his way. 'One false move,' is how he put it, being Bronco!"

"Okay, Francie. Thank you. I mean it."

My baby kicked, hard. I pulled up my shirt so Francie could see. She put her hand on my belly, felt him when he kicked again.

Chapter Fifty-Three

New Orleans was forgotten, not mentioned again. And Dale Drinkins, too, not a word, not an appearance. Maybe Francie really had shut him down. But Aarto made recon, he called it, rode down the trail every dawn and every dusk. The rest of us dropped our guards, I'd say, wishing so for the life we'd had so recently even while summer waned. There wasn't going to be any glass, so Francie made shutters—clever, perfect shutters that pretty effectively sealed her windows at night to be thrown open at sunrise, a little square window in the middle of each that Lucky fitted with stove glass, he called it, thick sheets of mica he'd peeled off a boulder exposed in a rock fall, nearly clear: we didn't need Drinkins. The windows reminded me of my little window in Cats—I could look out for hours and never be bored, a square frame on the forest, moving pictures. The shutters opened, the shutters closed, day following night following day. And a good thing they were there: one early morning an inch or two of snow, first of the season, arrived in a mighty squall, blowing through every crevice of the old lodge making drifts that getting out of bed we had to step over in bare feet. And of course, this made some of us think of boots, of thick socks, of heavy mittens, of scarves and watch caps, all the things we didn't have. And it made Francie alert once again. Only I knew why. As quickly as it had come, though, the snow was gone, sublimated into that desert-dry air.

Except for the delicates—tomatoes, cucumbers, nasturtiums—the garden survived the snow. The potatoes would wait till we wanted them. The kale would make it to Christmas, chard and lettuce and spinach, too, if we assiduously covered them at night. Food that could come with us, too, should we have to flee, a thought I kept to myself, because we would not have to flee. A thought we all kept to ourselves. Denial ran in each of us, one way or another. And honestly, the perfection of that existence made it seem nothing could ever go wrong. And that made us believe: Drinkins had forgotten us. No sign of Clay either, but each night in my prayers at the fire I asked for winter things, for more vinegar, for a safe passage to this world for my baby.

Afternoons I worried about just that, always a dark spot in the day, my back to the sun at Family Table, my front to the fire, slicing deerskin into snowshoe strips for Aarto, the last of our supply.

Brook trout made way to fill the deep holes Lucky and Aarto had emptied feeding us, and to the beaver ponds. The boyhood pals had implored the fish to come by singing their Viking trout song at full volume, and of course the fish heard and came to hand. Aarto wanted to preserve some, tried to invent a smoker using the woodstove in the lodge, succeeded only in making everything smell like fish. One day, teasing Lucky, I sang for mushrooms but the vurry next day found fortuitous blooms, hen of the woods, Aarto called them, massive things, ten and fifteen and twenty pounds, growing in leafy globe shapes downslope almost to the range lands, not a sign of another human. We harvested them by the bushel, and those we didn't fry in deer fat Aarto set about drying in hot sun, more baskets filled. For every day's eating, we put away food for three more.

Still I talked to the fire, lit the candles when no one was around, made up incantations: I wanted extra rice. I wanted more sacks of beans. I wanted to hear from Clay, wanted to know the official plan, since I didn't have one of my own. Francie was the official plan if you asked her. Aarto and Lucky were the official plan if you asked them. In wanting Clay, I wanted my dad, I guess. I pulled out Dad's dear letter and read it over and over, savoring stray thoughts of him: riding his shoulders, fishing in the mill ponds, learning how to drive, also his smell, which was sawdust and glue and varnish. He was going to be a grandpa. Lucky was going to be a dad. And I, I was going to be a mom.

The mornings got colder, frost on the porch posts, gray jays begging, practically pets. Lucky talked to them, and you swore they talked back.

Where are the wapiti? he'd sing.

Patience, the gray jays would reply.

And next morning again, Where are the wapiti?

Patience, Lucky Turtle.

And the next: But when will they come?

And finally, cold morning, the gray jay chorus flew down from their searching, replied: The wapiti are in!

Late one afternoon, late enough to worry me, reading *Hawaii* for the umpteenth time, Francie off collecting, I heard the pounding of the horses on the trail from the south, and shortly here came Aarto and Lucky, hurtling into camp like olden huntsmen on prize steeds, whooping and shouting, those idiots, half child's play, half real life, meat tied in the skin of the animal across Chickadee's rump, long, elegant antlers tied in on top, six spurs, nothing like the little craggy mule deer antlers Lucky'd been carving into spearheads and buttons and knife handles and awls, world without plastic.

They pulled those horses right up to Family Table in their excitement. Aarto began the report, so thrilled, even as I coughed in their dust: "Past the high meadow and down into the big brook—they were in the aspens right there eating forb!"

I loved mocking him: "Forb?"

"Leaves," Aarto said.

"Aarto missed," Lucky said.

"I missed," said Aarto happily. "My Viking spear is still unblooded! But Lucky's!"

"I rested down in the bottom so when they bolted the whole herd crossed just so. I waited for the least male, and he was last in the line." He lofted his spear, shouted its new name, Aarto joining in, "Elk Hand!"

"Nice," I said.

Aarto made a seashell of his own hands and blew into it, a high, eerie shriek and then a groan and a loud, satisfied grunt, then again, but longer, a winnowing trill, a bugle note wavering not quite to melody, almost, and again the happy grunt.

"Careful," Lucky said. "The wapiti women will come mate you."

That night and for several more we enjoyed beautiful roasts stuffed with hen of the woods, Aarto's wapiti meatballs, always a prayer to the animal, so much meat left to dry and to smoke: Lucky's job in the coming days. Francie made a soup of frost-fucked tomatoes, she called them, and meat scraps from the butchering, plus greens and beans from our stores and a handful of twigs Lucky insisted on, magnificent flavors.

Aarto and Francie would tan the new hide, talk of mittens, talk of hats.

The meat was the plan. The mittens, the hats, they were the plan. Aarto was the plan, and Lucky, and Francie, too, all with so much to offer. As for me, I'd come to see that the baby was the plan, dead of winter, and far from help—I wasn't offering much but trouble. Bunny Slayer was Doe Slayer was Elk Hand, that was the plan.

The wapiti were in!

Aarto remembered it must be near Lucky's birthday, not that Lucky cared—he claimed to not even know the date. Still we took it as reason for our feasts, several days of variations on our theme. Hunt night I improvised a birthday cake with Francie's help and with her help brought it to Family Table, stubs of those two blue candles in the center. Lucky pretended to have deep questions: Why all the wishing if birthdays were happy? And if you've blown the fire out, what is left to carry the wish?

"You make the wish, then you blow the fire out," Francie said. "Blowing it out is like hanging up the phone."

We laughed.

Something amazing: Lucky hadn't ever used a phone, so he said. Maria didn't have one. Camp didn't even have pay phones, miles from any lines. Dora had had a heavy radio phone on her desk. But who had Lucky ever been going to call? In the end we cut the cake with the candle still burning in its center, passed thick slices among us. It wasn't too terrible, maybe like a big pancake with extra sugar.

The wapiti were in!

Francie and Aarto snuggled and smooched, headed down to the lodge, soon a loud song, hilarious duet, delighted shrieking, then the usual thumps and crashes and uncontained laughter, fraught silence, then the familiar insistent rhythm of creaks and moans. Never got old, my eavesdropping.

It all made me so confident. "I think we're going to make it," I said.

"It will be a good winter," Lucky said.

"I think so, too," I said.

And at just that moment, the baby kicking in my belly, we heard the most eerie sound, a shriek and a groan and a loud grunt, then again, a longer shrieking trill, a bugle note wavering to melody, almost, and that satisfied grunt. I squeezed up tight against my husband, scared of the sound, and he said it was okay, and then he said it one more time, quietly, I thought: "The wapiti are in."

And from Francie's room, Aarto's deep boom: "The wapiti are in!"

I don't know. I don't think I've ever slept like that again, the bugling of the wapiti echoing all through the mountains and the woods, my husband's arms tight around me.

Chapter Fifty-Four

The elk-hide door scratched open, letting in a fury of sunlight along with a cold blast of wind, also a wave of irritation, the new strange irritation that had begun to overcome me at formerly tranquil times: hormones, though I had no clue.

I whined: "Lucky, forget it. I thought you were going to hunt. Look at this rice here. This rice is perfection." I took the rice off the heat using XS panties as potholders, showed him.

"Well, ho," said a voice I thought to be Aarto's.

My irritation fled: "Well, ho, yourself," I said.

But it was Mr. Drinkins. "Here's the little liar," he said, oddly calm. His large face, already red, going darker. His tough, tight wool jacket, buffalo plaid. He patted his belly, a taut drum like mine, rounder than mine, a powerful man, not a fat one.

"Excuse me?" I put the rice down super calmly, banked the fire at my own pace. I'd seen much worse than him, was the look I put on my face. "You are in my home. Mind your manners."

"Your squat, you mean. Squatters get no manners. Not from me."

"Bronco will not take your behavior lightly. And I do not take it lightly."

At my tone, at my words, the slightest tic crossed his features, like a skip in a film, one frame missing. Bronco? The little liar was still trying that, or was she for real? Anyway, he softened, a bigger transformation than I'd expected, almost begging: "I just want to see Franciella. And it's not like I ain't been looking. Help a feller out, will you?"

"After what you've just said to me?"

He hardened again, but barely. "I say the truth."

"You'd impose your disgusting kisses on a seventeen-year-old girl? What does your marriage mean to you, Mr. Drinkins?"

He started back to a boil, that face going red as elk blood on the firepit stones. He stepped closer to me, but even with his bulk, his little bit of height, he didn't frighten me. Nor did the gun strapped at his hip bother me when I noticed it, not even with his face so pinched, eyes burning. He was in romantic distress, I could see, not ready to kill anyone, and that gave me fresh power. Of course I wanted him out of there. I walked into him, baby belly first, hard against him. You could see something in him had asked for just that kind of treatment, for that punch in the nose from Francie, for all the blows he'd ever taken. So Francie was right: we did have the power, but it had to be played just so. Just what idealistic Lucky had been saying, I thought, our after-dinner discussions: a man of violence has no weapon if we are unafraid.

"Ma'am," he said. "Ma'am, I swear," he said. "She told me she was twenty."

"Out!" I said.

He felt behind him for the elk hide, managed to part it, tripped off the threshold, stumbled across the porch and into the yard, where he stood, blinking. His beseechment had debased him. His whole performance embarrassed him. Suddenly he wiped his eyes, blew snot on the ground, went back to where he'd started.

"Liar witch! Fucking that Injun. Stinking gash! You let that half man put that baby in you?"

He stepped back onto the porch, but I stood my ground. Then, fearful at last, vulnerable—so much for the power of righteousness—I faltered, stepped back just as Aarto came into my line of sight around the corral, mighty Aarto, wearing Clay's Stetson, moving fast. He put a finger to his lips, put a sudden hand on that beefy shoulder, his big fingers reaching clear down the front yoke of Mr. Drinkins's cheap jacket, put the other hand at the small of his back, might have been a grizzly the way Mr. Drinkins torqued, gasped, tried to duck away. But Aarto pushed on that broad back and pulled on that shoulder, knee in the thigh, twisting the man three ways, an elegant drop, trained assassin, and all maybe 240 pounds of his victim fell like the last dinosaur, great thud and shudder. Mr. Drinkins frantically reached for his weapon, Aarto's foot on his chest, but his weapon was gone.

"Howdy," our true Bronco said, six-shooter swinging from his free pinkie by the trigger guard. He handed the old, cold thing over to me. It was heavy, a revolver like the toys my brothers had played with, but steelier, dense. I opened the chamber, dropped the shells out into my hand, checked that there were no more in there—actions I knew from watching movies—slipped the cartridges into the bib pocket of my pink overhauls. Bronco moved his foot up to Mr. Drinkins's cheek, pressed that face hard into the dust.

"Bronco," I said dramatically, damsel no longer in distress. "Don't hurt him."

Mr. Drinkins stopped struggling, an animal in a trap: there really was a Bronco.

"Apologize," I said.

"You're making a mistake," Mr. Drinkins said.

"You don't say," Aarto did say, and twisted that foot some.

"Apologize," I said again.

Mr. Drinkins could hardly speak: "I'm sorry, Mr. Bronco. I'm sorry."

I said, "I'm sorry, Mr. Bronco? Apologize to me, Mr. Drinkins."

Another twist of Aarto's boot. He said, "Apologize to Mrs. Bronco."

Mr. Drinkins took a breath like a sigh, said, "I'm sorry, little lady. I'm truly and utmost sad and sorry."

"For what? What are you sorry for?"

His voice rose in pitch with every phrase: "For disturbing your day. For saying those things I said. I only want to see Franciella. I brought along something she wanted to see." He reached as best he could inside his jacket, pulled out a pair of envelopes, showed them quickly, tucked them back.

Aarto lifted his foot. Mr. Drinkins rested a moment, his cheek still in the dirt, gathered himself and slowly got to his knees, then slowly stood, like a pale mushroom growing, really a big person, never been manhandled, not like that, not since his father's torments, you saw. He brushed himself off, took a cautious step away.

"Don't insult Lucky," I said.

"No, ma'am. Never again."

And we stood there in the wind, too much to think about.

At length Mr. Drinkins gave a weak smile, said, "I hate to ask for my sidearm back."

I said, "I hate to give it back. You'll have to earn it. Simple as that." I tucked it in the bib of my overhauls, laid it on the shelf of my belly.

He appealed to Aarto: "That's a Smith and Wesson long-bore .45, practically an antique."

"Well, tarnation," Aarto said. He'd watched the same movies I had. "I reckon in that case you'll have to behave."

Mr. Drinkins patted the envelopes under his jacket again. "I call this behaving."

"What you got there, boy?"

"Francie wanted to see. It's just pictures of my house. And some papers. I thought she'd like to come down visit, is all."

I said, "Come down visit or live in your back room?" I said. "Who do you think Francie is?"

"She did give me a wallop," he said.

"What papers?" Aarto said.

"Oh, it's about my divorce, see."

So I took the envelopes and tugged out the papers and the little photos and had a look. Here was a little neat house, big pickup in the drive. Here was a tiny bedroom, two twin beds stuffed in, Jesus on a cross on the wall. Here was a little boy dragging a shovel. The divorce papers were generic, unsigned by anyone, undated, Mr. Drinkins's name filled in, shaky hand. I tossed them on the ground, tossed the photos on the ground.

"I seen your truck down in the fork," Bronco said. "Had a perfect bead on you there as you come up through the rocks. That's a long way 'round.

Don't know how you beat me walking. You'd think a man with honorable intentions would just pull in down below and walk up the road."

Mr. Drinkins ignored him, but you saw his eyes track at the thoroughness of Bronco's watch.

"Your poor son," I said.

He blurted, "Oh, Francie . . ." And then he surprised all of us by breaking down, fulsome, sudden tears.

Aarto went to him, patted his back. He'd seen the pain of men, didn't judge. Plus, we didn't want the interloper angry, Francie was right about that. We needed him agreeable. Broken would be fine.

Mr. Drinkins said, "It has been hard on me these days. My housekeeper passed. A squaw I came to depend upon."

I said, "A what? What kind of word is that? Show some respect. Show some *decency*."

"What am I supposed to call her? She lived in my house. She passed away not four days ago. That was her room there in the picture, just a-waiting."

Aarto kept patting.

Barely controlled, I said, "You like a Blackfeet woman if she cleans your house?" I was holding his gun, I kept realizing. Maybe should have left the ammo in.

"I did like her. She worked pretty hard. Tame as they come. And not twenty-five, not that she ever kept track."

"Oh my god, tame!"

"Tame," he repeated. "I thought Francie could take her room. But more than that. I'm to be a single man. You see the papers. You're standing on the papers. It's going to get mighty cold up here. And nothing your Injun can do to help you, neither. And not this cowboy here, not even him."

"How stupid do you think we are, Mr. Drinkins?"

"Stupid enough," he said, so careless.

"Just keep wagging that tongue," Bronco said.

"No, I mean formerly. I've a different view now."

I said, "I think it's time you left us. Bronco, don't you think it's time

Mr. Drinkins and his vile prejudice and his fraudulent divorce papers left us?"

Mr. Drinkins seemed genuinely stricken. But any good actor might. He said, "I just want to see Francie. And those papers, those are the genuine article. I have feelings for that gal. Please. If you think I'm prejudice, why do I want to see her?"

I felt my heart pounding suddenly, realized I was puffing out breaths. I said, "I suspect the answer to that is easy."

He switched tacks: "You need me, young lady. You don't know what trouble you're in! Newspaper article every day now! It's the Camp Challenge people. That pushy woman, the donut lady. You've embarrassed them. Me, I have kept my promise to Franciella, and I haven't said a word. And I can help. I can keep them off you."

"A plan's a plan," Aarto said cryptically.

Oh, right. He was talking to me. The plan. I nodded. I'd heard him.

So Aarto helped Drinkins to his feet, patted the dust off him. "We do appreciate your help," he said.

We'd made plans for every eventuality, Aarto's insistence, my concurrence, and here I'd almost forgotten. I hurried inside the lodge, hid the six-shooter where my gifts from Daddy were hidden in among the spruce boughs that made our bed.

"Well," Bronco said—Aarto said—"I got chores." This was a line he'd written as if in a movie script. A line he'd practiced. Because that was the plan.

I didn't want Aarto leaving, but we had to act as naturally as possible and welcome Dale as forgiven, as a friend good as his word, in the hopes he'd be so. The plan, that was the plan. Aarto walked away. I knew he wouldn't be far, but still.

I gathered the papers and the photos, handed them back to our visitor, who stuffed his pockets with them, led him to Family Table, stirred the coals in the firepit, added kindling. Mr. Drinkins wiped his face with the back of his hand, stood near. Debased and he knew it.

I said, "Francie will be back soon." A little bit of hope for him. That was the plan. Draw him in a little. Don't let him rush off angry. The plan, the plan. I pointed to the morning's dishes, played saucy, said, "If you're going to linger, sir, make yourself useful."

No more about his gun, no more about Francie, Mr. Drinkins gathered our dishes, such as they were, gathered them into the scrub bucket Lucky had made from bark, gave a positive sort of grunt, headed straight to the brook path. Which, how did he know so exactly where we washed dishes?

I heard Aarto's whistle, a mighty thing to rival the wapiti. He whistled again, and again once more. Lucky, of course, would hear it and not approach. Francie, if she heard it, the opposite—she'd hurry in. Because that was the plan.

We hadn't checked the coop for a day, and—acting normally, as per plan—I went to look, found the hens had provided nine eggs to add to the four we had left. So dinner with our guest could be omelets. Because he was going to be a guest. I remembered the cartridges in my bib pocket, picked them out one at a time, put them under the hay. Not even the chickens would find them there.

My rage slowly built even as I prepared the fire, intense rumination. Aarto's crazy planning. Francie's. My own. But really. To have to eat peaceably with Dale Drinkins and his photos and his curses and his fake papers. Poor Franciella, who'd have to play at being wronged, recovering bravely, all while holding out the faint possibility of remorse, just the right smidgen of hope, enough hope to keep Mr. Drinkins quiet without my murdering him. I stuffed the tears, broke eggs, made batter, banked coals into a wall at the back of the fire, put a chunk of elk fatback into our huge pan till it melted a little for grease, poured in the cornmeal batter.

Simple truth: food restored order.

Shortly I heard the tinkling and rattling again, and it was Mr. Drinkins with our load of dishes. He carried it to Family Table, laid it all out to dry.

"Set the table for four of us," I said.

And he did it, he set the table, picking among the dishes and mismatched flatware he'd just washed, asking after napkins, ha-ha.

"Get us a bucket of water, sir. That's kind of how we do it."

I turned the corn bread pan as Lucky had shown me: five thoughts east, five thoughts west, five thoughts north, five thoughts south. Thoughts were like minutes. You tracked your mind.

Mr. Drinkins loomed. His cheek was torn from its encounter with the gravel under Bronco's boot. I aimed to put him off balance: "Tell me more about this Crow maiden of yours."

"Blackfeet," he said warily. "We was close once."

"And what does that mean?"

"She was Injun, ma'am. It just weren't proper."

"You just won't stop, will you."

"You asked."

"I asked about a person. What happened to her?"

"She'd got beyond useful, I'm afraid. Some you put out to pasture. Some you put down."

I'd thought we were having a conversation, but this was not a conversation. This was a manipulation, a threat, some kind of extortion. I did not miss the turn in his voice.

"About that gun," he said.

"You'll have to take that up with Bronco," I said.

"A formidable case, that feller," he said.

"More than you know."

I tended to my corn bread, my back to our poacher. He'd made his threats. He knew I'd heard them. Give him credit for guile. We'd have to hold him close. We'd have to count on Francie's fortitude, on Aarto's training, on Lucky's equanimity.

"I'll be back," Mr. Drinkins said. He paced the yard a while, then seemed to make a decision, marched down the trail and around the bend and out of sight. Good if he was leaving. Bad if he was getting a new weapon. But shortly he reappeared, no fresh bulges in his pockets or at his belt, just the familiar old rucksack on his back, and awkwardly carrying something, a big sheet of what looked to be plain cardboard all wrapped up with masking tape. He leaned it on Family Table, great care: window glass for Francie.

"Done," he said.

The plan. I said, "You can give that to her yourself."

Honestly, he blushed. Looked like he could hug me. Sometimes you get to see a person another way, if only for an instant.

"Stay for dinner," I said, not too generously: it was one calculation after the next, it was the plan.

Chapter Fifty-Five

Lucky stayed up on the ridge among the sentinel rocks—he'd heard the whistle and so hadn't come in. Aarto knew exactly where to find him, brought him his blanket and knife. He could take care of feeding himself.

I put fatback in our skillet and scrambled all our eggs, added piles of salad with plain vinegar for dressing, not bad. The corn bread was of another order—best I'd ever done, Clay's government-surplus cornmeal—stood tall and steaming out of the fire, scorched at the edges and still warm. I divided it into five great wedges, one to save for my husband. Mr. Drinkins sat by Francie, not too close. And though she'd been jazzed by the gift of glass, she wasn't giving him any openings, didn't even let him in her room to see about installation, a builderly excuse about refitting the shutters to accommodate. Aarto seemed as easy in his pale skin as ever, ate cheerfully. I sat close at his side, put a wifely hand on his arm.

"We shore eat good," Bronco said. He smelled like smoke and sugar and some kind of gourmet mushroom you'd pay a hundred dollars for. We must have looked for all the world like a happy, expecting couple.

Up on the ridge Lucky no doubt watched over us, eating his raw fish and cress, sitting back on his haunches among the rocks, those ageless sentinels.

"I brought a little something," Mr. Drinkins said. "They call it *postres*." He lifted his rucksack to the bench beside him, a thing heavy with the essentials of survival. You could see a hatchet handle, a length of rope, a mineral hammer; you could hear spikes and turnbuckles and chains and old bones clanking as he rummaged, prospecting tools. At length he pulled out a bottle of liquor, like nothing I'd ever seen, big square thing.

"Tay-quila," he said, mocking someone he found inferior. No laughs from us. "One liter. I got 'er in Mexico last winter, like cactus in a bottle, so they say."

I'd heard of tequila because of the song, but I'd never stopped to think what it was. A little bit couldn't hurt. I took an experimental sip after Mr. Drinkins opened the bottle and handed it to me, foreign thing, taste of dirt and flowers, liquid desert, kind of awful, kind of beautiful. And the label, so pretty, cactus and an adobe hut and a pretty girl where you might expect a skull and crossbones.

"Don't be dainty," Mr. Drinkins said.

So—why?—I took a pull like a sailor. That desert taste, and better, the warmth surging up, like the fire had come inside.

Francie tugged the bottle away from me, took her own lusty pull. "No more for the pregnant girl," she said, that much wiser, and pulled again.

Aarto tugged the bottle from her, pretended to drink hard but drank not at all, obvious from my angle, burped theatrically.

And back to Drinkins, then round and round excluding me, Aarto and Francie both pretending—he'd signaled her somehow. There wasn't much to say, just the silent fake sharing of the alcohol, what little I'd had straight to my head. Aarto put his arm over my shoulder, smooched my cheek comically. He was so much taller than Lucky, and his arm so much heavier, those teeth looming in the firelight.

Francie glowered, took another real sip.

Dale slid closer to her, attempted a smooch.

She shoved him away violently. He tried again and she laughed—we all laughed—leapt to her feet, backed away from him, from all of us, nearly into the fire. Mr. Drinkins stood, too, and leaned in all puckered up toward her and she punched him square in the nose, not kidding around. He loved that, laughed with us, holding his nose, laughed heartily, his cheek scabbed from Aarto's boot. I wiped my cheek of Bronco's kiss, slipped my hand out of his. Lucky up there on the ridge. Francie and Mr. Drinkins at an impasse, but passing the tequila bottle back and forth.

"Come talk to me a minute," Mr. Drinkins said to Francie.

Cautiously she got up, walked with him into the shadows, no farther, kept him at arm's length, Mr. Drinkins imprecating, tones we could hear.

Aarto got up and broke sticks. He broke a lot of sticks, added them to the fire, added logs, though it was a warm night.

Francie pushed Mr. Drinkins away—apparently he'd gotten too close. She returned to the fire, Mr. Drinkins following. He searched for something to say, then finally: "You are a good team."

And Bronco said, "Thankee."

That struck me as so funny, Francie, too—anyway, we women set in to giggling.

"You'll miss this girl," Mr. Drinkins said.

"He got the papers," Franciella said. "Show the people."

"We saw," I said. "They are not impressive."

Aarto gave me that look: the plan. He said, "That glass looked pretty primo. Clear as."

At that, Mr. Drinkins fished out an envelope we hadn't seen. "Now we all got secrets," he said. He drew out the pages in there, handed them to Aarto, who handed them straight to me.

"A birth certificate?" I said.

"Keep looking."

"Eleanor Drinkins?"

She'd been born in 1971, whoever she was, so nearly ten years older than Francie and I. A passport, too, dismal crimped photo of a formidable-looking woman, her broad features barely visible, cold stare for the camera.

"Like I told you," Mr. Drinkins said. "Recently deceased, amen. But these here papers are good. Quite good. The passport was on account we were back and forth to Mexico."

"And your wife?"

"Oh, she's hale and hearty, that one. You misunderstand me."

"He wants to give me a new identity," Franciella said in just such a way: the plan.

"New identity," Aarto said, too ironically Bronco. "Now if that don't beat all."

"A new identity? Whatever for?" I said.

Mr. Drinkins said, "You kids are on the run. Don't gas me. No need. But right here is Francie's keys to the kingdom."

Franciella was nodding away, as if any of it made sense. She said, "Dale says I can move into Eleanor's rooms sometime soon."

Aarto clucked a cowboy cluck.

"Move in, why?" I said.

"Yes, that could use some explanatory phrases," Aarto drawled, channeling Clay Marvelette.

"Well, maybe this will seal the deal," Mr. Drinkins said. "A gift from Eleanor to you, Franciella. You'll have to adjust it some. But it'll go with your new life down in town." And he dug in that rucksack and pulled out a large, rolled suede item, spread it across Family Table where we all could see: a kind of gown, stitched in intricate beadwork, gorgeous beyond understanding. "That girl worked on this thing every spare minute going on ten year. It's a victory robe. Not many victories left for her. That and a headband and Francie'll pass just fine."

"Pass," Francie said.

"Just fine," Aarto said too unhappily.

Francie was incredulous but managed a light tone: "I'm going to dress up like a cartoon Indian?"

"No, no, like my housekeeper. She's most real. Or was. She worked hard on this."

"Yeah, and wait," I said, too fiery for our game. "How'd Eleanor get the name Drinkins?"

"Well, that's a long story. We adopted her. She was family."

"Everyone?" Francie said. She meant Aarto and me, both of us getting edgy, she meant play the game. Trust the plan, is what she meant. Also, trust Francie. And that did soften us.

Bronco went all shocked. "Adopted her, eh?"

Like joking, I said, "You mean you made her family so you didn't have to pay her?"

He flinched, busted, took a pull of tequila. "Mutually beneficial," he said, side-eye my direction. Was he trying to look lascivious? He was not good at lascivious, looked lurid instead.

"How'd she die?" I said.

"Plan," Francie said plainly.

"Sick a long time," Mr. Drinkins said after some thought. "Never clear what ailed her. She wanted me to have this. Said so. Wanted Francie to have it. Said so. Pass it along to that Black lady on the mountain, she said. Simple as she was."

Francie stood, unlaced the long gown, and too far into our game for my taste, pulled it over her head, wriggled and hopped and tucked till it was in place, laced it back up, too tight through her broad shoulders, too loose through her narrow hips, hanging to her ankles. She made a turn, girlish for her, looked like victory, all right. Underneath it she pulled her sweatpants off, held the leather up around her stone-sculpted calves. Eleanor, if that was really her name, lived on in that gown, the one true thing about Mr. Drinkins's story. Beads in the thousands, hundreds of thousands, sewn row by row in undulating waves across the shoulders, yes, easily a decade of fine work, mostly blue in various shades that graduated dark to light to dark again, more colorful at the bust, brown beads on red and ochre and light pink, geometric patterns, earthy colors. And were those birds across the shoulders? And mountain ranges across the belly? Along the hem a jagged but precise green-and-yellow-and-black procession of wapiti, antlers and all, forever migrating. Francie did a twirl, and the wapiti galloped along the ground, kicking up powerful dust.

I felt a chill run from my scalp into my shirt and straight down into my belly. Aarto felt it, too, had visible trouble retaining his bemused smile.

Franciella felt it, too, went dark, struggled hastily back into her sweats and out of the gown, laid it again on the table and across the bench between her and Mr. Drinkins, sat seemingly entranced by it, patted the leather, ran her fingernails between the tight rows of beads.

Mr. Drinkins sat close as he could, patted the leather as she did, trying to be natural, hand too close to Francie's. "Our girl made them beads, too," he said. "Or a great many of them. You roll clay, you stick a wire through each little tube, slice it up, fire it. I bought her the wire. The clay she dug someplace. She made a kind of Injun oven in the yard."

"Now not so fast," Bronco said.

"A Blackfeet oven," Mr. Drinkins corrected: it wasn't like he didn't know his offenses.

I said, "She died and no one took an interest? Died of what, Mr. Drinkins?"

He said, "God don't watch over all creatures, little lady."

"God's plan," Aarto said. "Plan, plan, plan." He rose, grabbed the tequila bottle like a pirate, pretended to guzzle but drank nothing, handed the bottle to Mr. Drinkins, who drained it.

Aarto stretched elaborately, then broke the night with a loon call so loud I had to cover my ears. Then another and another, uncanny. So out of place in the near-desert mountains that we laughed. He tugged Drinkins to his feet, and for a long time the two of them did calls across the animal kingdom. Loons and wapiti and moose and eagles, wolf and coyote and even whales—Aarto knew his whales. Mr. Drinkins had a fine marmot and an even better red squirrel, all the rodents. They boisterously built the fire back high, hooted out the various owls, Aarto keeping it going strong: the plan, the plan.

Late, Aarto declared it bedtime. I stood and he took my arm, and we were Mr. and Mrs. Bronco. Francie stood and Mr. Drinkins tried to smooch her. Again she belted him, and he fell back, held that nose, delighted, caught up in our web, might it hold.

Aarto took Mr. Drinkins's arm and rather forcibly turned him, walked him down the road and out of sight around the corner. You could hear them laughing down there. I drew Francie into the lodge. We decided we weren't worried about his returning middle of the night looking for more kisses. Like a lot of bad guys, Mr. Drinkins had a kind of chivalry in him, a code of conduct. Murder here, principle there. Anyway, we heard his truck start up and drive off, heard it a long way.

Drunker than he knew, he'd left those preposterously fake divorce papers on the table, but also Eleanor's startlingly real passport, the sad photos of his home. I stacked it all up and tucked them away with the antique six-shooter. Aarto rolled the gown—Mr. Drinkins had left the gown, too, truly a gift to Francie—and we brought it inside, all its strings attached. The belongings felt like leverage.

"I'll check on the horses," Aarto said.

In my room—Lucky's and my room—I stripped quickly, climbed into bed in my fresh pink underpants from Clay and size giant T-shirt. Outside we heard Aarto's yodel, neither man nor beast, and Lucky's reply from up on the ridge.

Aarto came in, all quiet. He stripped to his Swedish skivvies and T, climbed in beside me, my pretend husband, just in case our friend returned in the night. Aarto weighed double what Lucky weighed, a vast presence, the bed of boughs and fragrant pine needles and soft mosses collapsing us together in a trough. He smelled good, too, maybe the sagebrush he was always rubbing on himself, and the chill of the evening was on his skin still, his butt backed up hard against my thighs. I didn't want to spoon him so rolled away, difficult in the sagging bed, finally pressed my own butt against the long wall of his back.

He said, "Yore wriggling like a tadpole in a bucket."

"I feel more like a netted whale pulled up against the ship," I said.

"Well, it's true you're fat in the middle," he drawled, "but you're doggone cute at each end."

"Thankee, Bronco," I said.

"That's enough in there," Francie called.

We said our goodnights, Aarto breathing like canyon wind. And I tell you, I felt the greatness of him. I thought of Lucky, sent him a wave of love that I hoped he'd feel, swore I felt the wave return. At last, then, I slept, safe against the rampart of my own personal cowboy, let the monster even try.

Chapter Fifty-Six

Almost forty, and I had no vehicle. But my neighbor Jack let me use his daughter's college car while she was abroad, an impossibly tiny Fiat, color of a tomato. I visited the laundromat, washing and folding absolutely everything to give to Goodwill, lived on convenience-store groceries, ate up every canned or frozen thing in the house, went to afternoon movies—Walter hated movies, talked all the way through, couldn't give himself up to them ("They're just actors, Cindra"). The movies made me cry. They made me laugh. They were my emotional life. One of them gave me the housesitting idea. I got on a website that matched "quality sitters with quality houses," passed the screening, immediately found a posting in San Francisco, a diplomat's home, open ended, take care of gardens and pets, to begin March 1. Their houseman and cook were going with them to Asia. Once I was settled in, their housekeeper would come by three afternoons a week to clean in case I'd think no one would be paying attention. The houseman interviewed me, super stern, his English accented and formal, then, my having pleased him, put me on with the lady of the house. She was so interested in Ricky, in Ricky's heritage. They loved Montana, frequent fishing trips. There were eleven other applications of interest. She liked how I talked dirt—garden dirt, I mean—they liked my biography: widow, thirty-nine, seeks new life. They liked that my son was in school nearby. I suspect they liked that I was white like them yet checked a diversity box or two. For pets they had fish and land crabs and lizards, perfect. For references I had my neighbor Jack and my volunteer lawyer, Carl "Ronnie" Ronson, apparently sufficient: the houseman spoke to both. The last hurdle upon my arrival would be a conversation with their daughter, my age, unlikely to be a problem, said the lady of the house.

"A leap of faith," I said, meaning for me.

"We have insurance," the lady replied.

Late January I canceled all utilities as of one month hence and hosted a series of yard sales, the first formal, the last ten cents a bag, shower curtains and all. Neighbor Jack (not a Walter fan after years of petty disputes) let me store twenty boxes and one crate of Legos in his shed, adopted my houseplants. I brought the mailbox in, no forwarding address, left the house echoingly empty, the least I could do, ran through with a mop and a broom, gave Jack the keys so he could take possession of the last thing: my beloved mattress, complete with bedding.

I put everything I wanted—clothes, mostly, one extra pair of shoes, a single precious book, my Felco trimmers and garden apron, my pearl, our wilderness notebook, a ceramic turtle made by Ricky in fourth grade, the odd toiletries—into one medium roller suitcase, the rule I'd made for myself. Jack drove me to the T, the T took me to South Station, and from there it was Amtrak to San Francisco (to fly seemed too quick) and an Uber to my new digs, a seemingly modest stack of glass-and-steel boxes that climbed Telegraph Hill among terraced gardens.

The diplomat's daughter, lovely woman, let me in the back-side kitchen through a brick archway under vines, small windows to an overgrown but pretty tea garden, vetted me over finger foods, a lot of laughter, thank goodness—I was in. Upstairs she showed me the full-wall fish tanks, like windows in the dark back side of the home, incredibly colored reef fish and fancy shrimp, bright sea anemones waving placidly, reptile terrarium adjacent, big as a room, crawling with lizards and tree crabs and, yes, turtles, all maintained professionally—my job was feeding. The housekeeper would be by a week from Monday to meet me, not too early, ha-ha, "Florita. She's a lovely woman, Mexico City Mexican and as sweet as pie, but a field marshal, I'm telling you—be sure to tidy up for her!" And then to the front of the house, which hung as if floating, vast windows looking out on the bay and the whole world, Alcatraz out there, the Golden Gate, the Bay Bridge, too, which was the bridge to Ricky. My room was the bottom box, accessed via spirals, a terrarium itself, lots of glass, bathroom black, bed like heaven. When my hostess was gone, I flopped on it, slept through dinner, through the night, woke to the view, slept again till noon, then three.

I loved San Francisco unreservedly, being a lover of views, for one thing, and the ocean, for another, also fog banks, and spring so much further along than back in Massachusetts. I walked everywhere, got myself set up. Maria had said I'd find Lucky the seventh day I arrived. I struggled to believe, to make that mean something. Maybe that I'd find some kind of peace—Maria was ever allusive, one thing meaning another.

Because lest I forget, Lucky was dead.

Ricky came over the third day I arrived, which was a Tuesday, after a busy week for him, bottle of champagne. We sat upstairs in big leather chairs, watching the fish, drinking from the most elegant crystal, Indian takeout. After a couple of flutes and a lot of tikka masala picked up with naan, he said, "I found Donut Dora."

To which I replied, "Ha-ha."

"No," he said, "I really did."

I don't think he expected me to be unhappy. "Ricky, no."

"Momma, yes. She's my grandmother, for one thing, so I'm well within my rights. She's here in San Francisco. It's her town. It's where she met my grandfather."

"It's where she got in trouble."

"I found her on Instagram. We could DM her."

"What does that even mean?"

He opened his phone, opened her IG page, as he called it, and there was her reprehensible name on a fancy hardcover memoir, real publisher, dramatic cover, photo of her at thirteen with her index finger through the hole of a spinning donut: *The Karter Kids*.

He said, "What should we write to her?"

"We should write to her nothing."

"No. We will say Hello, Grandmother." He began to type, well within his rights, damn him, narrating all the way. "This is Mountain Turtle, also known as Ricky Zoeller Sing. I am the son of Lucky Turtle and Cindra Zoeller."

"Better not to mention me!"

"Of course mention you. Let's see . . . I'm a grad student at Berkeley Engineering, and my mom is here visiting. We'd love to get coffee, maybe, or meet for a walk."

I was ever rueful: "Coffee and a donut, Dora."

"Ha-ha," Ricky said. "It's sent."

"What?"

"It is sent."

"Ricky, goddamn it."

"You're angry with me."

"Exact."

"But if we don't do anything, how will we find Lucky on the seventh day you arrive when this is the third day already?"

"Sweetie."

He filled my glass. The champagne was exactly the thing.

"I'm tired of these fish," I said. "The constant movement, like they can't make up their minds and just settle down someplace."

"Then let's go look at the view, the static humans, and I'll tell you about school."

Downstairs we found two severe chairs that turned out to be perfectly comfortable, perfectly positioned, little table between them, the lights of the Embarcadero starting to twinkle, the lights of the ferries. The champagne, too, twinkle, twinkle.

Ricky checked his phone. He was always checking his phone.

"Ooh, she's answered," he said.

"What? I'm not ready."

"It's a fast world," he said. "Okay. It's all caps, no punctuation, your soul sister."

And he showed me his screen.

OH GOODNESS GRACIOUS HOW WONDERFUL RICHARD I DO
REMEMBER YOUR MOTHER SHE WAS OUR LITTLE RUNAWAY AND
RUINED EVERYTHING COME SEE ME IF YOU LIKE THIS FRIDAY AT
ONE P.M. MUCH TO DISCUSS JUST YOU

So, on the sixth day I arrived, as Ricky pointed out, he and I climbed out of a pleasant-smelling Uber, this time in the Presidio, beautiful house perched at the apex of the street, built out in back, the landscape falling away to the thousand rooftops below. He'd been talking a mile a minute, had to be back to campus by ten past three, looked as if he'd been up all night, his clothes like they'd been up all month, beautiful clothes nevertheless, sewn by a friend.

"She owns the building," he said. "Rental units upstairs, rental unit in the basement. She occupies the first and second floors, new steel deck out back, which must have views clear to Taishan."

"Focus," I said. "We're here to ask about Lucky."

"That *was* about Lucky!"

We climbed the high stoop.

Ricky, no hesitation, banged the polished knocker six times, one for each day of my journey. Shortly the door opened, and it was no servant but the woman herself, a little stooped, and that was it for aging, as tanned as ever, eyebrows raised high: we recognized each other. She didn't invite us in, even blocked the doorway. Behind her you could see it was a nice old apartment, big bright windows in back, the Pacific horizon. She wore a surgical mask, not the first I'd seen, but close, the pandemic and what to do still such a mystery, not for long.

"Grandma," Ricky said.

"Oh Lord," she cried. Because here was the only man who could move her, this one right in front of her, her only grandchild. She tugged her mask tight, and they fell into a hug—Dora Dryden Conover, a hug! Well, I'd seen that before. She held her breath, held him out to look. "You're a big creature," she said, audibly conserving that breath. She backed away, took a big gasp of air. "The news from Italy, terrible," she said, meaning the Covid-19 news, which very soon we'd all of us be paying closer attention to.

"Is my father alive?" Ricky said, always to the point.

"I said just you," she said sharply.

"Hello, Dora," I said.

"Your father is alive," she said only to my son. "But I'm afraid it's bad news. He's homeless. He's broken. He's irretrievable. I wouldn't go looking."

"Alive," I said, calling her out for the lie.

"If you call those shelters living," she said unrepentant. Then to Ricky alone, "Oh, Richard."

"Mountain Turtle," Ricky said.

She jerked her gaze to me. What rubbish had I been feeding him? She took another deep breath, stepped forward bravely, always with the theatrics, took his face in her hands.

"Your father was abandoned. Left to his days in prison. Now in a prison of his own. He speaks ill of your mother. He shouts at tourists on the sidewalks. He spits and swears. Tell her she best not go looking. She was the root cause. The repercussions ruined me as well." She stepped back, breathed. Stepped back a little farther.

"You look pretty comfortable," Ricky said, not one for drama.

Hers or mine. Because I'd fallen into tears. With her words she'd pushed me back through the membrane of magical thinking, self-recrimination: Lucky alive, Lucky harmed, my fault, this blondie with her beautiful life.

On Dora went, now safely back in her foyer, easing the heavy front door into our potential paths: "But there's something you can do to help. You,

Ricky. A battle we can win, though your father may be lost." She shoved the door shut behind her, a massive blue-enamel thing, precision fitted, her finger in the air to say, Wait.

Ricky put his arm around me, pulled me to him. "Alive," he said.

"Don't listen to the snake," I said.

"I'm hearing only the good words," he said.

And then the old viper was back, flick-flick of her forked tongue. She handed Ricky a plain folder labeled MONTANA. "Simply put, I need an heir," she said. "More important, Far Turtle needs an heir. These Free Men have gone mainstream. They are the local government up there, and the media, and the banks; they own all the businesses. Mind your birthright, young man. They killed Far Turtle, your kin. They ruined Lucky every way they could from a child to this very afternoon. They're not done with you either, is my guess. But at last, you must win for me, dear Richard, *you must win*."

"But what is it I'm supposed to win?"

"Richard, dear boy. Pay attention. There's a trumped-up lawsuit to strip us of Turtle Butte Ranch, articles of abandonment, they're calling it. These men want to seem like concerned citizens, but in fact they're thugs. They've made their own laws, but they can't change Federal law, and our claim is absolute. Your claim, I should say."

Ricky stood taller. "What about Lucky Turtle?" he said. "What about my dad if he's alive?"

"He's not," I said.

"Lucky won't take part," Lucky's own mother said. "Lucky won't see me. Lucky won't see you either, is my guess. After prison, the one you put him in, Cindra"—flick, flick, forked tongue—"I collected him, I took him in, I tried to open him back up, but they'd broken him. He lives from shelter to shelter and alley to alley. He drags a wagon hither and yon. He lives on the docks. He begs for food. There's nothing to be done."

"There's something to be done," I said.

"Well, it won't be you who does it," Donut Dora said.

"We'll find him," Ricky said, calm as topsoil. "And whatever's to be done, we'll do it."

"*You* will do it, Richard, just you. Ask your treacherous mother if she recalls the name Dale Drinkins."

"Do you remember that name, treacherous Mom?"

I laughed and said, "Oh, for Christ's sake. Dora, you're pushing every button."

She scowled, she glowered. "Richard, of course she remembers him. Well, now he's their fixer. Tried getting me out on a date. Well, in fact I went. Dinners in Billings after Lucky was put away. Thought he'd charm me. I learned soon enough. Never signed a thing, none of his phony papers. Your mother brought him down upon us. It's you who must take this on, Richard. Think of your birthright."

"Take what on, Grandma?"

"Please don't call me that."

"Win what?"

"We've a court date in ten days. The info is in that envelope along with authenticating artifacts. There's no way I can attend with my health. Your appearance here today is auspicious. You are in fact the heir. Where I was but an illegal wife. Our lawyers will be there. I've long since told them about you, and they're very excited we've found you. The goal is simply change of venue, Federal court. Where we will prevail. But you must be there. The lawyers will call."

"Grandma, I'm in grad school."

"It's your heritage, Richard!"

And that was it. Silhouette against the big light of her windows, she backed into the safety of her home, shut the door against considerable air pressure. How long had she been preparing this speech? Ricky, unperturbed as always, asked his phone for an Uber, and we walked downhill to the intersection to wait, still under the eyes of that house.

"Let's see," he said, and opened the big envelope, discovered more envelopes inside. The first held Lucky's grandfather's railroad ID: Robert Sing, address and birth date both listed as unknown.

"Authenticating artifact," Ricky said wryly, but put it to his heart, pressing hard.

Next envelope held four photographs, poorly kept, perhaps always in Dora's purse, tearing at old folds. Two close-ups from the same sitting, same sober gentleman, slicked black hair, shirt of mattress ticking, tightly closed collar, burningly intelligent eyes, delicate features, almost pretty, tight lipped in one, vague smile in the other: Far Turtle, Robert Sing, Lucky's grandfather. The next shot was of a kid in uniform, US Army, the name Sing above his shirt pocket. Lucky's dad, Thomas Sing, who'd rejected his Turtle name. The next photo was of him and Dora, his arm around her, dazzling beauties, both of them, children, really, the triumphant smiles of those who have escaped their fate: also the unending kiss.

Why no picture of Lucky? We studied the shot of the happy couple, soon to be parted. "See what's in her hand?" Ricky said. He thought it was a bouquet and this their wedding, but no way they'd been wed: I thought it was money, a huge thick wad of cash, pai gow.

In the next packet were more photos, those square old Brownie shots, some with deckled edges, all dated in the borders, midsixties: Thomas Sing's first photos. Not offered as examples of his living hand and eye but simply as evidence. Far Turtle with horses, Far Turtle with sheep, Far Turtle with two men. One of whom—oh my god—was Clay Marvelette, handsome cowboy, age about mine now. The other must have been Joh Johman, broad shoulders, big toothy smile, the only smile to be seen, ten years older. Far Turtle, then, ten years more, posing beside the house he'd built and been shot in, the little house that Lucky had grown up in until that date, demolished in sorrow by the time I got to Challenge. Ricky and I handed the photos back and forth in silence under hot sun, stared at each one a long time: Far Turtle.

"Nice of her to give these to us," he said.

"It's not nice," I said. "It's self-serving. And there must be many more. Thomas Sing was a photographer most of his short life, remember? She's got a cache somewhere. She and Far Turtle must have treasured them."

"Far Turtle is dead," Ricky said. "And Thomas is dead. But my father is alive."

"'Homeless,'" I said. "'Ruined.' It's nonsense. She only wants to hurt me. She only wants you to do her dirty work. Your father is dead."

"Mommy, he is alive."

The car pulled up and we climbed in back. Ricky opened the next envelope, drew out a brittle document, handwritten, perhaps by a scribe, dated 1933, the cursive so elegant that today it might be mistaken for a font. Ricky looked at it closely. "Letter of Understanding," he read. "I hereby place under the custody of Joh Johman the lands of the Turtle Butte Ranch as purchased from Aapo Johman and as outlined by the coordinates designated herein below and upon the enclosed deed of ownership. Be it known that this custody is in constitution a formality meant only to aid in the legal registration of said deed." And signed Robert Sing, same handwriting, Chinese characters alongside, indescribably beautiful, not so much for their form but for the realization that Lucky's grandpa had drawn them, sitting side by side with Aarto's, maybe another decade older, Joh, as well, who'd have been barely twenty-one. We touched the characters wordlessly—perhaps the old name was not lost after all—the car falling down the grand hill, our driver oblivious of the momentous doings in his back seat.

I said, "She's had this stuff in her possession all along."

"All along," Ricky said.

In the next envelope was the deed itself, original signatures.

The next document was Lucky's Seattle birth certificate. We looked that over closely, too: Lucky Sing. October 8, 1972.

"I've never known his birthday," I said.

"A Libra," Ricky said.

"Whatever that might mean. He was Lucky Turtle, he would say, and not a Libra or anything else."

"He's alive," Ricky said.

"If we can believe Dora."

"If we can believe *Maria*."

"Those are two big ifs."

"Well, let's go with it. Let's say we believe. Let's err on the side of believing. It's a non-zero possibility. I mean, why do we believe he's dead?"

"Death certificate?"

"From *Walter*, Mom."

"Oh, Ricky," I said.

"And why do we think he's in San Francisco?"

"Maria," I said.

And Ricky, so focused: "So that's better than non-zero. Now we're into non-negative. And if we believe based on non-negative possibility, then we know my father is homeless. In San Francisco. Momma, we can find him."

"How do you propose we do that?"

"There are homeless shelters. We'll visit them all. People on the street know one another. We'll ask around." And then, as the Uber driver carefully bumped over streetcar tracks (crowds coursing obliviously, a mask here, a mask there), Ricky drew out the thickest envelope, opened it, found it full of newspaper articles. The car climbed precipitously. No time to look. We'd arrived at the diplomat's secret driveway, maze of inclined streets under Coit Tower.

"You take all of this with you," Ricky said. "I have class at three-ten. Take all this stuff, look it over, and ponder. I'll be back tomorrow. I've got lab all morning, class at one, so after that."

"The seventh day I arrive."

"That's right. Stay positive, Mom, okay?"

"I'll stay non-negative, how's that?"

In the diplomat's house I watered plants, I fed the fish and the reptiles. After a shower, after a nap, after a snack of pet-store crickets, just kidding, I pulled out the newspaper clippings, several dozen, all short, all about my escape from Camp Challenge. The whole affair had been framed as a kidnapping, Dora Dryden Conover throwing her own son into the fire in multiple stories, calling him an "errant Indian." Her own son, let me repeat. "A misguided Native youth," she called him in an extended interview that turned into a plea for donations. A youth whose true heritage she knew, and intimately. I was identified in various articles as a camper, a minor, a model Challenge *inmate*, never named. She hadn't wanted to lose her grants! Lucky was identified as Mr. Turtle, which would have been amusing if it were amusing. Francie was identified as a minor from New Jersey and left at that.

But there was one more story, a young woman of thirteen who'd committed suicide at the camp, one Azalia Martinez. Ocelot, my little tough night buddy! I knew it wasn't true—Ocelot a suicide?—knew something else had happened to her, something official, something to do with the trouble that must have come after Francie and I disappeared, something to do with Vault. I couldn't go on searching, because there'd be much more, and every fragment would leave me bereft.

So, to action. I Googled homeless shelters, and one by one began to call, all around San Francisco and then Oakland. My question was simple, put to people who were used to frantic relatives (also, no doubt, uncaring relatives), warm people who wanted to help.

"Do you know a man named Lucky Turtle? Or just Lucky? Or maybe Lucky Sing?"

They did not. And likely wouldn't have told me if they did, though most were willing to walk a fine line. They consulted logbooks, databases, dug in their own memories, offered me next phone numbers to call. I mentioned the waterfront, as Dora had said something about the docks. But perhaps she was remembering Far Turtle's story, assigning it to Lucky. Finally the articulate young man on the phone at Sixth Street Shelter suggested a place that hadn't come up in my searches. A smaller facility, he said, privately run, with a strong focus on mental health. One of the better ones, with counseling, job training, social opportunities, community support, showers even. Harmony House, it was called, nice.

I talked at length with a woman there named Carol Washington. "Your husband!" she said. But she didn't know that name. "I'll put it out there," she said. And took my information, phone, email, relationship. "And you wish to see him? If he wishes to see you?"

"I do."

I stayed non-negative. Almost giddy in fact.

Ricky called and we talked so fast, confident we'd found the path. Afterward, to calm down, I worked in the diplomat's gardens, thinning, pruning, aerating the soil around truly exotic shrubs, raking the mulch high, moving terrace to terrace, all of it planted so beautifully, so logically, one level hanging into the next, pulling weeds, watering, coarse composting, every gesture I made aided by tools and supplies already in place, these good people, their good hearts alive in their gardens, the feral parrots squawking above, all the various hummingbirds coming to the feeders strategically placed, wind chimes quietly singing, grace.

As the spring gloaming descended I crept inside, craving brightness, washed my hands at the capacious stone sink in the kitchen, found some cheese in the small fridge, which had been left freshly overstocked by my kind hosts, found some crackers, found a cucumber in the large fridge, found a bottle of wine in the cooling tower, such privilege, opened it carefully, put a towel on my arm, reused the glass from champagne, climbed the stairs to sit with the fish, the loneliest I'd been since Walter's death. I thought to call Ricky, got out my phone. And on its face a notification, just a phone number, and inside a long text:

Cindra, hi. This is Carol Washington from Harmony House. So good to speak today. Our outreach person was in this afternoon. Outreach is our eyes and hearts on the street, as not every person in need will come to us, in fact not many.

We gave Outreach your information sheet and they say they might know your person or at least a possibility and will try to arrange a meeting. Probably you should be prepared to move quickly, as we have no mechanism for holding people, should this be the right person and should he want to visit. You are a beautiful soul, don't forget.

Chapter Fifty-Seven

I can't say the month or day, but it was a chilly morning, quiet of birdsong, Lucky and I in bed awake, things passing between us as if we were sunlight and window. In sleep I'd worked his thigh between mine, woke from my wild dreamworld clamping that taut, tall leg, gripped it tighter as he woke, too, that one sly thing in his eye, that thing only for me, and it was there and I gripped his thigh between my own and rocked looking square into his sleepy face, taking his kisses on my chin, my throat, soon my breath coming short and soon his, too. I climbed atop him. I'd learned to be more noisy, and Lucky had learned to say things, love and forever and beauty things, those little Lucky compliments. To which I was responding with theatrical cries when we heard Aarto come through the elk hide in his brusque way, flapping and scraping, footsteps loud and hard. I stepped up the shouting, showing off as Lucky pulled out in the midst of his—

But our bedroom door flew open, and Mr. Drinkins was there, me all atop Lucky.

"Dog fucker," Drinkins shouted. He instantly had me by the hair, pulling me back and off Lucky, had me naked on my knees by the bed, something drawing a sharp line on my throat. He shouted, "Where's my fucking piece? Where is it? Get me that gun, dog-fucking whore. And my papers, my goddamn papers."

Lucky rolled fluidly off the bed, stood to his full height, just this rail of a young man, calm and steady and naked, still half-tumid. He gave Mr. Drinkins the long gaze, said, "I will get your gun."

"You'll want to know your Bronco is out there fucking my beloved," Mr.

Drinkins said, desperate tones. Clearly he'd come up through the brook, clearly surprised them on one of their warm rocks, their bed of moss at the edge of the clearing, any of the million places I was always spotting them. Two kids in love, that's what Mr. Drinkins had seen, then two more. His hand shook, the knife wobbled, the blade pressed into my skin. He'd picked his battle, wasn't going to take on Bronco.

"I'm serious," he shouted.

I felt a trickle of blood, then more, blood dripping off my collarbone and onto my breastbone.

He wanted the gun to shoot Aarto, plainly. And plainly was out of his head and now would shoot Lucky, too. But I found him pathetic rather than scary, couldn't cry, couldn't speak, didn't say a word when I ought to have been yelling. He was so distraught that he didn't sense Aarto slipping up behind him, Aarto again, naked as Lucky, naked as I.

Aarto gave Mr. Drinkins a professional pinch to the neck, dropped the big fool to his knees on the floor beside me, the knife dragging itself across my throat. Lucky dove to reach under the bed. I was cut but couldn't tell how badly. Blood came oozing, not pumping. Okay. I pressed my hand on it.

My husband poked the old six-shooter against Mr. Drinkins's temple.

"Dress," Aarto commanded me. To Mr. Drinkins he said, "Who is with you?"

But Mr. Drinkins couldn't speak, could hardly stand. He hadn't had a plan beyond seeing Francie, making his case around those papers some new way, maybe retrieving his gun and the gown, had only reacted: nothing was as he'd left it. Aarto dragged him outside. Bleeding, I leapt into my pink overhauls, Lucky into his only shirt, only pants. He took my last pair of new white underpants and held them to my neck, walked me outside.

Where naked Aarto had already laid Mr. Drinkins face down in the dirt, big hand on his head. "Get me that lariat," our cowboy said.

I took over, pressed the cloth to my wound. Lucky found the lariat, simple stiff length of waxed rope, slipknotted. Aarto slapped the loop under Mr.

Drinkins's feet in a practiced motion, pulled it snug, pulled Mr. Drinkins's arms back, wrapped his wrists, made a calf of him, perfect control.

I stood close over Mr. Drinkins, I don't know why—it wasn't triumphal, exactly, more just fascinated, a chance to look fate in the eye. I pressed my hand hard to my neck, those fresh panties dripping blood between my fingers now. "You cut me," I said evenly.

Mr. Drinkins found my eye, found his voice: "Dog fucker," he croaked.

Lucky pressed his hand over mine on my throat, brought me to Family Table. The dish pot had boiled—Aarto put it on first thing each morning—so Lucky peeled my hand away, took the panties, dunked them in the boiling water, hooked them with a stick, stirred them around to rinse, fished them out, waved them steaming in the sharp air, cooled them enough to press again on my wound, rinsed them again, super patient, fishing them out, folding them, pressing them on my throat, rinsing, folding, pressing so gently and right where in sweeter times he had liked to kiss.

"Not so bad," he said.

Franciella appeared from the brook trail all dressed, carrying Aarto's shirt and trousers, his huaraches. She saw the blood leaking into the compress on my neck, my overhauls drizzled in blood, but didn't hurry to me, didn't appraise my wound, just marched straight to Dale Drinkins lying there hog-tied, kicked him emphatically in the head.

"Franciella!" he wailed.

"You said you wouldn't," she cried. "You made a solemn vow." She booted him again, bare heel hard to his cheek.

"Okay, I reckon that's enough," Bronco drawled.

Francie threw his clothes at him, mad at the world.

"Franciella!" Mr. Drinkins said more quietly. "I brought you your papers, didn't I!" He squirmed against the ingenious lariat, knot designed to tighten against struggle. "I brought your window glass."

"Papers?" Francie shouted. "That's the least of your broken promises. You said you wouldn't."

And Dale Drinkins begged: "I didn't. Not till I seen you. I *seen* you. With this cowboy." And he thrashed more against the lariat, began to choke.

"Settle down there, pard," Bronco said. He put that reassuring foot on Dale Drinkins's neck, pressed him harder yet to the earth, loosened the slipknot another notch—no need to choke anyone—all the while giving Francie a muscular straight-arm.

Francie came to me, pulled my hair back, knotted it, close look at my neck: "What has Dale done?"

Lucky took the compress again, ducked it in the boiling water, rinsed it with a swirl, fished it out, washed my hand, dunked the compress, fished it out, pressed it to my cut, the bleeding already slowed.

Mr. Drinkins rolled out from under Aarto's big foot, got a knee under himself, half stood. "Come with me, Francie," Mr. Drinkins begged. "Come off the range. It's all set up. We get a date. Justice of the peace. Twenty-four hours. Windows galore at my place. And you can come straight back here if it don't work out." He staggered to both feet, lunged at her, groaning with emotion.

Aarto calmly pinched that thick neck again—and Mr. Drinkins flopped like a marionette at the end of a performance. "She'll stay," Aarto said equably.

"Go ahead, kill me," Dale said. "Without my girl, kill me."

"You watch him," Aarto said to Lucky. He retrieved his garments, dressed quickly, and came to me. He inspected my wound, rinsed the panties in the boiling cauldron, continued the doctoring—more confident than Lucky or Francie, looked minutely, calm mutterings.

"It won't take stitches," Aarto said. "I got some first-aid in my pack. This Drinkins is crazy, you know. Crazy with love. A bigamist to boot, looks like."

I said, "Just don't hurt him."

"It's us going to get hurt." He washed the panties again, made a compress. "Ja, you're gonna be okay, little lady. Almost stopped bleeding. Need a couple butterflies at best. Francie, could you get the kit? It's got a cross upon it."

Francie went for the kit, seemed to take forever. View nickered, Chickadee paced, everyone upset. Mr. Drinkins came back to his senses, sputtering and rolling. Aarto knew what he was doing, doctored me quickly, antibacterial ointment and butterfly bandages and a big patch to cover.

Drinkins, it seemed, was trying to escape, as if he could roll all the way home. Lucky put a bare foot on that broad back, pressed him rather gently into the dust, tightened the lariat, yes, gentle as could be, authoritative, powerful with compassion.

"Injun, you'll be sorry," Mr. Drinkins croaked. "If you won't listen to God, you'll listen to his army! This is America, not some stinking reservation!"

"Dale, you be quiet," Francie said.

And Mr. Drinkins was quiet.

Aarto let my hair back out, used the drinking ladle to wash the blood away. He didn't hurry, didn't lose focus, rinsed my hair, tied it back with the thong from his wrist, gentle words—I'd be okay.

"Goddamn whoring Mormons," Mr. Drinkins said, misguided as always.

"Now that's enough shouting," Bronco said, just a cowboy doing chores, one more inspection of my bandage. He strode to Drinkins, bent easily and picked him up, simple as that, grunted and picked him up like a toddler in twisted jammies, carried him almost tenderly to the horse pen, big man bucking and struggling the whole way.

Lucky opened the corral and Aarto and his load came through, straight to the tether post in the center of the ring. Together the old friends lifted Mr. Drinkins high enough to loop the lariat over the post, then lowered him to the ground, maybe a touch less gently for all the struggling.

"Hog-tied and staked for branding," Bronco said, brushing his hands on his pants.

Lucky laughed. Maybe we all did.

Meanwhile, the horses paced and snorted, feinted at the bad-spirited man they'd found at their feet. Drinkins lay there shouting. You couldn't believe the epithets. He didn't like Indians, that was one theme. He didn't like Aarto with his girl, that was another. Aarto's head they'd find on a pike, like the sheep how they'd done at Turtle Butte, if you wanted a confession. He didn't like that I was pregnant and had lied to him plenty: my baby would be the size of a buffalo, tear me apart limb from guts. Francie, though. Francie, he'd take care of. She only had to come on down from the range and the Free Men would leave her be, live the life of Riley in the Drinkinses' back room.

Bronco said, "We'll just store you here till you calm down a little, pard."

Francie said, "Quiet, Dale," and he was quiet once again.

Lucky held up a large set of keys, Mr. Drinkins's keys, more sleight-of-hand. He jangled them, said, "I reckon his truck is down there at the second turn. Back in the rocks down there. That's where he always tucks it." He threw the keys to Aarto, who pocketed them in his fancy Swedish pants.

The horses pawed the dirt, snorted and stamped. They didn't like Mr. Drinkins one bit, and you must always take into account the opinion of your horses.

Chapter Fifty-Eight

I half hoped Francie would change her mind, untie Dale Drinkins in the middle of the night and let him skedaddle, that we'd be done with him, bygones being bygones, and could go on with our wilderness life. But no. She and Aarto were intent. Mr. Drinkins had revealed himself to us, and we to him. Lucky and Aarto's emergency plan was in force, and under way. Francie and Aarto would drive down to Billings in Mr. Drinkins's truck, catch the one o'clock flight to New York (at Billings Airport in those pre-9/11 days you just bought the ticket at the counter, walked across the tarmac, boarded your plane minutes before they pulled the stairs away), and from there onto Stockholm, where Aarto was a hero and could sort things out.

I was intent on New Orleans.

Lucky and I would ride the horses out, a challenging but partly familiar route south across the boundary of Far Turtle Wilderness, which was also the Wyoming state line and the top of Yellowstone National Park, one no pregnant woman should ever attempt on horseback, that's for sure, not without Lucky—but we didn't see it that way: I'd been riding all along, and Chickadee was trusty. I was seven months at most, not huge, not small. But Mr. Drinkins would report that there was a pregnant teen, so I'd have to disguise my figure. He'd report four of us, but we'd be two and two. And otherwise as well he'd report all the wrong intelligence to the police and to his posse. Which was the plan—Francie had fed him the careful disinformation Aarto had cooked up—and with the Free Men as deputies, the police would close their pincers on the lodge just about the time Lucky and I were getting on the bus to New Orleans from Denver.

There wasn't much to pack up. Aarto said to abandon everything but leave it shipshape. That way the police would find nothing to look down upon, the respect of others being the best defense, so he kept saying. To leave the food behind broke my heart. I made bread to carry and stuffed Lucky's rucksack pockets with as much of our elk jerky as I could. It was so good. We wouldn't need to carry water, all the fine springs and brooks everywhere, one canteen to bring into the world beyond. We were experts on wild greens, no problem, but brought a pile of lettuce and kale and carrots from the garden, nicely wrapped in chard leaves and tied with long grasses. Forever after when I see refugees on the news I think of them having to leave their gardens, terrible along with everything else, their gardens going on without them. And the hens, five of them. Lucky hung a huge sack of rice out in the open yard. The birds could pick through the burlap for sustenance after the scant insects were down.

"They'll feed the next creature," Lucky said, meaning Eagle, meaning Coyote, meaning whoever happened by.

There was the little blue suitcase for me, a voluminous yellow dress from the bazaar bag that might soon have been our cooking rags, T-shirt underneath stuffed with more odd clothing to give me an overhanging bust, hair tucked up under a handkerchief bonnet, also the Bible Aarto had produced from his survival pack to make my disguise complete: chubby Church Girl. Lucky wore a bright yellow tropical-tourist shirt, same bag of clothes. That and a yellow baseball cap with a big *L* on it made a nice disguise, his braids tucked down the back of his shirt—Church Man, just another vaguely foreign tourist backcountry in the Yellowstone. Law enforcement would be looking for a distressed and pregnant girl and a fierce Crow kidnapper, not these jokers.

We put what little cash Aarto had with the money my father had given me and split it all, nothing but finger-mangled paper anyway, Aarto stuffing their share into his big Swedish pants pockets. Lucky's and my share I stacked neatly back in Daddy's gift box, then into the big envelope, and stuffed it into the flap pocket on Chickadee's saddle where it hung on the fence. Seemed impossible we'd need money, but of course we would. As an afterthought, I removed my pearl necklace, gave it a kiss, tucked it into its sock and then into the envelope with the money in the saddle: that pearl didn't look Church Girl and only called attention to my wound, still pinched with butterfly bandages, still oozy, high dress collar to hide it.

All the while, Mr. Drinkins imprecated, moaned, cried for Francie. She brought him water, brought him a biscuit, more than I would have done. In the evening, the light still good, Aarto and Lucky saddled up View, threw Mr. Drinkins up on View's rump like a sack of rocks—that heavy and uncooperative—planned to transport him down to where Lucky had found his truck hidden.

He couldn't be left there tied up—he'd die, and no need. But of course Aarto had a plan. Mr. Drinkins was humiliated, also likely hungry, all his blood in his face. The bile returned: "You've kicked the wrong dog this time!" he cried, thousandth variation. "You'll be sorry, you will!"

Aarto had had enough. Also, he wanted his man cowed. He marched back up to the lodge, emerged with the empty six-shooter from its place under the spruce bows of my bed, marched back to Drinkins, put the heavy barrel on the sweated forehead and in his best cowboy said, "Is this thing your'n? Want to tell me how it works?" And he pulled the hammer back, nice clonk.

"Go ahead," Mr. Drinkins said. "I know that dog-fucking whore took out the cartridges."

But Aarto must have visited the chicken house and found those cartridges, that careful eye upon me that careless day. He lifted the gun, aimed up over the rock spires, pulled that trigger, huge echoing blast. I jumped. Francie cried out. Lucky grinned. The horses tensed—they loved a gunshot, they'd always hunted. Mr. Drinkins twisted violently.

"Missed," Aarto said.

But even warned and hog-tied and draped all sideways over View's back, Mr. Drinkins started in on a string of vile epithets, first about Aarto, stealer of women, then about Lucky, no need to repeat, some childish, some plain cruel, all of it impotent. Lucky was unprovoked, just put Chickadee's blanket on her, threw her saddle on, cinched it up. Aarto gave me the six-shooter and I tucked it in the saddle pocket under our food and atop my treasures.

"Franciella!" Mr. Drinkins cried angrily. Then begging: "Franciella." And then he repeated it and repeated it, his voice going higher, tears coming, a crescendo of supplication.

"Quiet," Francie said.

Not another word.

Lucky mounted Chickadee, let her rear and prance—she felt the excitement, the foreboding, too. View paced, his annoying load, stinking Drinkins, the unknown ahead.

Aarto climbed up in front of his unfortunate cargo and he and Lucky and the horses disappeared around the bend, farewell Dale Drinkins.

Back at Family Table, Francie and I fell into each other and our own tears came; we wouldn't be together anytime soon. "You promise me something, *mignonne*," she blubbered. "Promise me you'll stay with Lucky *contre vents et marées*. Promise me!"

I blubbered back: "What does it mean?"

"Through, like, thick and thin."

"Oh, easily," I said. "Promise me you'll come to New Orleans, a proper wedding."

"And you to mine," she said.

I know I keep saying it, but I was seventeen, Francie maybe eighteen by then: we were kids. We went back to our disguises. Francie had put the Blackfeet gown on, woven her hair in braids with jay feathers. If anyone was going to be looking, they'd be looking for a Black girl. We pulled her braids into a high confabulation and she tucked it under Bronco's cowboy hat, once Clay's. She did not look comical, important instead, even elegant, an emissary.

Lucky and Aarto returned in the dark, leading the horses.

"Where's your friend?" I said.

Aarto shrugged, said, "We filled his head with bad intelligence on the way to where we dropped him, which he thinks is near his truck but is not."

"He's got a long way to crawl," Lucky said.

"Are we worried about him?" Francie said.

Aarto nodded. Sure, we were worried. But maybe no need: "I tied him a way I learned in the service. It's called a fink hobble. Your subject can motivate but not access any knots in his bindings or reach anything he might use to escape. You know he'll try to cut that lariat on a sharp rock, but he won't have leverage. US Army tried it on magicians: beat them all. Still, we'll move fast. He'll crawl all night. Moon's up in a couple hours." And then Aarto let Bronco have the last word, Bronco's last words ever: "I'll about bet he don't rest. So we cain't rest, neither, cowgirls. We cain't rest at all."

Lucky said, "He said to tell Francie goodbye."

"Goodbye to him," Francie said.

I held Aarto a long time. He was so solid, invincible. Without him, we had only my suburban wiles and Lucky's wilderness skills, neither much good for the highway, for buses, for New Orleans.

Francie wouldn't let go of me.

But she had to, and finally we were off, she and Aarto on foot down through the trackless woods parallel to the road to find Mr. Drinkins's truck, Lucky and I over the mountain on View and Chickadee. We rode up over a pond we knew, letting the horses leave sign, brushing our tracks with pine boughs like amateurs, as Lucky felt no one would believe we'd not try to cover our tracks. His idea was to slow their going after Francie and Aarto, lead them on a chase after us, only for all sign to disappear. We drank water, a terrible mourning arising: the loss of our wilderness future. And rode the way we weren't going, the obvious way, several miles. At the edge of a scree field under steep cliffs (nothing but loose rock, no way to leave sign going forward, so none would be expected), Lucky dismounted, helped me down. We let the horses try out the scant grasses, brushed the way we'd come with careless spruce boughs, then put Lucky's homemade elk-hide hoof covers on the horses, remounted, and went back the way we'd come, all the way back to the pond, where you could easily discern that we'd watered the horses, that we'd taken a swim, even that we'd made love, and that we'd brushed the mud after to hide all that and then ridden up beyond the pond and to where else but the long, hidden trail that led out of the forest toward the tiny town of Marmot. Not even an airplane could see in that slot canyon. They'd have to follow us on foot or on horseback. We pictured whatever posse of marshals and militiamen tracking us, likely dozens, single file into the canyon, where they'd find the hoofprints Lucky and View had carefully laid down two days before. And then, mile after difficult mile, no matter their skill and hope and excitement and bloodlust, all sign would disappear. But they'd chalk that up to our increased caution, and to Lucky's expertise, and to the rocky soil, and on they would go, quickening pace, hot on the trail of nothing, reality dawning just about the time they met the rest of their gang coming the other way.

The elk-hide booties didn't leave a mark, not even in sand, at least not a mark anyone but a Lucky could read: weathered bear tracks, that's what a pro would think if he noticed anything at all. We didn't chance a direct route but rode high to stay on rocky footing and over the ridge on scree to the beaver impoundment we'd often visited foraging and onward into the tight little valley behind it, night falling, moon rising just before full. And then simply rode, mile after mile, eating our snacks of jerky in the saddle, stopping only to let the horses rest and cool, and for me to pee and stretch and complain a little, then more, all of the night. We crossed from the Far Turtle Wilderness into Wyoming and the national park, no trail but our own.

At dawn Lucky smelled a hot spring, turned us its direction, back up into a side draw, just a hot gush from the earth in Yellowstone country, too hot to touch. But down the hill some hippie long before had made a rock pool and as there was no sign of any person more recent than that, and as we hadn't heard any airplanes, and as day was rising, and as my back was vurry sore, we unrolled our two blankets on cushy pine duff above the pool, the horses loosely tethered and content in the sun amid thick pond grasses, and slept.

Chapter Fifty-Nine

On the seventh day I arrived, my phone rang early. I woke to a pretty voice: "Honey, it's Carol from Harmony House. Ms. Cindra? I'm sorry to wake you. But Outreach has found someone who might be your husband, anyway, someone named Lucky."

"He's there? He's there with you now?"

She muffled the phone. Then: "No, no, he's not here. Apparently, he's not cooperating. But Outreach has arranged a meeting. Noon today, if possible. Here at Harmony. Which is in, like, half an hour. Okay. Twenty minutes. You're fairly close. We can't make your husband honor the meeting, we can't even exert 'undue influence,' as they call it. I mean, we hope it's your husband. Outreach says the man is wary. Just, I mean, not having seen you in so long. He's actually coming a little earlier, but don't you. Let's let him settle in. So, twelve-thirty? I'd suggest you two talk here at the shelter for starters. You can make it?"

"Thank you, Carol. My heart is pounding. I can make it. I'll leave plenty of time."

"Outreach authorized me to tell you that your husband seems bright and with it, none of the yelling you reported."

"Well, that was reported to me. But I do deserve his wrath."

"You won't be alone with him, if that's a worry. That's simply policy. You're a beautiful person, don't forget it."

"Twelve-thirty," I said.

She offered the address, waiting for me to get it written down, I fumbling with the pen, all of San Francisco out there watching, and the fish in the tank circling endlessly, something scrabbling among the reptiles.

I busied myself in the gardens, dirt under my nails. I'd need a half hour to walk, not even that. I checked the time repeatedly, then failed to check when it mattered, had to dress on the run, just whatever clothes—I'd almost none.

By the time I got to Harmony House, Outreach had left.

"He was here all morning," Carol said, pure sympathy and affirmation, Black matron with flawless skin, taller than I'd pictured, far more beautiful, smart pink jacket. She stood behind a tall desk among a gentle group of clients, it looked like, three frazzled men holding newly issued clothing in neat piles atop single towels, a lone woman in filthy slippers, pair of new ones in hand, patting the new duds on the seat beside her, staring sweetly.

Carol said, "Just by himself, though. I guess the guy didn't come, your maybe husband, not so sure now."

"Kind of a saint, our Outreach," one of the men said.

"I second that emotion," another said.

A blue light came on above our heads.

"Men's showers are open," Carol said kindly. "Teddy and Eric, you two are first, but go on with them, James. And you two help James if he needs it."

"But where?" James said.

"Just follow," Carol said warmly.

Teddy or maybe Eric took James's hand and the men filed out.

I tried to picture Lucky like James, couldn't do it. To Carol I said, "So what do I do?"

"Oh, honey. Outreach took a couple little donor boxes of Cheerios, I think, for your Lucky. He said to tell you."

"Your Lucky like Cheerios?" the woman with the new slippers said.

"He likes to eat," I said.

"I'm waiting for the attendant," the woman said. "I'm not to shower alone. The green light is for me." She pointed.

Wrong Lucky, my heart kept saying. Dora must have gotten wind of a Lucky, but he wasn't ours. I couldn't hold a social face. I stared. Tears were coming, and we didn't want that. I heard Louis Armstrong calling from ahead, New Orleans. I saw Camp Challenge behind.

Carol patted my arm to get my attention, said, "Remember you are beautiful and that your life has meaning."

"I sure hope so," I said.

"Oh, yes," the lady with the slippers said.

"I'll be in touch," Carol said, so gently.

I hurried out past a new long line of men—it must have been shower hour—so many troubled souls, a lot of muttering and moaning and random curses, but conversation as well, and even laughter. I stepped outside into sunshine, fighting those tears. Fuck Harmony House. I pictured Dora, didn't want to. I marched back up the block. Fuck Outreach. I should have brought Ricky with me. So what, he had student labs. I'd need a shoulder to cry on, his. At the corner there was a commotion of sparrows feeding. On a small pile of Cheerios. Across the street toward the Embarcadero, another commotion.

Next corner, a line of Cheerios pointed the way. I crossed, entered a little park. Commotion of squirrels: Cheerios. A shrub with a branch broken downward. A single bluish pebble balanced on a guardrail. A bare footprint in mud beside a fire-hydrant puddle, a bit of broken glass stood up on end in windblown trash, a plucked tulip aimed toward the bay, more Cheerios, more commotion among the birds. At the Embarcadero I had to wait forever for a walk signal, then hurried across, scanning the lunchtime crowds.

A lady checking her phone. A blond kid shouting to his friends. A Buddhist nun. A man watching the ocean, leaning with his long hands on the balustrade, hot-dog cart to one side of him, tourist bus hawker to the other, a quiet spot in the mayhem, bright white braid all the way down his back to his knees. He was vurry thin, but maybe no thinner than when I'd known him: Lucky Turtle.

I didn't hurry. In fact, I walked as slowly as I could manage, breathing in with one step, breathing out with the next, my heart pounding like disaster.

At last, I stood at the cement balustrade beside my husband, put my hands on it as lightly as he did. We stood together a long, long time, just looking out at the roiling waters, the wind, the boats out there, the sky high with fair cumulus clouds not whiter than his hair.

"Still a tracker," he said at last.

I put my hand over his on the damp cement. His skin was dry as paper, just as I recalled. Quietly we watched the ocean for a couple of lost decades, not another word between us.

Chapter Sixty

Lucky and I slept nearly the whole day at our spa in the rocks and spires, his feeling that our sudden appearance in public just when expected could doom us, that the delay would throw off the timing of any search, create bad hearts, as he put it, meaning discouragement.

I didn't like that he hobbled the horses, strap of leather from ankle to ankle, but they'd been trained to it, and hobbled they wouldn't wander far, just enough to graze. "Keeps 'em calm," Lucky said. "And there's been some excitement."

We had a way of lovemaking that was just my sitting in his lap for hours, few adjustments, sweet desultory conversation, a rising and falling of passion, and rising and falling, and rising and falling again through sunset while the horses moseyed close, gentle snorts and nickers, keeping track each of the other. We ate our beautiful Far Turtle Wilderness food, never dressing, then lounged in the deep hot-spring pool, bigger than ours had been, in and out well into the evening, leaning our heads back on the rocks to watch the stars turn. Lucky wanted to hear stories of New Orleans. I knew vurry little but sang in a Louis Armstrong voice about what a wonderful world it could be and about the saints and recalled for him what little I'd heard about Mardi Gras: fancy costumes, beads flung through the air, jazz, hilarity, freedom, all of it hard to explain or make sound agreeable, except how happy we'd be. The moon rose east, and we climbed into our bedding, such as it was, slept in one another's arms.

In the morning, unseasonably warm, we dressed in our tourist outfits, yellow as sunflowers, stuffed that short sundress to change my shape busty, blue jeans underneath, teased my hair up high. Only then we mounted our valiant horses and continued onto the great volcanic dome of Yellowstone National Park. I held my Bible tight. Soon there was a trail, much covered with horse sign. We took the booties off the horses and continued, Lucky in his yellow baseball cap, big *L* for some forgotten team, and of course serendipitously for Lucky, add that flashy flowered tourist shirt. After a long time, we passed a horse train led by a ruddy guide who gave me a quick, friendly appraisal. He looked Lucky over too long, however.

"Got your backcountry permit?" the guide said.

Lucky shrugged, playing foreign.

I said, "We got separated from our group. This man was ill. I was trying to help him."

"What group?"

"Testamental Church of Wyoming."

"Testamental, huh?" The man's eyes were steel blue, knifed at the edges. He held a length of grass between his teeth.

I said, "Just a stomach thing, I guess. I hope not appendix. He doesn't speak much English."

"He rides well," the guide said, having softened some. He reached behind him on his saddle and found his first-aid kit, inside it found a dose of Imodium, he called it. "Fix you right up."

"We're good," I said.

"Those are Clay Marvelette's horses? I thought that ol' lizard got out of the trail game."

My heart. I said, "I don't know. They're from the group. I guess we rented them?"

Lucky held his tummy, groaned.

Yes, the guide had softened, a look of real sympathy, a man used to coddling tourists. He said, "Well, everyone knows Clay. Last two horses in this string of mine were once his, best of my lot. Have a look at the brands as you pass, the two paints at the end, Marvelette all the way."

Lucky slumped.

The man said, "Your friend seems to be drooping some there."

"Yes, I'd better get him to camp."

He said, "You are on the right trail. Just go till you hit the access road. Maybe five miles, less than an hour if you trot through the flats. Ride to the uphill side through there, though, for your mounts' sake: sharp shale to the downhill."

"God bless you and keep you," I said.

The guide tipped his hat, said, "Miss."

And we carried on. The last two horses of his string had Clay's brand, it was true. And on the last horse a pug dog rode proudly, eyeballs rolling to examine us.

"Oh!" I said. Just to see a dog!

Lucky grunted. We rode, slow pace.

"That's neat he knows Clay," I said after a while, knowing it was a danger.

"Well, see," Lucky said. "He knows me, too. Or ought to." And then he jerked his reins, and View left the trail and into the wash of a tiny brook. Chickadee and I followed, not a word. The dry brook course grew, guided us downhill until we were on the great flats inside the caldera of the ancient volcano, the heart of the park. "Always hated Wyoming," Lucky said, funny guy. The tension lifted, just ever so slightly.

A vurry beautiful river flowed ahead of us. The question of how we might cross didn't even occur to me: we'd cross one way or the other, or we wouldn't cross at all. On the other side of the river was a paved road, still a good ways away. Cars were pulling off, stopping.

"Bears," I said.

"Bears mean us no trouble," Lucky said. "It's the people to worry about."

Two grizzly bears, brown as brown and fishing, I thought, or maybe just standing in the water to get cool on the hot, hot, likely October day—peaceful, beautiful—and almost a relief to see the colorful clothing and happy postures and children, too, all standing at a stone railing to watch. We rejoined the bridle trail, crossed the river on a wooden bridge, following pretend-rustic signs all the way to the stables at Old Faithful—horse tours were big business—and there among others was Clay's horse trailer and truck, part of the plan, one made between Aarto and Clay long before, and known to Lucky. I'd only just been told. Lucky shuffled off and lurked in the huge crowd that was waiting for the geyser. In his brilliant yellow tourist duds, he blended right in. I played Bible girl, led the horses to the trailer, hitched them to the rings at the back of it, quick found the promised bale of hay inside, pulled it out onto the packed dirt, pulled the bailer twine off on one side, fanned the stuff out. The horses knew that trailer, all right, knew the taste of that hay, never so relaxed since I'd met them. I wanted to kiss Clay. If only Clay were near.

I put my face on Chickadee's flank while she feasted, didn't cry. That time was past. On the driver's seat of the truck was a piece of paper with the words *Pontiac Bonneville blue 1981* and a license number, Wyoming plate: that would be our vehicle, beautiful Clay and his friend Williams and Williams's mother, a plan Clay and Aarto had cooked up long since. Aarto would have called Williams from the airport in Billings the night before—everything working perfectly.

I had to pee so bad, didn't want to go in the building, held it—I'd pee on the side of the road soon as I could. I pictured us arriving at the bus station in Denver, pictured us parking at the far northwest corner of the lot as Aarto had instructed, pictured us boarding the bus separately, pictured us sitting in different rows, pictured our delight in arriving at New Orleans two days on. And pictured sending the next note to Daddy via Uncle Jeff: *Come see us.* I collected Lucky's rucksack, my suitcase, waddled in an exaggerated Church Girl way to the lot, waddled around the lot, spotted the car, unlocked it no problem. I put our stuff in the trunk. We could hold hands as I drove. Or where it was busy, Lucky could climb in back and hide.

My god, I had to pee.

I found Lucky standing stiffly near a probably Japanese family, not a bad idea in the overwhelmingly white crowd, stood behind him, told him where the car was.

"Blue Bonneville," he said.

In a few minutes a rumbling began. The famous geyser spit and fumed, then spouted, dramatic. I hadn't heard Lucky laugh for a while, I realized. He laughed and pointed, not even acting, and the people around him laughed, too. I waddled off, a long stroll, got in the car. To pee, to pee, I really had to pee. Shortly, Lucky climbed in the passenger's side, lay down across the seat, head in my lap. I hadn't driven in a long time. But I backed up smoothly and smoothly pulled away, simply following traffic, out of the parking lot toward Jackson Hole and Denver and our bus station, a smile growing on my lips at the thought of Aarto and Francie making their connection at JFK, heading for safe and tolerant Sweden even as Dale Drinkins and the county sheriff and likely several dozen self-righteous militiamen stormed our tidy lodge, Francie's fresh architecture, our chickens, our food, Family Table, all abandoned.

Lucky started kissing at my lap.

"Now stop that," I said.

Around a corner over the heartbreakingly beautiful Madison River, I noted that something was going on beyond a bend far ahead, briefest glimpse, just a lot of cars stopped and people milling. More bears, no doubt. Perhaps we'd see them closer up. But police lights came visible, next curve. I pictured a roadblock suddenly. My heart pounded and my baby's heart, too.

Lucky said, "What?"

The next bend took us into forest. Out of sight of the knot ahead, I eased the car into a fisherman's pullout above the river. "I think it's a roadblock," I said. "Maybe a mile ahead."

"If you saw them, they saw you," Lucky said.

"Lotsa cars," I said.

Lucky said, "It was that horseman on the trail."

And instantly I knew he was right. That guy had had a wild eye. And he'd known Clay, and Lucky, too. I made a smooth U-turn, drove back the way we'd come, my heart pounding in my neck.

"Checkpoint the other way, too," Lucky said. "Let us recover the horses—we'll go back. We'll go back into the mountain."

The horses! View and Chickadee, whom we'd thought we'd never see again. Suddenly I realized I'd left our cash in the saddle pocket, all of it, left my daddy's necklace, too, my pearl, *Hawaii*, neither so important as the money. We really did have to go back. We were in the money world again. A little carved sign pointed to a campground.

"Pull in there," Lucky said.

I put the blinker on, that's all I recall, and then suddenly a police car was swerving and screeching to a stop in front of us, more like a wreck in progress, blocking our way so suddenly that I had to swerve, too, the car drifting sideways, no seatbelts, Lucky flying across and nearly atop me. I shrieked and shrieked again, felt we would die. But our old blue bomb only came to a stop, so close to the cop car that the officer in the passenger's seat couldn't get out but banged his door against our bumper.

I didn't even think of backing up: we were done, and I knew it.

Almost worse in the moment: I'd peed my pants.

Another police car hurtled up behind us, then another and another as the puddle grew beneath me on the seat. Cops and rangers leapt out of every door, white people to a man (and all men), guns drawn. I knew to put my hands out the window. Lucky had barely sat up. He slid to his door, went to open it, first instinct to talk with the men, lips already muttering. As he pulled the handle, the door flew open, several pairs of hands reached in, yanked Lucky out of the car, several cops and rangers dragging him face down into the road, tugging his arms behind him, foot on his neck, then another on his back, then handcuffs, lots of yelling, Lucky silent.

Meanwhile, a cop in plain clothes pinned a badge to his chest, opened the rear door behind me. Far from yanking me out, he climbed over and into the passenger's side, spread his arms protectively. At the all-clear he showed me his badge. Over his shoulder I saw other cops lifting Lucky by his bound wrists and now ankles, dragging his face on the pavement, heaving him into the back of one of their cars.

"Lucky!" I cried. "Lucky!"

I felt the baby kick and kick again.

An electrified redheaded ranger stuck his head in our car. "Clear twenty-nineteen-fourteen," he shouted, or something: cop lingo.

And my good cop said, "Okay, okay. Calm down, Bozo. Clear twenty-nineteen-fourteen. Poor kid's pregnant. Injured, as well. Neck wound, slight bleeding. Her water's broken."

"No," I said. "I peed myself."

But he didn't want to hear, already sliding out Lucky's door, giving me a hand to help me follow, he and the redheaded ranger easing me to my feet super gentlemanly.

"Arrest me," I said. "It's my fault. Don't take him. He's done nothing wrong." Sudden useless glimmer of New Orleans. I spun all around, couldn't find Lucky. My cop guided me to his car, clearly a chief of some sort, accepted a Red Cross towel from a colleague, placed it on his passenger's seat, guided me to sitting. The redheaded ranger gentlemanly helped my legs in, as the good cop came around to take the driver's seat, super nice. The same men who treated Lucky so violently. Innocent Lucky. It was I who had done wrong, I who'd sealed my beloved's fate, this white girl that the cops could only see as victim, that darker person they could only see as dangerous, gentle or no, not the slightest threatening gesture, blond hair, black hair, protect, destroy.

"Lucky!" I cried.

"You're safe," the cop said. He clicked his radio handset, said, "Recovery affirmed. Twenty-nineteen-nineteen. Affirmed, do you read? Young lady's in shock. Expecting. Maybe in labor, even—water's broke. We'll forgo ambulance corps. I'll run her to the clinic myself. If you'd let them know we're coming."

"I'm not in labor," I said, pulling panties out of my neckline, scuffing my cut further. Of course it bled. "I only peed my pants. Sir? It's just pee. Arrest me. Arrest me! You've got the wrong person."

The cop, enjoying his emergency, didn't buy that, or didn't hear, delicately humped the car over the verge of the road to get around the crowds of his colleagues and their many cars, more arriving. We eased around an unmarked cruiser—black as night—and as we passed, I spotted Lucky, face gouged and gashed and bruised and bloodied, tourist shirt ripped open, gazing out the cruiser window skyward, ignoring whatever was being shouted at him.

PART THREE

Chapter Sixty-One

My dad drove all the way out to Montana, and I was released into his custody, incarceration date in Massachusetts congenially set for after I was expected to give birth. The drive back was a lot of silence. I'd finished crying. I'd finished talking. I was a different girl than Dad had known, browner and tougher and ready to take his side with Mom.

I lived with them till the birth, February 8, 1998. My baby was already named Mountain Turtle, I insisted, railing at my mother, who was disgusted. First Dag, now this. Even my father counseled against it, but so gently. I'd bring nothing but trouble to the child, name like that. I was still underage, of course, and powerless. The nurses at Watertown Hospital were a mixed lot, but a kind spokesperson delivered the news: I couldn't put that name on the State of Massachusetts Application for Birth Certificate. Baby Boy Zoeller was all they'd allow if I wasn't going to name him proper.

And so, under duress and a couple of monstrous weeks later (breast-feeding trouble, sharp isolation, torn perineum, urination unchecked), I named our boy Ricky after baby Ricky on *I Love Lucy*, that sweet actor baby, half Cuban, half wacky redhead. I was watching lots of morning television—morning was when my own Ricky slept.

But I gave him his secret name, too.

I was not allowed to contact Lucky and was given no information. I was not allowed to contact Francie and Aarto, no clue how in any case, curious unto misery about their fate. I was not allowed to contact Maria or Clay or even Dora, no internet, no phone, no stamps, no envelopes. My mother inspected everything in my room, flipped through the blank journals she'd given me as if they'd been gifts, examined every scrap of paper, took out a PO box so I couldn't beat her to the mail. I was so lonely, bereft. Not even the baby could solve that. The baby made it worse.

My court date was relatively painless, the sentencing a surprise—I was prepared for prison, prepared for the horror of leaving my baby with my mother. But Judge Pernal remanded me again, this time to what was called the Program. The Program was a pilot project in an era of enlightenment that didn't last long, a kind idea in a bleak, mostly white world. My baby and I could live halfway between prison and freedom so long as staff reported that I showed "promise and remorse," as the court called it. *Promise* and *remorse*, those were my watchwords. And so in the spring of 1998, baby Ricky and I moved to a single room in a modified dorm on the UMass Boston campus, the door removed for I guess security (suicide was a thing there, also sex, probably drugs and rock 'n' roll as well, not me). Nice for my mom, who could say I was off at school and forget about me. Nice for Dad, who could visit pretty much any afternoon he wanted, and did, sawdust in his hair after work. He was delighted to be a grandpa, gifts aimed way too old for an infant, even a toddler, like a fishing rod, a basketball. Everyone said how good it was I could make friends, but there were no potential friends there for me. I took an accelerated GED and started college all in the same months, real college, practical classes chosen for me, a social worker always at my side, baby held hostage in the dorm nursery: I was a flight risk, perversely my only source of self-esteem.

The Program's resident psychologist was Walter Linklater, a newly minted PhD. He was twenty-six, no older than Aarto, but oversaw a staff of grad students and interns. I mistook his manipulations for kindness, liked his white-smocked confidence, his sunny, scientific curiosity about every thought that might travel through the mazes of my mind, his unending interest in all I had to say, the more private the better. Even as my therapist, he was utterly transparent, always transfixed by the hair falling across my face, by my mouth as I spoke, big on the eye contact. I manipulated him, was how I saw it—I hadn't learned a thing from Francie's mishaps with that game. I needed him, needed his bureaucratic patronage, not yet eighteen and a mixed-race baby in tow. Also, as he liked to remind me, he could send me to prison with a nod and a signature. My life, I came to understand, was at his permission and by his disposal.

The way the rest happened is that my father died. He'd taken on more and more work—the Program wasn't free—had grown noticeably less and less healthy, uncharacteristically mentioned his exhaustion the vurry last time I saw him, and that night had a massive heart attack. Unforgivably, my mother waited four days to tell me so I wouldn't cause any drama around a funeral. He just didn't show up, he didn't call. I pictured him taking days off, relaxing. When she finally told me, I was devastated: the sun, already faltering, had gone entirely out. My mother soon revealed that she was involved with Reverend Turtman. She sold the house, moved with him to Florida, a blaze of scandal. I have never seen her again, mutual choice. My dear Uncle Jeff came and saw me monthly for near a year, loved my Montana stories, took on my bills, then he died, too, same exact cause as Daddy. So much for family.

Uncle Jeff's death and my mother's renunciation left me with no sponsor and no home to be remanded to at the end of Phase One, the inflection point between the Program and further incarceration. What choice did I have?

Walter had an apartment in his barn, something built by a previous owner, not fancy, but after a couple of months of bureaucratic impasse at the hospital, bills unpaid, he signed for me, so to speak, and in the absence of family, baby Ricky and I got weekend furloughs, pretty dreamy. Later, the boy having just turned two, and upon Walter's clinical but passionate petition to the court, we were remanded full-time to Walter's barn and to his care. For almost a year it was me and my toddler up there in the pine-paneled apartment (shades of Camp Challenge!), birds singing outside, coyotes wailing at night, beautiful long walks with the baby, old-school pram, social-worker visits Mondays and Fridays, probation officer Thursdays, Walter daily, helping out in so many ways, grocery shopping, changing diapers, even cooking and finding babysitters so he could take me to some clothing stores, and (once I was dressed like a lady) having me over to his house across the property for "socials," these deathly dull, no-alcohol dinner parties, food bland but elaborate, just like the guests. All the while my host would steal glances at me, a touch of heat in them at times, but only if he thought I didn't see. Truthfully, I thought him a fool for taking an interest in me, because, forget it.

I begged him to post letters for me—Francie, Lucky, Clay and Maria, Dora, even—but no. The law was the law, he said, and I was enjoined. When I asked to see the paperwork that said so he produced it, typed forms on state letterhead. He took over probation, why? He took over social work, why? He pulled me out of college classes before I'd even finished a year, why? Too expensive, he said, penniless me. With no other people in my life, something shifted in my attitude. I hate saying this: I felt I had to please him. At first just a little, then at all costs. After I turned twenty-one, Ricky in pre-K, Walter started taking me to morning movies shown in a lecture hall at Wellesley College, a college for normal girls, he said. In the movies we held hands. Week maybe ten, we kissed. In the car he explained that my attraction to him was natural, that it was the result of something called transference. He didn't say manipulation, which would have been more accurate. He said nothing about his attraction to me, furious unlovable ingrate that I was.

Except he popped a ring one day, just a shit bright thing from the mall. I refused to accept it—I was already married—in fact threw it out his car window, enduring image of him on his hands and knees in the weeds by Walmart, where somehow he found it. He was bad in bed, passive and brief, better than nothing, I supposed. I used sex like coin to find out things, those conversations after. What had happened to Lucky? Walter designated such information as antitherapeutic, said he was unable to find out in any case, that he'd tried, only knew that Lucky was in prison. I went through his desk drawers while he snored, liberated envelopes one at a time, collected a stash of stamps. His phone had a lock on it. I guessed psychologists had locks on their phones. In his address book I found the address for Camp Challenge, Dora Dryden Conover, director. He had a nice world atlas and I pored over maps of Sweden, found the village of Arild, which Aarto had often mentioned, composed a letter to him, another to Francie, general delivery village of Arild, dozens of stamps on each envelope, watched for the mailman, trotted out to meet him.

"Dr. Linklater says to take no mail from you," he said cheerfully.

The babysitter said the same.

I wrote Lucky, too, care simply of the Montana State Prison System, covering all locations, not many incarcerated Turtles, I supposed. I'd seen a mailbox at Wellesley and next movie excused myself to pee, raced to the box, mailed my letters, raced back to my seat heart pounding.

"What's with you, all out of breath," Walter said.

"Tummy ache," I said.

True enough. And side bonus, I didn't have to fuck him later.

I used that system week after week, mailed bales of letters.

"Dora Dryden Conover called," he said all stern one night at dinner. She was looking for Lucky, too, he said. He knew how to draw me in, phony developments in this supposed search. He said he had a call in with some people in Sweden. Apparently, I'd been sending mail there as well. He wanted to know how. And the thing was, I told him. He showed me the return labels: Aarto and Francie were unknown. And then he showed me a tidy stack of letters returned from the Montana Department of Corrections, all of them stamped NO SUCH INMATE. After that, there were no more movies. New lock on the door of his home office.

Ricky grew, moved from being a baby to a toddler to a four-year-old, a person you could talk to. We worked in my gardens together, my only peace, gardens in all the borders, begged Walter for seeds for a vegetable patch. Walter's theory was you could get produce at the farm stand cheaper and easier. He liked what I did in the yard, though, borders, perennials, the taming of shrubs. Still, my mental health wasn't great. It occurred to me to run away. It occurred to me a lot. I even got as far as the corner of the main road one time, Ricky delighted to be riding in his old stroller, fear overcoming me, a race to get back home. I was a psychological captive, Walter's plan: I'd soon technically be free, and he meant to keep me.

Ricky started school. Then suddenly he was six, missing front teeth. Walter went to the parent meetings with me. My supervision period had been complete for nearly a year, but we didn't speak of that. We moved Ricky and me into Walter's house, the big house, we called it, and Ricky got his own room. Reluctantly, I shared a bed with Walter. I made friends among the other mothers, or anyway acquaintances. All of them were wary of me, having been warned. What was Walter telling people?

Dora seemed to call Walter whenever I got most desperate, most angry, unmanageable. Acting out, he called it. She called him only at his university office, it seemed. How did I ever even believe this? Dora had never called, never would. Walter was manipulating me. He brought home little fake scraps of information, smallest rays of phony hope. Then the terrible call. Walter even cried, about as passionate as his lovemaking, not very. Lucky was dead, killed in prison, Montana State. I simply didn't believe it. Not a word of it. We knew nothing, and suddenly we knew this? They returned my letters, no such inmate, and now dead? Dora devastated? Fat chance. I treated Walter to months of recriminations. But then he produced the death certificate, dramatic presentation, only himself available for comfort. Which I accepted, because Lucky's death had killed me, erased me, nothing left but Ricky.

A suburban mom arose in my place.

Chapter Sixty-Two

Avurry sweet little girl and her grandpa came out of the Ferry Building with a nice-looking baguette in a fancy long bag. The grandpa let her tear pieces off the end, which she threw in the water. Several blew my direction. I bent and retrieved them, handed them back to the beautiful child, who tried again. Before long, an uproar of seagulls descended, the little girl delighted, her grandpa laughing, too, and helping her rip the loaf: life.

When I turned back, Lucky was gone. My heart skipped as I scanned the crowd, but there he was, serenely walking away up the Embarcadero, that Lucky stride, a little bowlegged, tall as ever, as erect, hair thick as ever, but white now, white as the wings of the gulls. I hurried, caught up, matched his pace, neither fast nor slow, and we walked together a mile or more, all the way around to the industrial piers, not a word between us. Along the way a security guard emerged from a warehouse, gave a wave, shouted: "Yo, Mr. Sing." And Lucky nodded peaceably. A woman with a dog waved, huge grin. Delighted, Lucky just pointed at the dog, who seemed pretty delighted, too. Cops touched the brims of their hats. A hot-dog vendor waved a bun before filling it for a customer.

Finally, at a pier under construction, Lucky helped me past a dumpster, electric touch of his hands on my ribs as he steadied me, then under a barricade and down a precarious construction ramp crossing open water, then along a battered walkway, the bay tossing beside us. Far end of the pier Lucky moved some plastic sheeting and revealed a mound of colorful clothing that I only slowly realized held a corpse.

Or not.

"Roberto," Lucky said. Nothing. "Roberto," he said again.

"Motherfucker," said Roberto, stirring.

"The construction folks want you out of here. Gave you a week, but now that's done."

"I told 'em," Roberto said, standing, loomingly huge, filthy, instantly agitated.

"We can help you pack up here," Lucky said. "We got you a bed at Harmony House. We got you a doctor appointment."

"You and your always with the doctors!"

Lucky enlisted me with a nod to help fold the enormous sheet of plastic, and we did, fighting the breeze and folding till we came together face-to-face, Roberto cursing us the while. We folded a second sheet, ignoring the smell of urine, then a third, worse, stacked them by a pile of dusty bags of mortar mix. Roberto paced, muttered, swore, his hair blowing almost comically. Unperturbed, Lucky pulled one last sheet of plastic only to reveal a wretched pile of belongings: American Girl horse doll, squashed egg cartons, lampshade collapsed, blue Tiffany box empty, selfie-stick broken, a number of whacked umbrellas, donut boxes half-full, donuts half-eaten. Finally, a roller suitcase, broken handle. Lucky wiped it with an old towel I didn't want him touching, unzipped it past several snags, no matter. Inside, a clean and nicely folded Lakers T-shirt with the price tags still attached.

"You didn't wear it?" Lucky said.

"Saving it," Roberto said.

"Saving it for after your shower," Lucky said equably.

"You and your always with the fucking shower!" Roberto said.

"You said you liked the Lakers."

"I love the fucking Lakers!" And Roberto kept repeating that, pacing, pacing. He loved the Lakers, simple as that.

Lucky was Outreach.

Why had Dora lied to Ricky and me?

Lucky patiently put Roberto's best and cleanest possessions in the suitcase, including the horse doll and four or five umbrellas, zipped it up, pressed the handle into Roberto's palm. The enraged fingers reluctantly closed around it.

"We have time for a walk," Lucky said.

"You and your always with the fucking walks!" Roberto shouted.

Lucky spread out the last piece of plastic and he and I put all the other refuse on it, wrapped it up into a huge, stinking ball that Lucky lifted easily, strong as ever. He led the way back along the construction walkway, Roberto muttering and swearing but obediently following, suitcase veering behind in crazy arcs. I kept my distance, some steps behind. At the dumpster, Lucky threw the packaged refuse in, and then we were a procession back down along the Embarcadero. The long trek in sunshine seemed to calm Roberto a great deal, and soon it was just a walk, no conversation, people greeting both Lucky and Roberto all the way to Harmony House, not a glance for me. Lucky had a key to the gate out front, and we let ourselves in.

"Mr. Sing," said a new woman at the desk, dot on her forehead, surgical mask over her nose and mouth. "Mr. Fassone!"

"Ya, Shakuntala, fucking bullshit," Roberto answered.

I dragged his suitcase up against the counter.

"Let's all wash hands!" Shakuntala said. "And let's all watch our language!" She air-kissed in the general direction of Lucky. "I see you found Ms. Zoeller."

"I did," said Lucky. "And Roberto, too."

"Roberto is an artist of some distinction," Shakuntala said. "Google him and see!"

Roberto grimaced, a vestigial smile: "Fucking always with the Google him!"

She pointed me down a corridor to the staff washroom, and there I washed my hands through several mechanical verses of Happy Birthday, then had a private cry. Lucky was alive, and he was Mr. Sing, and he was Outreach, too, and he'd grown so far past me, stupid privileged girl who'd believed for over twenty years whatever the monsters told her. I cleaned up and dried up and blew my credulous nose, forcibly shoving all the emotion back down my gullet. I opened the door, jumped to see that Lucky was there.

"I'd better wash up, too," he said. "Then I need to get Roberto showered and settled. This is his lodge!"

Softly, I said, "Hoppo."

Lucky, so efficient, the new man: "It will take about an hour. Get him into his Lakers shirt. And then maybe we could meet?"

"Maybe."

Slow smile. He still liked my jokes.

Something passed between us. I said, "Oh, Lucky. I don't want to be apart."

Shakuntala had slipped up behind us with Mr. Fassone. They leaned in to hear Lucky's answer, both of them fascinated.

Lucky said, "You and I have been apart a long time. One hour for Mr. Fassone."

"Okay. One hour, Mr. Sing. Meet you same spot there by the Ferry Building. I'll get some food for us. Do you want a sandwich? Personally, I'm starving."

"You were always hungry, Cindra." Those wilderness eyes, that slight irritation, the worlds in there, jagged new scar on his cheek, the current embodiment allowing only quickest glimpses of the young man I'd last seen smashed into a cop car in Wyoming.

He led Mr. Fassone away down the long corridor to the residence.

Shakuntala took my arm, led me back the way I'd come.

"Remember you're a beautiful person," she said.

"I'm not," I said, and stepped out into the San Francisco afternoon, certain I'd never see Lucky again.

My phone buzzed. Ricky, done with student labs.

"Oh, honey," I said. "He's fine. He's beautiful. He's working. He *works* at this place. Harmony House. Dora lied to us, sweetie. Your father is fine. I'm going to meet him for lunch."

"Dora told the truth. About the important part. He's alive. And we knew it."

"I'm worried he won't show up. He's being so distant. He was never distant."

"Don't do this to yourself," Ricky said. "He needs a minute. You took him by surprise. He'll show. You two take all the time you want, I'll meet him later, when you're both ready. For now, it's you and Lucky, okay? Fuck Dora. Fuck them all. It's just you and Lucky. I'm fine here, stress-testing electron welds with this kid from L.A."

I hung up, hurried to the Embarcadero, unreal, Lucky so close, the great sense that there were bigger things, that I was walking in not just a city but upon a planet, a planet spinning to the tune of that great, warm sun, which I felt on my face like love.

Okay, sandwiches.

Chapter Sixty-Three

Mr. Sing and I climbed the Filbert Street Steps up Telegraph Hill, dozens of frank and steep and quirky flights to the little park around Coit Tower, neither of us breathing too hard: people who walked, even if some had pink orthopedic hiking boots.

"I'm staying near here," I said. "Just housesitting. Taking care of plants and fishes and various reptiles."

Lucky said, "I've been up here sometimes, looking after campers, I guess you could say."

We'd walked that far without conversation. His teeth were still perfect, his smell still wind, physique still lank and long, his shirt better buttoned than back in the day, chef's pants instead of Wranglers, tough cloth. He held himself a little stiffly, his face maybe more rugged, but that was it for aging. Well, that and the bright white hair. He could be moody sometimes, I remembered that. Near the top, the last few flights, slippery stairs all shrouded with undergrowth from someone's garden gone feral, wild parrots chattering overhead, Lucky stopped and turned to face me. Focused on my feet, I about ran into him. He put his hands to my waist, lifted me to his step, then a step higher, like lifting me onto a horse. The extra step put us face-to-face. He leaned to me. Our noses nearly touched. I fell into the canyon of him. After a good long while, this non-kiss, he said: "You blame yourself."

"There's no one else I can," I said.

"There's everyone else." He touched the scar on my neck.

I touched the scar on his cheek. I'd learned to think before I spoke. I'd even learned not to speak at all. His eyebrows had not turned white, seemed fuller, darker. His breath was from mountains. My breath was from gum. We didn't blink. The overgrowth behind me was reflected in his eyes, dappled with light. Lunch was heavy in my hand, or I might have hugged him. He turned me by the shoulders, aimed me up the last stairs, and we climbed into the park, the grandly angled and grown-in hardscaping below the strange old tower, monument to firemen. I hoped he'd see I'd kept my figure, best shape of my life, vain thoughts. We climbed up and stood on the sweeping stone bench to see the view, stood neither close nor far.

He looked a long time, finally pointed, said, "Down over there is Portsmouth Square. You can't quite see the edge of it. Used to be right close to the wharf in my grandfather's day before all that fill—it's where he got loaded off the boat in his barrel and it's where he had his gambling outfit and where his boy caused all that trouble, including me, and now it's for tourists and immigrants alike, most densely populated part of the United States—how about that?—Chinatown, they call it. I guess the food's supposed to be good, and no one speaks any English."

He pointed out into the bay. "That island there, that's Alcatraz, but I guess you know that. Native people took it over at one time. They were still there when my father met Dora, they were there for that whole romance, far as I know. I've met some of them now, elderly. People said it was futile, only a gesture or a joke, but look. All the motion out there? The birds, the boats, the whitecaps from the wind, those ghosts of mist there, those trucks crossing the bridge, that cloud there, and that one, see, moving so fast? Those people changed it all forever."

We watched the changes, more coming, I hoped.

When at last we sat, we sat close. I opened the bag with the sandwiches, the chips, the sodas, all absurdly fancy, unwrapped everything atop our laps.

"Lucky, I'm so sorry," I said.

"Sorry for what," he said.

"For all you've suffered while I've just carried on."

"You suffered the same, and I just carried on, too."

I considered that, considered it a long time. "It was not the same," I said. "It was not the same at all."

"One thing at a time," he said.

"One thing at a time," I repeated.

He arranged his sandwich, opened his bag of chips, laid his slice of pickle just so. I did about the same with mine, a symbolic kind of alignment, Lucky watching closely.

"You've still got garden hands," he said, the compliment like a touch, so intimate.

I ate half my sandwich quickly, saved the other half not to seem a glutton, gulped my drink.

Lucky put his sandwich down carefully on its wrapper after each bite. When at length it was half gone, he wrapped the rest as I had wrapped mine, said, "That's excellent bacon."

"I asked for the Far Turtle Wilderness special."

He liked that. He kept checking my hands, liked the dirt under my nails.

I blurted, "Oh, Lucky. I wrote you. Nobody told me anything. I wrote via Dora. I wrote via Montana Prisons. But nothing worked. I never heard a word. Not from you, not from Dora. And then they told me you were dead."

"Yes. Dora said you wrote. She wasn't much good at writing herself, not after a while. She never once visited. I guess the camp was collapsing and that took her time. She wrote me at first, blaming. She said she was ashamed what had become of me, that my grandfather would be ashamed. So the tutor lady didn't much like reading me those letters and didn't much like helping me answer. Dora wrote they had put you away. She said you weren't allowed to write or call or anything at all. I thought it wasn't true. She said she talked to the head of the place where you were, and he said you had asked to be left alone, and anyway it wasn't allowed by the law for you and me to talk or write or anything at all, that's what he said. The tutor said she thought that wasn't true. He said that you and him had got married. Dora, though, she said this man called her quite a few times. She had a particular question for him, and finally he answered it. So don't worry, I know the truth. Poor baby was stillborn. The tutor and I mourned that pretty hard. And I really had to let go of you."

Walter, you little fucking monstrous prick!

I said, "Stillborn! He certainly was not. He is vurry much alive, just as you are, and I was told you were dead, the same. These liars."

"Our boy?" Lucky said. And then all of a sudden he gulped, he ducked his head, sobbed, a wracked, brief moment.

I was emotional, too. "Yes, sweetie. He's alive. And beautiful. And nearby. I'm sorry you didn't know. You'll meet him soon. He's twenty-two years old and he's in graduate school over at Berkeley Engineering. And if you want, you will see him tomorrow. He wanted us to have our time."

Lucky unfolded a napkin from our lunch bag, touched his eyes with it, blew his nose, so delicately. He poked me then, his finger finding my navel unerring. He said, "I knew he walked with us. I knew none of the writing was true. I thought I'd come get you when it was time, that's all. Get you both. When I was out and you were out. But it wasn't time till now, and instead you came got me."

"They told me you were dead."

"You knew it wasn't true."

"I knew for a while, and then I didn't."

"They had powers, like we said."

"They told you I was married. They wanted us apart."

"But look. We are not apart."

"And our boy is not dead."

"Our boy," Lucky said.

Fog had run under the Golden Gate Bridge and the travel deck was slowly engulfed, just the towers standing above in bright sun. The Bay Bridge was untouched, half the world rushing off in one direction, half the other.

He said, "What's this place you're staying?"

"It's right down the stairs here. It's huge. I'm just housesitting."

"Forever squatting," he said.

"Ha-ha. I picked this park because I wanted to be close. I mean, in case."

"In case you still liked me."

"Other way around."

He liked lifting me, maybe showing off his strength, lifted me off the bench and gently to the ground, led me to the Filbert Steps, down three flights and unerringly to the little iron gate that led to the diplomat's top garden. I didn't ask how he knew because he did not. I punched in the code, led him through the beautifully overgrown plantings to the big kitchen sliders, same code. We put the halves of our BLTs in the enormous fridge, so much other food in there, these generous people.

"The great indoors," he said, looking around. And led me up the stairs straight to the fish room, where we stood in front of that motive brilliance a long time. His chef's pants had one big pocket in back and I tucked my hand in there. He flinched, a subtle thing, so I took the hand out.

"I guess I don't know," he said.

"It's just me," I said.

"You and the fish," he said. "And these lizards over here. And snakes, I guess. And we have a boy. I felt it but didn't know. And I don't know him."

I hadn't even looked in the master bedroom as yet, but it was about as expected, enormous window, view architecturally unencumbered, as the daughter had phrased it, the San Francisco afternoon glimmering out there. But Lucky didn't linger over all that, pulled me into the bathroom, tub in there like a grotto pool, needing only brimstone.

He didn't ask, didn't need to, started the hot water running. It would take time, so we went back out to the view. "The tub will be full when that boat gets to the bridge," he said. A container vessel, enormous, really slow. He pulled off his shirt, let his chef's pants fall. I dropped my pants, tugged off my shirt, shy.

"Always you," he said.

No time had passed at all: whatever beauty I still possessed was his.

He took my hand, placed it over his heart. "Still alive," he said.

I pulled his hand to mine, same. The ship was halfway across the chan-nel, red-and-white eminence loaded high, huge Chinese characters on its side, the company name.

I said, "What do you think it says?"

"Maybe it just says 'boat.'"

"Maria said we'd find you."

"And when did you see Maria?"

"It's been a few years now, but Ricky and I visited, long story. Much to discuss."

"We'll have time," he said.

We orbited the big empty space, vurry slowly, unconscious circuit, my hand on his heart, thumb pressing his scar, his hand on my heart, literal arm's length, like ballroom lessons but slow.

He said, "I dreamed about Maria. I dreamed she was floating just an inch off the earth."

"She's still right here on the ground," I said.

"Yes?"

"Yes."

"And Clay?"

"Oh, Lucky. Clay has passed. Maria thinks he was murdered."

"I had that dream, too," he said, never surprised.

The ship was nearly to the bridge. I trusted Lucky that the tub would not overflow. The steam crept out of the bathroom door, at first unnoticed, then filling the greater room, the window fogging slowly.

"I haven't had a bath in how long," I said, small talk.

"Since that last one," he said.

It was true. "Husband," I said, insecure when he didn't reply.

We made one more ballroom turn, wiped the big window as our trajec-tory brought us close. The boat had reached the bridge. In the bathroom the tub was only a little better than half-full, steaming hard, too hot to touch. "We'll add some cold," Lucky said.

"Are we awkward?" I said.

"I don't know this house," he said. And then slowly, touching my ear: "I don't know this woman." Then touching his own: "I don't know my boy."

"It's our lodge," I said evenly as I could.

In the tub we sat neither close nor far. I slid to not be like that, pulled myself behind him, my chest to his back, tugged his blue hair ties off, no more rawhide, gradually loosened the tight braids, his hair falling like snowfields across his back. We lingered like that a long while, sweet smelling.

"What of Francie?" he said.

"I wrote her," I said. "I wrote her in Sweden. In Arild."

"Ah. But they weren't in Sweden. Sweden never let her in. They held her kind of luxurious for months, then deported her. She picked Haiti, as she would've gone to prison here. In Haiti she was held up a while, but a court found her American felony conviction fraudulent. So she was free. And then they fixed it here, too. Aarto had to save money but went to her in Haiti after a year. He wrote me at first. They built houses, they helped improve towns. They built public spaces. Things like that. Money from a Swedish charity of some kind. Money from the Haitian government. He wrote me, the prison tutor helped me write back. But I didn't keep the address, I guess I didn't really understand that part, keeping things—the tutor had always kept it. But when I moved to Kansas it was gone."

"Kansas?"

"There's a lot to tell you. It's too much right now in this tub. I'm half-boiled."

"We'll find Francie, we'll find Aarto," I said.

"I only just found you," he said.

In the cool shower, I washed those locks of his with actual shampoo, treated them with actual conditioner, some expensive brand, blue glass jars with no labels, sage scented, naturally. The Far Turtle Wilderness touch. I washed my hair, too, head thrown back, his hand on my heart again. We slipped back in the tub, closer now, added hot water as needed (the diplomat's daughter had been proud of the dedicated on-demand boiler), kept getting out and showering, slipping back into the tub, our own fragrant hot spring.

Evening came down. We finished our sandwiches naked in the kitchen, ate the things they'd left us, nice vegetables, fruits, cheese. We drank ritual water, meaning just that before each small glass Lucky said some important someone's name, all the various Turtles. And Clay and Maria. And Hates Roofing. And Francie. And Aarto. A lot of names, all common to us both. A lot of water. We'd be up and down peeing all night.

"Mountain Turtle," he said at last.

We drank to our son.

Before bed I brushed that snowy mane of his and rebraided it, two thick cords the way it used to be, down his front for power. His body was the same, just a new sickening scar across his neck and shoulder, running down from that cheek. Twenty-two years wasn't much. He'd dreamed we'd make love in the morning. So in bed at last we only snuggled, seemingly out of words. But I was someone who needed words. I put the light back on, opened the bedside drawer, pulled out the old notebook, handed it to him.

I said, "Maria rescued this."

"Ah," he said. "And Chickadee must have helped." He looked around for water.

"We'll drink to the horses tomorrow," I said. "Should I read to you?"

He took the notebook from me, petted it, cracked it open, touched my old rough handwriting.

"How about I start," he said. And then, not a miracle, only a tutor at Montana State Prison who believed in him, he read aloud, clearly and slowly, word by word. And word by word, sentence by sentence, the wilderness came alive again.

It wasn't all that much writing, not really. After the second time through, midnight, our snuggles having grown just a notch more intimate, legs interlocked the way we'd always done, I said, "I want to hear the rest, after the notebook ends. I want to hear what happened after they took you away."

"And then you tell me about you."

"Deal."

He said, "It's not a lot. I wouldn't talk, spent a few days on the floor of the jail there in West Yellowstone. Then they took me up to Billings in the exact same van you came in. They gave me a lawyer, and he was good. But the judge was Free Men, like Drinkins. There was no kidnapping, my lawyer said. Because you were voluntary at Camp Challenge in some way. Papers to prove that. You left on your own say-so, and so there was no crime. But in the end the little Free Men judge said I was guilty, just not as charged. Sentenced me to five years for unlawful sexual intercourse. With you. Well, I did that crime. And then he gave me five more for laughing. I laughed so hard even my lawyer stepped away from me. And that was that. Hard time, no parole possible. Montana State Prison, no windows in the cells. That was the hell, not to see out."

"And you served it all."

"Long story."

"We've got a long night, sweetie."

"Well, then. I served seven years there. My work detail was sweeping. That's important to know. I swept all day most days, yards and blocks and walkways. I was thought strange. The time went fast with the chores and the books and learning. But my seventh year, and yes, I was counting, a New Face came after me, new inmate with an iron rod he'd gotten some-where, which meant it was a hit job. Got me seventy stitches and one full month in the infirmary."

"A hit job."

"Someone outside paying someone inside, and the warden paid off, too. Free Men, that's how they do it. When I got out of infirmary, first morning, I knew I'd be killed, so I unscrewed that broom handle and sharpened it hours on the cement walls, made a Viking spear, caught that new inmate on the upper walkway from clear across the yard, right through the neck. You'd have loved that shot, fifty paces and vurry high. Warden said it was impossible, and an inmate couldn't be charged with something impossible.

Wink-wink, he said. I didn't know what wink-wink meant. The lawyer had to tell me, something like, I'm glad you killed that guy. Anyway, I was charged with rioting, because a riot did follow. The state added twenty years because that hit man was killed and some other men hurt. The judge had me in chambers because that second lawyer was incompetent—he said that—and asked for the story and I told him: all true. And he called me the last honest man. Then he explained that to me, something about a wise man, name of Diogenes, and a lamp, and maybe the judge finding himself wise and me honest. He cut the new sentence back to ten plus one from the old sentence and for my safety sent me down to Federal in Kansas. Good place, with Ping-Pong and a window in my cell."

"So that's where Kansas comes in."

"Kansas," he said. "Not bad. Good conversation when freedom is not an abstraction. A lot of interesting people."

"You killed a man."

"Broom Handle did that. She had no choice."

I let all that soak in, my husband in my arms, the night around us. At last I said, "But Lucky, why San Francisco? Of all places? When you finally got out?"

"Dora was my sponsor. Not so long ago, 2015."

"So you served eighteen years!"

"Yes. Eighteen of them. Dora was weary of me. I was too far inward. She called it depression. Therapist she hired called it PTSD. I call it sensible. I couldn't live with Dora and she couldn't live with me, though we tried. Harmony House was a little different then, took in transitions, as we were called. I lived there two years and swept up like at Montana State but had a room upstairs with a window and in the daytime walked all over and met all the People and some of them came back with me to get help. And then I did more of that. Finally the outreach coordinator retired and recommended me, and so I was hired, which didn't mean anything except for a little pay and I had to move out because employees can't live there. And the people started calling me Outreach, and so that is my name, if you want to drink."

I did not want to drink. I said, "And you had lovers?"

"I saw someone on the Embarcadero once after Kansas, but she didn't want to talk. She didn't like I'd been in prison and of course I said that first."

"Not a great pickup line," I said.

"Now you," Lucky said, unamused.

My story was nothing compared to his. I'd had our child, I'd raised him. I'd lived with Walter. Lucky didn't even ask, and good, I didn't want to say. That I'd lain with Walter was clear enough, why flog it. That he was dead was enough. And then Ricky had grown up and lived with us through school at MIT, our genius mama's boy, and now was in Oakland, not one Montana mile away from where we sat. "He was my work," I said.

"But you said gardens."

"Yes, I had a nice yard and liked to garden. A hobby."

"And you volunteered."

"I helped the town with gardens, yes."

"I'm proud of that."

We lay there in my host's fine sheets, lay close, no more work for words to do.

Soon sleep. Soon morning.

Soon again we made love, as in Lucky's dream. Pretty much just like we'd always done—forwardly, backwardly, hours of it interspersed with padding barefoot around that enormous house arm in arm after food, after fish in their tank, after the heat of the reptile room, after the cool of the garden, after the views out across the bay, after lists of names, after ritual glasses of water, after lots of peeing and baths and showers and long talks. Then we made love some more, really made the stuff—it filled the house like steam, soon to fill the yard and the neighborhood and the city and the whole, wide world: love.

"Wife," Lucky said.

Chapter Sixty-Four

The next morning, after another great, long night—things put to rights, as Lucky said it—nothing but fog in all the enormous windows, breakfast a series of snacks, the two of us lounging approximately atop each other in one of the loungers in front of the fish tank, compelling aquatic drama, good coffee, I called Ricky.

"Today?" he said before I'd suggested a thing.

"If you can," I said. "I mean I know it's Monday."

"Nothing more important," he said. "I'll dress up."

"Keep it simple, Bub. We're going out on rounds. Your father is Outreach. He's perfect. Meet you at Harmony House, just out front at noon. All to be explained."

"Oh, Mom, I love this. I'm so excited."

Lucky was nervous to meet Ricky, worried there'd be nothing to say. It was his idea to have the boy come along on Outreach, firmly within Lucky's world, the real world, not that strange big house.

Still, in the light of the aquarium we threw off the bathrobes we'd found, black sumptuous things, our dishes all around us, our many water glasses, the dishes from several meals we'd made, an old bowler hat Lucky had spotted on a high shelf in the kitchen and found nearly as funny as the built-in ironing board I'd demonstrated, new to him. We'd ironed his chef's pants after washing them, hilarious for some reason. And put butter in the freezer so I could show him how it hardened. And those twenty-plus years kept coming, poured from us, thank goodness for ritual water—I think we shed it all. And naked I climbed once more on my ironing board of a husband, his hands hot like an iron on my back, and he smoothed me and smoothed me and moved me and moved me. Those poor fish in their tank—they'd lived through San Francisco earthquakes but never temblors like that.

We heard a sound, that's all. Like a pot clanging. And footsteps— couldn't be footsteps—and suddenly, hands on hips, an ample housekeeper complete with uniform. Florita! The field marshal! "And what's this," she said.

"Florita," I said, covering up, covering Lucky up, her employer's bathrobes. "This is my husband, Lucky."

She inspected our ring fingers closely: nothing. "Did you have to disarrange every bed?" she said.

Lucky said something in Spanish, some long, placating sentence—we were lovers separated, now united—and I saw her soften, actually melt, at least for him. For me she was still hard butter, straight out of the freezer where we'd left it.

Sharply, she said, "I'll clean up. And let us postpone our meeting until tomorrow. Just a few rules and practices to discuss."

"I'm so sorry, Florita. Our meeting. I forgot. Rules and practices, of course."

"It's nothing," she said, turned on heel and clonked her way downstairs. We heard her in the master bath. The candles! The washcloths upon the floor! The many water glasses, the commandeered slippers! The blankets and sheets and towels everywhere in the master bedroom! All the stuff I'd meant to see to.

Well, never mind. She wasn't our boss. Lucky and I crept down to the kitchen, picked up our messes quick, then down to my room, same.

"Where did you learn Spanish?" I said, dressing.

"Kansas," he said. "I was housed with the Central Americans, and there were lots of ways to talk."

We left those robes folded on the bed, left a note: *See you Tuesday*, big heart and smile face. And an apology in Spanish, which Lucky provided—a man now with handwriting—also a bit of French I recalled from Francie: À *bientôt, choux*. Too cheeky? Lucky thought not.

At the shelter we collected the giant Radio Flyer donations wagon, waited for Ricky among the lunch crowd, all of them vying for the attention of Outreach, who chatted with each. I spotted Roberto Fassone, all cleaned up and clipped and dressed in donations, clearly dosed on something, sheepish smile, wouldn't keep my eye. A bent lady was angry, and the crowd gently talked her down; a young man was muttering and lost, and the crowd said sympathetic things.

"Just is," I heard one say.

A car pulled up, and Ricky slipped out, looked all around him in some excitement, spotted me, spotted us. He took in the abiding man—his father—wearing chef's pants too big for him, pink rope for a belt, nice shirt borrowed from our diplomat, snowy braids pulled forward.

"I'm going to cry," Ricky said. And then he did.

And of course I cried, too. We stood apart like that and cried until finally Lucky took my arm and walked me two steps to where we could pull in our son, long embrace, the three of us moved to perfect stillness. The Harmony patrons clapped, they cheered. Carol Washington appeared, unlocked the gate for lunchtime, long look at me, long look at Ricky, our whole history explaining itself. She touched her nose, pointed at our son. Yes, yes, Lucky and me, and this our son.

Ricky began to bounce. He said, "I knew it, I knew it, I knew it." He meant he knew that meeting his father would be this beautiful, that despite all we'd been told and all I'd insisted on so carelessly, his father was alive, and that we'd known it. That his father had survived prison intact, and we'd known it. That his father was not homeless, and we'd known it. We'd known it in our hearts. Guilt is a bad emotion, the one that arises in the body when the intellect hasn't listened to the heart, has acted without heart, and I was filled with guilt, let it fuel my tears.

"Mountain Turtle," Lucky said. And kissed him, square on the mouth, then kissed both his ears, pinched his cheeks. "My son."

"My boys," I said.

Ricky, struck silent, had begun to rock on his heels. Lucky understood that Ricky needed to settle down, moved us up the block and away from the tumult of our fans, the Radio Flyer gliding behind. We stopped at the corner, everyone settling, this little perfect family that hadn't gathered since Ricky's days in utero. His bouncing stopped. Our grins grew. There really wasn't anything to say. We just stood there. The sun moved several degrees across the sky.

What followed was a tour of Lucky's days, the back ways of San Francisco—all at a pace, urgent, footsore miles, Ricky taking his father's hand, taking mine. We collected "tickets" from pizza places and diners, food vouchers, they were, some lovingly decorated. We picked up bags of clean, folded clothing from churches, toothbrushes and floss and sample toothpaste from the back doors of dentists' offices, outdated remedies from drugstores and bodegas, towels from a big bath place, all the while checking on the People, Lucky called them, the unhoused, each a different story, located in places he knew to look, flocks under bridges, hard cases in dumpsters, entrepreneurs on street corners, their finds for sale on dirty blankets, the wounded morose in doorways and alleys, long conversations, directions offered to free clinics and free meals, directions accepted to all the various gates and stairways in and out of all the various holes where the People might be found. Everywhere he was known: Outreach. Some seemed to know his name: Mr. Sing. Not a one called him Lucky, no one, zero. He handed out food tickets about as soon as we got them, offered shirts and pants and underwear, the wagon full and empty again, then full again and empty, offhandedly produced new toothbrushes, toothpaste, bottles of water, demanded that several young men brush their teeth in front of him, which they mostly did. Ricky saw the method and joined in, chatting with one and all, hearing troubles, hearing stories, hearing prayers, backstopping madness. At the alleyway kitchen doors of some vurry fine restaurants we collected quality food, ate a little ourselves at lunchtime, chefs and workers emerging to say hello to Outreach, to meet his wife and son, water tributes everywhere we went, and onward, food for the hungry in our wagon, flowers from restaurant centerpieces tucked behind our ears.

I could see Ricky coming up with solutions, formulas, systems, so proud of his dad, but always the city planner. Back along the Embarcadero we were collecting a parade, a comet with a long, slow tail, Lucky a pied piper if the Pied Piper had a wife and a son, and probably he did, the most cheerful procession following us back to Harmony.

I said, "This is getting disconcerting."

"People just want to know," Lucky said.

"People just want to know what?"

"Why we're so happy," Ricky said.

We laughed, we laughed all day. Come evening, we dropped the wagon and a last load, which was boxes of cheap surgical masks: the pharmacist at DrugMart said to get our people used to them: this thing was coming. I'd mostly missed the news, Lucky, too, but Ricky filled us in: the terrible toll in China, the terrible toll in Italy. It wasn't just Donut Dora being nuts. I guess one or the other was all of us at first: crazy conviction, crazy denial. Adamant, Ricky made us put on masks. We wore them as exemplars, he said, passed them back through our followers. Many of whom put them on, takers of advice, many of whom did not, rebels without a clue.

As we got close to Harmony, a number of people fell away, but there were seven people to register, all but one in a mask, Carol Washington and Shakuntala tireless, their shift from eight to eight, the night shift more like guard duty. Shakuntala, up on the news, was pleased with the masks, and Carol, denial lifting, tried one on.

"Meet my son," Lucky said.

The women were enchanted.

Chapter Sixty-Five

B ack at the diplomat's house, grocery bags in hand, we meant to make a beautiful family dinner, build a fire in the garden chiminea, drink a bottle of red, red wine Ricky had picked out, and just talk till the words once again were gone, plenty of room for the boy to stay with us overnight, and plenty of time in the morning for family brunch.

But at the front door, I couldn't make the code work. At the back, my medium roller suitcase had been left out by the glass table in the garden. On the door a note:

Madame: Mr. and Mrs. Morris have requested that I change the codes on the locks and ask you to terminate. The reasons are as follow: You said you were a widow, then brought your husband in. You made unauthorized use of rooms and personal items. You left a mess. You disrespected me, the housekeeper. If you have any questions, please call Mr. Slzepkic, the house-man. He is in complete agreement. Don't worry over the fish or reptilians—though you failed to feed them this morning, I took care. *À bientôt* indeed, Florita.

My mouth fell open. I read the note aloud to Lucky. You know when you're totally in the wrong, how you want to be outraged? You want to stamp your foot as if you were the victim? Lucky was so amused at my sputtering he couldn't contain it. And Ricky, exactly the same. The two of them roared with laughter, *dos gotas de agua*, as Lucky said, no translation forthcoming, and then me too. So much for an elegant bath, so much for that comfortable bed, those sleek, caressing robes.

But Lucky collected firewood as in any other forest, built a fire in the chiminea while Ricky and I prepped dinner using matched barbecue utensils Lucky found in the shed, super fancy. The wine, thank goodness, was screw top. There were plastic plates and paper napkins in a plastic bin. When the food was ready—grilled stuffed chard leaves like fragile burritos, Ricky gone vegan—Lucky built the fire back up and we sat at the glass table and ate, and talked, and laughed, and let the evening fall, no plan but the food in our mouths, so good, so spicy, the laughter at our lips, the talk, the talk, the talk, years and whole lives to fill in. Not a soul came to bother us. We asked the fire for secret things. Then we cleaned up thoroughly, doused the coals, water from a hose.

Late, Ricky called an Uber. The driver didn't mind dropping Mom and Dad along the way at an old building in once-maligned Bayview, and Ricky, still laughing, headed back to his roommates across the bay. At Lucky's door we had to pay an extra twenty-three dollars, lady behind bulletproof glass.

"My wife," Lucky told her.

"My ass," the lady said.

I paid and Lucky led me up several flights of steel stairs to a tiny, tidy, salt-sticky room with a steel cot and a grand bay view out a window so narrow it was like an archer's slot in an ancient castle. Lucky had a duffel, and we stuffed in all his worldly possessions: a voluminous sweater, two more pairs of chef's pants, no doubt from one of the restaurants on the Radio Flyer tour, two long-sleeved shirts, two short-sleeved, all the same pale coral color, dental-assistant stuff, all nicely laundered and folded. No underwear, not Lucky. A pair of unused eyeglasses, still in the free clinic box. The duffel held it all, and after a difficult descent in the narrow stairway, it was no big deal to terminate Lucky's weekly lease and trundle in the sweet misty night to the hotel Ricky had helped me book on his magic phone. At the hotel, all that beautiful polished marble now to be seen as surfaces, they asked us to wear provided masks and use globs of sanitizer, some new world coming into view. Upstairs we peeled off the masks and everything else and sat on our bed and held hands in front of yet another view. "Like every room has its own square of the world," my husband said. "A window's worth."

"This is so good," I said. "This coming down in the world is so vurry good."

He said, "I miss the fish tank, though."

"I miss the robes."

"Yes? Me, I miss my horrible room on the bay."

"This will take some time, you and me."

"I think we should go home."

"Home," I said. "And what does that even mean anymore?"

He pointed out the window unerringly north-northeast. Montana, of course, that's what it meant. Just outside this window plus twelve hundred miles, nothing much to hold us here, our kisses no different from Far Turtle Wilderness kisses, and all the rest we got up to that night, no different unless better, these ageless yet aging bodies, this spinning planet, this hushed hotel.

Chapter Sixty-Six

We woke in the night, Lucky kicking in his sleep, and he confessed waking that he wasn't so sure about family life, nor the idea of Montana. He liked things as they'd been, liked being Outreach, liked life in the city, a man living alone, plenty of time to think. He missed his narrow window, the ocean out there.

"It's okay to be mad at me," I said.

"I'm surprised by it," he said, and he stewed, a subtle thing with him, inward. In the morning, way too early, first light, no further sleep, the room seemed small and hot and confining. Lucky wanted to walk and so we stopped by Harmony House, the night guard still on duty, friendly, fearless person all of five feet tall, big glasses. We collected the Radio Flyer and visited a commercial bakery, not for day-old merchandise as I'd expected but for their daily donation, the underorder, they called it, many big flat boxes of fresh danishes and little cakes and croissants and bagels, all still warm, the Harmony daily breakfast, if you added donated blocks of American cheese and bologna and reconstituted orange juice. We dropped off the pastries and walked more, bag of croissants to tide us, bottles of water, really good coffee from a kiosk, walked clear to Golden Gate Park, the gardens bursting.

"You should meet this lady," Lucky said, pointing up a hillside.

"What lady?"

The lady in camo coveralls and utterly hidden among the plantings, it turned out, a city gardener named Hill, career position, Lucky said. And now I saw this was no coincidence, that Lucky had had an idea. He introduced us.

I said, "So early!"

Hill was super present, super centered, clear eyed, clean, head shaved both sides, flag of orange in the middle, race indeterminate, certainly all American, flag on her shirt, flag on her neckerchief, flag tattoo on her wrist. She said, "My habit is early and odd hours so as to avoid conversation."

"Like this one?" I said.

That delighted her. "Yes, just like this one."

She was planting azaleas among some rocks and we got to talking—I knew quite a lot about azaleas from working with them in Massachusetts, also rocks.

"Just the vibe I'm trying to promote," Hill said. "A New England summer."

"Anyone sleeping?" Lucky asked her.

"Yes, dear Outreach, there is a little knot of folks down under the low boughs in the spruce grove, Haight end. Girls and boys, though, so I think they're just dharma campers. And I saw Big Jack, sleeping on the museum steps, too. Super early."

So Lucky went off to find Big Jack—and that fear came upon me, that I'd never see my husband again. I cried, want to say briefly, but no.

Hill was taciturn about it—I was such a fem—but waited me out, then just as wordlessly included me in her project. And I knew something about the soil amendments she probably ought to be using and the amount of shade she should seek, the thorough drainage. She moved things where I suggested, and I got into it, relieved to be doing something useful. And loving the talk, which was all plants, nothing but plants. That I'd just arrived in town without prospects, Hill already seemed to know.

After a long time, she said, "Listen, lady, my assistant was promoted and got his own section. They're hiring—got word Friday—and I'm quite nervous I'll get a talker or a dum-dum. If you have any interest, go to the city parks website and look for the Careers tab, totally hidden but don't worry, just keep looking, and apply with me as reference. Kathy Hillman. I can put a strong word in. You'll have to get certified—Level One is minimum to get hired, but you're great at this. You just take a class down here at the pavilion. I actually teach it? It's a career job, great bennies. I rotate some, but this is my park, and this is my section. And if you're my assistant, it's your section, too. List your experience as institutional, that's all. Garden Club volunteer will count. But just say institutional."

Sometimes a vista opens in front of a person. I said, "Thank you, Kathy Hillman."

She grimaced, said, "Hill." And gave me her card. Which said Kathy.

I pointed it out and we laughed.

"Lucky's been talking you up as long as I've known him," she said.

"Yeah?"

"Couple of years at least. I thought he made you up. And yet here you are at last."

"At last," I said, once again overcome.

We continued planting. We planted a long time.

I expected Big Jack, some eloquent story from Lucky of why we needed to accompany him back to Harmony, but Lucky returned alone, and from his gait I could see he was no longer inward. He was a little impatient with Hill's conversation, simply cut her off, wanted to show me a spot, goodbye.

Another long walk, that enormous park, the day getting hotter. I told him about the assistant gardener idea and he was so pleased he picked me up, threw me over his shoulder like we'd used to do, so funny. Still not a soul around, just a brightly dressed jogger or two, aggressive bicyclists in a peloton, a few moms with babies. On a knoll there was a stand of dense shrubs. Lucky put me down and led me ducking through a kind of twig tunnel, and after a long crawl we emerged in a clearing, the eye of the shrubby storm, big flat boulder to climb up on—kids had done so, and the vandals with their paint. "Sometimes I find one of the People in here," Lucky said.

But no one that day. Perched on the rock and looking north you could see just the tops of the orange bridge. "I used to come here," Lucky said.

"And just sit?"

"I'd think of you."

I snuggled close.

"In Kansas I had a spot, too. In the library. After the tutor. Library was always empty. I'd think how you and I were in the wilderness."

I knew just what he meant. I'd had a spot at the back of our yard in Massachusetts. You'd feel the sun on your face and along with the melancholy a surge of crisp memory, a strong presence. "That time, right? When we'd found the tarn? With the floating floe? You froze your knees."

He nodded, unsurprised, yes exactly that time, and said, "And also that sort-of sand dune far from any water?"

"Yes, yes, I was just thinking of that. And that place, the moss at the edge of the doe meadow."

"The high rocks that time? You got a bruise."

We went on a long while, spots we'd made love. And a little kiss turned into a snog, soon husband and wife wrassling, naked people at the center of that fragrant shrub galaxy.

"If we went home," Lucky said, stretched out after.

"Yes," I said.

"We could come back, yes?"

"Yes," I said. "Yes. This is our lodge."

"Hoppo," he said gently.

"We decide that together."

"It is decided," he said.

My phone buzzed and it was Ricky, proposing via urgent text that instead of meeting at the crowded breakfast spot he'd planned, we meet outdoors. He'd been reading up in the pandemic literature and sounded alarmed: "They're going to start shutting stuff down."

We met an hour later farther down in the park, Ricky carrying food.

Lucky and I explained what sitting clover meant, and the three of us sat that way on a picnic table at the head of the park—quite a bit of arranging, big kid—and ate the takeout Ricky had brought, tamales and tiny tacos, delicious. Ate and then sat there like that, back-to-back-to-back, napping a little, one sapped family.

Some indefinite time later, Ricky cleared his throat.

"Okay," he said. "I've been thinking. Lucky, you're my dad, and so I want to ask some advice of you. I've been talking to Dora. Your mother. I know that she makes Mom mad. Maybe you, too? But she's my grandmother, and I have been talking with her several times each day since we found her. She started it—calling me at all hours. But they are okay talks."

Lucky's shoulder blades flexed—sitting clover, you felt the unspoken.

Ricky's shoulders just felt busy, words falling faster: "Well, she wants me to borrow her car and go to Montana and straighten out this thing with Turtle Butte Ranch. There's a hearing about the deed. It's next week. Apparently new laws have been ginned up. Someone has to be there. The deed is in her name, I guess. I'm the one who's left."

"You and Lucky, you mean," I said. "If you own that land, you own it together."

"The land owns itself," Lucky said.

Ricky said, "Yes, yes, beautifully said. But the land will be raped, Dad. We have to fight or lose. It's spring break. They might even be closing campus. The timing is auspicious, Dora says. We three could all go."

"Son," Lucky said. Because Ricky had called him Dad.

"Much to consider," I said. But intrigued: home to Montana, and Ricky along.

Agitated, Ricky got to his feet. "*Please!*" he cried, for all the world to hear.

And wasn't the park bustling. Sports teams and more bicyclists and kids off to play tennis, guitar guys and food carts and joggers and cops. Right in front of us an elderly couple stopped in their stroll so the wife could button her husband's shirt correctly, loving little pat of his face when she got to the top.

"It's a long ride up there," Lucky said.

Such a sweet way of saying yes.

Chapter Sixty-Seven

Dora's car turned out to be an enormous Lincoln, a half-stretched *limousine*, not particularly new, lustrous bronze, vast in all proportions, square at the edges, polished and gleaming, tall whitewall tires with golden wheels, golden trim all around, the initials DDC on the driver's door in gold filigree. Upon the death of Dora's parents, Ricky had informed us (old *People* magazine article online), she'd regained access to the trust that held her child-acting money, some kind of small fortune, plus their assets, which had only been withheld in life, substantial.

Ricky wanted to drive, wanted Lucky and me in the back, liked the idea of playing chauffeur. My husband slid close to me on that couch of a seat. My impulse was to slide away, but that would have been *my* family—no one touching, no sign of affection, so. I cuddled up even closer, kissed his shoulder, just as I wanted to do, no hiding it, no withholding. I held both his hands. He leaned deeply into my neck. Ricky drove sensibly, picking his way through those tangled streets, his phone giving directions from his lap, the car all but floating on regal springs. After an eternity, we crossed the Bay Bridge into the future, or at least into Oakland.

"Lot of Native people from all over here," Lucky called.

Static in speakers above our heads, a startling voice, Ricky's: "There's an intercom, just talk."

I said, "Daddy says lots of Native people."

"I heard him. People he knows?"

"Some were ours, sure. I'd bring them back and forth if they turned up at Harmony. Most are just living like anyone else, though."

Ricky said, "Well, maybe anyone else with a foot on their neck."

Lucky cracked a smile. "Some live pretty well, Mountain Turtle. Though it's true, some live pretty poor. Some, it's their own foot on their neck. Not that you're wrong. That's a big foot, the one you speak of."

"One of my math profs at MIT was Cree," Ricky said.

"Those are tough people," Lucky said.

"Like the Taishanese," Ricky said.

"Like my grandfather, sure. He's the only one I know."

"There's a big store in Chinatown. The whole staff's from there. We'll go someday."

The intercom crackled off. The ride was super smooth. Ricky's eyes were upon us at all the stoplights, so much stopping and going. I felt my cup overflowing, all right.

"Good driving," Lucky called: he didn't trust the intercom.

Ricky tipped an imaginary chauffeur's cap.

At the Berkeley Engineering quad it felt so good to sit out in the car among other parents while our son ran into the Applied Simulation Lab, people from all over the country, judging by the license plates, an orderly evacuation. There were masks, sorry to keep bringing it up, not so many as there'd be soon, but. So many suitcases, so many boxes, so many desktops and outsize monitors, cardboard boxes full of projects, books stacked in arms, so many black portfolios, briefcases, bizarre constructions in every sort of material. Lucky took it all in, no interest in getting out of the car, the stream of students, of parents, of solemnity here, hilarity there. These were the Legos kids, the calculator crowd.

I said, "Mountain Turtle has found his tribe."

"This is no tribe," Lucky said. Then, "Reminds me a little of Kansas."

"Kansas?"

"All this certain kind of building." Prison, he meant.

I turned his face to me, squeezed his cheeks emphatically: "You're a college dad, mister. You better think hard about that."

He laughed, then didn't, pushed my hand away—everything was funny,

sure, but everything was poignant, too, all he'd missed, *just is* notwithstanding, a lot of pain, all the things that were but that might not have been,
and the other way, too. We untangled a bit in that back seat, the windows
cracked, the air so hot, an atoll in the storm.

To secure the future, I said, "One day let's ride bikes around the city."

Lucky scoffed. "Bikes, never learned."

"Oh, jeez, it's easy. We will name them Chickadee and View!"

My husband liked that.

Here came Ricky, box full of notebooks and laptops, twenty or thirty
flash drives on colorful lanyards around his neck: his students.

On a quiet street of tall houses, we stopped again and Ricky got out,
and soon the kid was back, no medium roller like Mom and Dad, but two
enormous old-school suitcases and behind him a tall roommate, blond as
the sun, lugging three stuffed garment bags, four hats on his head, numer-
ous scarves.

"Mom, Dad," Ricky said. "This is Gene-Gene, the Dancing Machine,
from Iowa." We all grinned at that, just Gene's expression, like he'd never
heard that one before, Iowa somehow funny, too, extremely buff and rugged boy in bare legs and T-shirt.

"See you three weeks," he said to Ricky. And pulled down his mask to
reveal a lush mouth, kissed my boy, so deeply, Ricky pulling him in, a long,
thoroughly romantic hug and then what could only be called mashing, this
new generation, then sudden tears. Ricky climbed in the car then and, with
Gene trotting alongside tragicomically waving, we drove off.

"My boyfriend," Ricky called back. "Isn't he the best?"

I pushed the intercom button. "You didn't mention," I said.

"It's new," he said cheerfully. "One day you're roommates, the next you're
in love. But he's so needy!"

It was an adjustment for Lucky, you could see it on his face. But he
laughed, called, "Then we are glad he didn't come along."

Miles went by, all the industrial everything.

"I'm growing," Lucky said.

I liked that, said, "We're throwing so much at you."

He said, "I'm good at ducking."

I laughed. "You'd better be good at catching, too." Then, after a few stop-and-go-traffic miles, I said, "How about me, does it seem like I'm growing or have grown at all? What do I even offer you? I'm not so good at ducking."

"Oh, Cindrawww. You brought me out of the dark. You were the garden girl. You fed us."

"Well, we all did. I mean, what do I offer now?"

"You taught me to think, think in words."

"You always thought in words, maybe just different ones."

"And you raised this boy up tall."

"I did, it's true. But now, Lucky. Like right now?"

His hand settled on my thigh.

Good answer. A creamy feeling settled in my gut. The city miles gave way to marching suburbs, the marching suburbs gave way to dry country-side. Lucky and I couldn't look at each other for smiling.

Our route took us through Nevada, and there, the mountains rolling into view, you could feel your heart expanding. Some part of Lucky seemed to leave the car to join the vasty landscape. We hardly talked, but drifted on our own thoughts, this family in a car. Lucky couldn't abide Ricky's tunes, which had gotten louder and thumped harder and harder, the car's fancy stereo.

I said, "Just tell him."

Hard for the new dad, but he did it, pressed the intercom button so he wouldn't seem to be yelling. "The music, son. I can't hear my own." Thoughts, he meant, thoughts as music.

Ricky didn't mind, pushed the necessary buttons, closed the glass divider between us, two worlds.

"He's a good boy," Lucky said after many miles.

"He is."

And after many more: "You know what Mountain Turtle told me? He thinks you and I should have a wedding."

"Oh, Ricky and his weddings. He would love that."

"Would you?"

"Would I love it? I don't know. Would you love it?"

"I would love it."

I said, "In that case, yes. I would love it a lot."

"He's already planning it. A surprise. Just some easygoing kind of thing for us. I can put it to a stop."

"A surprise wedding? How can you have a surprise wedding?"

"Well, it won't be a surprise now. But, see, I wanted to check. This is how I've grown. I ask you. You answer. But I like Ricky and me being in on it together. If it's yes, just say yes, and then forget it."

"Okay, yes. Yes, yes, yes."

"Got some other surprises, too, that boy."

"I won't ask."

Lucky pressed the intercom. "Come in, Mountain Turtle," he said.

Ricky popped the music out of his ears. "Yes, Poppa."

"Momma and I are going to get bicycles."

"Well, there you have it," Ricky said.

"Have what?" Lucky said.

"Exact," Ricky said.

More endless miles, my private beaming, my boys getting along behind my back. Ricky stopped at a grocery, came out with a dozen stuffed bags and a large red cooler. He filled it with ice, loaded his perishable items into it. We stopped for lunch another hour up the road and ate thereafter beautiful meals we created at roadside stops as I had done with my own Daddy, that long pregnant ride, that other going home, the hard one, ate beside lakes and rivers, ate at the tops of dams, swung our feet out over the various abysses.

Lucky liked Target because of the logo, same as one he'd seen in a dream, but that one grown in grasses and pressed into the land, lasting imprint of a pole house. We stopped there—clean bathroom for me, Lucky lingering in the candy aisle, skinny fucker with those perfect teeth. Ricky filled a shopping cart—I wasn't allowed to look. But he trotted up to me with a dress from far across the store, pressed it to my shoulders.

"Dreamy," he said, walking off with it.

I drove a while, Lucky's head in my lap. Then he took the wheel. Then Ricky again, then just the two of them up front all night, trading off. Did they sleep? Maybe not. There was a lot of conversation, vurry serious. I slept, long and hard, no problem, Lucky's garden girl, Ricky's mom, peaceful to the core, the back seat of that limo as big as a Hollywood casting couch, sorry Dora.

Well, not entirely peaceful—I woke ashamed of how Lucky and I had treated the diplomat's belongings, how we'd been booted, remorse having settled in. I'd seen myself in that house for a year or more to come. I'd seen Lucky and me in that house. I found the daughter's sweet emails, started a new thread: "Apologies, and an explanation." And exactly that, told her about finding Lucky, how I'd thought him dead, told her the whole story, how we'd reunited in their house, how the bathtub reminded us of our hot-spring baths, all of it. I proofread, revised, proofread some more, pressed Send. And though I knew I'd never hear from her, I felt better in my heart.

We stopped for gas often—that car drank the stuff, eight miles to a gallon, Ricky calculated, two twenty-gallon tanks, grotesque. Lucky's inwardness eased further; he even started getting out of the car at pit stops. Ricky's excitement eased, too, my boys meeting at a figurative Halfway Spring. Together, they strode into men's rooms, farm stands, tourist traps. Of course they drew stares.

"Go back home," an unshaven man said that midnight, corner of Idaho, maybe hoping we wouldn't hear, maybe just for the ears of his drunken friends, whatever bile draining from them all under Ricky's oblivious moon, under the sun of Lucky's unexpected smile, that gentle benevolence, gas station fluorescents:

"We are," he told them. "We're going home."

Chapter Sixty-Eight

I must have looked like a creature in a sci-fi film climbing out of that bronzy starship, pink preliminary sunlight coloring distant peaks west, the rear wing doors of Dora's limo slowly opening. We were three dazed time travelers taking it all in, Maria's place, that paint-garish mobile home perched on its outcropping, gardens lush, Turtle Butte looming in the near distance, all cliff and slide, the air between smoky with morning.

I was perplexed, as Ricky said he'd made arrangements at the resort where we'd stayed years before. Lucky had been driving, Ricky shotgun, the sleepless duo. We'd developed a kind of patter during the long ride, a family style emerging from Ricky's jokes between my naps:

"Lucky, my dear," I said. "This ain't the Big West Resort."

But Lucky was serious. He said, "This is where I know."

Ricky was matter of fact. "Maria said to come here."

I said, "You've been in touch with her?"

"I've been in touch with Born on Bison. Remember Born on Bison?"

"Of course I do. And you didn't tell your mom?"

"I did not."

Lucky said, "I dreamed it. We were standing right here by this car, only it was maybe more like an ocean barge."

"And you didn't tell Mom?" Ricky said, his sort of teasing.

"I told *you*," Lucky said. "After Target. And you said—"

Ricky grinned. "I said, Don't tell Mom."

I said, "The little family reunited not a week and already triangulating!"

Ricky laughed: the last time we would ever quote Walter, the last we would ever mention him.

"This is so great," Ricky said. "I have parents."

And so we all had to hug.

The old Aermotor spun as always, the constant wind, the musical creaking, the olden wood trough full as ever, dripping as ever, mud beneath, dust all around. And still the chickens pecking everywhere and always the mountains at far horizon north and west, sharp peaks, the yellow rangeland between.

Suddenly the sun broke the long ridge east and rose time-lapse above the plains. Clay's immense collection of junk went radiant all around us, stainless steel and chrome and gold leaf sparkling, mirrors and window glass throwing beams like lasers, the endless rust flamingly orange, a number of fresh wrecks since even those few years before, even without Clay—more than just dumping but a kind of homage: this is where metal came to rest. Some kindly soul with a giant backhoe or even a boom crane must've stopped by from time to time, I thought, sorting things like-with-like, keeping the alps not wide but high the way Clay had: tractor frames and baling machines, airplane cowlings and whole restaurant kitchens. At a kind of low pinnacle atop other vehicles, a pickup truck had been perched three stories up as if by helicopter, proud on its unbowed springs. I'd have known that blue door anywhere, the rest all rusty yellow, and I knew that homemade wooden bed: Clay's truck.

Lucky recognized it, too. "Hoppo," he said quietly, a benediction.

Ricky took it all in, the engineer's eye. "Isn't entropy magnificent," he said.

"I imagine so," Lucky said. "What is it?"

"One of the laws of the universe: all things seek randomness."

"Like, things fall apart," I said.

"But you can put them back together," Lucky said.

"Just not the same," Ricky said.

"Two turtles talking," I said.

The way they were grinning. Something was up.

Lucky lit the bath fire, pumped water into Clay's boiler-bottom caul-dron, let it heat way too hot, filled the farm tub. I went first, used Ricky's bathing kit, all sorts of fancy emollients and soaps, a good razor, then the boy, fresh hot water, no rushing him, then Lucky, who preferred it cold, seldom shaved in any case. We weren't too terribly private—but Ricky had brought towels suspiciously reminiscent of the diplomat's pool towels, thick and colorful. I'd have to write another note. I combed out both men's hair forever and braided them both double and forward for power. Ricky did my hair, insisted on a tight French braid and bun.

"Lucky, look how beautiful she is," he said.

And I saw in Lucky's eyes it was true.

We dressed fresh for the first time in days, chef's pants for Lucky, peasant blouse for me, vintage-store jacket and tie for Ricky, big padded shoulders. The sun climbed higher to elicit the creaking of sun-warmed metal, oily scents in the breeze along with the scent of sage and ponder-osa-pine smoke. Lucky and I linked arms like an old couple, took in the boy much the way we took in the landscape, an impressive figure, our son.

Turtle Butte, too, looming close.

Ricky grinned, and that set Lucky in motion, those conspirators. They led me to the patch of yard below the trailer. Lucky kneeled in front of me, checked in with Ricky. "Like this?" he said.

And Ricky said, "Yes, Daddy, go."

And from the breast pocket of his shirt Lucky produced a plain blue ring, presented it to me on his palm. "Will you marry me?" he said.

"We're married," I said.

"So marry me even more?"

"Yes," I said, playing a little bugged. "Yes, I will."

Ricky clapped his hands.

Lucky got up, slipped the ring on my finger—no time to admire it, he wanted a formal kiss and we shared it, Ricky looking on.

"We thought we could do it here," Ricky said.

"Oh, you thought."

"Because you never had a wedding."

"When did you blockheads cook this up?"

"We're not blockheads," Lucky said.

Well, try as I might to pretend to be cross about it, I was delighted, especially with the ring, some kind of stone, blue as water, thread of gold all the way around.

"Tell her where you got it," Ricky said.

"Gas station," Lucky said. "That guy with the table. It's lapis lazuli. It cost same as the tanks of gas."

"See how it fits," Ricky said.

"It fits," I said.

Ricky clapped again. "Mom, now you know why I was trying on all your rings!"

"You *clowns*," I said.

"We're not clowns," Lucky said.

Immediately we heard a car coming. Ricky took no notice. Lucky did, stiffened, turned his head to hear, to check in with me. But I already knew that particular wee-car wheeze: Born on Bison. The little Fiesta pulled up shortly, Bob waving out his window, beeping. Arms, in fact, were waving from all his windows. He parked, popped out.

"A wedding!" he cried.

"Oh, no," I said. "Right now?"

"Surprise again," Ricky said.

"Only if you want," Lucky said.

Three young women climbed out of the Fiesta after Bob, Maria's three attendants, three different shapes, college age, smiles like shy lightning, but not so shy they didn't race toward me, waving wooden spoons.

"Wedding spoons!" Born on Bison announced. "We were carving all night."

"And singing," the shortest of the girls said, also the most confident, bangs and short-shorts, bracelets up her arm.

"Tradition," the tall girl said, built like a boy. She claimed Bob with a hand on his back.

"Well, maybe tradition in Norway," the third kid said. She was dark skinned like Lucky, sun burnished, a little hard. She said, "Bob, give her the thing."

And Bob pulled it out of his pocket, a little animal skin, maybe marmot, sleek and a little gross. The girls touched me with their spoons as Bob presented the skin, and they did begin to sing, not some rare old song of the plains but a Beyoncé song I knew a little, great harmonies, talented girls. Bob, not so much, crooning and handing over his fur.

The girls tied their spoons together as they sang and tied Bob's fur in there, and it all went around my neck. "We're making it up as we go along," Bob's girlfriend said. "Maria said it didn't have to be Christian, but it couldn't be straight Crow. So it's kind of all the things we like?"

"This is Sinopa," Bob said. "She lived in Norway junior year."

"Dear girl," I said, sounding like Dora.

"The spoons are good," Lucky said. "The skin is good."

They all looked at me expectantly. "The spoons are really good," I said. "The skin, not so much."

Everyone laughed.

I said, "Where is Maria?"

The kids didn't answer, just sang their song. I mean, really talented. The girl with the bangs was called Kate—she kept touching me. Alsoomse, the hard girl, inspected me closely. Sinopa pushed Bob at me. Bob was supposed to kiss my hands, hilarious how he could not but instead kissed the air near them.

Lucky looked so guilty—he and our son had been plotting the whole ride, Crafty Turtles!

And now here came a pickup truck, huge and brand new, pulling a first-class horse trailer, not a sound till it was upon us, that's how new, cloud of dust I'd not noticed, some tracker I'd turned out to be, reckless four-wheel drift. To belie the speed, an ancient gentleman unfolded himself and got out so slowly—you could almost hear the creaks and pops. "Sorry to be late!" he cried.

"You're not late," Bob called.

"I thought noon," the old man said.

Suddenly I recognized him, too: Reverend Bridgewater, the Camp Challenge pastor. Hadn't he been old even back in the day?

"It's far from noon," Bob said.

The reverend hurried around the vehicle to his passenger's door, opened it, helped down a tall, striking figure: Maria. Ricky squeezed my hand. The spoons clattered around my neck. The fur was silky. It smelled, not badly, nostalgically in fact, but smelled. Maria approached upon the reverend's arm, came straight to me.

"I've been in to see the doctor," she said. "The reverend here came and got me. Nothing to do with you." She touched my hands first, clutched my spoons formally, put her forehead to mine. Everyone else just stopped. She seemed to know the old way. We fell into each other's eyes a long time, then she kissed my mouth, my ears, backed away, biggest smile I'd ever seen on her, maybe the only.

"Our bride," she said.

"Our aunt," I said.

"Blessings," Reverend Bridgewater said.

"I remember you," I said.

"I hear I remember you, too," he said wryly.

Now Maria went to Ricky, took his hands as she had mine, touched her forehead to his so fondly. "Mountain Turtle," she said. And only then did she turn to Lucky, take his hands. "We dreamed this," she said. "We always did." They touched their foreheads a long, long time in our silence. You saw how old she was, sister of Walks Far. They'd been born at the deep, far end of the twentieth century, when you thought about it, same planet, different world.

Maria put my hand with Lucky's, squeezed. I could feel the ring new to my finger. I could feel that I'd wanted it. I could feel that I'd get Lucky one, some gas station flea market somewhere unknown. I could feel that the ring mattered, that it made a difference. I could feel that all the things had come out just as they had come out, the only way they could, and this ring blue as water said okay to that, amen.

"Shall we proceed?" Reverend Bridgewater said.

Maria gave him a pitying look.

"We told the guests noon," Bob said gently.

"Everyone but me," I said. "Me, you told nothing. What guests?"

Everyone laughed—they were all in on it, all of them!

"You would have said no," Ricky said.

"I don't feel manipulated," I said. An old joke between us.

"We're married either way," Lucky said.

The young women wandered off, a serious project, plucked grasses and tiny purple flowers that grew close to the ground. I wished to join them. Just to be so easy, to sit on the ground so focused and pluck beauty as if it were a harp.

Born on Bison tried to seem like nothing was afoot, pretended to wander purposelessly to the horse trailer, opened the sleek latches, pulled the ramp down, positioned it, then backed out a sweetly dappled horse.

"Chickadee," Lucky said.

And Chickadee heard him, yanked her reins right out of Bob's capable hands, charged over, pulled up hard, pushed her nose into Lucky's shoulder as if to knock him over. He took her great head in his arms. "Yeah, Chick," he said.

And I said it, too, "Chickadee," and gave my little clucking, and she threw her head back, torn between Lucky and me. I nuzzled her as she nuzzled Lucky, pushing us in her excitement, a big staggering reunion.

"Horse never forgets," Bob said, regaining control of those reins. "You'll have time to visit shortly. But for now, let me water her—I'll put her to trough back behind the shed. Horses are big on reunions but don't care for weddings from what I've seen."

Another car arriving. You could hear it was a rental. I would explain, but this is not the time. Around the majestic piles of metal it crawled, a small green thing, two people silhouetted inside. An old fear arose: strangers. No rush, it stopped, backed a little, pulled up to a different spot. And the driver's door opened. Even less rush, and a long leg emerged. Then a dapper Black man, crisp white-linen suit, tall and slender, a little tentative, shoulders to carry the world. He pulled himself out against a doorframe too small for him, skull shaved, super elegant, suit and tie, bright white shirt. He didn't acknowledge the knot of us standing middle of the yard, but circled around the car, opened the passenger's door to a fit of loud cursing, painstakingly extracted Francie.

Francie!

I shrieked.

"We're not here for you, Cindrawww," she called.

Chickadee heard, pulled away from Bob. Another of her people, different life. She didn't go to Francie, but to Lucky, and watched the arrival with him, Born on Bison throwing up his hands.

At last I cried. I tried to laugh but cried and pushed through the people and, spoons clattering around my neck, went to her, my Francie, her hair braided tight and full of beads, clattering like me, hurrying toward me. She was so much to hug after Lucky and we held each other so long. She smelled like Francie, like clover and hammers and trees split by hand.

"The missing girl," she said.

"I wrote you in Sweden!"

She said, "Oh, don't start apologizing. Your shrink there in Massachusetts, the Program, was it? What kind of pig? In case you think I didn't try."

"And you in Haiti!"

"Mother Haiti. A beautiful life. Perhaps a bit fractured as of late. Meet my son. He is called Arild."

"*Bonjour*," said Arild, super shy, big smile to reveal enormous teeth just like Aarto's.

"He speaks Swedish better than English," she said, overcome, "but he's Haitian through and through. And this is your boy?"

Ricky rushed up. "Francie! It's been so nice texting with you!"

Francie pulled him in, hugged him tight. My blessed tears poured down. I took Arild the same and held him long. Bob and his friends gathered around, the reverend, gazed upon the babies of the Far Turtle Wilderness, Arild and Ricky. Maria, now, too. She touched Francie's ears, patted her cheeks, grabbed a handful of those beaded braids and rattled them together lovingly. "New Jersey," she said. Clay had called Francie New Jersey.

"No more," Francie said. Her tears wet the shoulders of her dress, my beautiful friend all grown, T-shirts long gone.

I kept checking the little green rental, already knew, already bereft. "Aarto?" I said.

"Aarto is dead," Francie said, blunt as ever. "He was ill many brave years and slipped from us just last summer, *chérie*. It was cancer. *Chérie*, don't cry so."

"Don't you," I said, and buried myself in her.

Lucky approached. She pulled him in, too. And Lucky cried as we did.

When she'd gathered herself, she said, "We've got a court date, as do you. About the ranch. With Aarto gone, well, Aimo couldn't come from Sweden, and Aapo the younger is a drunk. So I'm the spokesmodel. The Free Men, sister. It's your fight, too. It's our fight together. A fight we will likely lose. Those shits run the show here now."

"Much to discuss," said Ricky.

"Yes, much," I said. "But let us speak of Aarto."

"Aarto," Francie said.

"May the Lord bless and keep," called Reverend Bridgewater from across the yard, only deaf when he wanted to be.

"Good night, friend," Lucky said, he and his sidekick Aarto on a boy-hood adventure, wands of Timothy grass stuck in their teeth, the two of them scrambling among river boulders after brook trout, pockets full of fishing gigs and little folding knives, flints to make fire, nothing but life ahead of them, no monsters they couldn't slay.

"Hoppo!" Lucky cried suddenly, startling everyone, breaking our huddle.

And "Aarto!" everyone responded, that attuned.

Bob, sweet boy, rushed to the drinking trough and filled the pitcher there so Lucky could drink the name. The pitcher went around and those who would drink, drank, that is one and all, the young women, too, who'd made bracelets of grasses and tiny tough flowers, desert purples and pink, palest green. They put a bracelet on everyone's wrist, several on my own. Of course I still have them all, the purple holding forever. This San Francisco dresser, this beam of morning sun.

The young women began to chant in high repetition, reedy, practiced harmonies, crows squawking somewhere, the Aermotor squealing, the wind in the grasses like strings back behind, my delicate new bracelets, my sturdy blue ring.

"If the bride would come with me," Ricky said. He walked me back out into the junk and out of sight of the guests. On the hood of an old Buick he'd set up a dressing station, and there was the white shift from Target. He looked away while I stripped out of my peasant shirt and Wranglers and spoons and put the dress on, one piece of clothing in which to get married, nicer than I'd thought, thick cotton stiff with sizing, simple as rain, SEWN IN VIETNAM, the label said. Ricky touched up the French braid he'd given me. Now a flower crown, pins for the wind. "My cousins made this just yesterday," he said, placing it on my head. He meant the young women: Sinopa, Kate, Alsoomse.

Now footwear, not meant to match any dress, actually cheap RV slippers, but the color exact. He tore the gas station price tags off. I didn't wear makeup as a rule, but Ricky had a little, gave me bright red lips, eyeliner and shadow, a little rub of blue, a brush or two of glitter stick, he called it. I bent to peer in the old car mirror.

"Wow, Mom," Ricky said.

I thought so, too.

He put the spoons back around my neck, the marmot skin. He touched my new ring. The noon wind, steady as an ocean current, pushed high-speed clouds like time-lapse up above. The metal scraps all around us banged and creaked, the windmill squealed, dust devils lifted leaf scraps and holy dust in our faces. My sweet new dress ballooned. I thought I might take off, fly up high where I could see everything, everything there was.

It was Ricky who would give me away, and so he took my arm, and as the windblown young women sang and the junk ticked and clattered, we walked upon the face of the planet, turned the junk pile corner, everyone having made a circle around the reverend, who asked once more if it was noon.

Chapter Sixty-Nine

After our ceremony, a privacy I'd rather not share, the blessing of food. So much food, yanked from coolers in every vehicle, even Dora's limo, artfully hidden from me by that engineer of deception, my son, including an actual wedding cake, which he'd made by stacking descending sizes of frozen cakes from Target, a couple of Polly Pockets holding hands on top, a third sitting on the edge of the second tier. The hair being interchangeable he'd put long wigs on the male figures and made little braids, black and white, pulled them forward for power. My Polly was a nice white lady in a white plastic dress.

After the eating, and laughter, and continued song (those young women were like camp counselors, irresistible and increasingly confident), everyone, even Lucky, had to come up with a song. His made Francie cry, that croaking singing voice, two notes: "Three people in the moun*tain* / Three people in the wood / Three people in the moun*tain* / Three people and two hor-*ses*." The tears because Aarto had made us four. Five if you counted Bronco, which Lucky did in subsequent verses, the joke that brought us back to gaiety. Ricky after that took Francie to the trough under the Aermotor and talked with her at length, a warm, vurry sober conversation. I knew he was gathering evidence of my life, comparing my stories to hers. Accuracy was his thing, secrets, too. Arild joined them, listened closely, a lot of translating going on.

My story was, I could not let go of my husband's hand. He wasn't inward, but definitely bashful. Born on Bison was up to something, dragging various barrels and buckets and tubs into the yard. When he was satisfied, he stole up ceremonially and ceremonially snatched the spoons off my neck, then used them for mallets to play that scrap like drums, super-simple rhythm. Alsoomse took up the beat beside him, and pretty soon we'd all found some piece of Clay's big scrap-metal heart to bang on. And our sisters Kate and Sinopa created a dance—didn't just hop and wriggle, but really created a dance, soon dragging poor Lucky in with them, and then Arild, even more awkward than my husband, and then Maria, slinky as you please, then the reverend, stiff and tottering, and Ricky spinning Francie, who was not exactly a toy top, more of a tropical depression, increasing winds. I, of course, was practically Twyla Tharp, whom I'd seen with Hates Roofing at age nine, and thought divine. The drumming did not dwindle, but rose and rose and rose till suddenly Bob brought a spoon down hard on an old car hood he'd suspended like a gong, not so resonant, last note, the end.

Reverend Bridgewater seized the moment, looking like a hymn had just ended too soon, the minister who'd forgotten his sermon. But he stood tall, all of us expectant, that hot plains wind hotter yet, our sweat evaporating before it could fall.

"I propose a nap," the good reverend said.

"A nap," we all shouted, general laughter.

Then, without a word, Maria led the entire wedding party slow and stately back amid vintage Coke machines and Mobil Oil flying red horses and three work-worn manure spreaders to a partly crushed Airstream camper of fine fifties vintage, the distinctive aluminum capsule freshly parked under cottonwoods at the camouflaging edge of Clay's scrapyard. I say freshly parked, but the old fine thing had no tires and clearly had had to be dragged into place by backhoe—that dedicated groomer of junk, whoever it was—the soil disturbed all around it, freshly placed wooden pallets making a walkway to an old industrial sink turned turtle, stainless-steel step-up to the bashed stainless-steel door.

Maria stood up there, said, "Let us remember Clay Marvelette." And with that she reached up into the trailer's old rolled awning cover and pulled out a handgun she'd hidden there, as long as her shoulders were wide, a big old antique six-shooter, which I immediately recognized. She spun the chamber dramatically, bone-skinny wrist wrapped in a brace, her arm wavering with the weight of the weapon as she lifted it. We all ducked as the gun swung in front of us. But finally she got it aimed in the air toward Turtle Butte. Bob stepped forward: too late. A monumental explosion shocked the air, hot slug flying cleanly through the cottonwood branches, shattered leaves floating down. The old gun leapt from Maria's hands in violent recoil, bounced off the face of the Airstream, clattered to the stones at her feet, skittered into the weeds, where it hid like a coiled snake.

The reverend looked killed, but was only surprised: "Maria," he said, "what on earth?"

Maria said, "You always shoot a gun at a wedding."

"Okay, Maria," Bob said. "Where the hell?"

She said, "It's Lucky's, come back with Chickadee those many years ago."

"That's not mine," Lucky said. "Never owned one."

I said, "It's a Smith and Wesson long-bore .45. It was owned by Mr. Dale Drinkins. If you want to know."

"Dale Drinkins?" Born on Bison said, college kid well versed in the legal business of his Nation. He said, "That thing could be evidence. We need to get it to the Montana State Highway Patrol." He shuffled in the weeds, found the gun, picked it by the bore with a ready rod of scrap metal.

"Maria," Sinopa said, dearly sincere. "You don't worry where the bullet will land?"

"Oh, I know right where it will land," Maria said. "It will land at the feet of my sister, Walks Far."

Whatever that meant! Still, we all nodded sagely.

"Let us pray," the reverend said.

"Let us not," said Maria.

Bob bowed his head, the old six-shooter held high on its evidence rod. He said, "Of sickness, Sun, may among us there be none."

Lucky said quietest words in my ear: "Soon I get you back."

"I'm going to kill you," I said like a kiss.

Maria still commanded the stage, which was a sink. The Airstream radiated heat. From her extremely narrow Wrangler pocket, a delicate operation, she drew a folded sheet of foolscap, dramatically unfolded it. "Lawyer paper," she said, holding it high to show one and all. "There have been some doings. Bob, young friend, please come up on here and read it."

Some doings. Lucky chuckled. He knew what doings.

Ricky clapped. He knew, too.

I was the one who didn't.

Arild, so tall, bobbed with happiness, just the way back in the time beyond his father had, dear Aarto.

The reverend struck a pose, chin high—he knew the secret thing, too.

And Francie, nodding and slight-smiling and raising her eyebrows like someone with a handful of contraband Robinsons.

Even our bracelet makers went silent.

Even the plains, the wind a sudden stop.

Bob changed places with Maria on the upended sink, took the piece of paper, studied it a moment, read the important parts: "Assign of Deed. Marvelette Ranch. Plus or minus twenty-four thousand acres as delineated by the coordinates below, bounded by the Crow Nation to the north and east, Turtle Butte Ranch south, Federal grasslands west. By Maria Marvelette to one Mountain Turtle, known as Richard Sing-Zoeller, American citizen."

I gasped, everyone gasped: this wasn't the expected surprise.

Francie stepped up. "My gift," she said, and handed a similar piece of paper to Bob.

He read, nearly identical: "Assign of Deed. Johman Ranch, plus or minus twenty-seven thousand five hundred acres," and etcetera, once again given to Mountain Turtle, what? Then Ricky stepped up, handed Bob a last piece of paper, this one pink: Dora. Same wording, all of it orchestrated by her lawyers. Bob read: "Assign of Deed. Turtle Butte Ranch, plus or minus one hundred thirty-four thousand acres, delineated by the coordinates below." Beneficiary: Mountain Turtle.

"A hundred thirty-four thousand acres?" I said.

"Sounds like a lot," Reverend Bridgewater said, ready finally for a sermon. He spoke slowly, well-thought phrases, well-timed breaths. "But consider that it's one of the smaller of the old ranches. Purchase price in 1933, after the Lord's wet decades gave way to the persistent dry: one cent an acre, with several large, essentially desert swaths conceded, as they put it, assembled as was typical from many small grants and assigns the US government had awarded to earlier settlers willing to *inhabit* and what they called *improve* lands formerly, as they saw it, Crow. Ricky, your great-grandpa paid nine hundred ninety dollars for the entire ranch, his railroad money and perhaps gambling assets."

"Not perhaps," Maria said.

"May he be forgiven," the reverend said.

Ricky climbed up on the sink, stood beside Bob. He said, "Thank you, thank you, Maria. Thank you, Franciella Johman. Thank you, Far Turtle and Lucky Turtle and thanks to Dora Dryden Conover. Thank you, Bob, for all your help these last hectic days. I'd just like to say that a city boy like me has no business owning these three historic ranches. So, with permission of my grandmother and my father, Lucky Turtle, already received, and with the aid and support of the Crow Nation, and with the help of Born on Bison—Bob here—and as of pretty much this moment with my mom's knowledge and right of veto, we are preparing an amalgamated gift: the three ranches will be united and offered for sale to the Crow Nation, price, one dollar."

Everyone cheered. Not me, couldn't, sobbed instead, no veto.

"It's taken some navigating," Bob said, trying to tamp things down, grinning despite himself. "And there are still some legalities to work out. But we are confident they will be, plenty of lawyers, and I've been authorized by the chair and officers of the Crow Tribe Executive Branch to accept on principle and to extend warm greetings and thanks." Chickadee nickered and whinnied and snorted back out behind the pump shed, must have freed her tether, because here she came, trotting right into the frame among us. Bob leapt down from the sink and got hold of her halter, no big deal, she as joyous as us all.

"What about our nap?" the reverend said.

"Ah," Maria said. "The business at hand." She tugged Bob by the inseam of his pants down from the sink, tugged Ricky the same, strong as ever. She motioned to me and Lucky and we climbed up there, our turn.

"Enter," she said.

Good, no speeches.

The Airstream door was riveted and sleek and newly polished, the recessed door handle apparently freshly oiled and adjusted. It pulled easily, the latches clicked smoothly, the door simply opened.

Inside the trailer a honeymoon suite awaited, even the crushed-spaceship nose of the thing hung with garlands of paper flowers and swags of dainty fabric. All the fixtures and furnishings of the old camper had been removed to make way for a queen bed dressed magnificently in hand-stitched quilts and pillows, woven blankets, crisp new Target sheets, smoldering sage burners made of local clay by the cousins, so fragrant. Above was the open sky, the trailer burst open during whatever accident had befallen it. On a little steel worktable rested an overflowing bowl of fruit, a dozen candles of all shapes and sizes, mostly half-burned, one white, one new, one blue, box of matches, also a pitcher of water, tin cups.

"Someone musta dropped all this off," Maria said to laughter, following me in. And then the others, one by one climbing up on the sink and entering the trailer till we were stuffing the small space. Last was Lucky Turtle, the two of us lined up opposite across the bed, all the women on my side, all the men on his, Ricky at the foot of the bed between us, Chickadee's head in the door, her big brown eye.

"This is my lodge!" Lucky cried.

"This is my husband," I said to laughter.

"And this your shelter for so long as you wish," Maria said, pointing to the open roof just above the pillows—it was no shelter at all and that was the point.

And cut to the lovers alone in the old Airstream, wind and pricking-bright stars through the gape in our roof, dinner and flowers delivered by the singing cousins, exhaustion.

Chapter Seventy

We'd thought to linger a little in Montana, but Lucky missed his people, and Ricky wanted to get back to his new love, Gene. We might have stayed on a week or two despite all that, but Kathy Hillman, San Francisco city gardener, texted to inform me that she could hold a job for me only so long, a job I hadn't quite known I wanted. And so Lucky and I redefined the concept without much talk, collected our willing son, and headed back to San Francisco: home. My certification course was delightful, as it turned out, even if conducted via Zoom, the test calling for the identification of plants by species, genus, family, and order, the qualities of soil, the carbon cycle, the water cycle, planting zones. Ha-ha, I failed. But Hill carried me along and tutored me crossly for another quarter, and second try I passed, went from provisional employee of the San Francisco Parks and Recreation Department to assistant horticultural specialist, Golden Gate Park Division, twenty-two bucks an hour, city benefits, including very generous maternity leave, completely Covid-proof employment, because we do essential work outdoors in a park that can be closed on a dime.

Hill is wonderfully grumpy everywhere but in the dirt, and the two of us go whole days without speaking anything but Plant. Best is, she'll leave me in charge of some impossible soggy border, and then it's days alone, root trimming, top pruning, digging drainage, planning and drawing, trips to the greenhouses, our shared green golf cart full of tools and snacks, sometimes Lucky leaning: he always seems to know where to find me, breastfeeding time, our baby on his hip, but more about that shortly.

He is Outreach, and he is Mr. Sing, and he is married to me, and we have two children far apart in age and he likes it that way. More shortly, shortly.

The pandemic fit our timing: we quarantined in the diplomat's house by the Filbert Steps under Coit Tower, good for a year at first, now renewed, as the diplomat and retinue, safely back from his assignment in Asia, have taken to his mountain estate in Colorado to ride out the pandemic "absolutely as long as it takes." They have a caretaker cottage other side of the hill as well, ours when they are back. Their privilege has thus become our own. The answer to my email to their daughter, Libby, came as we were packing up the limo for the drive back from Montana, our prospects uncertain. Libby said she was so moved by my message, by the reunion with Lucky, by the presence of our son, and that those things would have been enough, but already what I'd done with their gardens in two days had dazzled her, her exact word. Also, because of the pandemic, the thoroughgoing California shutdown, Florita would be joining the family in Steamboat Springs as part of their "pod," these new concepts. And would we consider taking up her duties, accepting a small salary? Yes, yes, of course, for the duration, Lucky and I cleaning and keeping the place supplied and in order, essentially just cleaning up after ourselves. And of course tending the gardens and feeding the pets. And now baby, sweet baby. But more about that shortly, I repeat, repeat in some joy.

Ricky had a rough year Zoom teaching but used the time to develop the work needed for his dissertation. He and sweet Gene are in *our* pod, and so we saw and have seen them often enough. They have Dora's limo, she glad to keep it in her name and carry the insurance, and they use it to cruise to the desert, where, back at the start of the shutdown, they found a shack to improve, somehow convincing Dora to invest. Soon, I think, those boys will marry. With the limo and among easing restrictions back in Berkeley, Gene has started up a weekend party service, You Drink We Drive, and he makes enough to pay for the gas (Lucky's joke). Actually, he's managed to pay their rent and buy materials for the desert place. He's dutiful with his mask, his customers behind glass. Ricky the same with his students, now back in person, all sorts of precautions, everyone immunized, let it hold. I hope for the best, the best for them, the best for us all. May the pandemic ease, and worldwide.

Ricky's well on his way to his PhD. He's stayed close to Born on Bison, and that future lawyer has been a resource for our son's dissertation, something arcane to do with civic planning, political power, Federal infra-structure, and the Nations.

We hear that volunteer crews have removed every trace of Camp Challenge, lumber repurposed, the Vault filled in. Crow tribal rangers patrol the new holdings, poachers and speculators beware. The high tip of the bluff where the Challenge chapel was, the turtle's head, had always been a holy site, and is still, visited only on secret days and by kids crossing into adulthood both alone and in the company of chosen aunts and uncles and cousins and elders. The wooden Christian cross is still there, and the ecumenical Easter service still a thing, God being God, as Bob likes to say.

I guess I've given away that we prevailed in court, pretty open and shut once the case went Federal. But get this: Mr. Drinkins and all his Free Men went down hard. That six-shooter of his coughed up enough ballistics for a murder warrant: his big new house raided at dawn, computers and phones seized, new weapons with their own stories to tell, an ongoing forensic chain, indictment, conviction, incarceration. There. I will never mention his name or the name of that syndicate of theirs again.

As for my dear, dear Franciella, she's back in Haiti navigating new tumult there, may peace prevail. We talk every week. Lucky and I are plan-ning a trip. Not right away. He's never been out of the country, never been out of the American West, and of course there have been travel restric-tions, and of course the baby, the baby, the baby. Ricky wants to go, too. Arild, we hear, is part of the thriving NGO Aarto and Francie founded in Mother Haiti: it's all about housing, schools, communities, common space and common resources, and Ricky's gotten involved there, too, designing, consulting, offering expertise, also internships for his students, may peace and health prevail. Dora's a major donor, by the way, which of course is Ricky's doing.

She loves that kid, and I don't stand in their way. But enough about her.

I talk to Born on Bison. He calls me Auntie and I'm vurry charmed. Recently he called to tell us about Maria, who'd been doing pretty well on her own out at the Junk Ranch, having refused to move to assisted living in Crow Agency, though she'd let herself be reunited with the tribe. She had all-day help from various cousins and friends, also Crow Elder Services, but on one of Bob's mornings she was missing. She'd always said that when her time came, she'd just walk out into the land and lie at the feet of her sister Walks Far. So on that assumption, Bob and large numbers of volunteers (including people from the bowling league in Billings) hiked and rode and drove in innumerable grids out there, tens of thousands of acres, no luck.

"Finally, the chair said leave her," Bob told us. "He said she's fine out there with her sister and that wherever she might be is right where she belongs."

Lucky cried, he cried for days, me too. On the seventh, Ricky and Gene came over and we built a fire in the diplomat's chiminea, sat with it all night, passing baby back and forth among us, our family.

Chapter Seventy-One

But let me back up.

To the morning after our sardine-can honeymoon. Lucky rose early, saddled up the limo, hooked up the horse trailer to the gold-plated ball hitch, led calm old Chickadee up the ramp. Maria loaned us a couple of blankets—the saddles were all gone—and packed us a lunch of wedding leftovers, jug of water from the trough.

That limo has special springs, sits pretty high, so we barely noticed the bashing and crashing and bottoming out, the road into that obscure corner of the Far Turtle Wilderness so little used there was grass in the ruts, Lucky pointed out. It had been a dry season, so the crossing brooks were small and no mud, the old limo proud as a Brahma bull, rocking its way through the switchbacks and swales, trailer swaying behind, Chickadee back there dancing. I'm glad it was Lucky driving, that's all I can say. The boulders were still in place at the old homestead, our lodge. We parked there and eased the beloved horse out of the trailer, surprised when she bolted and raced around the corner and up the hill ahead of us.

"Likely looking for View," Lucky said.

Sure enough, when we caught up, she was stamping at the gate of the old corral. Lucky put her in her traces, tied her there where she could mourn. The lodge itself looked about the same, tough and simple, though in the intervening twenty-some years someone had replaced the elk-hide door with a wooden one, boarded up the smashed windows in Franciella's addition. Not a hard guess who'd done the smashing nor who'd come along later and done the fixing. Didn't matter. I found I couldn't go inside—too heartbreaking if our bags of rice and flour and sugar weren't there, too heartbreaking if they were.

We got Chickadee in her blankets and climbed on together and rode her down the still discernible brook trail, where we found Francie's garden wall washed away except for the last dozen upstream stones; the topography of our garden spot had shifted. But the greens growing all around, I suddenly realized, were arugula, *our* arugula, perennial, garden-variety northern-zone arugula gone feral these two decades, another all but permanent presence.

The horse drank freely. Then we climbed her back to the clearing and up through the lodgepole pines to the high meadow, the place Lucky had speared his first animal, really nothing but a rocky opening conducive to grasses. The wildflowers were just getting started, still snow at the edges of everything, just as when we first arrived, the peaks surrounding all the same, a kind of eternity in that. I wondered which of the trees now standing dead Lucky and I had touched and leaned upon, and which of the thriving trees we'd trampled as saplings, and I wondered if humans were like trees— a forest being a forest much longer than a tree is a tree.

Lucky raised two fingers.

Game.

We listened, Chickadee, too, her nostrils flaring. Then I smelled it, too, something feral, the horse backing nervously, Lucky keeping her in place with clucks. The brambles shook.

And then the bear emerged, first his head, then the impossibly wide shoulders, brown all shot with gray, then the rest of him, slow, oblivious progress, an enormous grizzly intent on whatever berries he was grazing.

"Hoppo!" Lucky called.

The bear looked up, sniffed the wind, rose up on its hind legs, stared myopically, pivoted slowly, found us, all of us staring, sniffing, fixed like that a long time, horse, bear, man, woman. Slowly the bear dropped back to all fours and, unconcerned, went back to his berrying, pushing his way into the brambles, soon out of sight, the plants shaking with his progress through them.

We watched a long time, then mounted our girl and simply rode away.

"There's generally a bear," I said.

"Generally," Lucky said.

Not so many miles away, we tethered Chickadee loosely in a familiar grove and found a certain mossy area, same as ever, soft and thick as our honeymoon bed, spread the horse blankets, ate our lunch, good things left from our wedding. We lay back then and napped and woke together and kissed and tangled our legs and arms and you know how these things end up.

Lucky placed a hand over my middle when we were done, put on his Maria voice, said just about what we knew she would say later when we saw her back at her place, intoned it like her: "There's a girl inside here. And her name is Walks Far Turtle, and she'll be back one day grown, and we will tell her all the stories."

"Maybe not all," I said, inclined to believe.

"Maybe not," Lucky said.

Acknowledgments

Let me start by thanking my uncle, the reverend Bill Burkhardt, my mother's little brother, both of them now long departed. For several of my high school summers he showed me his Montana, from wilderness to church and back again (they were the same to him) and introduced me to the people who showed me the rest, some of it the underside, but always in nature, which was balm. And I thank one of those people in particular, who did not survive youth, and so remains ever young, though perhaps resurrected and even redeemed in these pages, where he continues to find a way to teach me. He said, "Never say my name," kind of kidding, kind of not, and so (that old psychedelic moment a pact, no matter the joke), I won't.

Thank you, Kathy Pories, editor and friend, for pulling this book through a couple of tough years, and thanks to the whole team at Algonquin and Workman, all of you, who've had my back four books' worth now, special bow to Jude Grant, copy editor and timeline hawk.

And thanks, Emily Forland, my agent, for patient advice and encouragement, and of course thanks to everyone at Brandt & Hochman.

Warm thanks to the sensitivity readers for *Lucky Turtle*, both official and unofficial: Alicia Fisher, Michelle Flythe, Joseph Lee, Yue Liang, Mae Zhang McCauley, Yvonne Adhiambo Owuor, Jeffrey Young, and many others, including a number of students and colleagues over the years, all of whom helped me see the world more clearly.

And you couldn't do this work without writer and artist and research and soul friends as early readers: Kate Colby, Melissa Coleman, Evgeniya Dame, Melissa Falcon, Roberto Fassone, Susan Gregg Gilmore, Megan

ACKNOWLEDGMENTS   407

Grumbling, Chris Hillman, Lauryn Hottinger, Bill Lundgren, Jen McInerney, Eloisa Morra, Amy Neswald, Debra Spark, Matthew Thomas, and many others who read or heard the first scraps and cheered me on, also pretty much everyone at every library I've ever set foot in.

And of course to the Starfish, the Hand, the Band, our writing group: Monica Wood, Kate Christensen, Lewis Robinson, and Sarah Braunstein, forever family.

Deep gratitude to the Civitella Rainieri Foundation and everyone there, especially Dana Prescott, Ilaria Locchi, Diego Mencaroni, and Marco Mewshaw, for support and fellowship during the writing, also a quiet desk in the castle.

And of course love and boundless thanks to Juliet and Elysia, who keep my heart full, inspire me with their art and acting and dance, and make me laugh every day. Now, guys, let me work!